Carmel Bird is one of the most exciting and original writers in Australia today. With the publication of *Cape Grimm*, her first literary novel since the Miles Franklin-shortlisted *Red Shoes* was published in 1998, she again confirms her place as one of our foremost writers.

Carmel is fascinated by the power of memory and the capacity of mundane scenes, incidents and sensations to trigger it into life. She loves the truth-telling power of fiction and its ability to mine and represent the past perhaps more effectively than the single-minded pursuit of documentary fact. As she has commented in an article titled 'Fact or Fiction': 'Life is a crude inventor; fiction will only be convincing if it is more artful than life.' She has also described herself as 'interested in the play between fact and fiction, interested in the moment when the metamorphosis takes place, when the grub of fact becomes the butterfly of fiction'.

Her previous novels include *Red Shoes*, *The White Garden* and *The Bluebird Café*, all of which were shortlisted for the Miles Franklin Award. Carmel has also published several volumes of short stories and two guides to writing fiction: *Dear Writer* and *Not Now, Jack – I'm Writing a Novel*. She has edited several anthologies including *The Penguin Century of Australian Stories* and *The Stolen Children — Their Stories*. A selection of her short fiction, *The Essential Bird*, will be published by Fourth Estate in 2005.

Cape Grimm

OTHER BOOKS BY CARMEL BIRD

Open for Inspection
Red Shoes
The White Garden
Unholy Writ
Crisis
The Bluebird Café
Cherry Ripe
The Common Rat
Woodpecker Point
Automatic Teller
Births, Deaths & Marriages
Dear Writer
Not Now, Jack — I'm Writing a Novel
Daughters and Fathers
The Stolen Children — Their Stories
The Penguin Century of Australian Stories
Red Hot Notes
The Mouth
Cassowary's Quiz

Carmel Bird

Cape Grimm

HARPER PERENNIAL

My thanks to the Literature Fund of the Australia Council for the granting of a Senior Fellowship which made the creation of this novel possible.

Harper Perennial
An imprint of HarperCollins*Publishers*, Australia

First published in Australia in 2004
This edition published in 2005
by HarperCollins*Publishers* Pty Limited
ABN 36 0009 913 517
A member of the HarperCollins*Publishers* (Australia) Pty Limited Group
www.harpercollins.com.au

HarperCollins*Publishers*
25 Ryde Road, Pymble, Sydney, NSW 2073, Australia
31 View Road, Glenfield, Auckland 10, New Zealand
77–85 Fulham Palace Road, London, W6 8JB, United Kingdom
2 Bloor Street East, 20th floor, Toronto, Ontario M4W 1A8, Canada
10 East 53rd Street, New York NY 10022, USA

National Library of Australia Cataloguing-in-Publication data:

Bird, Camel.
Cape Grimm.
ISBN 0 7322 6993 8.
1. Religious communities – Tasmania – Fiction.
2. Mass murder – Fiction. I. Title.
A823.3

'Angel Cake Song' lyrics © Jennie Swain
Cover images courtesy Corbis/Australian Picture Library
Cover and internal design by Gayna Murphy, HarperCollins Design Studio
Typeset in AGaramond by Kirby Jones
Printed and bound in Australia by Griffin Press on 50gsm Bulky News

6 5 4 3 2 1 05 06 07 08

Dedicated to the memory of Dinny O'Hearn

Contents

'In the whole array of living things there is only one terrestrial order that is homeless and is alien to any land. This creature is the moonbird.'

CARRILLO MEAN *The Flying Sheep of the Pacific Ocean*

'The north-west cape of Van Diemen's Land is a steep, black head, which from its appearance I called "Cape Grim".'

MATTHEW FLINDERS *Journal*

'There is the story of one's hero, and then, thanks to the intimate connection of things, the story of one's story itself.'

HENRY JAMES

Prologue

Berlin
24 July 1850

My Dear Lady Franklin,

I return to you my best thanks for your kind letter. It was most comforting and remarkable for me to learn from you of the popularity which *Die Kinder-und Hausmarchen* have found among the children of far-off Van Diemen's Land. My brother also wishes me to extend to you his gracious thanks. That you should personally have read the stories to the little ones in the Queen's Orphan School at Hobart Town is a matter for my heart's rejoicing. Like the memory of a dream, or like unto something I have imagined, using your eloquent description of the scene as the source of my vision, I see the children gathered in the firelight as they listen to the tales through the delightful medium of your voice. We are humbled by your confidence in the stories. I contemplate the globe of our little world and in my heart I smile when I realise that the tales themselves are able to travel to the four corners, voyaging between the covers of books, carried also in the minds of those who have heard them, transported by such gentle ambassadors as yourself.

Your accounts of your own travels and those of your intrepid, visionary and most courageous husband, Sir John, have implanted in my heart a strong desire for a visit to those distant shores of the

Antipodes, to see with my own eyes some of the wonders to be witnessed in those parts. I confess to you, however, that in my own case the length of the journey and the rigours thereof, as well as my responsibilities to my family and to my work, present themselves to me as serious impediments to such an undertaking. I have much admiration for those who put out to sea, placing all their trust in the grace of our loving Father in Heaven to deliver them safely to their destination.

Please do me the honour of accepting a small contribution to the funds dedicated to your search for Sir John in the Arctic wastes. I share with you and also with many other folk the earnest belief that your dear husband and his faithful men will most surely be discovered alive before many more weeks have passed. May Our Lord in His infinite wisdom watch over him, and also over you, dear lady, and may He swiftly bring your sacred enterprise to its happy conclusion.

I would also beg you to accept, as a token of my great pleasure at the thought that the tales have by your efforts given instruction and pleasure to the children of Van Diemen's Land, a presentation copy of a new English translation, the *Nursery and Household Tales*, bound in my own favoured crimson watered silk casing. All your efforts in general to bring the gifts of language and literature to the people of your dear husband's former province are a part of the great work in which my brother and I, and all philologists and storytellers everywhere are engaged. Though the universe is full of sound, with the air whistling and howling, the fire crackling, the sea roaring, and every animal making its own specific noise, only man has speech. While primitive expressions of joy and sorrow, laughter, sighs and tears, are common to all mankind, each language and each story is a creation, always subtly changing, always renewing itself, an outcome of mankind's God-given ability to think.

May God guide you and may you be soon reunited with Sir John, to live in joyful good health for many long years to come.

I am your sincere and faithful friend,

Jakob Grimm

CHAPTER ONE

Dust

Much of eastern Australia is turning to dust.

Once there was a fair country where the people lived in peace and in prosperity until there came a time when a strange child appeared and the land was turned to dust, to dust and ashes. A strange and powerful child came and the land fell away into dust and ashes, and the child gazed at the land, gazed with his great gleaming aluminium eyes. The sun beat down upon the surface of the land and no rain fell for a thousand days, and for a thousand and one nights no rain fell. The crops withered in the red earth which opened up with patterns of cracks, the cracks in the visage of a wild old woman. The cracks yawned open. The earth yawned and no rain came. And the cattle died, and the sheep — and the trees began to hum. Then the forests exploded into flame and the words in all prayers were 'bushfire' and 'drought'. *Dear Lord, save us from the flames; Dear Lord please send rain. Holy Mary Mother of God, intercede for us.* Then there came the fearful word of 'famine', and then came 'plague and pestilence' and next were added war and tribulation. And sorrow and sadness and loss. Heartbreak. Somewhere in there were the locusts and the winds. The winds, the hot and cold winds blowing hot and cold across the land.

Behold I will send upon them the sword the famine and the pestilence, and will make them like vile figs that can not be eaten they are so evil.

That is one way of putting it, as recorded by the Prophet Jeremiah. Many people believe that stories will somehow save the world, and maybe they will, maybe they won't. I don't know of any story that has the kick back of an assault rifle, or the reverse ability of a nuclear missile.

The child in the story about the dust appeared in the far northwest of the little world of Van Diemen's Land where the Roaring Forties meet the rugged rocks, where round and round the rugged rocks a ragged rascal ran. Van Diemen's Land dangles at the bottom of eastern Australia, like a jewel on a pendant, and the child in the story was born in Van Diemen's Land, now generally known as 'Tasmania', in the second part of the twentieth century, in 1959. I am not that child, although I too was born in 1959, but I am simply the teller of the tale as it unfolded, as the winds blew and the waves rose, and the sun beat down on the great southern continent and the red waves of the central desert blew forward to the coast, and somehow, everything was reduced to dust. And ashes. My name is Paul Van Loon.

In my father's office there's an old map on which the southwestern wilderness of Tasmania is labelled 'Transylvania'. This office is at our flower farm in a small place called Christmas Hills in the northwest of the island. I have always had a fanciful turn of mind, and it's not hard for me to imagine the mythic qualities of Transylvania merging naturally with the landscape of Tasmania. For in this place are mysterious and impenetrable swarthy forests, woods of deep and black-green shadows where demons lurk and angels hover nervously. One of my great interests lies in the connection between psychology and poetry, and I am in many ways well placed to pursue this interest, since I write poetry, and in my ordinary working life I am a psychiatrist. 'Ordinary working life' — where did I find such a phrase? I think I watch too much television and read too many newspapers so that my use of language is being infected with and bleached by the jargon of the day. The old map of Transylvania, like maps in the Bible, is tinted with a pastel purple wash, with areas of watery malachite, ash and primrose, and is detailed with fine drawings suggesting cauliflower thickets of dense forest woodland, lumpy multiplying mountain ranges, filigree lacework showing the veins and arteries of rivers. The mountains conceal vast mineral wealth, such as is mined by teams of industrious dwarfs, and the forest will build ships and many thousands of houses and make enough paper to construct not one but several pale pathways to the moon — and the rivers, like great snorting horses, will provide enough electricity to blow up the planet.

Since I was a very small boy I have always loved that map of Transylvania, and have dreamt about it, conjured it up in moments of reverie, moments of stress, times of joy. When my father dies — he's sixty-three and shows no signs of slowing down or bowing out — I hope to hang the map of Transylvania in my own office. My grandfather was one of the Dutch on the Burma Railway in the war, and he lived to be eighty-six, so we Van Loons are made from tough stuff. As far as I know my grandfather never spoke about the war, and he died with his secrets, experiences, memories and forgettings locked away in his sinewy old heart. He had a watch that had belonged to one of his companion soldiers, and when he died that watch was buried with him. The gracious mysteries of the map of Transylvania suggest a place inviolate to the forces that might turn a land to dust. This is a place of grey and lilac rock scabbed with moody lichens, a place of drifting mists, milky haze, splashing waterfalls and living lakes and rivers, carpeted green fields, leaping rainbow fishes chasing the flittering flying carpet of newborn moonfaced moths. Clouds of mournful sheep, ash-green clumps of still and whispering treetops, dark as velvet. The wisdom and breath of ancient thoughtful trees. There are four thousand lakes — it seems to me that's an enormous number of lakes. And deep mournful forest ravines where rumours of pre-history murmur and burble, seething softly with the imagination of some great brooding spirit. Nesting underground on the islands that dot the ragged coastline are the restless creatures we call the moonbird, the muttonbird, the shearwater, homeless, forever winging in a great figure eight around the Pacific Ocean from north to south, south to north, their aerial path describing the image and symbol of eternity.

'Much of eastern Australia is turning to dust.' With a straight face the woman reading the autocue of the television news repeats those words. It sounds credible; I can easily believe it. One of the true horrors of modern life is the fact that every night, night after night, straight-faced newsreaders look into the receptive eyes of all the world and spill out, spin out, the stories, speaking of seven Israeli children gunned down on their way to school by Palestinian militants, two hundred and forty-five people killed in an earthquake in Colombia, as fire sweeps through most of California, and Belgium is being washed away by the worst floods in one hundred and fifty years. Numbers, always numbers. If you watch and listen long enough you will have heard spoken every number that ever was — that's a thought. Night after night they do the numbers on TV with that cool straight face, that smooth, bright, clean, level, hypnotist's voice. The number of dead, the number of homes destroyed, the number of years since history started, the numbers of the weather, the number of years lived by Cleopatra, the numbers of finance, the number of people struck by the disease, the number of goals scored, the number of minutes it took the horse to run the race, the number of angels, the number to ring should you wish to order pizza. The price of health insurance. The price of petrol. The price of matches.

You can easily see why people might go mad. Possibly there will come a TV time when everything will turn to numbers, like star dust, and will disappear in one great piece of arithmetical and brilliant wonder.

After the news explaining that much of eastern Australia is turning to dust, there are some pictures of cracked earth dotted with dead trees. From the yearning tip of Cape York in northern Queensland to the sugary dots of Maatsuyker Island in southern Tasmania, the woman in the nice pale-pink jacket suggests, the wind may soon come and blow the whole thing away. El Niño has brought the drought to eastern Australia, she says. And to Colombia, even-handed, he has brought the flood. On the same day — it's the first of June 2002 — the newspapers document the tenth anniversary of the Mabo decision, referring to a High Court ruling that 'Aboriginal title to land had survived British settlement'. Now it is just called 'Mabo' and it was the dramatic beginning of a lengthy process in the life of the land and the people, black and white, a process that so far has benefited mainly the lawyers, as these things so often do. Today's newspaper records that, according to the smooth talk of a white speaker, Mabo has brought 'a lot of uncertainty', while a cautious black speaker says 'the exercise appears to have failed' and adds that indigenous people are 'still living in the dark corners' of Australia.

I have a sense that I too am living in a dark corner, speaking to you from the obscurity of a small place called Black River. Here in the dark corner we have Paul Van Loon, commenting on the events of the day; and here in the light corner we have the ubiquitous girl in the pink suit, bringing you the smiling evening news.

Dark corners and uncertainty. These shadows mark the flip side of life's bright moments and firm facts. The way I see it the whole thing is probably some type of fairytale — life I mean — a fairytale, a dream, a strange and bitter-sweet once upon a time, a journey by the hero in search of paradise. Monsters and wild storms and battles are encountered along the way until the darkness closes in, and the land returns to dust and the girl in pink can wash her hands of everything.

I wonder if I am the hero of this story? I suppose not, hope not. I'm the narrator, the storyteller, the Brother Grimm, and I will lead my readers along the path through the forest, will show the way the people behave — this includes myself, my own behaviour is not exempt — and show what happens, and how things turn out in the end. What do they say at the end of fairytales? 'My tale is done, and away it is run, to little August's house.'

Ten years is a short time in history; it's a long time in a human life. It is in fact ten years now since Caleb Mean destroyed the village of Skye, and that event is the one that really sets my narrative in motion. The fire at Skye, in my world picture, as a focal point around which and towards which the histories I will describe all move and tend, back and forth, round and round, waves rolling in against a cliff.

In the central Australian deserts, according to today's papers, half a million feral camels are running wild. The Claudina butterfly has been placed on the endangered list. Meanwhile, out in space, Mercury, Venus, Mars, Jupiter and Saturn are in straight alignment. In Colombia twinkling blocks of snow-white cocaine are fashioned into the likeness of the scene of Christ's Nativity, and shipped to distant destinations. Famine in Africa, unrest in the Middle East, melting of the polar icecaps. In Asia the deadly golden apple snail is threatening rice crops. A giant squid comes from the ocean's depths to surface on a beach in the southeast of Tasmania. In the past century only about fifty examples of these creatures have been found, and they were dead, but apparently they exist in dramatic living splendour in huge quantities deep deep down in the ocean. Bits of them have been salvaged, and recently a scientist in New Zealand tried to raise some baby ones in captivity, but they died. In their gliding, embracing, strangling, swallowing millions they explore the waters around Van Diemen's Land. Mysteries drift in all unseen places, deep in the ocean, high in the sky, thick in the darkness of the blackest forest. The deep blue pearly water — is that how it goes, the song? I think about the sea a lot, as might be obvious by now — I'm afraid of the open sea, and when a slimy pink prehistoric monster turns up on the beach I am reminded all over again that there is a great deal of danger out there, deep deep down.

To the northwest of Australia, India and Pakistan are facing off with nuclear weapons. On nineteenth October last year more than three hundred and fifty refugee parents and children, wanting shelter, wanting asylum in Australia, drowned when their boat, which came to be known as the SIEV-X, sank in international waters, north of Christmas Island. 'If I die in the sea,' said one little girl to her father, 'don't leave me here alone.' This has been a year, the paper says, of most unusual mass strandings of paper nautilus shells on the west coast of Flinders Island in Bass Strait. In Lima fresh rose petals sparkling with dew have miraculously appeared in the arms of a statue of Saint Rose. Water has been discovered beneath the surface of Mars. Scientists are planning to distribute by helicopter, in September, baits of Fipronil in an attempt to control the crazy ants on Christmas Island. The ants have effectively wiped out the crimson crabs which are a key species in maintaining the ecological balance of the island. At this point, the newspapers note, the Australian cricket team is due to play Pakistan, also in September.

From my own office window, here at the Black River Psychiatric Detention Facility (BRPDF), way out in the distance, I can see the sea. If I die in the sea, don't leave me here alone. The words of that drowning child keep coming back to haunt me, keep ringing in my heart. I look out to sea and I think of her. If I die in the sea, don't leave me here alone.

The Norwegian architect, Thor Gulbransen, who in the late eighties designed this building where I write and work, constructed the place such that the heart of the interior of the main building would resemble the interior of a nautilus shell. He worked closely with Sophie Goddard, the Director of the facility. Sophie was at the time establishing a world reputation for her work with the criminally insane, and she had a particular interest in the physical design of the buildings, seeing this as central to the treatment of the prisoners. The place is really quite beautiful, but has caused considerable controversy, since people are inclined to get excited about a bunch of criminal lunatics living in luxury inside a great new work of art shaped like some magic shell. There is a distinct hint of the work of Gaudi in the irregular soft shapes of the inmates' quarters. The architect called these rooms 'chambers', each one individual in many ways, each one inviting, embracing, stimulating, the walls softly moulded, the lighting discreet — all in all there is little about them to suggest that these rooms are prison cells. The colours go through a range of pastel lilacs and peaches and limes and primroses and so on, but we quickly abandoned the 'chamber' idea and went back to 'cells'. These are cells, and the inmates are dangerous rejects from society because they have done incredibly mad and unspeakably terrible things. In another time, another place, Caleb Mean himself would have been executed, and in the United States he would be on death row. I liken him to Charles Manson. But the last Australian execution took place in 1967, and in spite of anything people do, they will not be murdered by the state for it, but will live somewhere like BRPDF in pastel chambers surrounded by people such as myself who aim to understand them and to play a role in the repair of some of the damage that has been done (to them).

Thor gave the cells names from Norse mythology, but they were too confusing for the staff. Apart from being utterly ridiculous —

do you want Caleb in a room called Bifrost or Loki or Njord? These days the cells are simply numbered, like any other prison cells. And Thor put in a tower, and he put what he called 'eyes' into the tower so that the staff at least could contemplate the world outside, the sky and the ocean and the misty forest. In my own fantasy they are the eyes of one great giant squid, the largest eye in the animal kingdom. Imagine that, the biggest eye of all. My office eye is a slit, a slot, rectangular with soft rounded corners; the eyes of squids are truly fully round, round as saucers or as the lids of paint tins.

I am reminded of the eyes of the dogs in *The Tinderbox*, eyes as big as teacups, as big as millstones, as big as the Round Tower in Copenhagen. We grew up on European stories, and I still have my childhood copies of Grimm and Andersen in English and also in Dutch, well-worn volumes in which the tales of *The Red Shoes* and *The Snow Queen* and *The Juniper Tree* are contained between beloved covers. Thinking of the window and the sea and the sea monster, the Kraken, my own imagery becomes confused — am I, the watcher, therefore myself a great sea monster peering from the deep? Am I afraid of myself, as well as being afraid of the sea? 'Worse things happen at sea,' my mother used to say, when any little thing went wrong. Well yes, worse things certainly do happen at sea. I spend a lot of time gazing out towards the ocean, dreaming, imagining. I need this kind of drifting thinking time in my work. I comfort myself with Mozart flute and harp concerto, the pinnacle sound for me of sophisticated beauty as well as being the sound of deep heart-stirring, as I stare out at the primitive blue distance, as my mind goes blank, as my imagination swirls and riots. Just the one piece of music, I'm obviously an obsessive.

People must not suppose I've got wide sheets of windswept glass offering tourist vistas of Bass Strait here — no, this eye of mine is just a medieval slit high up in the white turret that rises from our criminal psychiatric fortress in the forest. It is an aperture through which to shoot an arrow at an enemy. As a joke we sometimes call my office 'Rapunzel's Tower'. We abandoned, as I say, the Norse references, and went back to numbers, and to the more familiar images of Grimm, close as we are to the bleak cape that marks the Landsend, the Finisterre of Van Diemen's Land. So gradually Thor Gulbransen's concept was adapted to our use.

On the door of my tower room there's a hand-carved board made by my father, a father who is incredibly proud of his upwardly mobile son. The design on the board is by my mother who, besides working on the flower farm, runs a business making floral aprons and embroidered oven mitts. 'Dr Paul Van Loon' says the sign on my door, and all around the edge there runs a stylised carved and painted border of tulips and poppies. It's just a piece of kitsch, Thor would be horrified, but I am stupidly fond of it, and when people visit us from elsewhere it is always a useful talking point, although there are moments of embarrassment when it is assumed the board was carved by a patient in the craft room during sessions of occupational therapy. It doesn't matter very much to me and so I sometimes let them think that anyway.

My father is the son of Dutch immigrants who came here after the Second World War, doing their time in the camp at Bonegilla before coming to Tasmania. Hence his joy in what he sees as my lofty position in society. His father worked on the Hydro at Bronte Park, making our family part of the special and only time when the population of Tasmania grew at a faster rate than the population of the rest of old New Holland. I offer here, for the record, a simplified version of the family story more or less as it appears in the front of the old family Bible, leaving out the uncles and aunts and tracing a straight line to myself.

Joost Van Loon, schoolmaster, married Claesgen Sofie Siebenhaar in 1901. (Claesgen's older brother Willem had in fact emigrated to England and then to Australia, ending up in Perth in 1891.) The son of Joost and Claesgen, Piet Joost Van Loon was born in 1911 and he married Gisela Schuyler in 1938. Their son — my father — Piet Hendrik Van Loon was born in 1939 and he married my mother Karel Maria Engel at Christmas Hills in 1958. I was born in 1959.

I went to the mainland to do my training, and then I travelled overseas. My colleagues have expressed strong doubts about this whole project, saying that writing a story that is so close to my own life, and revealing material that has its origins in my work will do me no good at all. Unethical they say, and nod their heads. Well, be that as it may — time will tell. Sue me, strike me off — whatever. I don't even have to publish it if I don't want to. In my travels I visited Britain and the USA, Mexico and several European countries. In the village where my father was born, I found no living relatives, but there were a few people who remembered the family. All memory of my mother's people, it seems, has completely disappeared from Amsterdam. Yet I did discover, on the side of a very old building, an elegant and faded sign, 'H. de Beer, Handschoenmaker', and I knew this was where my mother's mother used to work, making gloves. A few pairs of those gloves miraculously survive to this day in far off and improbable Christmas Hills. My mother keeps them in a drawer of her dressing-table — they are fine kid, embroidered, with rows of impossibly small pearl buttons.

I never imagined I would take a job back home in Tasmania, but when they opened the facility at Black River, it seemed too good to resist — it's one of the most impressive new centres of its kind in the world. I think my mother was disappointed that I wasn't going to be some hot-shot society shrink in Sydney or maybe New York, but I know my father was really pleased that I decided to come back.

My father and his brothers and sisters, and my mother and hers as well, were treated pretty much as outsiders here when they were growing up, refugees from a strange place, unwanted second-class citizens. My mother and her younger sister, my Aunt Margot, used to sum it all up by telling the story of a girl called Cleome Gordon who had a gang that would hide behind a huge chestnut tree on frosty mornings and jump out as the migrant girls came by, yelling insults and showering them with sharp pebbles, broken bottles and tin cans. My own schooldays were bad enough. My right eye was 'lazy' and so I had to wear a pirate's black eye-patch over the left one. The other kids loved to tease me, but I didn't feel particularly foreign or unwanted. Although several members of my family were a source of embarrassment, they were nevertheless treated by other kids as quaint and interesting. Some of the boys really loved my funny old Aunt Edda. She made good sweet spicy Dutch gingerbread and gingerbread men, for one thing, but it was more than that — she naturally inspired such love and affection. When she went to church in the little local hall she wore a brown felt hat that was laden with tiny flowers of all different colours, and from these flowers, at the back of the hat, there bobbed a little robin red-breast. He was a source of fascination to all who sat behind her in the pew, especially children. These Sunday excursions to the tiny Reformed Church were a time when the men of the family were all spruced up, their foreheads gleaming with soap, hair plastered down, grey suits with collar and tie, brown shoes cleaned with Nugget polish on a black brush, and buffed with a black velvet cushion. They all had a white linen handkerchief folded in their breast pocket. They all looked — I don't know — just very very Dutch. And proud, and kind of sad. Clumsy and sad. I was a second generation Dutch boy, and by the time I was growing up the family had learnt the trick of coping, and the world here had begun to absorb us, to need us, to value us, but we had to work for that, and all those years the family spent with the Hydro were no joke. I learnt to suppress any eccentricities, to merge with the colours of my surroundings. Not for me a robin red-breast on my hat.

My father and uncles, who did not really believe in the God of the Reformed Church, gradually gave up their suits and their churchgoing and spent a few hours on Sundays drinking their home brew and fishing on the Duck River with their sleeves rolled up. I used to go with them, and those times are some of the sweetest of my life, sitting on the jetty, baiting the hooks, waiting for the fish to bite, sniffing the dark tobacco of the men's pipes, half-listening as they reminisced in Dutch, waiting, always waiting for something to happen, to break the spell. We also had a little boat with a Seagull motor, and sometimes we would go out to sea and I would dream of high adventure and discoveries and whales and glory. I would look down into the deep deep water and shrink in fear from its unknown terrors. I pretended to be brave.

The end of my mother's story about Cleome Gordon was that when she grew up she became a dressmaker and married a small-time gangster with an Irish name in Hobart and he eventually slit her throat. This was one of the great true life morality tales, containing within itself the vividness and the satisfying elements of a fairy story mingled with a horror story. It serves as a kind of moral tale of vindication for the immigrant over the cruel, flash power of the ruling class — such as it was. My mother likes to tell the story, embroidering the details, and she always surprises me when she seems to revel in the gory bits. Apparently Cleome's ballgowns and wedding dresses were much sought after far and wide, but Cleome did what was called 'too much running around' and the gangster husband put an end to her.

During my parents' teenage years at Smithton High School the Dutchies were generally laughed at for being Dutch. And being called Van Loon didn't exactly help. Even my mother's name 'Engel' would not have been exempt from mockery — just because it was foreign, not because anybody would make the connection with the angels. My mother remembers fondly and wistfully two beautiful dark-eyed Jewish girls who befriended her, two sisters called Zillah and Eva. They were so kind and so sweet and so clever and they made her life bearable, teaching her English and sitting with her at lunchtime. They moved to Queensland and she never saw them again, but I bless them and thank them for their grace in the midst of what was my mother's bleak Tasmanian teenage migrant life. Generally she and her brothers and sisters were mocked for talking Double-Dutch and Gobbledegook, for eating thick slices of bread wrapped around slabs of bitter chocolate, for their clothes, their hair, even their teeth, which were bigger and stronger than any other teeth around. Most of us in our family, including me, have white eyelashes, and that always was, and sometimes still is, a subject for derision and mockery. It particularly bothered my sisters who spent their teenage years experimenting with make-up, and devising clever ways to get mascara to work, like mixing it with linseed oil which almost ruined their eyesight. Nothing ever seemed to work or to give the right effect on the Van Loon eyelashes. And I had the added problem of my lazy eye and the eye-patch. The right eye got stronger in fact as time went on, but an eye-man I talked to recently told me that it might have gotten better without the patch anyhow.

After a while the other students came to like our Dutch cooking. My mother swears her family introduced hazelnut chocolate spread to this country, and we also gave the neighbours a taste for home-style smoked or pickled herrings which are very very Dutch. I don't really know much Dutch history myself, but I *do* know that in the thirteenth century El Niño brought the herring industry to the country and launched Holland as a maritime power. How about that!

People in Christmas Hills didn't care, or even realise, that Tasmania itself was once long ago named after a Dutch navigator. First of all a Dutch sea-explorer, Abel Tasman, named the island, as people from outside will name things, on the twenty-fourth of

November 1642. He called it Van Diemen, in honour of the Governor of Batavia who had sent him on his voyage of exploration and discovery in the Great Peaceful Ocean. And there's a little island off the east coast of Van Diemen's Land called 'Maria', named by Tasman for Governor Van Diemen's wife. Tourists now go on guided walks on Maria Island which has become very trendy. The really interesting part about this, I think, is that Abel Tasman was madly in love with Maria Van Diemen, the boss's wife. I like to think that, when the name was later changed from Van Diemen's Land to Tasmania, Abel and Maria were together at last, taking off their stiff white lace collars and getting down to business in heaven.

I'm quite sentimental about these things, and sometimes even fanciful. There's a fine and treacherous threshold between honest sentiment and foolish sentimentality, and although I try to follow the former, I confess I sometimes lapse quite badly into the latter. For instance, I used to think in a quaint way that Maatsuyker Island was named because it and its neighbours resembled sprinklings of sugar, but I recently read somewhere that Tasman gave it the name because when he saw it the tea-trees were blooming there, and he thought the fluffy white flowers looked like sugar. But I also imagine it's possible that the name was simply in honour of Joan Maetsuijcker who was one of the Batavian signatories to the papers granting Tasman his voyage. You could write a history of the human imagination, the human heart, just by telling the stories of the place names of Van Diemen's Land. They resonate so sadly and wistfully with ancient observations, hopes, fears — Jerusalem, Paradise, Mathinna, Bay of Fires, Chain of Ponds, Tinderbox, Black River, Christmas Hills, Cape Grimm.

The whole country of Australia was once called New Holland, but it isn't Dutch any more, and a form of English is spoken here these days. Yet if you go back to 1840 you can see the Governor of Van Diemen's Land had a kind of hope that things would not be so narrow, so black and white, cut and dried. The foundation stone he laid for a little museum in Hobart was written in English, French, Italian, German, Latin and Greek. The Dutch had already faded from view at that stage. But I think it is a beautiful inscription, so full of foolish, sweet and scholarly hope.

I spend a lot of time here staring out to the terrible sea, thinking nothing, or contemplating my own fears, imagining the monsters of the ocean floor, imagining the boats that brought the explorers with their expectations, noble and ignoble, brought then the soldiers and the convicts and their jailers. As a kind of face-your-fear therapy I try to imagine the bottom of the sea as it is everywhere around here littered with the wrecks of boats, shattered and whole, furred and fuzzed with slimy green, quiet-sprouting barnacles, and I have sometimes in sleep dreamt of figureheads, fabulous wooden women, their hair blown back, their gowns billowing behind them in the ocean spray, their blind wide eyes like the eyes of crazed fairground horses forever staring through the weeds and rocks and unknown corals that jumble and twist and loom in the soundless, lightless world to which they have been abandoned perhaps for eternity. Eternity.

As well as staring out to sea, I spend a lot of time in the facility gym — I am addicted to the rowing machine — and we play tennis here in the summer. We also field a rather scrappy staff cricket team that plays the inmates. The inmates always win. I regret that the pool doesn't have views of the ocean, but everything here generally looks inward. I have described the place as resembling a fortress or a castle, but that really applies only to the outside — what you get inside is more like one of the sets for James Bond. Gulbransen was apparently addicted to Bond movies as well as to the organic shapes of his hero Gaudi, so that no doubt explains it. The outside romantic look is consistent with the current marketing image of Tasmania. It is as if the grim facts of a history that is not so old must be re-presented as sweet and charming, even amusing. I guess it's much the same all over the world. It's one way of coping with ugly facts. You can hide them or you can dress them up in fancy costume and sell them, since people are forever looking for things to buy.

I have the time to read a lot. I read the papers with a greedy obsession, and I watch too much television. I read a rather incredible number of books, I dream, write poetry, and I listen to music. I study the professional journals and keep in touch with colleagues in other places. Recently I was offered a job at a state prison completely unlike this one, in Florida. I found the offer quite tempting. There are prisoners there on death row, which makes it highly attractive — I would be most interested in them. I sound as if I never do any work but, as well as looking out the window and listening to music, I do spend much of my time with the patients, and a hell of a lot of time in meetings with my colleagues and administrators.

One day I expect I will move on, will take up my travels where I left off. Maybe go to Florida? I often have a strangely vivid (so vivid, so vivid) dream of a bright green and white backpacker hostel that must be somewhere in dream-Greece. Even as I am dreaming it, I am aware that it has the sharp quality of hallucination. It is there that I find my dream soul mate, my woman with amber-eyes, singing softly to me in the twilight. This brings me to reflect on some of the history of my personal life.

Once I was married to Paloma García, but what began romantically and dramatically in Mexico ended a year later in New Mexico with some bad blood and some hard feelings. All concerned — me and Paloma and the Other Man — were somewhat the worse for wear. At least I was the worse for wear, maybe they weren't. My mother certainly was — she was already knitting her special sort of lacy white baby dress in joyous expectation of our non-existent offspring. The dress was not knitted in vain, as it has served its purpose many times over, since my sisters regularly produce batches of bouncing young.

Paloma and I met in the unlighted emergency room of a nightmarish hospital in Mexico City during the earthquake of 1985. Looking back now I can see that we were caught up in the romance of having escaped death and of being thrown together by fate under extreme circumstances. She was wearing a thin dress the colour and texture of the pink fairy-floss cloud dress worn by a girl I fell in love with when I was six, my Cinderella girl. I was lost in an enchantment. I tell myself Paloma's dress had nothing to do with what happened, it was just a nice coincidence. The air around our first embrace was filled with the groans of a man dying on the floor beside us, his blood flowing warm and slippery and pungent beneath our bare feet. There was the stench of shit and decay with a sharp hint of a nauseatingly sweet disinfectant. We ran, both only slightly injured, from the hospital and kept going, finding a bicycle under a pile of dust and rubbish, and riding together out to the suburb where Paloma's uncle lived. We passed the dead and dying on the way. There was nothing we could do but keep going. Three months later we were married. It's all a blur now.

When we had been married for a year, and were on a short holiday, staying in Taos where I was doing homage to D.H. Lawrence, she deserted me — oh that bleak, that desolate word — to follow after a tall handsome Spanish Jesuit who was, or so he rather quaintly said, detaching himself from his original vows. Well, they had language and religion more or less in common. It took me a good five years to recover from the heartbreak. Heartbreak — there is another one of those plain and dangerous words. Heartbreak.

It was a radiant morning, the morning Paloma left me. She walked out through a dark red door in Taos, into the arms of Jesus the Jesuit who was carrying a small basket of oranges and a single red rose. How could something so corny cause so much heartache, so much world-shattering pain and anguish? Five years to recover. Five years. It's ridiculous. However I did recover — all you suicidal rejected lovers take note. The experience, as it happens, did me good. It's a well-known fact, but one that often needs to be restated, that the broken heart is just one necessary trauma among many in the development of the adult human being, like the pain of getting wisdom teeth, perhaps.

In any case, while those Greek sirens of the dreamland backpacker hostel call to me from the deep of sleep, I labour on alone in the sparkling daily gleaming whitenesses of the facility, listening to the dreams, the thoughts, the fabling warbling narratives of the patients, making judgments and decisions about their mysterious lives.

Meanwhile, much of eastern Australia is turning to dust. Seven million tonnes of topsoil, I heard, blew away in one enormous duststorm. Almost in the same breath you hear dust and El Niño. Here at Black River the words 'El Niño' have a different meaning from the newsreader's one. Our most important life-guest, our star, is Caleb Mean, who has been known all his life as El Niño. Because of Caleb and his title and the significance of El Niño in his family history, I have made a study of warm currents and weather patterns and catastrophes, as well as a study of the Catholic image of the Christ Child. I came to know about the role of El Niño in the Netherlands herring industry, for instance, not because of my Dutch heritage, but because of my study of Caleb — Caleb Mean, El Niño of northwest Van Diemen's Land.

I have elected to write an account of Caleb, who was nicknamed 'El Niño' by his family when he was born in 1959. I say 'nickname' but it was really more like giving him a title. I sometimes carelessly conflate 'Caleb' with 'Caliban' the missing link, because for one thing Caleb Mean is startling in his oddity. I have met some very unusual characters in my time, but Caleb is, for good reason, the strangest and most fascinating to me.

I confess that he is part of the reason I decided to take the job here at BRPDF. I have wanted to know what made him tick for a long long time. I never will, but I can try. He was treated by his family as if he was the South American version of the Holy Child, the Infant Jesus who sits up on his throne, wearing a pink silk dress and covered in cockle shells. He sometimes used to wear a straw hat with shells on it, a pilgrim's hat, a replica of the hat on El Niño de Atocha. We are the same age, Caleb and I, and I have known about him all my life — he was famous around here, a strange looking boy with huge teeth, and smooth shining electric-blue eyes with long black curling lashes. He sometimes wore the robes of El Niño, and sometimes he wore a shining silver and white suit, all his costumes were made from cheap taffeta and satin, according to my mother, who would know. He led prayer meetings and rallies, always gleaming with a preternatural radiance. I met him several times when we were children, and there would often be articles about him in the paper, sometimes serious, sometimes teasing and joking. I used to read these greedily, and with a sort of envy for his exotic, powerful and privileged life. I have spent many years trying to make sense of the phenomenon of Caleb by clinical and therapeutic means, like many of my colleagues both here and abroad. The result is a vast file of colourful contradictions and very little real illumination. So instead of a psychiatric report, I am giving a poet's telling of the story, which I hope goes wider and deeper than any case-study. I am looking for the shape of the shadows of things, of lives, of the ways things happen. Sometimes in half-dreams I enter the terror of being caught by the chill strings of my heart in the shifting shape of a shape-shifting Caleb. He morphs into a photographic negative of a photograph of myself. And once I heard a voice that I identified as his voice calling, echoing from a great distance, and that voice was calling: Nineteenfiftynine and already too late!

Caleb Mean is my great challenge. He is very difficult to understand, let alone explain. Impossible perhaps. I love a challenge!

Sometimes I feel that in writing these stories I give the account not only of the people and the events at Cape Grimm and nearby, but of Cape Grimm country itself, this place where the very winds and the very air are caught and sifted and measured and recorded. For Caleb and his deeds really are fashioned of the air — of the history and the geography, and they are made from the rocks and the trees and the water. And the air, oh, the sweet pure magical air. The air and time. Ticktockticktockticktock. Bewarebewarebeware. Tidesturn,tidesturn, tidesturn. Burnandonedayyouwillburn. Such was the rhyme we used to sing, the counting rhyme, the beat of the human heart. I don't know where it came from, that song. Am I being too fanciful — about the links between Caleb and this place? I don't know. It is a strange and eerie place, and I must tell the tale. Caleb's story reaches back into the history of his family, and like a lot of stories, I suppose, this is as much about me, the author, as it is about him, the subject. I know I'll be unable to resist breaking into the narrative as the story develops, and I have already begun laying out for readers some of the history of my own family. The two histories, of the Means and the Van Loons, are different, yet both families fetched up here on the rocky northwest coast of Van Diemen's Land, and that seems to bring them together, or so I think. The Means were here in the mid-nineteenth century, the Van Loons coming a hundred years later. This begins as a story of migration, of people looking for a home, finding it here on the far northwest of this island. Cape Grimm I see as a pinpoint focus, a convergence of lines of lives leading from all corners of the globe over time. You can do that to any place on the map, but I have chosen to do it with Cape Grimm. Because I am here. Because it is a kind of nowhere. Because it is home.

My practice in much of this writing is, as my colleagues love to tell me, unprofessional. I sometimes consider retiring from my day job in order to plunge head-first into the sea of writing fiction. And I also think of maybe going into private practice where I can be more free, and in a sense more secretive, somehow. I also think of giving up psychiatry altogether and becoming — what — ah, I don't know. Whatever the morality of this project, now that I have begun I certainly intend to continue. I must go on. For years I have done no other writing but articles for journals, and also the poems that pour out from my unconscious. The present project is another matter, with a different purpose, a new and different pleasure for me. No doubt there is an element of self-delusion lurking here. I am in love with the idea of telling the story, with giving myself the freedom to construct with words as I have never before constructed.

Some scholars say the oldest story to be found in manuscript is the tale of *The Shipwrecked Sailor*. The date of the manuscript is disputed, but in any case the tale is written on a very ancient Egyptian papyrus scroll, telling of a sailor who ended up on an island where he was saved and befriended by a serpent of bright gold. This place was called the Island of the Soul. That's the oldest story, and I can imagine that the story I am telling might even be part of it.

If I die in the sea, don't leave me here alone.

Am I writing against that loneliness? The child in the sea off Christmas Island had only her little human voice, and for the world at large, those words of hers are all that remain, but they are words never to be forgotten. When she spoke them she threw out a line to me, up here at Black River in my Rapunzel's Tower. I see that in quite visual terms, the little child in the water crying out to her father, the words becoming a line of eerie vermilion type, like the words the angel whispered into the ear of the Virgin Mary. Hail Mary. The child's words arc out from the waters off Christmas Island to the valleys of Christmas Hills where I take up the story. As I try to unlock the mysterious logic in the story of Caleb Mean, I am, in a sense, for the sake of the little one who cried out in the sea, looking for the key in our lives that turns and twists and unleashes our misfortunes. The destiny that left her there to drown, the impulse that compelled Caleb to set his own people alight. I will not leave her there alone. I will explore destiny, and good, and evil, and time, and tide. I have both a wide canvas and a curiously narrow one.

This is a big project, I know, but I have been worrying at it like a loose tooth for a long time now, and if I don't get on with it I might go mad myself. I think it could be quite easy to go mad. I live with the madness of others every day, and everybody knows that psychiatrists suffer from some of the ills of their patients. There must still be members of that lost child's family on earth, so the effect of her drowning on the SIEV-X will reverberate forever somewhere. For one thing, her father lived to report her words, otherwise I would not know them.

But my first task is this one: to trace the twisted history of Caleb Mean, to untangle, to find the shape of things. Instead of going into Caleb's head, I will go out into his past and out into the world, and that journey will take me far and wide in time and space. I will look at the stars and I will imagine the deep, deep ocean where the Kraken slumbers. There is talk of global warming, with much evidence. I wonder, as the planet heats up, and the Kraken prepares to take over the oceans, and the fevered earth, if the tempers of human beings might not be on the rise. Is everybody getting angrier? Is Caleb's conflagration just a symptom of a terrible flaming anger that is taking hold of the world? I love action movies. I do. Is the world turning into an action movie? I think perhaps it is. Maybe.

I took down my well-worn copy of the complete works of Hans Christian Andersen to check on the eyes of the dogs in the story of *The Tinderbox* and I discovered that whereas *The Tinderbox* is the first story collected, the sixth last — Number 150 of 156 — is called *The Great Sea Serpent.* I read it for the first time, and it turns out that the serpent there is not the Kraken I had imagined it would be, but the telegraph cable 'that stretches from Europe to America'. It lies 'perfectly still, as if it were lifeless, but inside it is filled with life, with thoughts, human thoughts. Human thoughts expressed in all the languages of the world, and yet silent, the snake of the knowledge of good and evil.' Just like Jules Verne and H.G. Wells, Hans Christian Andersen had his eye and his finger on the future. I had not fully realised that before. He saw in the transatlantic telegraph cable the snake of the knowledge of good and evil worming its slithery way beneath the waters of the world.

Meanwhile, much of eastern Australia, speck by speck, is turning to dust.

CHAPTER TWO

Mask

'Their vestments of spiders' webs shall not abide the
force of the Lord's wind.'
JOHN KNOX, *Epistle to the Congregation of the Castle of St Andrews*

I had already heard a great deal about Caleb Mean and felt I already knew him when I met him for the first time at a picnic. Before this day I had only seen him from a distance. Memories of this picnic take me back into the pleasant wandering realms of my childhood. It was summer holidays in Christmas Hills, the day I encountered Caleb, and our whole family — from the grandparents down to the littlest babies — were out at Duck River for the day, eating and drinking and fishing and swimming. I was about eight in a land of milk and honey. Our feet were bare, flies tickled our skin, and our white blond hair stuck up in tufts, letting the sun straight through to our pink Dutch skulls. The girls, protesting, wore sunbonnets which were one of my mother's specialities, but the boys were too tough for hats. Some of us were playing one of our favourite games under the helter-skelter shelter of a she-oak that grew above a big rock, away from the family group on the picnic rugs. We were on the dusty ground at the foot of the rock. The game was called

'Mask' and the main players were the Victim and the Interrogator. The rest were the Jury. The Victim had to put on a mask and answer questions invented by the Interrogator, the point being that all your answers had to be lies. The Jury kept score. When they decided you had told the truth three times, or had hesitated too long over your answer, you were out. You had one last chance to tell the truth, one last chance while everyone chanted our rhyme: Ticktockticktockticktock. Bewarebewarebeware. Tidesturn,tidesturn, tidesturn.Burnandonedayyouwillburn.

The nature of the questions meant that when you told the lie the others knew the truth anyway. Either way you were exposed, and you looked stupid.

The mask itself was a balaclava, hot as hell, made by Aunt Edda — strictly speaking she was a great-aunt — who lived over at Woodpecker Point, and spoke embarrassingly terrible English. 'Yu git th' idee?' she would wail after every second thing she said. I always squirmed inside when I heard her in public with her grotesque double vowels and the funny buzzing of the 'zz'. She was always cooking, buns and 'keks', always keks with cinnamon and vanilla and nutmeg. 'Littol keks for good children,' she would say, and I would try to blot out the way she talked, greedy for her cooking. Loving her for her keks, her shellbark layer cake and her shoo-fly pie. Yet I loved her too. 'The flowerz and the zunshine bring the colourz, children, and the shadowz and the gravez. Yu get th' idee?' We did understand her perfectly, but it was hard for people outside the family. She would tap the side of her spectacles with the middle finger of her left hand, as if to ensure somehow that the listeners got the idea. She kept a few sheep from which she got the wool to spin and dye and knit and weave — and we would even be taken on excursions to distant towns for the purpose of scraping lichen from the old gravestones in the cemeteries. She said the lichens gave her the finest dyes, but for us the visits to the graveyards were just another reason for other kids to make fun of us. We were known as Double-Dutch graverobbers, among other things.

The headstones in the cemetery at Stanley were some of the cleanest in the area because we scoured them. They were also dangerous because they were completely undermined by rabbit warrens. We would go to the beach below the graveyard for a picnic, baskets of Dutch gingerbread and ambrosial egg and bacon pie and, before we were permitted to eat a thing, we had to take to the graves with our pocket knives, collecting the lichens in special wicker baskets lined with the broad leaves of the palm trees that grew along the path to Edda's front door. Edda used to say that the lichens from that particular spot, from that graveyard looking out to sea, were among the finest lichens in the world. I don't know how she figured that, but you couldn't argue with her. 'Zientifick,' she would say, 'it iz perfeckly zientifick. You get th' idee?' Her other great scientific exercise was fixing her dyes in the urine of sheep or goats. All this happened in a shed under an old plum tree, and I leave people to imagine the fumes and the smell. We would do anything, anything at all, to get out of helping in the fixing shed. Edda refused to use commercial or synthetic dyes, claiming that her methods were God's own methods, as used by the people in the Old Testament (and the Greek myths). He was a strictly vegetarian god, with something rather Buddhist about him, as far as colouring his fabrics went, for Edda would not use, for example, cochineal, but worked on getting her reds from plant sources. She was known to use tea and coffee and seeds and grasses and wine and fruits and flowers — marigolds, red roses, the dark blue of the iris — never shellfish or blood. And she said squid ink was of no use to her. She had a friend who used to send her bright russet and terracotta lichens — which are smeared like paint and clotted like blood across the rounded tear-stained rocks along the coastline of Flinders Island — and she treasured those, giving cries of a kind of holy joy when she opened the little parcel. I have to emphasise that her work was really beautiful, and I wish I had kept some of it, if only to reassure myself that I am not imagining its quality in the glow of nostalgic memory.

One other wistful memory I have of Edda is that she would tell us of how, when she was a young girl, she went to Paris with her family for a wedding. It was in the church in the Rue du Bac, and Edda was very impressed by the prettiness of the pale pictures of the virgin on the walls. Then outside, as the bride and groom were being showered with rose petals, and the bells were ringing, a strange man shouldered his way through the happy crowd and seemed, Edda would say, to make a beeline for her alone. He was wearing a grey hat and a black cloak from the shoulder of which fluttered ribbons of many colours. He bent down and whispered in her ear, offering to sell her 'time'. In French he offered her, for the price of one franc, ten years of life.

But you don't even understand French, Aunt Edda, we would say, and she would say — ah, but that was the miracle, I *understood* him.

And you paid him?

Off courz I paid him. I take off my glove and I open up my little red velvety purse and I count out my coins, one, two, three, all of them, they are jinglingjangling in there all through the weddingz. Exactly one franc, it was as if he was knowing. He gave me a grey piece of paper with Latin writing on it. A certificate of time it was called. I fold it up as tiny small as can be.

So where is the paper now?

Ah, the paper. I looze the paper, but I have the years, I have my ten years extra.

You can't prove it.

I do not have to prove it, I am here, you zee, that provez it. You get the idee?

And she would pass her hands over her eyes as if to summon the man in the cloak from the shadowy lichen-dyed cloak of her own dreams and imaginings and hopes. Whenever I recall Aunt Edda, I feel my heart lift, feel my own spirit infuse with the lilting childish optimism of her voice, with the glow of something like truth in her round pale eyes.

Tell us about the baby and the cat, we would say, and she would tell us about the floods in 1421, the Saint Elisabeth floods. It seemed to us that she had been there, that maybe she was the baby girl in the cradle.

And the dyke break up and the waters they come surging through the windows and the doors and slapping and walloping up up up to the nursery floor and the nurse goes flop and she does not have a minute to even zgream she is gone. Only her little white frilly bonnet — Dutch girl — goes floating and bobbing, still as little potato in her knitty pink jacket. And up up from the floor floatz the little rocking wooden cradle where baby Edda (was that you? Ah, I am not saying) baby Edda sails out onto the tricking ricking rocking water. She is doomed. She will drown. The winds fly down on her and spin spin her round and round and the waves go up and the waves go down and all along the wide water the windmillz cry out like great big giants in pain and they wave ze arms whirly whirly clackety clack clack clack! Then zuddenly, zuddenly the little grey cat come from nowhere flying along the rooftopz, wheee she goes, straight she flies — out to the rocking rim of ze little hood roof of the little Edda's cradle. And all through the night, and all through the day of the great Saint Elisabeth flood, that little cat she runz, she runz backwarz and forwarz and backwarz and forwarz and the rocking cradle sails along on the terrible waters and I tell you, the baby iz safe and sound and warm and dry and she never even cries. She never even cries a very little bit-bit. And the brave little grey cat and the brave little baby they live happy ever after.

We had an uncle who lived on the west coast of Van Diemen's Land at a place near Strahan, and from time to time he would parcel up some lichen from the graveyard on the headland there, and send it to Edda in the mail. You would have thought someone had sent her a packet of diamonds, she would be so excited. The colours she got from the lichens and all the other things were all shades of rust and ochre and saffron and grey and lilac and green. They were very very beautiful, I realise that now, the sort of thing that arts councils prize highly, and that sell for a fortune in tourist outlets. But back then we hated the colours of our clothes, and we also hated the knitting patterns that were so different from the things other kids were wearing. Sometimes the differences were subtle, like a certain kind of collar Edda used to do, but the other kids could pick them every time. The needles Edda used were made from tortoise shell — what, I asked her once, the shells of real tortoises? And she said in astonishment that of course they were real tortoises, what else? 'What would ellz they be, you zilly boy?' Tortoise shells for knitting needles and hair combs, elephants' tusks for the keys of the old piano. The wonderful world was full of all manner of useful material.

From the forked branches of a gum tree at her back door Edda used to hang the dyed fleece out to dry. It was known as the haberdashery tree, and whenever I see one of those particular gums I think of Edda, remember her tree dripping and dangling and flapping with clouts of coloured wool. After the spinning came the winding into skeins. For this a child had to stand for a long time with its arms held up as if about to embrace a lover, hands stiff and draped with wool, while Aunt Edda stood in front rapidly winding the wool into a ball over the fingers of her left hand. We cried because our arms ached, but she was relentless. While we are on the subject of Aunt Edda, I must add that her brother, Uncle Willem, must have been inspired or infected by the idea of the lichen, because when he became a herbalist, he used to go to a place in Russia every five years or so to collect the lichen from a particular stand of trees. He put this stuff into one of his cures for cancer. I think it's worth noting that he lived to be one hundred and three. He was a Hobart eccentric, living for years in rooms on the top floor of Hadley's Hotel, and celebrated for his impeccable grey suits and burgundy silk cravats with a diamond pin.

Aunt Edda appeared to be a childless widow, and I just assumed she was. But she had in fact had a daughter. One day I was looking through a box of old photos.

'Who's this?' I asked, having unearthed a whole series of hand-tinted pictures of a fat, round-faced, blonde child in a pink and green dress, her arms around a large dog.

'Put those away,' my mother said in a quiet and warning tone, 'that's Dorothea.'

'Who?'

'She was Aunt Edda's daughter. She died when she was very young.'

'How? I didn't know Aunt Edda had any children. How did she die?'

'As a matter of fact, if you must know, she ate a hydrangea.'

'A hydrangea?'

'Yes. They're very poisonous. Now put those pictures away. And promise me you will never say anything about Dorothea to anybody. Let sleeping dogs lie. She has been forgotten now, and that's for the best. Poor Edda was destroyed, but she had to get on with her life. It broke up her marriage. There were no more children. It was a terrible terrible thing, Paul.' My mother was weeping.

It is so vivid to me, that scene with my mother, the tone of her voice, the sadness of the pictures, hastily tipped back into their box, never to be seen again. I had known that Aunt Edda's husband was killed in an accident on the Hydro, but this was a whole new dimension. An unknown dead child, poisoned by a common flower.

It was one of those key moments in childhood when you see the abyss opening up at your feet. I suppose it's called growing up. No wonder Edda was a bit nutty — but as I say, she was also very loving and sweet. In retrospect I realise how wonderful it was that she could pour so much love on us. But it was also eerie that she would send us to the cemeteries all the time.

My thoughts have often returned, in moments of reflection, to Dorothea and the hydrangea. Her parents and forebears had survived the wars in Europe, had travelled to this strange remote and hostile place on the edge of civilisation to fashion a haven, ultimately to carve a bright future, had found a safe place for Dorothea to run and play in the sunlight, far from the guns, bombs, pollution, starvation, death camps and insanities of the old world.

And then one day, as sunlight quivers in the tops of the eucalypts, as it dapples the path, and dew sparkles on the grass that is sugared and sprinkled and spangled with daisies, through the gate, past the bleeding furrow of a swathe of Flanders poppies, skipping on chubby legs, her hair a saintly nimbus, her pinafore a sensible shade of mustard, comes Dorothea. She is three years old.

Leaning over a new stone wall, sheltered by a stand of thick reptilian ferns, is a luscious bush of puffy ragged hydrangeas, ready-made bouquets for brides and ladies. Dorothea settles on the wall, and she reaches out to cup the flowers with both hands. Her guardian angel, thinking the child is part angel herself, and therefore safe from lightning strikes and falling trees, snakes and tigers and raging rivers, has left her to her own devices. Dorothea arranges a small tea party for the fairies who live in the hedge. Her neat little fingers nip from the hydrangea bush the tight curled flower buds, and then she places these in tidy piles on plates made from leaves all along the warm stones of the wall. Time passes and the fairies do not eat their portion; Dorothea nibbles hers, nibbles theirs, until only a few traces of the buds remain.

Dorothea hops down from the wall and returns to the house, where she sits on the verandah on a small willow chair next to her grandmother who is shelling peas. She nibbles on a pea or two. And shortly doubles up with a pain that is attributed to the effects of the fresh peas. What else did you eat? Flowers. Dorothea goes into convulsions, with fever, violent vomiting and diarrhoea, is put to bed, the doctor called for, she goes blue. By the time the doctor arrives she is in a coma and beyond help. They find the hydrangea buds in her apron pocket, and the remains of the fairies' feast out on top of the new stone wall.

Dorothea's pictures are put away, lost until I bring them to the surface many years later, and her short life and her tragedy have had the time to acquire the haven and the patina of legend. I am still afraid of hydrangeas, and during childhood I was phobic about them. At the sight of their powder puff pink and blue bunches the memory of the photographs of Dorothea and her dog comes swiftly to the surface of my mind, hangs before my vision like an hallucination, a warning of treachery and danger. I still think 'hydrangea' rhymes with 'danger'.

I searched for Dorothea's grave in the cemetery at Woodpecker Point, and when I didn't find it I tentatively asked my mother where it would be.

'Oh,' she said, 'they buried her in the orchard. You know the little statue of a girl with a duck? That's where she is. There's a beautiful climbing rose that goes all over the fence there — I think it's Reine Marie Henriette.'

'Why didn't they put up a headstone?'

'Well, Edda wanted just the statue and the roses. I don't know.'

The tone of impatience and discomfort had returned to my mother's voice. It's a tone that says stop asking questions if you know what's good for you. So that's all I know, really, about Dorothea.

I told my brothers and sisters about the life and death of Dorothea, and Anika, my most sentimental sibling, and I went out to the orchard and paid our respects to the weathered statue of the girl and the duck, and we picked an armful of the brilliant cerise blooms from Reine Marie Henriette who had gone completely mad all up and down the orchard fence. We took the roses home, and my mother knew where we had got them from, but she said nothing. There would forever be unspeakable pain surrounding the memory of Dorothea. She is a tender loss, a gap in the emotional landscape of the family. I begin to understand why Edda told the story of the baby in the cradle with the cat. And as I think of Dorothea now, my thoughts run ahead to the chasm that is the lost village of Skye, where many many Dorotheas died, where one hundred and forty-seven people were incinerated in 1992.

I must now return to the day I first saw Caleb Mean, the child who would grow up to eliminate his family, his community, in one cataclysmic hit. Come with me to the picnic at Duck River. The ski-mask we had for the truth game was a hideous rust and slime coloured stripy stocking that covered your whole head, with red-rimmed holes for eyes and mouth, and a little red tuft on the crown for decoration. Somewhere in Peru there's a glacier where people go to worship at a shrine of El Niño, and they wear truly grotesque masks just like ours. Well, I, free at least of my pirate's black patch, was sweating under the woolly mask — and under the probing questions of Anika, trying to lie my way out of questions about tobacco and alcohol and sex and violence and theft and lying itself — when a vision appeared as if out of nowhere. It was a boy with pale gold hair which was cut short and that stuck out at all angles like the leaves of a pineapple, or perhaps the spines of a hedgehog, and he had fine English skin, huge pale ice-blue eyes, and a mouth full of the most enormous dazzling teeth I have ever, even to this day, ever seen. And although his teeth were ugly, his smile was incredibly and strangely attractive. He was dressed in a white suit, like a little band-leader, with silver lapels, and he was suddenly there, above us, beside the old she-oak, gleaming with a supernatural radiance. He looked ridiculous, yet he had the power to suck our whole attention towards him. There was never a moment when we might have laughed or thrown stones at him. He was a magnet, a star shining above us. And there was about him a look of the wild-haired boy with the huge long fingernails on the cover of *Struwwelpeter* — awesome, angel/demon, and yet, in him I think we saw something of ourselves. That was the truly strange, compelling and disturbing thing, that when we looked at Caleb Mean, we were looking at ourselves, our deepest hopes and fears, our souls.

We looked up.

I imagined at first that he had come upon us by chance when he was out for some celestial stroll, but when we discussed it afterwards we decided he must have sought us out, must surely have come after us. He had his say, which was actually brief enough, but it seemed, coming from his lips, to be a magical incantation that could make time stand still. Then he raised his arms in blessing and returned to a white panel van that had crept up towards him, his father at the wheel. We were part of their mission to the world. Why didn't they stay to enlist us? I don't know. Perhaps he was just practising on us, perhaps we were merely a step along his way. Were we his entertainment? He certainly was ours. Astonished, I peeled the mask from my prickly red face, squinting in the light. We all stopped as if frozen or paralysed, staring up at the figure above us, and he, calling more or less to the air and the clouds, shouted in a voice that rang with hysterical conviction: 'He telleth the number of the stars; he calleth them all by their names.'

We didn't know the Bible well enough to realise that he was reciting Psalm 147. It sounded so beautiful and magical, pouring from the lips of this skinny boy in his shiny clothes. And that was all he did — he called the Psalm to us, his audience transfixed below the rock. Then he blessed us with his open arms and his sparkling teeth, fixed in a frightening grin, then he went. I have after-images of a swirling silver cape, a crackling of sparks as his heels struck the ground, a plume of dust as the van sailed off, gathering speed, sailing in a kind of haze, disappearing over the horizon. It wasn't really like that, I know. It was a mundane enough departure, yet the storyteller of the mind likes to import the trappings of drama and fantasy — something comic-book, something nightmare, something of sinister promise.

We stood there blinking for a minute, then we ran back to the picnic spot to tell everyone what had happened. We were all talking at once, but the folks could understand well enough that the Preacher Boy from out at Skye had paid us a flying visit, and they were none too pleased. The settlement at Skye was viewed with deep suspicion, even fear, and the legend of the Preacher Boy was one of the more colourful scandals of the place.

'That boy never went to school. It's criminal what they're doing to him. There are laws that say children have to go to school, but those people can do as they like, they can get away with anything. They should be reported to the authorities.' And so on. The smoke from the men's pipes drifted in the air, a silent accompaniment to the fascinated outrage of the women.

They had 'been reported' plenty of times, but the authorities considered them harmless, living as they did in apparent peace and harmony on a stretch of country that was to all intents and purposes otherwise god-forsaken, on the sea coast, just outside government land. My family had a special interest in them because one of my mother's cousins — a weird and beautiful girl called Betje — had 'got mixed up with them' and had eventually married a strange man called Jethro Mean. My family could not know, as they gossiped and discussed the wrong-headedness of Caleb's education, that the lives of Betje and Jethro and their children were in fact so skewed that they were on a course to grotesque disaster and tragedy. And leading them on would be the Preacher Boy who had just mesmerised all of us from the top of the rock.

The other very memorable time I saw Caleb Mean as a child was one day at an Agricultural Show in Burnie. I was about six, on the merry-go-round, sitting in the swan-boat with my brothers and sisters, and there, up ahead on the wildest white horse with the maddest fire eyes and the flying foamy mane tipped with gilt, sat Caleb, so regal, so shiny, so silver, his head thrown back in a kind of ecstasy, holding on to the gold barley-sugar pole like a great straight sceptre. The carousel went round and round and the white horse rode slowly up, slowly down, to the blaring music of the fairground, amid the smells of the cows and the sheep and the fairy floss, pink as clouds in the sunset. You had to look at him; you could not look away.

As the carousel turned and turned, and as the world moved round and about me in a slow and distant blur, from the corner of my eye I caught a flash of live soft pink, a quick pink girl, small like a quick brown fox, who ran alone all alone up to the wild white horse, and as it was prancing by, its rider gazing in rapture at the distant world of his domain, the child skipped, jumped, leapt up onto the running-board, and she grasped the straining neck of the shiny white wooden horse. The huge white bow in her hair bobbed as she moved. Her dress was pink cotton, cotton candy, fairy-floss, cloud cotton, and she clung to the neck as the carousel turned and the music blared and tinkled and whined, and she hung there, a girl with no ticket, no right, no place. She was ignored by the prince on his wild white stallion, but she was the focus of many eyes in the crowd. Where was her mother, her father, her granny? She must be a pale pink orphan in white socks and black shoes and her billowy dress with the wide white collar and the faint impressions of small orange birds fliffing and fluffing around the hem. I saw all this with a delicious clarity. I thought I could smell fairy floss, that tickling whiff of kerosene. And I saw that the girl in pink, drawn by magic to the prince on his horse, was the princess, was radiant. And the world seemed to fall back in the face of her daring leap onto the merry-go-round without a ticket, risking her life, risking falling under the spinning platform and being mashed up in the works.

I was actually a weird kid myself, and I used to hear about Cape Grimm, connecting it with the Brothers but confusing the stories with narratives from other books, and imagining that Red Riding Hood and Cinderella and even Goldilocks and the Little Mermaid lived up at Cape Grimm, the home of the Brothers Grimm. And I loved Andersen's Little Mermaid. I loved her so much. Charles Dickens always said he wanted to marry Red Riding Hood. That sounds a bit too domestic for me and how I felt and what I wanted. I wished so deeply to be with all those amazing girls, to bask in their glow, to stand beside them and defend them from trouble and pain. Well, that's what I imagined or pretended I wanted. And I would climb a favourite apple tree that grew up into the roof space of an old shed, and I would get under the roof and read those lovely books — the illustrations linger to this day in my memory, the dark and scratchy evil George Cruikshank etchings, the Doré image of the giant murdering the babies as they sleep, the gnarled and dreaming drifts and branches of Arthur Rackham, the weirdly elegant and strangely threatening palaces of Edmund Dulac. I thought I could become an illustrator and take myself and others into new dimensions of reality and unreality, but I couldn't really draw. The fairground girl in pink was better than anything I had ever seen in a book.

The princess on the carousel radiated light, and I saw her aura mingle with the light that surrounded Caleb Mean. Mingle just a little. But Caleb never even looked at the girl — and as the mechanism and the music began to slow down, ready to stop so that everybody could hop off or buy another ticket, a woman in a white hat and white gloves came yelling out of the crowd. And Cinderella clung on tighter to the neck of the stallion, and Caleb ignored everything, staring aluminium steadfast ahead, his eyes radioactive circles of terrible spinning light. The woman, her white kid handbag falling to the ground, leapt forward and snatched at the child in pink, prising her fingers from the horse's neck, pulling her away like a plasticine doll (my computer wants me to type 'Pleistocene' but that isn't what I mean) and yanking her onto the grass by the side of the merry-go-round where she turned her over and started slapping her on the back of the legs with the handbag, which she had swiftly retrieved.

'Stay . . . away . . . from . . . those . . . people, that . . . boy,' the mother thumped out the words. The child did not even cry. She just crumpled up and then stood, forlorn, on the grass, and her mother took her by the hand and led her away. 'StayawayfromthatboyItellyou. If you don't stay away from him I will thrash you myself, do you hear?' And the little girl was a ragged shaking bundle of toy rags on the end of her mother's white glove.

The whole thing lasted for only a few minutes, but it is lit in my memory like a scene on a stage, an isolated moment captured in brilliantly glowing time, a sequence of film, a fragment, yes, of dream. It is possibly sealed off in that way because of what happened next, the punctuation mark of finality and shock. The girl, my princess, and her mother went from the carousel where the dangerous El Niño and his followers, as well as me and my brothers and sisters, were riding, riding, riding horses and swans, over to the open field where a crowd of other folks were gathered. People were sitting on tartan rugs and drinking brightly coloured cordials while watching the acrobatics of a little team of light aircraft. It was a perfect afternoon for the air show. Large and graceful birds gleaming in the heavens, glittering great insects, a small boy's dream. *Zoom zoom zaroom*, the planes flashed across the clear free sky, making patterns, now together, now separate. *Zoom*. And as the last little aircraft — its name was *Dumbo* — whooshed down low, climbed, somersaulted, pirouetted, everyone looked up and smiled with pleasure. Then *Dumbo* began to cough, to splutter, to fall, and *Dumbo* fell, it said in the newspaper the next day, like a stone onto the princess and her mother who both died, as they are fond of saying in the papers, instantly. From over at the carousel I heard an explosion, screams, glimpsed a flare of flame, saw the slow obsidian billow of the plume of smoke that brushed tragedy across the sky.

I looked up the old papers and read about it a few years ago. There was a photograph of the woman and the girl — solemn, the same big white bow in her hair. Mrs Roberto Rinaldo and her daughter Francesca. They had been living at Skye, it said, until recently. Poor princess. Her father, it said, was a foreman at the Burnie Paper Mill. As such terrible events will do, her death and the image of Caleb on his white foamy stallion were linked in my childish heart, and they remain forever twinned in my memory, lit with the supernatural light of tragedy and loss. I don't even know the real story behind the child's ride on the merry-go-round, and the mother's hysterical outburst against Caleb and his family. I can guess, but I can never know.

When I think of Caleb's fatal last sermon on the cliff in 1992 I recall also the other time when I saw him, on the day of the picnic, with a particular and eerie vividness. And I think of that sermon often. The words he spoke in his final speech were first rehearsed and recorded on video, on a tape among hundreds of tapes found at a place on the outskirts of Skye known as the Temple of the Winds. He also recorded their final version when he spoke them in his clifftop performance. It's a bit like the photographer who takes the picture of his own death. I have made a study of the words, the tone, the emphasis, in order to try to come to some understanding of his mental state. I compare the sermon with the text he shouted to us at the picnic, and as I do, sometimes thick slabs of my mother's cinnamon apple slice, cold, with great blobs of yellowy cream, come sweetly back to memory.

CHAPTER THREE

Air

'My mother she butchered me. My father he ate me.'
BROTHERS GRIMM, *The Juniper Tree*

This is how it was that night on top of the cliff at Cape Grimm. Caleb the Preacher Boy had become the Preacher Man, and had destroyed his people — and the reality of that is still beyond my comprehension. His narrative had come a long way since the recitation of the Psalm at the picnic; it had moved through poetry to millennial madness, drawing into itself all the drama of the delusion that he is at once the isolated leader and the key and central figure of the universe, the King of the Golden Mountain. I still don't follow what brought this dangerous and tragic man to this point, but my work suggests that many factors and ingredients came together over more than five generations to produce the events of that summer night in 1992. Perhaps in some weird way it was the time and the place for that thing to happen — although that often seems to me to be a very skewed and bleak way to look at the events that make up the movement of human lives.

Caleb sits, high in the darkness, mounted on his horse, on the summit of the lone cliff, facing the sea, facing the forlorn and silken sky. The clear, clean, cold night air, the icy waning moon, the stars a scatter of tinsel in the fine pure air. Behind the man on the horse, across the stubble, rocks, lichen, yellow heath, stands the Cape Grimm weather station, like a tall soft-grey bathing box surrounded by cyclone fences. Light will bounce from the diamond framing wire spaces of the mesh, flashing messages of enclosure, of escape, to the sky, to the angels, to the night birds and the night animals. Presiding over everything is a lacy silver radio tower, a giraffe-insect, a wild windmill, a praying mantis gleaming in the dark.

A light is burning — comfort, hearth, home, a light is burning — in the weather station at Cape Grimm; there is one man inside, working the night shift. This place is where the air is collected, evaluated, measured, sent on to be re-measured, compared with other air, stored. And the air, which blows here across the Southern Ocean, touching no land, is frequently found to be as close to pure as any air in the whole wide world. There is nothing, nothing, between here and Africa which is eight thousand miles away. One of the computers in the silent weather station is named Jakob, and the other is Wilhelm, in remembrance of the great collectors and tellers of stories, the Grimm Brothers. Attached to the side of Wilhelm's monitor are the words of a song on a yellowing piece of paper torn from a story book: *My mother she butchered me. My father he ate me. My sister, little Ann Marie, she gathered up the bones of me, and tied them in a silken cloth, to lay, beneath the juniper tree.*

On the metal filing cabinet beside computer Jakob there is taped a small print of a painting by Tom Roberts, the original of which hangs in a country art gallery, in Victoria, at Benalla. Brushstrokes of children, two girls in white pinafores over gold-brown dresses, beneath a tea-tree twisting and writhing above the rocks on the edge of the seashore. Nearby a row of tiny houses from whose steep roofs wisps of hearth-home smoke is rising. Lights glimmer through the bushes by the tumbledown fence — comfort, hearth, home. And all across the horizon stretch mist-blue trees, low hills, with a miniature town intact, red roofs, white church, the school where other children are busy at their lessons — *Geography, History, Arithmetic, Nature Study for Tasmanians* — the butcher slicing meat, the bricklayer laying bricks. Mothers feeding babies, fathers chopping wood, boys playing cricket, dogs running wild along the beach. And the girls on the patch of stubbly grass beneath the tea-tree on the foreshore, wearing their hats and white pinafores and little black boots, are making a daisy chain.

'Playing in the Garden 1888'. The sea, the glimpse of patch of sea is blue-pink-lilac duck egg speckled in the thin still light of early afternoon. Grandmothers in dark shawls are making oat cakes and knitting stockings by the fireside. Children playing 1888. It is a piece of music, it is a game, the game of 1888 in Ulverstone Tasmania where, just out of sight, Tom Roberts has set up his easel and is painting in oil on canvas. If he forms a telescope with his curling hand he can catch and frame the piece of world, the time, the place, the tree, the children, the sea, the light, the busy far-off town — the church, the school, the dog on the beach. He can glimpse the daisy chain as it shivers in the air, draping from the hands of the child on whose hat there sits a decorative red poppy, on whose pigtail has been tied a bow of poppy-coloured silk. Pinky orange poppy blooming at the end of the pigtail at the back of her neck, in the soundless snatch of sunlight in the paradise glade on the edge of the well-known world. Playing in the garden. White daisies in a daisy chain, swinging in the air. Step forward, Poppy Girl and drape the living necklace on your sister's shoulders, decorate the little one with a string of dying marguerites, wild culling from the forlorn and humble garden behind the beehive oast-house cottages where the black kettle sings on the hob and the grey cat sleeps in the heavy kitchen heat. And in the patch of sunlight, thin upon the yellow grass, a clump of primroses, the paint laid on the canvas in such a way that in a certain light the flowers appear to form the head and body of a little dog, a little dog that turns its eyes to whoever is looking at the picture, which looks out at Tom Roberts, looks out also at every viewer, at me, at the empty room in the Benalla Art Gallery when all the visitors have fled, and only the ghosts remain.

Not so far away from Benalla on the map of Australia, in Bendigo, hangs the picture of the first primrose ever brought alive to the colony, and on the filing cabinet, below the print of the children playing in the garden is stuck a faded, feathered postcard of that primrose picture. The yellow flower in the terracotta pot glows with a supernatural light at the centre of the scene which is busy with nostalgic visitors come to the dock to marvel that this fragile tender bloom could travel all the way from home to this far far place, sprightly, unharmed, fresh from its Wardian case of mahogany and glass. The opulent dark hair of one woman shines as she bows her head before the primrose, caressing the leaves with her cheek, her eyes downcast, her silver earring enormously pendant from her aristocratic ear. The head of a dog is raised from below in homage to the flower. In virginal blue, with soft white head-shawl, wide-eyed a young woman with a face for all the world like the face of Queen Victoria, gazes into the heart of the innocent primrose, enraptured, lost in prayer. Such is the life of an English flower celebrated in the colony in 1855. The colours in the picture have faded over the years, and Africa is still eight thousand miles away across the Southern Ocean.

Below these two pictures on the grey filing cabinet someone has taped the top of an old matchbox on which appears the figure of a young girl. In her left hand a basket of primroses yellow and blue, in her right she elegantly holds a tiny posy selected from the flowers in the basket. Her grey shawl and grey bonnet resemble the clothes of an old woman, her hair is tangled on her forehead, and she tilts her head to one side as she smiles shyly up: 'Primroses, buy one, Sir?' Her arms are bare. The background is indistinct, misty, lilac, dreamy, but the story in her eyes is sad, and long, and terrible. The primrose is often called 'the flower of the key to heaven' — a sad irony.

These four forgotten scraps of paper — the song, the children, the primrose, the child with the basket — are more or less the only evidence here of a human response to anything other than the quality of the air, for life at the station is focused, as is right and proper, on the primary and important purpose of observing and measuring aspects of the weather. And the papers dangle there like the tattered and faded wings of a broken moth, gathering dust, subject to foxing, curling, cracking — distant recollections of other worlds, left there by absent hands who laughed and loved and maybe dreamed and understood. Telling somehow some narrative of dreadful vulnerability, who knows why. Was there one storyteller or many, and what roads have they taken now, and did those roads turn, twisting round and round upon themselves to wend their way back here again, back to the weather station at Cape Grimm where it all began with a song: *My mother she butchered me. My father he ate me*?

The date is February fifth, 1992, when Caleb speaks to the stars of the southern sky above this remote and rugged place, 40°45'S; 144°45'E. His horse is dark, with light scattered markings like pieces of silver faintly gleaming in the darkness. He records his own words on the Sanyo M–5645 in his pocket. Seeking logic, I wonder why he was recording if he truly planned to leap off the cliff into the sea. But you can't apply any rules of logic to the human mind under stress — it is hard enough to apply those rules at any time. Caleb is not thinking straight right now. It is around eleven o'clock, or, as Caleb states it, it is the eleventh hour, the hour of the marigold.

His words as I record them here will lack the ringing voice, that vital spark, the magical ingredient that drove them, as his words were always driven, like flaming arrows into the hearts of those who heard. His words had the quality of primitive music, they went deep into the blood, the nerves, and they worked as a power all their own, they were vibrant, luminous, necessary for the life of the ears into which they poured. Was it only in the timbre of the voice? Was it also in the electric glints in the speaker's eyes? Was it located in the erotic energy sensed in the way he moved his body, the way he stood on a platform, the way he sat on his horse? What was it that persuaded one hundred and forty-seven people to obey that voice and lay down their lives for him like sheaves of wheat before a mighty wind? His own focused ecstasy as he addressed the sky from the clifftop while the village behind him flamed, a thousand torches in the darkness, while smoke and ash rolled and flurried through the air — that ecstasy could hold the stars in thrall.

'I am an owl of the desert. The stars and souls are not mute. From the heavens comes the behest to instil in the air the mystery of all things. God is ocean infinite, infinite cloud. There are songs, there are stories in the air. Listen, listen to the mighty script of the universe. Listen to the saints and the wise men, the wise women, listen to the wisdom of the child. Saint Rose of Lima said "God is infinite cloud, ocean infinite." As I speak to the potent silence of the stars, a shudder is passing over everything that breathes. Joyful souls released from the torment of the earthly journey take glittering flight and swiftly rise with soundless echo into the infinity of space and time. All heaven is watching. Stars, cloak your eyes, for the souls are coming. These souls, these souls in gleaming, rushing flight, these souls on their pathway to the light of light. We are human and yet we came from the sea, from the mist, and we were made from the raw material of the stars. And into our bodies, the great spirit breathed the light of the soul, and we moved and we joined hands, and with holy joy we spoke together to the great universal good. And in our voice was fire. Fire! Fire! Stars and moons and all the suns and planets are on fire with love. On fire with love. And the fuel of that fire is the spirit of the imagination, the images borne of the high human mind. Seek always the Golden Mean, the natural number of all living things that grow and unfold in steps. Seek out in the ocean the nautilus; on the sweet earth, the sun-flower with its spirals of fruitful seeds. Seek out the number and enfold it within the secret imagination of your heart. All movement is in the spark, the ignition, flame, flint of the imagination. And lo! with the imagination comes the end of death, the end of evil, the perpetual cleansing by the divinity of fire. When we are gone, and our hearts are numbered among the brightest of the stars, there will remain the great Milky Way of the chambered imagination, the pure fire of fires. Fire of fires. Star of stars. I am the owl of the desert. And the true gold in the base crucible is Air. Spirits melted into nothing. The secret of the Golden Ratio is Air. Air is the breath of life, and life is the speaking of the Word. Air! Carry the sparks of our brethren to the outmost edges of the breathing universe. Air! Carry these words to the angels; carry them on the spiral winds, the everturning pathway; and carry these souls to the point of calm. For the wind can not blow everywhere forever across the surface of this earth. Somewhere must rest the fixed point that is the true point of salvation. Souls, seek out the fixed point. Imagine yourselves to God. Transform into yourselves. Transmute into air. I am the King of the Golden Mountain. The Word. Take the angel, take the demon, and fashion from the words the sacred Golden Mean. The acrobatic lacewings twist and spiral through space and time. The Air is the story. And the King of the Golden Mountain said: All heads off but mine. For the King must rule the mountain, must rule the seas, and I must commit the souls of the souls to Air. I promise you calm seas, auspicious gales. And behold we have seen the great festival of dreams when the burning brand is seized and the question is asked: "What are dreams?" Woe to him who seeks to answer the question, for dreams are the shadows of the devil's plans, and he who seeks to dream is evil, and will be exterminated by the fire of the furnace. Souls, seek only the fixed point. Listen to the music of the moment. That music will commit all souls to Air. And I will move on; the woman and the child will move on in trinity. We will make the great leap from the high cliff, into the far and holy Air. Nothing is ever lost, for everything is eternal. The new age of the spirit, the prophet Joachim's Golden Age, the age when priests and ceremonies will disappear, when the Air and the spirit will be one — this Golden Age is here and now. Now and here. The task is finished, and time will tell. The words I take with me as I complete my journey, my mission, my contract with earth and heaven, those words are "angel and demon". And with those words I commit our souls. I commit our souls to the wild and scattered freedom of the Air.'

CHAPTER FOUR

Story

'A butterfly is a messenger of love.'

PERUVIAN PARABLE

Caleb was born under the rainbow.

On the evening of the birth, in 1959, Caleb's grandmother, after hearing the ill omen in the cry of an owl, had a vision that told her the child was the chosen one, the prince, the preacher, the prophet. She seems to have ignored the ill omen of the owl. The vision was a radiant manifestation of God in the form of a vast white umbrella from which flew, in multicoloured clouds, flocks of butterflies. As they moved they spelt out the name 'Caleb' on the turquoise cloth of the sky. The word was a gleaming transcription, lit from within as with a sacred flame. From her own childhood learning the grandmother would intone the names of all the species she saw, none of them native to the area. The flurry of opalescent wings resembled a cloud of insects released, tossed from the violated glass cases of a lepidopterist's museum. Esmeralda, Blue Night, Purple Mort Bleu, Cleopatra, California Dog-Face, Orange Albatross, Red Lacewing, Cairns Birdwing. And the grandmother heard a voice that spoke to her from the air:

'Observe the path of the insect as it approaches the light — the path is the number.' There were tropical, South American, wild scarlets, dazzling blinding blues, treefrog greens — and they swirled and shone and glinted, gliding and wheeling in the sunlight of illusion, billowing out from beneath the great umbrella, the great ghostly, no-colour-glassy-shelter with its sinister ribs etched against the light. Pale shadows hover, shine, shimmer. And singing through the patterns of a million wings the grandmother heard next a clear sweet lullaby, where time and space were one, where good and evil mingled to promise now one direction, now another. Now sunshine, now storm — and look, look at the rainbow, the seven shifting colours of the light's refractions. If you fly above the earth the bow of the rainbow becomes now a full fuzzy circle, now a bright circle of split light moving from red to violet. Oh, beautiful, breathless, beautiful. It is the song of time and space. Rockabye baby time and space. And Caleb was born under the rainbow, a holy child, a sacred gift, a prophet. Old Testament Noah saw in the rainbow the covenant God made between Himself and humankind, and perhaps Noah was right.

The name of the grandmother who saw the rainbow and all the other sights and sounds was Minnie, wife of Joseph Mean, born Minerva Mercedes Annie Paxton in Skye in 1900. She was a distant relative of little Annie Paxton, who was the child celebrated in the family and elsewhere for 'walking on water'. In 1849 Annie Paxton stood on the leaf of the Victoria Regia lily at Chatsworth, thereby demonstrating the strength of the leaf's construction. This leaf was Annie's father's inspiration for the design of the Crystal Palace. A blurred copy of the etching illustrating Annie's moment on the leaf hung in the parlour of the house where Minnie grew up. The frame was a dark mysterious blotchy tortoise shell, glowing with pale amber patterns, and underneath the image of the girl on the leaf was printed a verse from *Punch*: 'On unbent leaf in fairy guise/ Reflected in the water/ Beloved, admired by heart and eyes/ Stands Annie, Paxton's daughter.' Minnie was born into a rural Tasmanian family where the prodigies of such sciences as botany and etymology were part of the fabric of life. There was also a rich and strange mixture of history and literature and theology informing the whole of the extended family's daily life. One of the most fruitful sources of the family's wisdom was the private library of Philosopher Mean, a great collection housed in a stone tower in a remote place on the coast. It was a building and a book collection that had moved into myth, and news of it would sometimes appear in journals or television programs about the strangeness of life on the planet. 'Believe it or not!' they said, and went on to describe the fabulous tower library in all its strange richness on the edge of the known world, battered by the tempests of Bass Strait.

Those bright insects of Minnie's vision of God-the-white-umbrella are not the only miraculous ones lodged in the family memory. There are in fact too many appearances of these things in this family for the sane mind to absorb. They are, for something intrinsically so light, a heavy burden, and they drag in their wake the overuse of verbs such as to flutter to flock to flit to flurry. There were some Blotched Blues suposedly seen in reality, by an ancestor in a time of great distress.

These Blotched Blues are a legend in the family, along with other beautiful wonders that have visited across the years, illuminating the history, illustrating the text, like the embellishments of flowers and fruits and birds and insects in a medieval *Book of Hours*, the *Story of the Means*. Unlock the ancient silver clasp of the sturdy book bound in leather marked with crosses, turn the vellum pages, fresh as minted morning across the murmuring years, and read the story inked in black and blood-fine scarlet letters, look at the pictures of the leaves and flowers of paradise, the creatures of the crocodile-dragon mind, see the fresh gleam of antique gold. Smell, if you will, the aroma of the miracle of time.

CHAPTER FIVE

Fire

'Thou shalt be visited of the Lord of hosts with thunder,
and with earthquake, and great noise, with storm and tempest,
and the flame of devouring fire.'

ISAIAH 29:6

The story of the Means begins in 1851 on Puddingstone Island in Bass Strait, which is the water that lies between the mainland of Terra Australis and the island named for Van Diemen.

It was on remote, forlorn, uninhabited Puddingstone that Caleb Mean's ancestors, Minerva and Magnus, met for the first time. The Blotched Blues are only part of the Legend of Puddingstone Island. They come along in the wake of a great storm, and before the miraculous survival and rescue of Caleb's distant and most significant ancestors.

Waking visions run in the Mean family, while dreams during the hours of sleep, are more rare and fragile. The stronger the waking visions, the weaker the dark night dreams. Caleb's own waking visions were powerful images of heaven and hell, and strange insights and truths of nature. Sometimes he saw in the heavens a great light which was infinite, and in the midst of it, a large and beautiful rainbow, above which there appeared a second rainbow, and above the second rainbow there blazed a shining cross. Beneath the first rainbow appeared the majesty of the figure of a god whose body flamed with rays of light and tongues of fire, and Caleb stood in wonder, and he was consumed, and yet he was unharmed, and he walked forward from the vision, and told what he had seen. At night Caleb did not dream all. His sleep was a time of floating absence, a cloud of nothingness. Like the echidna, Caleb was free from dreams. There are scientists who claim to be able to prove that not only do butterflies dream, but that the cabbages on which they lay their dots of white eggs are also capable of following the narratives of unconscious nocturnal images. It is worth noting that Havelock Ellis in his book *The Criminal*, referred briefly to the phenomenon of the lack of dreaming in society's transgressors. The more confirmed in crime, the less likely to dream in sleep, although the condition of total dreamlessness is thought to be very rare. Ellis, following the lead of Santo de Santis, was inclined to believe that the blankness of the non-dreaming criminal was caused by an anaesthesia of sensibility in the conscious life. Caleb is not any ordinary or regular criminal, and could be classified as lacking a so-called normal sensibility. He might be, after all, a kind of god. Do gods dream? They probably don't need to. Caleb says his night mind is 'an infinity of figure eight, like the movement of the Moonbird'. Like the Moonbird forever following its figure eight flight around the Pacific Ocean, moving from Bass Strait to the arctic waters of the Bering Sea and back again — and back again — across the open sea and sky, Caleb's sleeping homeless mind goes nowhere, never settling on the earth. The questing, restless souls of ordinary people may roam about in dream, following the journeys the sleepers do not take with open eyes. But in sleep Caleb's soul rests, gathering strange energies and gifts unto itself. And like a sleeping echidna, the sleeping dreamless Caleb goes floating free. Is he perhaps his own dream? I don't know the answer to that question — this is strange Daliesque territory.

Because of Minnie's vision of the umbrella and the name 'Caleb' which came flying through the air, the child was accepted as El Niño from birth — and so he never had a chance to develop in anything like a normal way, being the Prophet, the Holy Child. And if he said he did not dream, he did not dream. His brainwaves have been monitored and measured ad infinitum, but as yet medical science has no way of establishing what a sleeping person is in fact *seeing*, although the matter of the dreamlessness of the echidna and other monotremes is definitive. If Caleb and the echidna see nothing; nothing is seen and so Caleb does not dream. That is the end of the story and the beginning of the story. It is its own figure eight.

Caleb is the youngest son of Joshua and Elena Mean, one of the seven families in the tiny community of Skye, a village on the Welcome River, to the southeast of Cape Grimm. Caleb El Niño, the Holy Child, and he was raised in the expectation that he would lead his people to salvation. Some folk said, privately, that he was forespoken, that he suffered the curse of the favourite, the blight of unearned praise. I think there is much evidence to support that point of view. On his thirty-third birthday, February fifth, in 1992, after ensuring that all cats, dogs, horses and livestock were free to escape the fire, he assembled the Skye community of one hundred and forty-seven people at the timber Meeting Hall in the centre of the town. He had with him a document, signed by all members of the community old enough to write, agreeing to what was in effect a suicide pact. The men were dressed in their all-black clothing, the women in white, the children in red. All girls between the ages of thirteen and eighteen were dressed in white, and wore the veils of brides. These veils had been kept in blue tissue paper in deep drawers in the Meeting Hall, and were brought out on ritual occasions. Some of the brides had been marked on the left shoulder with the small blue tattoo of a bluebird, signifying that they had at some time been specially chosen by Caleb for his sexual favours. They carried fresh and shining dark-green sprigs of rosemary in intricate wreaths. Two dogs, unwilling to be parted from their owners, were also drugged and they too died in the fire.

Caleb was careless or carefree of the fact that the community's valuable and beloved library and archives were likely to be destroyed. They had become meaningless to him, all knowledge being carried in his head. At the Meeting Hall he addressed the people in his most powerful and seductive, soaring kind of lecture, assuring them of their status as people chosen above all others to fulfil a mission and a destiny, to move from this earthly plane to a higher realm through the medium of fire. Perhaps they imagined that at some level his talk was metaphoric. It is difficult, even impossible, for people who have not been subject to the power and magic of a charismatic leader to understand how the people might be so beguiled.

The wine the fasting brethren drank that day was spiced with opiates. When all were drowsy Caleb left the hall, locked his people in, and, as the sun was going down, he set fire to the narrow trench of petrol with which he had already encircled the building.

One of the first things to ignite was the row of Chinese fireworks strung across the front of the hall. Exploding and popping like the beginning of the end of the world. Hot jets flew into the night sky, shooting and whooshing, until they paused, hung for a moment, and then burst into wild vermilion and orange palm trees, raining down slow fierce poetic showers of burning leaves as if a great orgasmic angel was making love to the jasper arch of the sky. Flames exploded through the roof, exultant in the darkness, exposing almost immediately the skeleton of the beams. The bonfire that had been set in the field behind the hall caught and bloomed into a spitting, violent and passionate demon life. And then, as if in a pact with Caleb, with God, with who knows what, the wind coming in from the Strait, the wind which had played gently over the village of Skye throughout the afternoon, suddenly gusted up, and opened wide its jaws, wide, wide, and it hurled the full force of a howling breath right into the heart of the whispering flames that leapt and danced around the foundations of the Meeting Hall, out into the bonfire, and then off it went, a frolicking and roaring dragon thrashing its way into the village, through trees and sheds and wild exploding parked cars. A small flock of sheep was incinerated in an enclosure at the back of the general store.

Without looking back Caleb rode his horse through government boundaries to the top of the cliff that is Cape Grimm, the cliff near the weather station. There he watched and listened as the congregation down in his village died in the trap of flames. The cries of death carried in the cold starry air; gold and crimson and strangely malachite and indigo the flames leapt towards the heavens; sparks and flurries of flying charcoal glowed, glittered, floated, spurted into the darkness as the little town leapt into violent blazing life-in-death. Whirling midnight moths of tissue swept up into the sky. A glimpse of hell, a sudden view of a fairyland lit by the sizzling fat of human bodies, accompanied by the whinnies and shrieks and moans of children choking in crawling billows and wraiths of smoke, lungs and eyes filled with stinging poison as they woke from dreamy slumber to the swirling inky spitting clouds at the doorway to deep oblivion. Billowing. Blooming. Flowers of noxious smoke. Tongues of talking flame. Flying embers glowing bright in the deeper glow of the scarlet sky. Great grey sails and billows crowding the space, swallowing the air, the smoke blooming, the children choking, the pain of cruel knives in their lungs. The children were choking to death, drowning for want of the pure air collected and so carefully measured at Cape Grimm. Their earthly future rushed away, disappearing in a funnel of hellfire. Everywhere the smell of burning timber, plastic, leaves, the stench of burning flesh.

The air being measured in the weather station was polluted as it had never been before, and the pollution was recorded around the world. The smoke from the burning community at Skye rolled up and out towards the cliff and sailed, hung in the atmosphere, and sailed, a fleet of tall dark mutant ships, lumbering majestically away high above the sea which wrinkled, wrinkled deep and secretive, far below.

A little way off from Caleb, waiting since late afternoon on the clifftop, was his cousin and lover Virginia, and their baby daughter Golden. Virginia was mounted on a chestnut mare. She had the child before her, and slung across her shoulders was a backpack containing a mahogany box in which was stored a pair of antique pistols, their powder and shot. If real trouble promises big, they would always say in the family, pack the old pistols in your saddlebag. Rising from the sea before them were the rounded humps of the Doughboys, silky rocks sleeping as the water flowed around them, sweetly sleeping in the shapes of wise and slumbering whales, firm guardians of the ocean. The burning village off in the distance, the silhouette of the weather station, a tall silver castle, wooden, glowing in a wreath of moonlit vapour, to the left. And swiftly from the heavens came the police helicopter, a new dark clack-whup thrumming insect-sound, approaching, relentless, descending. Wailing in the distance were the firetruck and the police van, headed for the empty village where the Meeting Hall was burning brightest, where the fire was running through the timber buildings, a fierce wild celebration of hell. Later on some firefighters said the noises, shaped by the remoteness and the darkness, the noises were one of the most terrible parts of the whole conflagration.

The two horses stood statue still; the three human beings shadowy effigies, tranquil, tense, paralysed, hypnotised, waiting for a sign, a gesture from the stars. The child in the woman's arms stiffened, threw back her head and screamed, then she fell silent, and the loss of sound was like a dark, dark gap, a monstrous mouth, opening in the air. In time another helicopter. And another. These two came across the Strait from Victoria. Black, white, red and yellow flies, dragonflies — the helicopters hovered in their sinister heavy way, looking for places to land on the open heath.

Guns are here, and the searchlights and the cameras. The lights slice through the smoke. Caleb does not move. From above in the choppers they can see, through wisps of smoke that have drifted here, parts of the flattened scene — the man in black on the stallion, gazing out to sea; the woman in white on the chestnut mare, the child in red before her. The child appears to be asleep, the two horses with their riders resembling wooden toys in a paper landscape. The searchlights from the helicopters swoop across the open rough and ragged heath, slicing, intersecting, godly rays, cold, sharp blue, piercing the frozen picture below. Now and then, by a trick of the darkness and the light and the smoke, a haze, a nimbus of pale gold surrounds the man on the horse. The group is set for some voice to say: Camera! Action! Everything is poised as if on a hair between reality and dream.

Cameramen hang from the sides of the helicopters. The glossy machines land with ease and elegance on the open ground, and from them stream armed men — police and media, hunched over as they run, both in the familiar uniform of emergency. The images of the horses and their riders are now translated into footage that will fly back to base in Melbourne and then flit invisibly through the air to be seen in airports and hospitals and jails and cafes and living-rooms all over the world. An electronic message. A newsflash. A documentary. A tragedy. A mystery. An image. A commodity to be swallowed like an oyster by a world greedy for horrors. An image to play and play over and over again until it doesn't hurt any more. Animated cartoon.

Balanced on that hair between reality and dream, dream and reality merge, and the result is safe forever after on video. It is still possible to shock and hypnotise people for a moment with those swift bright violent pictures and a rat-a-tat-tat on the screen. The guns and the cameras; the cameras and the guns — twin technologies at work. In a couple of hours the ground truck will arrive, and live footage will be broadcast to stop people in their worn, familiar and fragile tracks, to awaken the sleepyhead, to appal the innocent, to inspire the lunatic with the story it will tell. Live footage, like a live wire, will spurt the information round the globe. Miles and miles of moving pictures telling living stories even as they happen, can be flashed from anywhere to anywhere else, keeping the world at large informed about the things that are happening right now in the world at large. For a few strange moments in 1992 all lines lead to Cape Grimm. The burning beacon that is the Meeting Hall at Skye can be seen anywhere you happen to be, and you will, for a minute or two, be transfixed by this torch of living human beings, and you will listen in horror and amazement and dumb wonder as a steady voice explains to you that this fire was visited by the preacher on his flock. The leader of the community put his community to death, and good people everywhere ask why and how this happened, and why wasn't he stopped long before it got to this. Until the questioning voices die away, and the story fades, and new stories flow from all corners of the earth, and a new magic carpet of moth-bright images rolls out.

There is a need, a lust, a love in the world, a longing to be provided, fed, nourished with strange dark wild terrible images, more and more, over and over. Even little children long to hear their mothers read them the stories recorded in Germany by the Brothers Grimm, the *Nursery and Household Tales* where the boy searches in the trunk for an apple, the mother shuts the lid and slices off his head. Later the mother cooks him in a casserole and serves him up to his father and his sister. What an astonishing and disturbing thing. The TV screen can deliver, at any minute of the night or day, moving pictures of such stories in real life, stories that are unfolding in the attic-of-torment just around the corner from the house where anyone might be living. These stories can be taped, stored, and played, played over and over. Play and rewind and fast forward and play, until the stories lodge in the heart. You can visit the nightmare again and again, as you have power over the images in your videos, stopping and starting them at will. And you are insatiable, filled with the need to know and see, the lust, the love of the darkness and the horror and the abject. The need, the lust, the desire and fascination. Every skull can be a casket of monstrosities, every heart a chamber of uncanny flying fish.

CHAPTER SIX

Word

'The flow pattern around Cape Grim is complex, particularly at low levels where the vorticity in the upwind profile is significant, and causes elevated stagnation points.'

BUREAU OF METEOROLOGY, *Baseline*

A perfect stillness, silence prevailed at the centre of the dramatic flourishes and rasping clatter of choppers and cameras in the swirl of smoke up on the heath. The man on the night shift at the weather station was hunched behind a window, binoculars sweeping the scene before him. He had put through a call to the office in Smithton, but was waiting for it to be returned. He needed to report what he was seeing, needed to receive instructions. It seemed to him that the scene outside was something out of a dream, some incomprehensible clash of medieval horsemen and modern warfare. He imagined, in fact, that they must be shooting a movie in the area — that's what he thought, and it was a reasonable thought and he figured he should have been told about it. Nobody had told him about any movie. This is government land and the operations at the weather station are top secret and you can't just come here in the middle of the night and set things alight like that and start flying helicopters around the place. What about the air? This place is all about the air, after all. Yes. The smoke — was the smoke real? This would play hell with the instruments, the readings. The business out there on the clifftop — well, part of the point of everything here was supposed to be — well — the isolation and the quiet and the silence. The air, the lovely sacred air. They were out there on the heath polluting the beautiful air. This place is for Atmospheric Research, answering to the Bureau of Meteorology, Department of the Environment, Sport and Territories. It is the Baseline Air Pollution Station which engages in highly significant Climate Monitoring. It holds a Certificate of Merit from the Keep Australia Beautiful Council, and you can check it out at www.wunderground.com

The man on the night shift could see the fire across in the distance, and he thought it must be some terrific bloody movie. He should ring somebody about this. Then as he thought about it, the phone rang. With one hand he reached for it, his gaze still fixed on the fantastic play on the hill.

'Len? Len? Are you OK, Len?'

'K. Yeah. Is that you Darron? Yeah. But I tell you . . . '

'Stay where you are and check the locks. There's a maniac up there somewhere. The nutcase from that place down the road at Skye. Something's happened there. A fire. People are dead. People are dead, Len. Are you with me?'

'You mean — Christ — you mean this is real? I figured — well, doesn't matter what I figured. There's a hell of a lot of action outside. Police everywhere. Cameras. But — it looks like some movie or something. Are you sure? I figured there was a mistake. We should've been told about this. So long as it's not aliens or whatever.'

'Aliens?'

The line was crackling and spitting. The words dropped out behind some of the static.

'It's for real. Like I say, check the locks and don't go outside.'

'But can't I *do* something? Are they going to set the station alight?

'Calm down. No. It's just the loony from Skye. He finally flipped. Sit tight and keep calm.'

'It's all very well for you to say. Can you hear that, for chrissake? Can you hear what they're saying?'

The magnified calls of the police officer in charge of the operation were blurred and distorted. The man in the weather station kept his binoculars trained on the scene, and the figure on the dark horse appeared not to hear or understand the words that were flung at him. The police closed in, but he sat there, he sat, his gaze stonily fixed on the far horizon. They closed in also on the woman and child on the chestnut mare, the child asleep, the woman shadowy immobile, a statue, dazed, drugged, who knows.

Then with sudden and shocking energy the man on the horse raised his arms and shouted to the sky. The sound did not carry to the weather station, but was heard around the world in due course, played over and over and over, edited, re-edited, played and played again. He screamed:

The Word! The Word of God is scarce and it is precious.

The whole scene stilled as if lifeless for a few seconds, then the police moved in to surround both horses, forcing the riders to dismount. The cameras tracked the scene as the police bundled all three figures across the stubble and rocky surfaces to a van. Then the van was locked by sudden magic, and it began to move forward, it nosed, sailed, crawled off into the night. Some helicopters stayed for a few minutes; others were off, chasing the van.

'God, they've gone. They took the three of them in the van. One of them was a baby. Now what's going to happen? It still looks like hell out there.'

'I reckon you don't open the door to strangers, unless it's the police. There could be more psychos out there in the dark. And those media guys will want a comment from you, because you're the eyewitness, the innocent bystander in the weather station. But you know, well, rules are rules. They can't come in, no matter what. They'll have to do their job without any help from you. They'll probably find out where you live, though, and come poking around. I seriously reckon you shouldn't talk to them. Ever. They'll be round at your place tomorrow, I guarantee it. Keep quiet, I reckon. I always knew that guy was crazy. It was only a matter of time. But we don't need to get mixed up with this. You never know where it'll end. So don't talk to the media — is all I am saying to you. Don't talk to the media.'

So Len and Darron never spoke to the media, but they spoke to everybody else, family, friends, blokes down the pub, and the stories multiplied. And the night Len watched the scene from the window of the station went down in family, pub and local legend. A few years on there was a website dedicated to Caleb, and there were a couple of pictures of Len.

'It doesn't even look like me.'

'Well, it does a bit.'

'Bullshit, I never looked like that.'

'You did you know.'

On the site there were pictures of everything. Pictures of the Meeting Hall before it was burnt and after. Pictures of Caleb as a preacher boy in a silver suit. Pictures of Caleb's dog, also called Caleb — the name means 'dog' the text cutely explained. In one place there was a little typo, and instead of 'Caleb' it said 'Caliban'. There were pictures of the sadly charming and nostalgic, not to say very strange, Temple of the Winds. On www.CelebrityMorgue.com there were also some interviews with Caleb, one of them by myself, although I have no idea how it got there, since I have never released such a thing.

People, fascinated by the events, wondered to each other about Caleb's sermon on the cliff.

'"The Word of God is scarce and it is precious." What'd he mean? What d'you think he meant?'

'Buggered if I know what he meant. He's mental, remember.'

'Right. Mental. But it sounds — well — it sounds like poetry or something. It's probably in the Bible. You get religious nuts that do those things sometimes, don't you, and they base it all on stuff in the Bible.'

'Yeah, the Bible. Probably.'

CHAPTER SEVEN

Secret Chronicle of Virginia Mean I

'The story of the People's Temple is old, a matter of flux and reflux, of eternal returns.'
ITALO CALVINO, 'Suicides of the Temple'

Note: In my work I have access to much material that is classified as private. Throughout this story I will quote extensively with full permission from the author, from the diaries of Virginia Mean, and will also qualify some of what she says with further explanations, particularly of the historical background to her story. The diaries first came to my attention when I was contacted by Father Benedict Fox from the Catholic Welfare Office. He sought my opinion as to the state of mind of the writer, knowing me to be one of the team of doctors working with Caleb Mean. In the first instance I received photocopies of the diaries without the knowledge of the author, but as time went on I was able to establish contact with Virginia, and entered into an informal therapeutic correspondence with her. I have attempted to preserve Virginia's particular style of writing, which readers will see is somewhat old-fashioned in both vocabulary and syntax, owing to the strict and formal system of education under which she has been raised, and the isolation of her family over several generations in the religious enclave of the village of Skye in the far northwest of Tasmania. The words and sentiments are essentially those of Virginia herself, however in the interests of clarity I have, occasionally, needed to edit the text. She began writing the chronicle at the end of the first year after the fire at Skye, in 1993. Her courage in trying to heal her own life, and her devotion to her daughter, are remarkable examples of the resilience of the human spirit, and the ability of human beings to recover and to move forward with hope in the wake of the most devastating and traumatic events, events that are largely beyond the comprehension of many readers. Virginia's life has been extraordinary and highly unusual from the outset, yet ultimately, I believe, she will make a full recovery from past damage, and will offer her own valuable and distinctive contributions to society. What form such contributions will take remains to be seen.

The following narrative is Virginia's story.

Paul Van Loon

I am unable to speak, unable to bring myself to open my mouth and utter, give voice, explain the progress and significance of the events of which I have found myself a part, or in which I have found myself to be a player as well as an observer. There was a time when I sensed that I was outside myself, watching my life unfold, stand still, unfold again. Unable to use my voice, I therefore write this chronicle, this diary, in which I seek to document my observations, my thoughts, my feelings. Silence is a shield, a defence; it is also a weapon. In truth I am unable to analyse the source of my mutism, since I know I wish to communicate the story of what happened — but my vocal cords are silent, silenced for reasons of their own following the shock of the events of that terrible night. The words I write are gathered into fragments, short sequences with which I hope to record my own history, the narrative of my daughter's life, the tale of how I have loved, how my life has undergone changes so swift and so dramatic that my mind reels before the memory of them, and my tongue is stilled. I believe that the strands of my narrative may resemble the short sad lines of a medieval lament, although there lie, within this history, moments of joy, moments of pleasure, times of illumination and ecstasy. My mind has been unable to absorb and process all that I have seen, all that I have experienced — and therefore I am mute. It seems the words have died even as they make their progress from my heart. I find myself repeating this, over and over as I put these words down, telling myself that I have no sound in my throat, not a word in my mouth, not a single phrase of song on my tongue, nothing that will trill within the dome, the seashell pearly hull of my breathless skull, my secret, hornbone skull. I expect there is a name for the condition from which I suffer, if indeed suffer is the word I seek. I have given my voice to Caleb, and I will not speak again until I see my own true love. And now all I know is that although I can not speak, I am able to write, to take up my pen and fly across the paper with a freedom I have never before felt with the written word.

If there were times in the dead heart of the night when I sensed myself coldly retreating down the spiral staircase of life towards the bottomless pool of death, the jasper waters of endless and eternal oblivion, I am now freed from them, those times, and I am able to ascend, step by winding step, towards the light, guided only by my pen as I fill the furling leaves of this book, this warm and loving book with its creamy paper surfaces and its dear dark cover, raspberry red. Beloved book of hours and days and months and years.

I recall wistfully the hours, the months I spent with my teachers, with Caleb, reading aloud the music and poetry of the Bible, and the magical cadences of many of the great works of literature of the world. After due reflection upon what we had read, we would discuss the beauties and the meanings of the works, and from my years of drinking from the fountain of the words, I believe I have at my command a certain skill with the language, and a longing to express myself on paper. It is with profound relief and gratitude that I apply the pen to the paper, scratching the burdens of my spirit across the surface, for my silent mouth can only kiss the air. For much of this ability to free my thoughts I am grateful, grateful to Caleb for he taught me to read and to write. Caleb — how I love the sound of his name. I have always loved him. I believe I will always love him. I *am* Caleb. We are Cathy and Heathcliff. Dante and Beatrice. Paul and Virginia. Petrarch and Laura. Lancelot and Guinevere. Romeo and Juliet. Abelard and Héloïse. I am thinking aloud my flailing thoughts and making an attempt to interpret and characterise the bond of love that exits between us. Caleb and Virginia. Is it possible to say 'I *am* Caleb'? I wonder often about that which I have written. It is so exaggerated, that I doubt I really understand what it means. And yet I do, I do understand, deep in my own heart, I know love's meaning.

Gentle, innocent, affectionate — these are some of the words that I would choose to describe Caleb, yet I have heard others celebrate only his power, his intellect, his vision, his charisma. His great beauty and his strength. He was extremely tall, some would consider him almost a giant. Others would revile him, this I know. But I remember so many different things about him — the way he played the fiddle and the bagpipes, the way he swam like a beautiful fish in the river. His favourite sport was cricket, and he was a fearsome bowler in the rare matches the Skye team played against church groups who came in sometimes from Smithton and Stanley. It was many months after the fire before I could begin to relate my story, many months of shock and bewilderment and sorrow. Many long months of icy stillness. As I write now, I imagine I whisper, with the voice I have lost, whisper the story to a stranger. Listen, Stranger, listen to my story.

I yearn to chronicle the beliefs of my people — with the loss of the people, disappear the truths we have lived by, truths for which my people died at Skye, fled into a vast eternity. I mourn for the family I have lost, and yet I must rejoice that they have passed before me to their ecstasy beyond the stars. I shed tears — for the dear people so bitterly lost, the sweet laughing faces, the children, and for the fruits of our labours — the toys we made, the books and the painted signs. I confess now that I had a great love for all the dolls I made for trade, those astonishing little personalities figured from simple cloth, so desired, I believe, desired by children all over Australia. The Skye Dolls are on many Christmas trees — well, they used to be. At least there are still thousands of them in homes far and wide, but the new ones, the recent ones have all been reduced to the soft black misery of ash. The tears of a great rainbow well of sadness come to my eyes when I think of the dolls, and I weep for those dolls of cinder and sorrow. Once upon a time, Caleb told me, when there was war, ships carrying dolls were granted immunity on the high seas. Caleb told me, Caleb told me — always my thoughts return to Caleb, my love, my darling, my self. Caleb.

And with those dolls and everything else have gone the paintings. Oh, the paintings. In the 1930s there was an incredible woman called Sweet Dahlia Mean who recorded the history of Skye in a series of a hundred primitive paintings that resembled in some ways the work of Grandma Moses, although some of the subject matter is not really very pretty. These pictures decorated the walls of the Meeting House, and sometimes as I explore my memory I see them, one by one, bursting into wings of flame and flying off to heaven — one by one as the souls of the dying people leave the earth. So far as I know there is not a single piece of Sweet Dahlia's work in existence anywhere in the world. Hence they must live in my head alone. Ah, but they must also be located in Caleb's head, yes? Most of the faces in those pictures used to remind me of owls — fat, thin and squinting owls.

There was the picture of the shipwreck with the monster coming up to swallow the boat whole, with Niña flying through the air in her white cotton gown, and Puddingstone Island where Minerva met Magnus and the story really started. Beneath the ocean a terrifying picture of drowned green people through whose eyesockets swim fantastic coloured fish. There's the rescue and then there's the sweet sad little wedding of Minerva and Magnus at the Presbyterian Church at Circular Head. A picture of the family outside their first bark house at remote, remote and windy Skye. Magnus and Minerva and seven children and a horse and two dogs and a garden full of vegetables and hope. Then the building of the Meeting House, the coming of the next family and the next, seeking a kind of sanctuary from the towns and the forests and the mines, seeking Magnus the Father and Minerva the Mother, and the structure of a good new religious way, apart from the prejudice and pomposities of the official faiths of the time. Then the building of the Temple of the Winds, and the joyful processions of little figures making their way out there to celebrate the Feast of the Sacred Imagination. Minerva and Magnus and Niña visit the local landed gentry in their funny little rose garden at Highfield. Down the generations the faces never change, and even the clothing scarcely alters. The children of all ages sit in the painted schoolroom, the self-same schoolroom where I sat. The blacksmith and the doll-maker and the market gardener are in their shops. The apothecary stands beside his big stone jars. The most beautiful pictures are those showing the people working in the poppy fields. These I love. The little figures are almost swallowed up in the dreaming dusty-green and silver-coral seas of leaves and petals in the meadows out past the Temple of the Winds, out where no outsider ever goes, where no outsider ever imagines going, out where Caleb took me on the first walk we ever went on when I was five years old, deep into the waving stems of the poppies in the fields. They are gone, all gone, the pictures of paradise on earth, all gone. Goodbye, goodbye sweet Sweet Dahlia Mean, goodbye to your pictures and your thoughts.

Caleb is gone now, I think he is gone from me forever and forever. He has not died. He *could* be dead, but he *must not be so*. He is forever and ever amen behind the bars of the psychiatric facility, on the Black River in the heart of the deep dark forest. For he is judged to be insane and murderous by the standards of the society that rules the land. There was Skye — for so many years in peace behind its own sweet walls of simple innocence — but all has come to a strange and terrible end, leaving the brethren in paradise and leaving us — me and Golden and Caleb — in a new blur of outer darkness, a world of fracture and mystery. I must live in this cold world without Caleb by my side. I have with me his daughter Golden, who is a sacred trust for me, a gift, a temple. She is our own miracle, the fruit of our passion, the holy promise of the future. I fear for what the world might do to her, a child, for she is innocent, and yet she is the child of such a father. She is the 'mass-murderer's daughter' — I must write those words even if they strike the deepest wound into my heart. If people were to recognise Golden, I believe she could be stoned to death for what her father has done. Caleb's blood in Golden's veins — there is a fearful potency. Like father, like daughter people would say, would whisper, would imagine in their dark hearts, in their misunderstandings and their understandings, in their thirst to punish. From fear of what they might do, I have told nobody that Golden's birthdate was one of the signs Caleb consulted when calculating the auspicious time for the final apocalyptic fire. He calculated by the date of his own thirty-third anniversary, which was also the date of Golden's blessed birthday. It is strange that the date also marks the anniversary of the day when Magnus and Minerva Mean arrived in safety on Puddingstone Island in 1851. Golden was Caleb's favourite child, and so he chose his birthdate and hers. What guiding fate had given her this date for entering the world? Golden is the child who wears the sacred family bracelet, fashioned from the blackened sinews of a wallaby and bearing the tiny arm of an ancient china doll.

I may not visit Caleb, and his own child may not visit him. He is forbidden to write letters to me and I to him; so I do not write to him, save for what I might say here in my journal, for they must never know what passes between us. We will communicate by the power of thought alone, as we have always done. Perhaps this is what is called telepathy, people may call it what they wish to call it, we have always been joined by unseen waves of thought. As a child Caleb used to have the gift of bi-location. If he still has that power, he may even yet be able to visit me here, and nobody will know. Perhaps he still has that power. I do not know, and I would not say. To the world I am the silent one and mine is a secret chronicle.

They stared in stupid horror and amazement when they learnt my age was seventeen. I must seem much older by the standards of the world outside Skye. I have studied many of the classics, and have studied also the great philosophers and the composers and the artists. We followed a very strict regime of study and, although still young, we were expected to be adult and responsible, to be sensitive to the smallest details of the natural world, and also to groom our own imaginations. We had lessons called 'Listening and Looking'. Our parents and other teachers would take us out into the garden, or into the bush, or to the beach, or onto a far and lonely hillside. They told us to close our eyes and to remain very very still. Listen, they would say, Listen to the music of the world and the heavens. Then each of us would tell what we could hear — the rustle of the wind in the leaves, the lapping of the lake, the cry of a gull, the whirr of an insect, hum of a bee, murmur of an unknown song. The beating of each heart. A footfall. The drop of a pebble. The pounding of waves. Then we had Looking. The feathered scribbling on leaves, the shades of blue in the turning heavens, the movement of an ant in the dust, the radiating edges of the pages on the underside of a mushroom. We spoke of these things, then we wrote of them. We studied the works of many scientists and poets and other writers. One of Caleb's favourite writers and thinkers was always Maurice Maeterlinck. We read his work on bees and ants and flowers, and we performed scenes from *The Blue Bird* and other plays. Caleb sometimes said he had conversations with Maeterlinck, who died ten years before Caleb was even born.

Because I am only young they have treated me gently, have let me be. It was clear to them that I had been Caleb's innocent slave, and I believe that being so young, living through so much, perhaps I frightened them. Young mothers were not unusual in Skye, were, in fact, quite common and accepted, even expected, but out here in the world such things are considered wrong and dangerous. Golden is quiet; she knows only what a child knows; they will not breech her understanding. Yet I know that Golden will be a subject of interest to the doctors and the criminologists all her life, and to the media no doubt. She must be insulated from all this if possible. The child is the child of Caleb Mean, the man they see only as the man who drugged the villagers of Skye and burnt them to death in their Meeting Hall. They probably imagine that if they wait long enough, watch and listen hard enough to Golden, daughter of Caleb, she will tell them some of the things they think they want to hear, will furnish an explanation for what has happened. They will never understand. Understanding was obliterated in the conflagration, purified in the light, in the flame, and it is gone.

All of this society says Caleb is insane, dangerously, criminally insane. I know that he was sent by God to save the world, but in some strange way he was defeated. He is locked away forever in the white and windowless fortress up on the Black River. Folks call that place the Crystal Palace. If I did not know it was a prison I would imagine it to be a fabled fastness, some sparkling sugared Alcazar surrounded by a force field of armed guards and dogs and the magic crystal eyes of electronic surveillance, the Magical, Impenetrable, Impermeable, Impregnable fortress. Castle Magical, home of the sleeping-beauty-prince, My Prince.

I love him. I have always loved him. He taught me how to read the stars, taught me how to play the dulcimer. I would play the strings, and he would play the ancient pipes of Scotland that have been in the family, a family that sets great store by its history, for so many generations. Together he said our melodies were light to illumine the endless night. I will love him forevermore, love him as he taught me to love the deep pink roses which have grown for generations in the front garden of the first house ever built by Magnus Mean. I will write my poems and songs for him, for he whom I will never again hope to see upon this earth.

CHAPTER EIGHT

Water

'If I die in the sea, don't leave me here alone.'
CHILD REFUGEE, SIEV-X, October 2001

Caleb's grandmother, Minnie Mean, was born in 1900 in Skye. She was the one who saw the vision of the multicoloured butterflies streaming from the white umbrella of God. Minnie was named after her great-great-grandmother Minerva who sailed from Liverpool in 1851 and was shipwrecked in a storm in Bass Strait, and ended up on the rocky beach of Puddingstone Island off the northwest coast of Van Diemen's Land. Puddingstone Island was named by Henry Hellyer who was an explorer in Van Diemen's Land during the early part of the nineteenth century. The pages of the early histories of the Great South Land are seeded with the lives of men who set out into a most strange unknown, who sometimes died, who sometimes discovered wonderful things, who certainly graced all they saw with names. Puddingstone Island. Much of the island is made up of rock which consists of large round red pebbles, black pebbles and white pebbles, cemented together with hard white clay. The cliffs are covered with succulent edible pig-face, and there are small stands of dense tea-tree, dark and twisted, which is a great survivor in the weathers here in the middle of the ocean.

The original Minerva for whom Caleb's grandmother was named was miraculously saved from death by drowning when her ship went down long, long ago. In this family, signs, wonders, visions, miracles are, if not commonplace, then not entirely unexpected.

The site of this miracle was Bass Strait, where there have been many, many shipwrecks, and anybody who wants to read about some of the others can go to www.oceans.com.au

A gale took the barque *Iris* to the bottom of the Strait in 1851. As the ship, having sailed from London docks, entered the Strait, the world was in a mood of darkness, as if a cloud had descended out of nowhere, and a furious tempest arose and blew for almost an hour, after which the wind dramatically fell, and in the sudden calm the sea itself arose as if sucked towards the heavens by a gigantic and ravenous mouth, great black-purple bruise of a maw that gulped all in its path. Mountains of inky water rose and clashed against each other in whirlpools of furious foam, high, high above the ship, enclosing the vessel in a vortex of steely turbulence. Waves, sheets of swarthy icy glass, rose on all sides, lit by ghastly flashes of lightning that filled the scene with a horrible, brilliant, deathly glow, a sudden hallucination. The ship was thrashed and battered and broken by torrents of bitter rain and then by cloudbursts of giant hail, until it rose up, a mere wooden toy at the mercy of the play of the waves, twirled, it seemed, in the air, and pitched over as if fashioned from biscuit dough and filled with a breath of air. Human screams were raised in a hellish harmony that was part of the symphony of the storm, and the cries ripped through the air in a choking cacophony. Then silent frozen people tried to hold their breath as fantastic towers of water rose and crashed and fell in boiling foam. The howls of the dogs, the majestic terror of the horses as all were overwhelmed and sucked into the boiling, freezing ocean. The captain's pig went flying through the space between this world and the next, crying a terrible unearthly cry that was sucked into the clangour of human and animal and angel cries as all reeled and roiled around the rumpus surface of the sea.

Then something happens. The quality of the terror changes and an unearthly grumble, a grotesque and slimy murmur has been set in motion far beneath the waters of the Strait.

Through the blackness of the turbulent frothing waters come the whipping and thrashing of the tentacles of a most astonishing blubbery rubbery puff of sea monster. The creature's arctic eyes the largest eyes in the world, its beak stronger than steel, and the bodies of women and men and children are lashed in the deep pink passionate and succulent embrace of its tree-trunk spiral arms. The *Iris* is a broken coffin, spilling its corpses into the abyss, to be swallowed in an instant, in a flash, into the waters of the Strait, some gathered up in a fierce ecstasy by the monster's raging bliss.

The storm awoke the Kraken and he came to exact his toll. Seen yet unseen the giant grey squid looped up out of the ocean, swept up its prey, and torpedoed down again into the cold cold Stygian darkness of the deep. To sleep again. To dream. To wait and wonder.

The storm abated as quickly as it had arisen. Sixty-two crew, forty-five passengers, nearly all were lost, and yet three passengers survived, squeezed out by some miracle, some freak, between the crushing arms of the great animal that had come from the bottom of the sea. These three were flotsam from the ship, the ship that had so suddenly gone, taking every twist of rope, every ragged patch of sail, every black cigar box, every beating heart but three.

These three survivors were Minerva Hinshelwood, Magnus Mean and an orphaned baby girl whose history was unknown. She could have been any one of four baby girls on the *Iris*. Who will ever know which one? Her unknown history gave her a fairytale quality later on in the family, and it was a quality that became exaggerated, embroidered upon, as the decades passed. If you don't know who you are, you can imagine anything. If you don't know where your great-great-great-aunt came from, she might be a Russian princess or the child of Irish fairy-folk. But I am getting ahead of myself. The baby is still just a piece of flotsam in Bass Strait.

Minerva Carrillo Hinshelwood was born in Peru in 1830. She was the only girl in a family of six boys, four of whom went to sea — captains of ships or just plain sailors taking life as it comes. One brother was a lawyer who became an explorer. The other one was a priest, and he died young. Minerva, the only girl, had an English governess, and she listened as if to strange legends when Miss Monkhouse spoke of high tea at the village hall, of boating on the river Thames, and of glimpses (hushed and joyful tones) caught of Queen Victoria herself. When Minerva was only seventeen she set sail for England where she became for a time a singer and dancer, an exotic South American beauty in dark-pink silk with emeralds in her hair. Her parents had died, her brothers were wanderers, and she never saw or even wrote to any members of her family again. Her life became like part of the romance she sensed in the stories Miss Monkhouse had told her in her soft English voice.

Magnus Mean was born in Minginish on the Isle of Skye in 1829. During the famine of 1841 the family, a family of weavers, moved to Glasgow from where Magnus eventually made his way to London, and then sailed alone to Van Diemen's Land, his plan to become a farmer with sheep and property of his own. He spoke English as well as Gaelic, and some members of this family of crofters were educated enough to read the Bible and the newspapers. As a boy Magnus loved to read. A memory that often rose to the surface of Magnus's mind was of the Sunday afternoons when his sisters read aloud from the Psalms in English. The edges of the pages were rosy pink and gilt, and Magnus derived a sweet pleasure from the way they moved and shone, from the whisper of the pages, *shush-shush*, from the murmur of the women's voices as they softly spoke the verses. 'From the end of the earth will I cry unto thee, when my heart is overwhelmed.' On the table of his memory there was a white cloth and a cake with red jam, and steaming hot tea in a dented silver pot, one of the few family treasures. And always in his nostrils was the aroma of the weaving hall, the softness of the raw wool, the sound of the spinning wheel, the dark scrape and clunk of the loom, the slow magic of the pattern as it began to form in the cloth.

Magnus read many books and papers about sea voyages. He read of thrilling and successful journeys, and he read also of the disasters. In the *Glasgow Herald* was the re-telling of the story of a most notorious shipwreck. It happened in 1838, when a ship went down in the Torres Strait, and a few survivors landed on an island off the coast of New Guinea. The exhausted men fell asleep, only to be awakened by savages who held knives to their throats. The one man who finally lived to tell of what had happened recalled being forced to watch as the natives devoured his companions. 'I watched them eat the eyes and cheeks raw, blood running down their chests.' There was fascination for Magnus in the horror of that. Many tales of ferocious cannibals made their way into the Scottish press, stories from all parts of the Empire, including New South Wales. Magnus often read these stories, along with tales of pirates, tales of torture, death by starvation and thirst, and he was strangely attracted by the danger, by the sense of adventure, by the challenge of the unknown breath of the Antipodes.

The final decision to emigrate was made when Jenny, Magnus's bride-to-be, died of tuberculosis in Glasgow. The recollection of that pewter twilight when they buried her often rose up in his sad memory. In an effort to mend his shattered spirit and ease his broken and tortured heart he would put his homeland behind him and make a new life on the other side of the world, following a different dream, seeking extreme adventures in the wild places of the earth. In his deep sadness, part of him longed to confront the terrors and the dangers, to meet the fury of the sea, to feel the knives of pirates and savages at his throat. He would see his companions eaten alive, would await the moment when he would witness the splitting open of his own abdomen.

Magnus had a good and sensible and orthodox aim as well, and a serious streak of optimism. He meant to go to the southeast part of the Great South Land, to settle in the district of Circular Head, on the lands assigned to the Van Diemen's Land Company. Great green and golden imaginary acres drifted gracefully through the swirling skies of his water-bright dreams. He imagined he might sleep in his plaid in the heather on the sweet bright moorlands of the Great South Land. These dreams were far from the reality of the gloomy forest and the primitive makeshift hut that fate, after other adventures, had in store for him.

He left behind in Glasgow three sisters and his mother. Maggie, his youngest sister, said she would follow him to Van Diemen's Land. When she eventually learnt of the shipwreck of the *Iris*, her nerve failed her, and she realised she could not face the five-month sea voyage from Glasgow. Magnus would never see his family again, although he wrote to them, and they wrote back to him, the letters taking many months to come and go. They begged him to return to them, but he never did.

Minerva Hinshelwood was a married woman, wed in Liverpool to Edward Herbert Hinshelwood who now lay dead deep down in the black waters of Bass Strait. Pale handsome Edward who had loved to see Minerva dance and loved to listen to her sing. He was a romantic, had paid no attention to stories of cannibals or even stories of shipwreck. In his heart he knew Minerva was a strange choice for a wife to transport to the colonies, but Edward was not a practical man; Minerva was not a practical woman in any ordinary way. Yet there was a side of Minerva that was characterised by plain common sense and practical ability. She could run a household; she could minister to the sick with the skill of a witch or an angel; she believed she could garden and also cook. Minerva and Edward planned to take up land in Port Phillip.

'Let me make myself quite plain,' Edward's father had said. 'If you marry this woman, Edward, I intend to cut you off without a penny.'

His mother wept and asked the vicar to pray for him. His sisters tried to interest him in their charming pretty friends, some with money, some without.

'The boy is a complete fool,' people said. 'Throwing away a fortune for some woman of ill-repute.' In their hearts his friends had a sneaking admiration for him — the madness, the daring, the beautiful woman. But why could he not marry an heiress and simply keep Minerva in lodgings until he tired of her? Well, for Edward it was not a question. He had fallen in love with Minerva and his mind was made up.

Edward was not particularly suited to farming, being an amateur botanist and entomologist with an ambition to catalogue the mysterious insects and animals, flowers and plants of the fascinating and promised land of Port Phillip. With him he had several of the new glass and mahogany boxes in which grew and flourished plants he hoped to grow. Minerva was delighted and fascinated by these plants. On the voyage out Edward studied the flying fish, the dolphins, the great stingrays, the seabirds. They were the kind of nineteenth-century couple people now love to find existed and flourished back there in their family tree.

On the eve of the new year Edward and Minerva, filled with hope and joy, stood on deck entwined in each other's arms and breathed in the sound of the sixteen bells as they rang out in mid-ocean, mid-heaven. Omens of all the great goodness to come, promise of prosperity, of children, of discoveries, of adventures in unknown places.

Edward had long desired to witness the sight of the thick eerie tentacles of a slimy Kraken of which he had read in verse with his tutor. Was it a myth? He planned also to study the moonbird. He made close observations of the weather, the sky, the fragrances in the air. He catalogued the stars, sketched the ship, the passengers, the sea, the horizon, the moods of night and day. It was Edward who first noticed that the albatross that followed the ship had four white feathers in a line on one dark wing, and four in a diamond formation on the other. Edward was a man who was filled with wonder at the varieties of nature — and Minerva was in his eyes one of the greatest marvels on earth. She was to his poetic mind and heart an iridescent creature flashing before his dazzled eyes, a source of light and life, and she was his alone.

To Edward's distress and to Minerva's fascination and horror the albatross was caught on a line that was baited with a piece of pork rind cut like a swallow's tail. The bird was a creature that measured fourteen feet from wingtip to wingtip. Its head was huge and heavy, its powerful curved bill a thick yellow-tipped apricot. It was killed, skinned, then the skin was plucked, thick rivulets of blood moving across the decking in shiny globules. Minerva could not look away, was captivated by the sight, and she observed that the skin was fine, soft, white and very beautiful. Whiter than what? Whiter than milk and soft, softer than kid-skin, slimy in death. The graceful creature, whose great and powerful wings had never beaten as it rode the wind, lay on the deck in its separate pieces, for separate purposes, the blood washed away with buckets of water, the meat thrown into the sea. In a long purple and red arc the guts flew out across the open sky, ribbons spiralling down towards the shining silken surface of the sea. There was a quick swoop and squabble and shrill squawk of birds that came from nowhere to take the sudden gift. A flurry of clean grey and white. 'We eat the eggs,' the first mate said, 'but the meat is only for the birds — or for the starving and the mad.' The hollow wing-bones were taken for making pipe stems, and the feathers would be quills to be sharpened for writing. The feet would make excellent tobacco pouches. 'The head,' the Captain said, 'is a real curiosity. I don't collect them myself, but perhaps you, Mr Hinshelwood — he turned to Edward, holding out the severed head of the victim — perhaps you would care to keep this as a memento of the voyage? Your great interest in the animal kingdom? You spotted him first, I hear. Those strange markings on the wings. They say it's bad luck you know, to kill an albatross. Are you the superstitious type, Mr Hinshelwood?'

Edward was speechless with emotion, with rage and grief and bewilderment. Minerva could see that he was almost ill with disgust at the killing and dismembering of the creature for its useful parts. She expected him to refuse the offer of the skull and to lecture the Captain. But, his hands trembling as he did so, he took the grotesque but lovely tragic thing, cradled its heaviness in his spread palms. Water streaked with blood ran between his fingers. He nodded to the Captain, and went below with Minerva at his side, below to the airless quarters that they shared with three other couples. He wrapped the head of the albatross in a blue silk cloth, a cloth embroidered in white flowers on Sunday afternoons by his youngest sister.

The sky, mussel blue as darkness moved across it, was laced with ribbons of pale crimson and rust. Edward's breath came in strange feathery rasps, his heart contaminated by what had occurred. Something, he sensed, had snapped deep inside him when the Captain handed him the head. Yet with his rational scientist's approach, he planned to dry the head and study it, to record its measurements, its textures, its poetry, not, as the Captain inferred, to keep as a memento. Its only memories were freighted with the ugliness of what had been done, alive in the mind's eye with images of grinning sailors with bloody knives, accomplices to the carrion birds that came in for the leftovers. The whole picture would remain as an ache in Edward's heart, and he imagined that he had brought the whole thing about by discovering the bird for the crew. He had set the evil in motion, and he had ended up with the creature's proud, sad, severed head. He wept as he explained this to Minerva, and she cradled his own sorrowful head, and in the softness of her embrace, he slept. Over the ship the bruised sky opened, emptying great sheets of icy rain onto the world. And finally Edward slumbered like a sorry child.

That was then, and now Edward was gone, was drowned, lost, dead, gone. He had, at the time of the wreck, been suffering from the beginnings of a fever from which several passengers had died on the voyage. Minerva and Magnus separately, unknown to each other except perhaps vaguely by sight, both witnessed with horror the burials, the bodies dropped over the side of the *Iris* with hasty ceremony and short prayers. Usually at night. The first was a young woman. There were children whose little forms, weighted with ballast and wrapped in blankets or shawls, made no sound as they fell into the ocean, slid from the arms of their fathers and mothers and went drifting down forever into the bottomless swirling soundless darkness of the sea. As Edward lay in his berth, his eyes wild with pain and a black terror, Minerva had a sense that he feared the fever as a punishment for his having abandoned his home and family, for having followed his heart utterly in marrying Minerva. Perhaps it was punishment for sighting the albatross, and for other transgressions committed, both known and unknown. Now Edward was gone and to Minerva it was strangely as if he had never been. As she searched the waves of Bass Strait for a sign of him, she knew she was utterly abandoned, completely alone in the universe, with just the blue fragment of the wing of a little Claudina at her throat on a silver chain, a gift of love from her dead husband Edward Hinshelwood.

That's the way the story's told, from what I can piece together, and the Claudina on the silver chain came down to Virginia, and then to Golden, but I am getting ahead of myself.

There was the tragic end of one of life's chapters, and the beginning of what would be the romance of Minerva and Magnus. Some tellers weep for Edward, lost with his cases of moths and insects and books and seeds and leaves and fossils on the deep seabed, lost with the head of the albatross cradled in his hands. All that was light and air and green and sweet, all that was Edward and his hopes and ambitions and fears, rolled into the thick and never-ending darkness of the deep. Edward, so gentle and kind and fond of life and love and music. Some girls, hearing the story, long for Edward, imagining him to be so intelligent, so handsome, so attentive, so loving, so poetic; yet others thrill to the thought of Magnus, tall, wild, rugged, handsome also, fierce, brave. Whichever category of man they imagine, they imagine themselves into the slender golden body and powerful spirit of Minerva.

Fate, chance, fortune brought Minerva and Magnus, destiny's flotsam, together on the shore of Puddingstone Island. Minerva had prayed in the storm, her mind and heart a heavenly space filled with fervent intercessions to El Niño and his Mother. Magnus prayed to God the Father in Heaven, his prayers loud and urgent, snatched by the black and salty wind. Minerva and Magnus were two spirits borne by the wind to a scrap of land in the waters of Bass Strait, saved from a sea that raged and foamed and swallowed everything in a night. Their love and romance proper did not begin until much later, until they had been rescued, reached dry, dry land and had time to reflect in a kind of tranquillity on the ways of fate and fortune. This really was pure legendary romance, the union of Minerva and Magnus who were thrown together by a fate that they did not resist. All her life, on the slender silver chain around her throat, Minerva wore Edward's gift, the pendant that contained the dark blue from the lower wing of the colour-patched Claudina, a native of the Amazon rainforest. It was a brilliant blue triangle set in silver. The upper wings of this creature were splashed deep pinkish-red on black, but the lower half was midnight-velvet black imprinted with the unreal luminous blue of hallucination. Magnus never asked her to take off the pendant, this memorial to another man, a drowned husband, and she never did. When she died she left it to her grand-daughter, and eventually it graced the throat of Virginia Mean, who was born in 1975. To Virginia it seemed a miracle in itself, that such a small and fragile treasure as the wing of a South American insect could travel the world, and then continue to be passed down in the family without ever being lost or stolen or sold. Because of the silver pendant 'Claudina' was a name that was often given to girls in the family.

The two survivors of the wreck of the *Iris* clung together to one broken piece of timber, wild-eyed, unable to speak, swallowing water, freezing, and by working their arms to guide themselves, they finally came to the shore, exhausted and sick, and they climbed onto the rocks on the eastern side of the island. Magnus's thick clothing was heavy, drenched with the waters of the Southern Ocean, and he had lost his tartan plaid. Minerva was dressed in a dripping nightgown, drawers and slippers. The dawn sea was still, and a strange silence hung over the island. With an air of formality they introduced themselves, constantly staring past each other to the empty sea, or looking into each other's eyes as if searching for an answer to a riddle. At last Magnus could utter a few words.

'There must be others. There will be others. We must look for them.'

Minerva, knowing in her heart that Edward had drowned, could not bring her lips to form his name, but in her head she heard him humming the way he hummed when he was happy, and the tears, hot and hopeless, welled again and again, stinging her eyes. Knowing she was foreign, Magnus assumed she could not understand him, and there was much about his accent that she found incomprehensible. She bent low to the ground, feeling faint and ill, and a stream of yellowish-green water, thin and curdled, gushed from her mouth. Her bare hands, and her feet in brown slippers were so cold she could not stand, could no longer grasp anything. She fell into a faint. Fearing she was going to die, Magnus took her hands in his and worked her arms, beat her palms together.

She appeared to him to be praying, and in time she regained full consciousness, opening eyes of onyx velvet to look at Magnus whose face and beard were caked with thick streaks of blood. Minerva and Magnus walked around the tiny island, climbing over rocks, slipping, falling, going forward, but they found no sign or trace of more survivors. Magnus had lost his boots in the wreck, and his bare feet were cut and bleeding. Minerva discarded her soft leather slippers which clung to her feet, were smooth treacherous, and worse than useless on the rocks. She tucked them into the belt of her long, sodden and bedraggled drawers. Her feet also were soon scratched and bleeding. Her hands had been bruised and cut in the storm, and her fingernails were torn.

Minerva kept stopping and staring at the water, willing Edward to rise up before her eyes. And always looming somewhere at the edges of her mind was the unbelievable image of the thrashing parts of a great pink-grey sea creature, as if the churning, lashing waters had released a primitive secret, as if the storm had given slippery birth to a fat implacable evil. The image was forever out of reach, just out of focus, maddening in its refusal to come forward, to be examined. Did she really see a giant squid? Did the Kraken really power up from the ocean floor and hug the *Iris* to its deadly bosom? Or did the twirling darkness of the thrashing waves throw up hallucinations to occupy the spaces of unreality, to explain the unexplainable, to, in a perverse way, comfort her, give some meaning to the loss of everything? Much later Minerva told Magnus of her visions, but he remembered nothing like that. He had perhaps been stunned by falling timbers and had by a miracle floated free, seeing no monster, hearing none of the shrieks and moans and prayers as the ship made its last journey to the bottom of the sea. Or perhaps he saw and yet could not recall. The giant squid became, as you would expect, part of the folklore of the family, gathering a mythic strength and yet losing solid credibility as time went on.

Minerva and Magnus discovered, abandoned by the receding tide, three pieces of luggage: a leather bag, a wooden box, a tin trunk. All three were pushed up against each other, as if they had been the burden of one of those great, fantastic, and heaving waves, dumped together by the rocks, surrounded by bits of broken timber and flopping shreds of sail. Had they burst from their place in unison, or were they objects from three different sources, three different ships perhaps? There was really nothing to say that they had come from the *Iris* at all. Except that they had an air of freshness, of not having lain in the weather for any time. Minerva and Magnus found also a scrap of tartan cloth. A tin dish. And a baby.

The child was lying as if dead or sleeping, a doll-like creature, sopping, a crust of vomit across its cheek, cradled by the succulent pigface that grew in carpets and tufts and webs all over the island.

The boat lies at the bottom of the Strait, small pieces of scrappy timber floating in scummy drifts on the surface of the waters, making their way into narrow spaces between the rough and rusty rocks that frill the edges of the islands that lie scattered through the Strait. A small straw bonnet sails, a cheeky duck on the surface of the water — now almost completely still. All bodies save those of Minerva and Magnus and the baby have disappeared forever. No set of teeth, no eyeglass, no wooden leg, no chestnut wig — nothing but the forlorn straw bonnet bobs on the rocking waves. Three whole humans only, marooned together on Puddingstone Island, a fresh-made family group. Man, woman, baby.

It was as if the ship, the crew, the passengers had never existed, as if they were but figments of the hot imaginations of the lone surviving trio. Dogs, horses, chickens, pigs, monkeys, cats, children, agile sailors, the piper and the boy with the violin — all stilled and silenced by the sea. Gone was the strange and beautiful tortoise bought by one of the crew in Cape Town. Minerva simply named the baby La Niña, girl-child, for the time being. They began to call her Niña. It was Minerva who took charge of Niña, who suddenly became a mother to a child there in the middle of the ocean, who gathered the baby to her and who then said with urgency and desperation that they must look for shelter.

It was as if some part of a mission had been completed, and they must now move on to the next stage. Where they must find their home, their shelter. The wind began to moan. The child began to cry. She was alive, and she was hungry, and the sound of her cry was the most urgent and the most primitive of sounds. The hunger in her cry tore at Minerva's heart, ran like a jagged blade through Magnus's brain.

Magnus could only stare dumbly at the baby in amazement, and a kind of horror mingled with hope as he realised that perhaps she would die, that she would almost certainly die. Perhaps they would all die on the hell-spotted rocks by the sawtooth sea beneath the thick bleached canopy of the heavens. Above them loomed the arching no-colour of the southern sky while deep down serpents larger than imagination thrashed in steely dark-green shadowy ocean depths. The stillness and silence was only an episode in the strange weather at the end of the world. They knew that tonight or tomorrow almost certainly there would again come curls of surface foam, mountains of moving, slicing, pleating water, black with a glinting edge. Perhaps bodies would be released from the wreck, and would float to the surface before their eyes. Minerva had seen newspaper etchings of wrecks and bodies, as had Magnus, and they both silently tried to suppress the grotesque images of black-grey bloated corpses bobbing eerily on the waves of the mind. The will to live is stronger than love or sorrow, and Minerva and Magnus would not give in to the phantoms that could pull them back down into the ocean.

Minerva stood beside the water with the baby in her arms, and sometimes the baby cried, and cried and cried, her voice the voice of all things abandoned in the universe, the cry of despair in the hollow darkness of primal nothingness beneath the arching void of heaven. Minerva removed all the child's clothing and held her in the sea-water lest her small body die for want of moisture, then she lifted the top layer of her own nightdress, and cradled the naked creature in its sorry, sopping folds.

No whisper, no bubble of sighing air would ever rise from the splinters and bones of the *Iris*. What shards of memory would stay with Niña, soft milky fragments gold and white of a warm and innocent time? Her mother's skin, her mother's breast. Someone singing in the half-light: 'Rockabye-baby-bye.'

Niña remembered deep inside herself the soft lining of her father's jacket, the joy of the sun shining through the glass of a little room somewhere in County Down or County Clare or County Tyrone or Cornwall. The cheep of a chick. The mew of a kitten. A little white dog. A patch of green wall, fragment of wallpaper, painted with pink roses and red. A silky cushion by the fireside. The motherely glow of the candle in the pewter candlestick. Somebody was calling from far away: Caroline! Caroline! Line! Line! Line! And there was gentle rain falling, falling, falling in the twilight outside the window. Sweet Caroline. Baby Niña?

A small boy is laughing, laughing out loud in the sunlight under a chestnut tree in flower. New pennies chink on a chipped china saucer. There is the rocking of the waves, the calling of the thunder, the terror of the storm, the stark and staring eyes of the fainting mother, the father beside himself with panic and black fear. Then, Baby Niña, in some strange super-human seizure of the mind, by some non-human, some unearthly inspiration, your terrified father holds you by your back, swings his arm in a mighty arc and releases you into the high, high air, hurling you from the suck of the sinking ship, high, high into the whistling air, above the swishing scummy foam, out out out into the whirling world he throws you out, he throws you overboard to seek your stormy story fortune in the flying air. Child overboard! The demented father has thrown the child overboard into the howling dark!

Two iridescent angels in embroidered cloth of gold catch you, for a little miracle has occurred, and they ferry you, these angels, to dear Puddingstone Island through air as thick and thin as air in Chinese mythology long, long ago. The black crack of the adamantine tempest — and the whole world splits and spits and you fly, a baby angel in your cambric nightgown, unconscious in the freezing whirling air, light as a leaf, heavy as a teardrop, and you land on your back in a bed that is a great clump of tangled seaweed caught between two snaggles and snarls of rock, covered by a shawl of pigface.

The child's shoulders and heels are bruised in the fall; her head lands on a soft squishy wad of pale green succulent leaves that are mixed with dark strappy pungent seaweed. She has emerged from a gushing, twirling world of shifting shadows, crenellations, lacy froth and the shrieks and howls of sorrowful demons. She will never see the weird wild seaweed caught in the hair, strapped across the eyes of her doomed and drowned and drifting family. Icy waters stop their mouths which will yet cry out with silent cries, forever seeking their child, their little sister, their baby Caroline, Baby Niña.

They set out with you, your father and mother and brother, to seek their fortune, your fortune. Far, far away from neighbours and cousins, seeking a new beginning, fresh adventure, untold security perhaps. Perhaps. You are all that is left of all those hopes and all those bright ideas. This is your destiny, alive and not alone on Puddingstone Island, which is a pile of peter-piper-pebbles in the Strait. You are now Niña, the baby of Puddingstone Island.

So Niña the baby was saved. The angel who looked away that sunny day when Dorothea nibbled on the buds of the hydrangea was most actively present on the night of the storm, the shipwreck, the appearance of the monster from the ocean deep. That angel plunged through cloud and wave, lightning and hail, and as Niña left her father's open desperate and grieving hands, angel hands took her gently and flew with her in that perfect arc towards Puddingstone Island, placing her as carefully as possible on the bed of succulent pigface. Demons were busy that night, hand in glove with storm and squid; angels were busy, bringing together a new little family in this far away strange place, and arranging also for some useful luggage. For what would be the good of saving the baby's life if she didn't have at least a nice warm blanket and somebody to wrap her in it? You can see a sort of logic in it all — Dorothea's story was perhaps trivial when compared with the dramatic story of Niña. Nina survived the storm and the serpent and the sea; Dorothea died in her own garden from eating a lunch that was set out for the fairies — who can really make sense of that? God is supposed to be watching out for the fall of the sparrow. Poor little sparrow Dorothea. Lucky little sparrow Niña.

CHAPTER NINE

Secret Chronicle of Virginia Mean II

'And the woman fled into the wilderness, where she hath a place prepared of God, that they should feed her there a thousand two hundred *and* threescore days.'

REVELATION OF ST JOHN THE DIVINE

A thick wood of dark trees surrounds the facility out at the Black River. The forest sets it as a place apart, marking it off for the lodging of people who have done such terrible things they can never be allowed out into the world of ordinary folk ever again. They are not just mad, insane, not just criminal, but they are doubly damned for they are the criminally insane. The wood is the wood that is found in dreams and in fairytales.

There was once a beautiful palace, as white as clouds, as cold as ice, and as mysterious as mysterious could be. It shone like mirrors, glittered and twinkled. It was like something made from gleaming sugar, and a pale owl cried in the forest at night. When they were building this palace I remember reading of it in the *Circular Head Gazette.* Some people living in the district were much opposed to having a mental hospital and prison at Black River. Then there were people who were very angry because they said the facility was so opulent, was so luxurious and modern, a work of art. They thought that offenders such as Caleb should be tortured and put to death, an eye for an eye and a tooth for a tooth, should not be permitted to live out their lives in a home-like place where they are well fed, and where they have many comforts such as centrally heated single rooms with televisions and computers and CD players, and where there is a heated swimming pool and full gymnasium. It all looked most seductive and desirable in the pictures in the *Gazette*, if the pictures were telling the true story, and it is possible they were not. I have grown more suspicious of everyone since I left Skye, more wary of the things people say. I used to trust, but now I realise that I can no longer take things at face value. It's difficult for me to discern the marks of duplicity and deception, but I believe I am learning. A shell of snail-cynicism is protecting me now.

I learnt from the newspaper that the eiderdowns at the palace-prison are filled with the softest feathers from the moonbirds, and people are particularly angered by that detail. As if there was something about the moonbirds that forbade their feathers to be used by unworthy members of society. The palace was designed by a man from Norway, a man with the name of a god — his name was Thor. Much of the story I read spoke of how light enters the building, and I was quite fascinated by that detail, 'bringing the light into the darkness of sick minds' it said. When I read the article in the newspaper I did not imagine how important the building would ever become to me, that it would be the dark dungeon of my darling heart, the castle of his permanent enchantment, the guardian of his silence, guardian of my own silence as well. I do not really understand why he can not write me a letter, or why at least I can not write to him. Why are we not permitted to use the telephone? I always understood that prisoners had some access to maintain contact with the world beyond the prison walls. But Caleb is considered to be so dangerous that he must not contaminate the air with his voice, or stain a sheet of paper with his thoughts. His links with the world must be severed so that he can perhaps be changed, be rehabilitated — if I am here to speak that language in which he is now trapped. He is forbidden to write letters, and because of the fire at Skye he is forbidden to use matches. It is just as well he does not smoke — if he did, perhaps somebody would light his cigarettes for him. But they should realise that he would never be interested in burning anything in the prison. His task is done, his mission performed, but they do not understand. I do have one slender line of communication with one of his doctors who is able to send me formal reports. I am also permitted to respond to his doctor in writing. So that is at least a small sliver, a glinting shard of hope. I do not know how much to write to him, how much of myself I should reveal.

Around the perimeter of the trees, stretches a stark white concrete wall, electrified, and swept, during the hours of darkness, by creepy blue lights that probe the forest. There is a tower that is pierced by one slit, one window, looking out to sea, like in the tower of Rapunzel, while all the other windows I believe face inward, turn their back upon the world. Natural light enters the building through thick glass slabs up on the roof, but the greater part of the light inside the palace is artificial. The whole of the building burns inside day and night with clean bright electric light.

Caleb could easily imitate a lunatic — for he could imitate anyone, imitate anything, by action or sound. He could imitate the cleverest doctor in the whole of the universe. He could always produce the cry of any bird, the roar of the waterfall, the snarl of a rat. The laugh of a child, the sigh of a mad musician, or the cadence of a poet. He could be any politician, any movie star, any lost and wandering beggar. He was born with the gift of words, but it was much, much more than that. Caleb truly is a magician and a prophet and I believe him to be the most beautiful man in the world. He was described in some newspapers as one of the most vicious killers on the face of the earth. It also said that in the prison he must use a clear toothpaste so that he can not hide any weapons inside the clear plastic tube. I thought that sounded like a rather magical idea in itself, and I imagined fairy daggers lying quietly inside a tube of toothpaste.

I do not really know why I write about him in the past, for surely he can still do all these things that I describe. Unless perhaps the doctors have drugged him — perhaps they have drugged him right out of existence, or cut out his tongue. Such things do happen. Yes, they do those things to psychiatric patients for their own good and for the good of society in general. Dead. Perhaps Caleb is dead. Because of the rules I have received no letters, no telephone calls, but more significantly I have also received no telepathic thoughts or images. The absence of thought messages suggests to me that Caleb must be either drugged or dead, since we have always been able to communicate in this way. I am told that I will never ever see him again, and that I might as well forget all about him. How can I do that? How might I learn to forget his beautiful naked body in union with mine the first time we loved, the last time we loved? Those afternoons in his white, white meditation sanctuary perfumed with clove, where the girls in white play their dulcimers for us as a stipple of sunlight sifts in through the leaves of the cherry tree. How to forget? Under the window is growing wild a bed of poppies, flowers of sleep, and we drowse and love all afternoon, all evening, as the quiet lullaby of the dulcimers plays our love song. The notes of the music linger in the luminous air.

How to forget? How to banish from my mind's eye the memory and image of Caleb in his silver suit striding along on his way to the Temple of the Winds, under the great white umbrella, through the long grasses on the clifftop, while the pale salmon-coloured butterflies whirl about him, flecks of snow in broad foamy flurries? How to forget? Those salmon butterflies were made from wire and tissue paper, fashioned by my Aunt Tamar, and they were a most important part of the scene, part of the performance. We never pretended they were real. Yet there were times when Caleb had no paper insects, but he could persuade people to think they saw things, to imagine the beauty of the miracle that attended his own birth, and perhaps they did indeed see them. Caleb's imagination is powerful and is able to project what it sees, thereby instructing the minds and thoughts of others. The reality of imagination, of the unconscious mind, is one of the central beliefs of our faith. We have such ceremonies as the Festival of Dreams that was inspired by an ancient tradition of the Iroquois tribe, and which came into practice in Skye early in the twentieth century. It is an opportunity for people to release anger and to behave violently but safely. Within the people of Skye there is always one, usually the leader, who has the gift of non-dreaming, and Caleb has this gift. The gift frees the unconscious mind for its greater works. The Festival of Dreams gives the gifted one the liberty to commit acts (which may be seen as violent acts) without suffering any repercussions. During the Festival one person can physically or verbally assault another, but must stop as soon as the victim guesses the content of the first one's dreams. The first person must be honest about their dreams. I was always honest, but I suppose now that there were possibly people who lied. I do not know. Since Caleb has no dreams, he can not be challenged, and is free to impose his violence upon others for their own and ultimate good.

In my mind's eye of memory I can see Caleb naked among the wreaths of incense, among the flowers and summer fruits of our secret, secret bower. Here there are no musicians, no witness to our union. His body is taut and pale and smooth as ice, yet lit from within with the fire of God. I see him in his public role, presiding over the village feasts, preaching, always preaching, gathering about him his groups of devoted followers who bow beneath his radiant and sumptuous smile which is a sign of wisdom and of the grace of God. And between us we made our child, Golden. She is my only child, although Caleb had many other children among the community. Logically, Golden was the only one he chose to save. He said to me that he would sacrifice all his sons, all his other daughters first, but he would take Golden with him on his final journey. She would not burn, but would fly with us in our great leap from the cliff. I mourn for those children now. Caleb said that Golden has a special mission, a special meaning, a calling, that she has the gift of prophecy. In my heart of hearts, I hope that she does not have that gift, for such forespoken gifts I know are sometimes curses. If Golden could lead the life of a normal child, my prayers would truly have been answered.

Although I believe with all my soul, and I am bound to believe, that what Caleb did was right, when it happened I was so very shocked. I had not realised how I would feel. All our families, all our friends, all the brethren of our community of Skye — they are all gone. It is almost impossible for me to comprehend this. Groups of tuneless children singing folk songs beside the river. My sister Bethany is dead. I say that to myself over and over — my sister Bethany is dead. My sister Bethany and my little brother Zimran. I seem to see them through smoked glass, as if looking at the sun, and into my memory leaps the day that Bethany and I sat underneath the mulberry tree making daisy chains, and Zimran was lying baby-roly-poly on the rug, and we gave him a crown of flowers, and a necklace, and he gurgled with pleasure, then began to scream in pain because he had been stung by a bee in the long summer grass. My mother came running out of the house wiping her hands on her apron, flour — what on earth!

Well, they are gone. It is not possible, but it has happened. And all the children, so many dear people, are passed over, they are dead. I know they are in paradise, but in my heart I feel only their loss. One hundred and fifty is the optimum number of members for a community of hunter-gatherers. Caleb knew that when this number was reached, with the birth of baby Nathaniel Thunderstone, the time had truly come for the community to be sent forth by fire. One hundred and forty-seven to burn, three to fly away.

Yes, I dwell in dull amazement on the fact that even we — and Caleb — were meant to go, according to the plan Caleb had made. The idea is repugnant to me now. The plan was that we would all ride over the cliff and fly off, riding the winds, and our bodies would arrive at last in the sea and be lost, merged with the ocean, laced with foam, blessed with the deep waters from which all life once came. Our souls would be in paradise with the blessed souls of our families. Our bodies returned to the deep where the *Iris* lies, guarding the secret of Niña Mean, the secret, perhaps, of the whole history of the Means of Skye. Niña, Niña, who were you, who are you? There we would be, mingling with the bones of our ancestors, Caleb, Golden and me, and also Caleb's final words on the tape in his pocket, his message to the universe. Instead of jumping we gave ourselves up to the police — I mean that we just stayed quite still and the police collected us like obedient children and put us into two cars. Something had changed, after the fire, after the helicopters came, something that stopped us from jumping and flying and dropping into the sea. It is difficult for me to remember and describe all this because I was quite entranced, I had moved to a higher level, beyond conscious understanding, into a strangely vacant space, like the sky itself, like hollow sun-sapphire space and the weaving strands of time.

So much love and beauty has been incinerated — in the name of love and goodness and eternal life and light. Perhaps we are the unlucky ones, after all — that must be so, for the others have all fully translated to the light. We remain here on the earth in spiritual darkness, in pain and sorrow and exile. The air did not hold us up, and our mother the sea did not take us in her arms, and now I am so lonely here, so very, very lonely. I live in a sad hope that one day I may be permitted to see Caleb again. Then a great fear comes over me, a fear that they have perhaps executed him after all, have done it secretly, by a special law and dispensation. 'He died in custody, died in his sleep,' they would say, 'leapt to his death from the castle tower.' I imagine they can do that, can do whatever they wish to do. They would inject him with drugs and just let him fall asleep and fade into oblivion, dissolve into nothing. Then I think — but how could they do that to a being such as Caleb? It would not be possible. Then I realise very sadly that I no longer know what is possible. I remember all over again that I am alone in this vale of tears, in this world of wickedness and woe. I have resolved to try not to think of Caleb, but to exist in the now, for my life is beyond my control, and my very thoughts must concentrate upon the daily task of strange survival.

In the time between then and now, between when my horse did not fly out across the waters of the Strait and now, when I am at last able to write, and almost to feel, almost to think, there stretches a cold and empty arsenic world of trampled threadbare no-time. Everything has stood still, and my breath is held, my eyes are wide, and I am waiting for the next unknown.

I lay in the silence of a grey-white room, and there were bars outside the windows, and I was watching with dull eyes the moving shapes and colours of the sky. The sunlight and the moonlight cast the shadows of the window-bars across the walls of the room, and I watched as clouds drifted, as storms frowned and lightning split the mind of heaven in jagged fitful phosphorescent green. Once, at the beginning of a tempest, yellow and white flowers blew in streams and flurries in the sky outside the window-bars, flowing past my gaze, whirling now and then in a little dervish dance. Was it hot or was it cold outside? The temperature in the room was always the same. I could not smell the earth, I could not sense the rocks that must lie deep at the base, at the bone-creaking foundations of the building. I could not imagine the haunted rivers and whispering, rustling, spectral streams that must run somewhere nearby in the world of the hospital or prison where I was kept. A woman in grey was seated by the door.

Sometimes there was a bowl of lilies, huge and glowing, like ladies on thin stalks, visible to me in waving rainbow shapes through a thick glass window. Sometimes it was a vase of white roses, sometimes a tall jar of bright green and scarlet leaves shaped like enormous hearts. I could hear the shush shush of hospital machinery, the clink of cruel metal things, the soft voices and the shouts and laughter of the people working in the corridor. There was no real sound, not a dog, not a bird, not a rustle of leaves, not even a clap of thunder that I could detect through my dungeon walls. I was a living corpse, silent, fed through tubes, wondering, wondering — what will happen? I imagined spiders walking, curtsying on long legs, dancing taut and delicate across the white hospital quilt. Then I would remember Golden and I would want to scream, yet my throat was silent and the scream died in my heart. Golden was somewhere. Where was Golden? Golden my dancing baby girl. And I heard voices calling, calling, but I could not understand what they were saying, yet I know they were the voices of my family, all the brothers and sisters now translated into the light, living in my memory, shrunken to fit inside my spinning head, to sail along in my bloodstream forever. They are now among the glorious People of the Light, travellers in Fairyland, workers in Ferryland, creations of the mind of the great Saint Virgil. What were they telling me, those voices of the People of the Light? What are you singing, People of the Light? What have you seen? What do you say? When will I be free? And where is my baby, my Golden, my baby Golden? I wept my silent tears until, in a mysterious twilight hour, my baby was returned to me.

The woman in grey — her name I know is Alice — saw the actions of my weeping, of my sobs, my sighs, my groans, my moaning thrumming silent song of sorrow and despair. My sudden bursts of noiseless laughter, laughter that shakes me all over, but which does not light up my eyes, does not echo in this sorrowful poison-prison-room where life is punctuated by the sudden smell of prison hospital poisoned food. I know all this. I know when my eyes shine and when they are still, misted over with a veil of secrecy, a pall like the pall of death. Very occasionally I would open my mouth in a noiseless scream and I would attempt to sit up, like a woman experiencing some terrible nightmare, drifting in a landscape of ethereal light, weighted down at the ankles with heavy stones. Then the nurses and doctors were called to administer special soothing drugs and other medicines to me. That was a kind of relief from the sadness and the boredom and bewilderment. I can hear Alice breathing. She is like a piece of flotsam in my world, some piece of wreck that has floated in, washed up on the edges of my kingdom, barring the way out, the way in, a giant breathing grey nuisance spiderface sitting next to the door, understanding nothing, imagining she knows everything. She has power over my body, but my mind is free and she makes eternal notes in her eternal notebook. I believe I must be an unsympathetic character in a play or an opera she is writing. Furry-faced grey jailer genius writes prize-winning play hailed as a masterpiece on Broadway opening in London, Milan, the Sydney Opera House.

They took my clothes and gave me a thin white nightgown. They took the guns away from me, naturally, but I still have my blue pendant. And Golden. Sometimes I think that those things are all I really need to keep me anchored in time and space and hope and love. My pendant and my little daughter Golden. And yet, and yet, sometimes I wonder what even they might mean, Golden and the silver pendant. Golden needs me. That idea, that truth, holds me in place. All the teachings and meanings embedded in me from the past, all the wisdom of our ancestors seems to whirl around inside me, and all around outside me, and I am a reed, a cobweb, a speck of nacreous stardust in the storm. Our family history is dominated by storms, and we have weathered the tormented days and nights of many many tempests blowing in from Bass Strait. I used to love the storms, and I would stand high in the Temple of the Winds and revel in the drama of the skies. The fire was the final washing away, the purification, the final obliteration, the final blessing.

I am living now, with Golden, in the care of Gilia and Michael — old people, strangers to me, kind people, somewhere in the wilderness, and I am safe. They are the friends of Father Fox who rescued me from Alice. I am now safe from Alice, and from all people who would wish to hurt me. I have been told the only thing left in one piece in Skye was the Temple of the Winds. How I love my memories of that place. High up on the walls, near the ceiling, there is an old mural painted by one of my ancestors, showing the eight winds, four men and four women, imitating the style of Michelangelo. I liked those pictures so much when I was little, and whenever we went out to Four Winds Hill I would lie on my back, the shell and bone patterns of the floor uneven but warm beneath my spine, and I would look up in pleasure at the frieze round the walls. The motto of our family, strangely Welsh, not Scottish, brought with Magnus Mean long long ago, is written in gold ornamental script over and over again underneath the paintings: 'Heb Dhu — Heb Dhim' which means 'If I have God I have Everything'. One small window in the dome, a eye to heaven, is made from thin, thin slices of iris agate, which is a prismatic light gate, cut from a stone found by Magnus when he was looking for gold over at Fingal. My sisters and I would lie on the hillside outside the temple and stare up at the night sky, up through the clear pure air of Cape Grimm and we could feel ourselves falling up, up, up into the stars, so white, so clean, so near, so close to home. And there I would lie with Caleb.

I will never see the temple again, because I can never bear to return to the ruined town. For all I know the place may have been set aside forever as a perpetual crime scene. Is that possible, I wonder. Can they (the police? the local council?) decide that a piece of land is tabu because it is spiritually contaminated? I do wonder about that. But I daydream about the Temple, I imagine and remember the days and nights we spent there. Our ancestor Minerva began the building of the Temple, back in the 1860s, inspired by the Doric temple constructed by Lady Jane Franklin at Lenah Valley down in Hobart. It soothes and comforts me to remember that Minerva built our remote and holy temple — out on Four Winds Hill.

It is a tall compact room with a vaulted ceiling, open on eight sides to the air, the winds blowing freely through from all directions, the columns encrusted with the shells of mussels and scallops. On the external apex of the domed roof is a wooden carving of three knots, the knots that are said to contain the winds — undo the first one and you get a moderate wind, undo the second and you get a gale, undo the third and you get a hurricane. When I described the Temple to Gilia I said there were eight sides because eight is a Fibonacci number.

'What's that?' she said.

I tried to explain what they were, the Fibonacci numbers. It is funny the things I do not know of her world, and the things she does not know of mine. I expect her to know everything I know, and many more things besides, but it does not work like that. My father was very fascinated by the numbers, by what he called Sacred Geometry, and he would often say 'This sunflower, this shell, look at this, it is following the sequence.' Many of the designs in the shells at the Temple follow Fibonacci sequences — as do the designs of millions of shells, I imagine, and as do also a great number of plants. There are whole nautilus shells carefully preserved in the ceiling of the Temple of the Winds because they are not only beautiful, but they are perfect specimens of the equiangular spiral. They are really breathtaking and they are arranged on the ceiling in such a way that they make another whole sequence of the spiral. If you lie on the floor and look up you can lose yourself in the design. Nautilus are made from the secretions of the arms of a type of octopus, and are really flotation devices for the octopus young. Sometimes they are dumped in great numbers on Bass Strait beaches, and when we were little we once collected hundreds of perfect specimens from the beach at Woodpecker Point, and we sold them by the side of the road just outside Penguin. When I told my father about that he became very angry, and he said I should have brought them to the Temple of the Winds instead of casting them out into the dark world where they would lie lost and forgotten on the shelves and mantelpieces of beach houses, gathering dust and dead flies. Gilia was surprised when I told her we were allowed to wander about the countryside. We had caravans and we would go off selling our toys and signs and honey and cloth. People thought we were gipsies. Maybe we were. In the caravan I was sometimes very afraid of my father's sudden temper — he had extremely sensitive hearing, and in that very confined space he hated the sounds of us eating — eating is so unspiritual he would say, and the sounds of it somehow reminded him of death.

'If you are going to eat apples,' he would shout, 'go outside and do it, do not stand around here munching and crunching the things within my hearing, eating your way to the grave with your teeth showing, without grace and within my hearing. Thank you!'

All the surfaces of the Temple of the Winds are embellished with whole and broken shells from the beaches along the coast, as well as shells brought in sacks and boxes from all parts of the world over many years. The eye may follow the journeys of stripes and waves and striations, spots and glassy blushes. There are the three-dimensional iridescent swirls of emerald and turquoise, mysterious crimson shadings on the paua shells. In pride of place, central to the apex of the dome, is the Rainbow Paua, in acknowledgment of the *Iris*, the wreck from which our family first sprang. There are brick-red spatters that will not fade from the surfaces of the mitre shells, and they form geometric designs on the walls, and form pictures as well. Pictures of flowers, particularly sunflowers, and lotus flowers, of bowls of fruit, exotic birds and mountain scenes decorate the interior of the Temple of the Winds. The colours are soft — white with greys and browns and corals and mysterious purples and blues and greens, all overlaid with a dusty bloom, a salty, moonshine haze. These colours are my favourite colours, and the shells at the Temple of the Winds are some of my dearest favourite memories, are lodged in my mind and forever linked to my people. I close my eyes and bring back the patterns, the colours, the secrets of the sea that are eternally whispering in the shells. And there are fragments of glass, all colours, that twinkle. There are stones, smooth as eggs, and pieces of broken pottery with coloured patterns of roses and garlands and birds and even little scenes of old-fashioned country life and Chinese legends. There are strange insect shapes built into the patterns, flocks of palest flying insects captured in the lines and whorls of the walls. Was it, after all, a dream-temple, nothing but a chimera conjured up in the collective mother-of-pearl imagination of the people of Skye?

This imagination was the obverse of my father's outbursts of temper, and it sometimes seemed to me that my father suffered from a profound lack of trust in the beliefs of the community. He was unlike other fathers, my uncles and cousins, who all appeared to follow the teachings on the world to come and our part in it, teachings that have grown up in the community since Magnus and Minerva first began to build Skye. If my father had not died the year before the fire, I wonder, I wonder — perhaps the fire would never have come to pass. He was not a charismatic in any way, but he did have a certain ability to persuade other people with what he called his 'basic common sense'. So why did he stay on and lead his life at Skye? Why did he not pack us all up, me and my mother and my brothers and sisters and move away, away? Just get in the caravan and rumble off into the wide blue yonder, never to return? Ah, the answer to that, I believe, is that it was very very difficult to leave because so much had been indoctrinated from birth, and the world of Skye was the whole world, although I have heard my father yell at my mother:

'This place is a paper nautilus and we are trapped in its chambers, sailing along to nowhere, peering through the walls at the high waves, waiting, waiting for the winds to tip us over and we go down. Down-down-down into the graveyard of the *Iris* and all the other rotting wrecks at the bottom of Bass Strait.'

'Hush now, Matthew,' my mother would say, treating him almost like a child, 'the Truth will one day be revealed to us, and until that Time of Light, we must persevere in cheerfulness and hope.'

And she would make him some camomile tea and attempt to soothe his brow with kisses and warm drops of lavender oil. They loved each other. Perhaps that is also why he stayed, for she would never never leave, she believed very deeply and simply in everything that was taught, and it also seemed (at least to me) that every nerve, every vein, every hair on all our heads was linked, tied, knotted up into the fabric of the village of Skye — cut us loose and we would bleed to death, would wither and shrivel and fade away into hopeless ranting helplessness.

And mostly, I realise, my father also toed the line and played his part in the communal life. His death was sad and strange, and ironic when you think about it, for one day he was sitting with my mother on the cliff and they were just looking out to the dreamy turquoise of a sea festooned with the slow lace of waving foam — it was a warm day in October — and watching the mollyhawks, the shy albatross, in their dignified courting dance on the rocks far below. My father, concentrating on the beauty of the dance, took a huge bite out of a big green apple and it caught in his throat and before my mother could do anything he had choked to death right there and then, where the high land meets the water down below, where the rocks have snapped off to form the edge of our world.

CHAPTER TEN

Gold

'What need is there to weep over parts of life
when the whole of life calls for tears?'
SENECA

There came a point in my reading of Virginia's Chronicles where I felt she had learnt to trust me, and I knew I must enter into a correspondence with her if I was ever going to understand more of how Caleb Mean's mind worked. Virginia is, after all, the only sane and living key to the community of Skye, and to have gained her trust is probably some sort of coup, people in closed communities being traditionally suspicious of the outside world and its ways. There are other Means scattered through the countryside and the backwoods of the northwest, but the community itself remains the mystery it has always been, and it still exercises its fascination for me. My father used to know (and disapprove of for a number of reasons) Bedrock and Carrillo Mean who lived at Copperfield and who ran the Bedrock Press that published so many of Carrillo's books, of which there is a vast number on every topic under the sun. Every topic, that is, except the community at Skye which seems to have been a skeleton in Carrillo's closet and thorn in his side, as far as I can gather. Just as I caught some glimpses of Caleb when I was young, I also saw Carrillo once, although not Bedrock. Bedrock was Carrillo's twin sister as well as his wife, a detail that so appalled my father he became a vehement Mean-hater for life. Once my sister said that perhaps the Means were like the Ancient Egyptians in their attitude to marriages within the family. This comment probably only succeeded in turning my father against the Pharoahs, about whom he knew very little.

Carrillo Mean came out to Christmas Hills to buy bulbs and seeds from us. Father was happy enough to sell them, in spite of his moral prejudice. The visitor was tall and handsome, with white-white skin and bright auburn locks — I say 'locks' because his hair was thick and long and springy, standing out from his brow in sparkling angelic rays. I knew he was Caleb's second cousin or something, and there is a strong family resemblance. I was bedazzled by his presence, and also because he was related to the Preacher Boy. I followed him and my father round the farm, probably hoping to gather some inkling of the glamour and mystery I sensed in the lives of the Means. My mother seemed to fall under his spell, and she picked an opulent bunch of zinnias, all shades of pink and red, which she presented to him. He held them in both hands like a bride, a blood-stained nuptial bouquet. I believe it was an amazing sight to witness Bedrock and Carrillo Mean side by side, as they were identical apart from their gender. There is a sad story attached to them. Their young daughter disappeared from her bedroom in the middle of the night and was never found. I was very young when Carrillo bought the bulbs, and I don't recall much of what he said, but I do remember that his voice was what I could only call mellifluous, and the words sounded to me like poetry, although he was presumably only describing the kind of plants he wished to buy. The part I remember was when he said he wanted some mauve foxgloves that would 'shoot up like a melancholy rocket'. I remember it because my father took to quoting it whenever the name of the Means came up. 'Shoot up like a melancholy rocket,' he would say, and laugh a kind of bitter little laugh. One time Carrillo won a local poetry writing competition with his epic 'Playing With Fire' and I read the poem when it was published in the *Circular Head Gazette* but I couldn't understand it. I was about twelve, and had planned to write to Carrillo in admiration, and in the hope that he might write back and ask to see some of my own work, but as it turned out I was far too embarrassed because I didn't even get what he was on about. He was always in the local news for one thing or another, and he also had quite an international reputation, going into the more academic side of psychology, in fact. He founded a well-respected centre for the recovery of lost children in California. Bedrock never recovered from the tragedy of the loss of their child, and I think she still lives alone somewhere in one of the ghost towns, making incredible patchwork quilts, one of which my sister bought, much to my father's disgust.

But as I said, Carrillo was never part of the community at Skye. His branch of the family escaped early and settled at Copperfield and Woodpecker Point, but there were other families who moved *in* to Skye, marrying Means, and bringing new blood, and, in at least one instance, gold. I had heard the stories about a miner who found a large nugget of gold at Beaconsfield and somehow ended up being wrecked off the west coast on his way to try his luck at Mount Bischoff. How he got to Skye remains a mystery, but he did, and he fell in love with Rosa Mean and stayed and married her. This turns out to be a true story. Without what came to be known in the family as 'the Beaconsfield gold', the whole enterprise of Skye might have foundered before the end of the nineteenth century. As it was, Magnus and Minerva read the miner's gold as a miracle and sign of God's blessing, and the future of the community was confirmed. Rosa and her miner, a Chinese man whose name was Charles Beaumont, had eleven children, nine of whom survived childhood, and six of whom remained at Skye. If you have ever heard of the violinist Atocha Beaumont, who played in London, Paris, New York and Berlin, you have heard of one of Rosa's daughters.

That golden nugget ensured the future of Skye. It set down the foundations from which would rise the child Caleb, who would be born under the rainbow, who would be the harbinger of so much woe. Who would have thought?

Virginia calls me her pen-friend which I think is very touching.

CHAPTER ELEVEN

Secret Chronicle of Virginia Mean III

'We live already in the shadow of future events.'
MAURICE MAETERLINCK, *The Great Beyond*

I have heard of a butterfly — and I have seen pictures — that lives in Africa, and it is called the Mother-of-Pearl. I imagine lying somewhere in a quiet sage-green place where the light is soft and clear like the notes of a distant flute, and my eyes are open, and I am visited by quiet loving flocks of Mother-of-Pearl. To go straight across the open, open sea from Skye to Africa! To lie in a silent place where the wings of insects shimmer, translucent palest green, blushing with whispers of dark violet, and they make a sound like *paper-paper-paper*. Their wings resemble the petals of the opium poppy, and I fall into a sweet and mystical slumber.

When the winds blow through my Temple of the Winds, it sings and sighs, and sometimes it roars. When it is silent in the moonlight, it is an eerie, magical, mysterious place like the floor of an ancient sea. The surface of the floor is composed of the vertebrae of whales caught in Bass Strait in the early part of the nineteenth century, white, hard, yet soft, geometric, warm and lovely. The place is guarded by the spirit of the homeless moonbird and is believed to be situated at an entrance to another universe. On the Night of the Dead which we celebrate in February the floor is strewn with the petals of calendulas, the flowers of the eleventh hour, leading here from the graveyard so that the souls of the recent dead may find their way to this haven, and beyond. In our houses on that night we serve bowls of fish soup with calendulas, and we celebrate the lives of those who have died by saying the Fish Prayer, a prayer that moves from one member of the group at the table to another. 'May the sacred unknown creatures of the deep guard you and keep you forever more.' We are taught to be unafraid of the sea, yet in truth I am afraid.

I speak as if all this was still part of my world. I hope that one day I may return to the Temple of the Winds, across the wind-beaten tawny gorse and twisted prostrate bushes, across the Honey Meadow where the flowers blow in the summer sun and you can hear the happy yellow songs of bees. I may lie on the pavement and melt into eternity, return to the no-time when the star-god fell to earth and became the father of the original peoples of this island.

The night of the fire the police took us and drove us for hours and hours, bumping along, to the airport at Launceston, and then we were flown to Hobart. I have almost no memory of that night except that it was a black, blank tunnel that went on forever and ever, and I imagined I could smell the fire on my skin, on my clothes, could feel the smoke smarting in my eyes. I could not answer any of their questions properly, and I was put in isolation, with a guard. Sometimes Golden was with me, and sometimes she was not. She was only two years old, and it must have been terrible for her. This continued for days, and then for weeks, and the police and the doctors and strange women came and talked to me, but I was often drugged and whole nights and whole days, fade and blur when I try to think about it. I never saw Caleb again. They finally told me he was 'unfit to testify' and was put away 'never to be released' in the new facility on the Black River. He is more than clever, and will certainly escape from there one day. It is they who are crazy to imagine they can contain him.

They decided I was crazy and consequently unfit as well. In a technical sense I am I suppose innocent of the crime of killing the people at Skye. I am not insane. I *am* innocent, truly innocent, but not insane, yet many of the people around me since that night have thought I must be insane. For a long time I never knew exactly what Caleb was planning to do in response to his thirty-third birthday. His language is poetic, his meaning sometimes obscure, and by the time his meaning was clear it was too late to do anything. What could I do? And I still love him. That is why they say that I must be insane. Perhaps I am stupid and crazy they say. Am I crazy? Am I stupid? Clearly I am not. I waited for Caleb on the cliff with Golden, and the air was pierced and filled with strange and otherworldly screams carried in the still darkness, filled with ash and smoke, and I could see the fire in the village, and I was frozen to the place where my horse was standing, a bruised mist of purple and sulphur between myself and the reality of the night.

Somewhere between the night on the cliff and the time when I became conscious of my surroundings in a hospital or prison in Hobart, I lost the ability to speak.

The first person who really made any sense to me, after the fire, was Father Benedict Xavier Fox from the Catholic Welfare Office. I had to trust somebody. I trusted him. Now I am uncertain of what my expectations were of a priest from the Catholic Church, but I have a strong recollection of my first response to him. With Father Fox I felt safe, deeply safe, for the first time in a very long while. He told me they could not decide what would be the best thing for me, where I should go to live, and what would become of Golden. The day when he came to visit me, there in the room with Alice the guard who so unsettled me, was a true turning point in my life.

Father Fox is a very tall man with black hair and a square face with freckles and square hands, blunt square hands. There are freckles on his hands, and sandy hairs that glint in sunlight. I found myself staring at the hairs on his hands and wondering why they were not black like the hair on his head. He was wearing a black shirt with his white priest's collar, and he was smiling, truly smiling with his whole face. His shoes were shiny black. When he spoke my name — Virginia — it was music, music that I loved to hear, and which he seemed to love to speak. Suddenly my eyes were brimming with tears. It was so long since I had seen somebody smiling. He appeared in the doorway, and he spoke my name, and he was beaming like a shining, gleaming, smiling raven. I saw my salvation in the aura that hovered about his form as he stood filling the doorway of my prison room which was generally populated by frowning scurrying anxious bothering ugly oppressive folk and the spider woman Alice. Golden was lying asleep in her cot beside me.

In his hands Father Fox held a plastic bag containing a yellow knitted sheep with a bell around its neck for Golden, a bottle of ginger beer and a packet of chocolate teddy bears and a beautiful fancy flowery nightgown with lace and satin bows. The nightgown resembled nothing I had ever seen in my life on earth. It was like a breath of paradise, sprinkled with small flowers, winking with tiny green leaves, and decorated with bluebirds all around the hem. I held it in my hands and it took my breath away. At home in Skye families made their own clothes, buying the fabrics from a shop in Burnie, or spinning, weaving and dyeing our own woollen cloth. Everything was used several times, until eventually an ancient skirt, for example, would re-surface in a patchwork quilt where it would appear to last forever and forever. My old dresses and nightgowns were sound and simple, in keeping with our beliefs and our way of life. Beauty and embellishment existed principally in the realm of the imagination, and there they knew no bounds. I had never dreamed of owning, of holding in my hands, of wrapping around my body, a drifting, floating, whispering garment such as this was, from a shop somewhere in Hobart. Hobart Town we always called it, a place where I was incarcerated with my child, and yet a place where I had never been before, a place of mystery and glamour and impossible strange music. The packets of biscuits were more familiar to me, as occasionally such things were seen within my Hobart prison walls, but they were also a much desired luxury. In Skye we mostly did all our own baking, and we enjoyed many treats. My favourite, and also Golden's favourite, is the shoo-fly pie. The recipe is my grandmother's — always when I write of members of my lost family I must stop to weep and to reflect and to pray. I believe with all my intellect that they have moved on to a glorious place, but in my heart I have a dark and heavy feeling that they should still be here on earth. Perhaps this is simply a reflection of my own self-regarding desire to be surrounded by the people I love. I felt like crying when I saw the bottle of ginger beer Father Fox brought me. Actually I never liked my mother's ginger beer which was celebrated in the community. I always preferred the ones we bought in milk bars whenever we went to Stanley or Burnie, but now I am sorry, so sorry. I cry over the strangest little things. I think it helps.

I wrote notes to Father Fox on this matter, and he replied that perhaps I would find comfort and meaning in giving thanks for their lives and in praying for their eternal souls. I asked him also how he knew I liked Gillespie's ginger beer, and he smiled the way he does and said that it was common knowledge about me and my fondness for Gillespie's ginger beer. That was very strange. He gave me a shining new copy of *Wuthering Heights* with a romantic picture of Cathy and Heathcliff on the cover, sweet and full of tragic promise. This book is one of my most favoured stories. Did he know this? How did he know? The first time I read it, many years ago when I was very young, I was unable to stop reading it, and then unable to stop myself from thinking about it for a long long time.

Father Fox also requested the people in the prison — I describe the place as a prison, but in truth I do not know what it was — bring me a television set. He also gave me magazines such as *TV Week* and *Vogue*, saying they were the first stage in my new education. I confess I found them to be full of wonders. They were so shiny, and they had a delicious aroma, spicy, and they took me into worlds of the imagination that I had never known before. *TV Week* is very jumpy, but quite easy to read, and it seemed to be almost instantly familiar to me, which is quite strange I think, since it took me into a world that had before been so alien. *Vogue* is like magic. I leaf through it over and over again as if I am looking for a secret or a clue to some lovely mystery. The people are so beautiful. And there are images of jewels and shoes and perfumes and dresses and ideas that can pick me up, place me on a magic Arabian carpet and transport me to worlds beyond worlds. I drift and wander through Aladdin's cave where there are riches dripping from the walls and the trees in clumps of green crystal as the middle of the sea, great chunks of ruby red and smooth as the ruby in the heart of God. But the most common image is that of the watch. The point at which technology and adornment and luxury and mortality converge. Time was so different at Skye, it stretched back before thought and measurement, moved in its twist of figure eight, back onto itself in the shape of eternity. But in *Vogue* there is a real obsession with gleaming elegant timepieces by famous fashion designers and the watches are either thick with diamonds or they are smooth and almost faceless, and they are shocking.

Father Fox was talking to me and observing me closely as I accepted all the gifts, and as I turned over the pages of the magazines. I know he was watching me. My eyes said thank you, and I wrote the word very firmly on my notepad. Father Fox smiled at me some more and drew a picture of a funny dog.

I realise that my thinking is possibly forever out of step with the world outside Skye. The world outside had for so long been the prison hospital walls, the prison bars, the prison labyrinths. And then suddenly the world outside is *the world outside* and I am in that world. I am going to become obsessed with watches and seconds and minutes and hours and the time of this world. I long to own a *Nomade* made by Hermès, oh how I long for that. It is not bejewelled, it is like the silver steering wheel of a magic car because of the way two watches are displayed together in the picture. I love Roman numerals. I realise that I have no real concept of society in general, for that is the way we were always meant to be in Skye, ignorant of the wicked world. Our thinking was superior, and we knew of matters that were wrongly overlooked by the people beyond our world. That world of Skye is now no more, it is gone forever and forever. I mourn for that world, I mourn for my lost sweet family. I cling to the goodness of Father Fox, praying as he says to pray, reflecting on the goodness of God who has given to me and to Golden the opportunity to survive a holocaust, to embrace the beauty of the world beyond Skye. For there is great beauty here.

If I am to survive in this world, I have much to learn of its ways. I am as a child. This is a most interesting position in which to find myself. Golden and I will grow up in the world together. Golden needs me, and she anchors me as I float in the flinty sea into which I have been tossed. She needs me and I need her. I have to be strong for her, for when my world disappeared, so too did hers, and she is imprinted with the knowledge of that world, even though she can not articulate her loss. I placed the yellow lamb in the cot beside her and she stirred in her sleep and turned her face into the pillow.

While Father Fox gifted me with the nightgown and all the other treasured objects, Alice was watching. She sat on her chair by the door, and her long nose was pointy with intense disapproval. Her eyes — close together and round like stones — glittered with repressed rage and other choked-up emotions that I could sense radiating from her. For Father Fox represented a Higher Authority. He was from the Catholic Welfare Office who had, I believe, taken it upon themselves to champion the cause of Virginia and Golden Mean, since our case fell outside the interests and capabilities of all other bodies. He was not attached to the prison, not attached to the police, not the doctors, not even the press, not anybody to whom Alice could appeal. Father Fox was able to follow a regime and a law known to himself alone. When I realised this I thanked God for bringing me to the attention of Father Fox. Sometimes there is a nice reason and logic in the universe.

He smiled, and I smiled, and I felt the corners of my mouth lifting in joy and pleasure and trust. And a week or so later, as if in a dream I found myself floating, with Golden in my arms, drifting, flying past Alice on her doorway guard-chair, out of the prison, past doors and gates and sad bad people, out into a bleak wide courtyard where a car was waiting. A man called Vincent then drove Father Fox and me away, away up the magic carpet road of Hobart Town. Out the window I saw rows and rows of houses and gardens and streets with shops and banks and busy people. The driver is also a painter and they call him van Gogh because his name is Vincent. I wrote on my notepad asking Father Fox whether he painted sunflowers and he laughed out loud and said sometimes he did.

Then Father Fox asked me what I would like to eat — what do you fancy? — and I thought for a long time and then I wrote down fried mushrooms and fresh coriander and a cup of peppermint tea. And Vincent said he knew where you could get that, and we drove to a house somewhere and some Catholic nuns were there and they prepared the sweetest and most refreshing meal I can ever recall. Golden woke up and played with her lamb and the nuns played with her and nobody asked any questions and it was warm and I was in a dream. It was like a miracle. The house had a smooth tiled floor that gleamed dark red, and a cool green cloister, almost white, icy yet inviting, suggesting prayer and joy and medieval paintings. There was a garden with a statue. Nobody expected me to speak, and I felt so very safe and comfortable. We had strawberries.

Father Fox explained to me that he had devised a plan so that he would be responsible for me for at least two years, in hiding. In hiding. I was not sure I liked the sound of that, but he said it was the only way of ensuring safety for myself and Golden. He told me afterwards that much had depended on my responses to the gifts he brought me in the plastic bag. He said he needed to know whether I would give an indication of being able to adjust to life outside the institution, life outside Skye, life in the ordinary world. He said he watched my reactions, and he decided I could be relied upon to recover and to live with ordinary people. It would not be safe for me, he said, to be freely living in the world until much later, until the emotions surrounding the fire had faded. There were people, he told me, who wished to hunt me down and hurt me, hurt me and Golden. I understood that. He would take us where we would be safe. Perhaps it was not so strange that I was able to place so much trust in him, since the beliefs of the Catholic Church had always had a place in the beliefs of the people of Skye. Minerva Hinshelwood Mean brought the flowers and prayers and candles and saints of the Church with her when she married Magnus Mean in the sad little Presbyterian ceremony at Stanley. How odd that must have seemed to her. How brave they all were then.

I have a new name now, and Golden has a new name. I am known as Claudina and she is Stella. It was strangely easy for me to make this transition emotionally, and Father Fox organised all the papers with — I don't know — lawyers and police. The name of 'Mean' however was something we also had to discard. Searching for a family name, a new family name is really rather strange. Father Fox and I opened the phone book at random and the funny thing was that the first name I found was Fox. I wrote down on the pad that it was obviously an impossible name for us to have, but Father Fox laughed and said perhaps it was wise not to argue with coincidence and destiny. 'Two new little Foxes,' he said, 'I like that.' He did look most delighted by the idea, and so it came to be. Then I grew nervous and I looked again at the first names. Is Claudina not secret enough, I wondered, since there are Claudinas in the family, but Father Fox said he thought it would suffice. Golden likes being called Stella. Or perhaps she does not really notice very much, being a carefree child much like any other child. I do not know. But the name Claudina links me in a most beautiful way to my own necklace, the Claudina necklace that has been in the family forever and forever. The necklace binds me directly to the first Minerva, and it reminds me every day and every night of my family. My poor lost family. I pray for them in hope. Stella is also bound to Niña by the twisted sinew bracelet she wears on her wrist. Perhaps I should remove this bracelet from her, but I have been unable to do this. Perhaps I will live to regret my hesitation. I am physically marked as a member of the family, for on my left shoulder I bear a small tattoo of a blue swallow — Caleb marked all his girls in this way and, on his own shoulder, he has the bluebird too. Only two tattoos remain on this earth, his and mine. Father Fox said it is possible to get tattoos removed, but I do not wish to do that.

So we are now Claudina and Stella Fox, and we will receive new 'birth certificates'. It seems to me that they would be sort of forgeries. I know so little about these things. How strange it is to have new identities, yet I am able to accept it quite smoothly, as a natural event. Father Fox has said that it will be better if Stella never knows who she really is, who she was, who she used to be. In this way she will resemble the Baby Niña of long long ago. Niña never knew who she was, and we never knew who she was, yet she is one of my own ancestors. The event that cut her off from her past was the wreck of the *Iris.* Stella's breaking moment is the fire in the Meeting Hall. One by water, one by fire. I think a great deal about Stella and the fire and how that is a vast secret for a mother to keep from her child. But it is a secret I must keep. My mind races on to imagine how it might be in, perhaps, twenty years time, how Stella could read an account in a book or an old newspaper of the holocaust at Skye, and how she might think about it and talk about it, and how I would need to remain silent, protecting her from the truth. I am not sure how I would do that. Then there is also the fear that perhaps she *does* recall, deep in her childish memory, the events of the night of the fire. I must trust in the future to take care of itself.

Less and less Caleb inhabits my dreams. Perhaps he lives in Stella's dreams, and will she know him? Shall he call to her in her dreams, telling her where she has come from, what she has known? Did Niña find her father and her mother in her dreams; did the old woman Niña visit the gardens and beaches of her babyhood as she slept in the wooden house on the west side of Skye, beneath her wandering homeless moonbird quilt? As the dead sleep among the stars, do they dream of me and Stella Fox? Do they know us? Do the dead know us now?

Stella and I both had our hair cut very short by one of the nuns in the house where we ate the strawberries. Stella looks very sweet and pretty, but I feel that I look strange. I gaze in the mirror and I almost do not know myself. Perhaps that is a fortunate thing. We recently came to live in the wilderness with Gilia and Michael Vilez who are very kind good people. Michael is a doctor who has retired from his work, and Gilia is his wife. They live now in a remote place in the southwest of Tasmania, I do not know the precise location. Gilia and Michael call it Transylvania, and I believed that to be a joke until Gilia showed me an old map where the word 'Transylvania' was written. I have disappeared from the world, and I know not where I am. I might be in Transylvania. I think of the verse in Revelation where it says: 'And the woman fled into the wilderness, where she hath a place prepared of God, that they should feed her there a thousand two hundred and threescore days.' That is a very long time.

I am dependent upon Father Fox, and upon Gilia and Michael for everything. Will this be forever? Forever is a very long time. Not forever. Not forever. For one thousand two hundred and threescore days. I believe that stretch of time will be my destiny, my time in the Tasmanian wilderness will come to an end and Stella and I will go out into a new life. I have almost forgotten that I am mute. I wonder how people manage to live in the world when they are silent, not deaf, but choked with too much knowledge.

As much to lull myself as to entertain Stella, as much to help myself to forget Caleb as to fill Stella's little life with happiness, I ask Gilia to sing nursery rhymes and hymns to us, and to tell us the stories from Hans Christian Andersen and from the Brothers Grimm. Over and over again we have listened to *The Steadfast Tin Soldier*, and I am unable to understand why we love that one so much. It is about the one toy soldier who was different from all the rest because he was missing one leg. The paper ballerina he fell in love with was beautiful, and he thought she had only one leg too, but he was mistaken. And they ended up together, the tin soldier and the ballerina, in the cold ashes of the hearth. His little tin heart was welded to the jewel from the ballerina's crown.

'Shall I tell you about the paper ballerina, Stella?' Gilia says, and she reads the story all over again, and Stella and I listen, enthralled. Gilia and Michael must be saints, I believe, they are so good and patient. May God hold us in the hollow of His hand.

CHAPTER TWELVE

God Sees the Red Umbrella

'Always carry or wear a waterproof coat and strong clothing to prevent cuts from sharp or jagged rocks.'
WESTCOTT, SYNNOT AND POWELL, *Life on the Rocky Shores of South-East Australia*

It was February fifth, 1851, the day Minerva and Magnus and Niña found a haven on Puddingstone Island. Magnus had removed his heavy sodden jacket and placed it on a rock in the hope that it would dry. Minerva tied her trailing, bedraggled nightgown in two knots at either side. Barefoot and in long full white linen pantaloons she resembled a long-haired dancing sailor boy. If they didn't die from dehydration and starvation, they could die from a chill, from exposure. In hope and excitement they examined the objects thrown up from the sea. Minerva drew Niña close — lone, serene Madonna and child. The storm died down in the night, and in the middle of the morning, there was a faint warmth and a strange stillness in the air. A great flock of bronze-blue-purple butterflies appeared above the island in a silent cloud; they wheeled and swiftly disappeared. They moved at great silvery phosphorescent speed, flying like twisting thistledown. Minerva stared after them, as if longing for the freedom of their air, dreaming of her own lost world, desiring the possibilities of flight. These are the Blotched Blues of family legend-in-the-making.

'I looked up and saw them, blue, flying like thistledown, glinting in the sun, rushing off as fast as they came,' she would say. And the many things that were in the bag and the trunk and the box are listed in the legend, like a list of gifts in a fairytale. If subsequent generations of storytellers have added to the contents, so be it.

Magnus and Minerva pulled the leather bag, large, thick, from where it was lodged between rocks. If there was no food in the bag, then they may at least resort to eating the bag itself. The contents were dry. Magnus took them out slowly, one by one, and laid them on the speckled surface of the rock. Minerva sat by, cradling Niña against her breast. From a hollow in the rock she would take up a little water, warm it in her own mouth, then spit it onto her fingers, and give her fingers to the baby to suck. Or she would dribble the liquid from her own mouth into the baby's. As she did this she watched the treasure emerge as if from a magician's bag. Four gold sovereigns, a silver pocket watch stopped at ten minutes past ten, a small pair of lady's scissors, an oval hand mirror made from ivory, an ivory comb, a silver snuffbox, a gold necklace with an amethyst pendant, a small pair of white kid gloves. Minerva was longing to find something to eat or drink, and she felt a kind of hysteria rising inside her while these charming useless reminders of another life, a life so recently and suddenly dissolved, appeared in the light, and lay like dead things from another world, another time. Nothing was identified by an owner's mark or name. Perhaps the greatest treasure in this bag was the rough woollen shawl, pale celestial blue. Minerva seized upon it; it was the baby's salvation — well, half of it anyway. Warmth, but not food. Minerva gently wrapped Niña in the shawl. Niña stirred and murmured in alarm as the cold air bit her flesh, and again as the soft dry cloth embraced her. Then suddenly she opened her mouth wide and a frightful scream flew forth, and she screamed and screamed and screamed as she had not screamed before, her mouth wide and red, its tissues vibrating in a terrifying and monstrous throaty dance.

Scratched onto the lid of the tin trunk were the words: 'Barnaby Coppin, Hobart Town.' Magnus smashed the lock with a stone and opened the trunk. Inside lay, wrapped in a shroud of brown linen, twenty-four iron umbrella frames. He counted them out in amazement. Two green linen umbrellas. Two brown and white gingham umbrellas. Magnus pulled them all out, and they counted them as they went, as if doing an inventory for a shop. They began to laugh, with a kind of hysterical laughter at the absurdity of what was before them. A pink silk parasol with lime-green fringe and bamboo frame. A scarlet leather umbrella on the apex of which was a many-petalled red leather rose. The trunk was watertight and so everything was dry, the linen shroud a marvellous dry treasure. It could be a blanket, a sail, a shelter, a tent. Magnus opened the red leather umbrella and ran with it to plant it in a crevice, as high up on the island as he could. It stood there, a scarlet toadstool among the grey-green silent tattered windswept dreams of the lichen and the grasses and the pig-face.

'Who would see it?' Minerva asked, with a gesture not of hope but of helplessness and near despair.

'God sees it,' Magnus said unblinking. 'Somebody will see it. If God sees it, somebody will come. God sees it.'

Because his speech was the speech of a highlander who had also lived in Glasgow, and because Minerva's English was something she first learnt from her English governess in Peru, they did not always understand each other. But when Magnus said God could see the red umbrella, Minerva understood him perfectly. Their Gods were different but the same. Fate had brought the three of them to the island. Had they come there to die? Would it perhaps have been better to have drowned with Edward and all the others? This dreadful, dreadful thought was enough to pull Minerva's spirit down.

The bag of the unknown woman with its remnants of a lady's life; Barnaby Coppin's umbrellas; then the box. This was the most valuable of the three things salvaged from the wreck, thrown up by the ocean that gives and takes. Three gifts from the sea — one object each for Magnus, Minerva and the baby. Minerva's spirits rose again, and Magnus sighed and nodded as if in a kind of blessing, for within the opened box they found blessed food and drink. His most earnest prayers, so far, had been answered. Hope rose in his breast as he prayed now for rescue.

The box was stamped with the name: Rosa Hoffmann.

'We can thank the Lord for Rosa Hoffmann,' Magnus said solemnly. Minerva glanced at him. His plain Scottish Protestant way of looking at things was utterly foreign to her. He spoke only of God and the Lord, while Minerva's lips were busy with soft and loud invocations of the saints and the Infant Jesus.

It seemed that Rosa Hoffmann was a meticulous and forward-thinking woman. The box contained, wrapped in a white silk cloth, sewn into an oil cloth, a tin of tea leaves, a stone jar of honey, one of raspberry vinegar, one of treacle, an apothecary's jar containing syrup of muskmelon seeds, Middlewood's Royal Abyssinian Flower Soap, a glass bottle of dark port wine, two wax candles, a bag of flour, a small green bottle of olive oil, a box of salt, a jar of calendula balm. A small bottle of ink. Four quills. An empty journal. A green flask of smelling salts. A hunting knife. A bottle of vetiver water. A mahogany box marked 'Parker of Holborn' containing a pair of pocket pistols. A few cups and plates of blue and white china, the dark blue patterns bleeding into the white. Glass phials containing seeds, marked: calendula, opium, foxglove, tansy, marigold, lavender, lettuce, cabbage, carrot, comfrey, mustard, dandelion, turnip.

Three books — an English translation of the story *The Deserted House* by E.T.A Hoffmann, *The Mabinogion* bound in brown leather, and a small fat blue volume of the *Nursery and Household Tales* of the Brothers Grimm, storybooks from a life already far, far away. Each book contained small black etchings that illustrated the stories, adding a dimension of mystery, magic, menace. The inscription in the book of fairytaless read, in a round and confident hand: 'For my dearest Rosa, on your thirteenth birthday, may life smile upon you, From your loving Mama.' Again the shipwrecked travellers set out all the objects on the rock. The sight of everything sent Minerva into a mood of bewilderment and confusion. Here were so many reminders of civilised life, but without shelter and the society of others many of these things would be ludicrous and useless on this lump of rock in the middle of the nowhere sea. Magnus said nothing. With gentle warm fingers Minerva smoothed the calendula ointment on Niña's round forehead, and on her bunched-up hands. The ointment and the stroking had the effect of calming the baby's cries. She wiped some honey on her finger and put it in the baby's mouth. Then Magnus found the last object in the box, a slender blue bottle of laudanum. This was the most useful and beautiful object of all, a bottle of forgetfulness, the greatest gift for the pain of memory, the terror of despair, a possible cordial for the baby.

These things, these discoveries in the containers sent up by fate to the shore of Puddingstone Island, Minerva later recalled and recorded in her journal. Perhaps she forgot some things; perhaps she put in things that were not there, things she imagined, things she wished for.

Thank God for poor Rosa Hoffmann, lying on the ocean floor off Puddingstone Island, trapped in a tangle of broken timbers, wrapped in the arms of a flesh-eating octopus. Perhaps part of her life had been smiled upon, for a time. If only she had thought to include a tinderbox in her luggage, for the castaways, her inheritors, had no fire. But each one sipped a little of the laudanum, soother of pain and anxiety. And the baby fell into a still, sweet slumber in Minerva's arms. Then the silence enveloped the three of them, a silence deep with terrible possibilities and some faint shimmer of hope.

As Magnus spread across the rocks the curious collection of objects, he and Minerva at first failed to notice that the air was much, much warmer, and that ominous clouds were rolling towards the island. Black cloudbanks were stealing in from the horizon and a dull glow was beginning to light up the edges of the scene. A hot, hot wind bearing the smell of burning forest. The sun was blotted out and soon thick fragments of leaves, charred, like fossils in ash, began to drop and then to rain upon the sea and the rocks. The afternoon sky became as black as midnight, and terror again gripped their hearts. Terror and bewilderment at the sudden switch in the mood of the universe. Gone were the seabirds, as one hallucination or dream or nightmare followed another. In the silent darkness the three lost people huddled together in a kind of peaceful terror, Magnus speaking now and then to God; Minerva whispering to the saints, taking careful sips from the blue bottle. These prayers, they later said, were heard. God and his angels listened to their prayers, and answered them. They wrapped themselves beneath the linen shroud, with the laudanum, the port wine, the stone jar of honey, the baby — and waited. Man, woman and child, they waited for something else to happen. Magnus was by nature patient, Minerva was not. For her it was a great effort to be still and to do nothing. Indeed, what could she do? The night air was thick with a terrible burning perfume, and with floating particles of ash.

It was the longest darkest night of unknown meaning, but at last day broke, and a pearly blue sky, clean and shining, gave the lie to the dreadful darkness of the night. The rocks and scrubby plants on

Puddingstone Island were now covered in dark ash, blanketed in a coverlet of the stark black impressions of ferns and delicate charcoal leaves and startled insects. Some dreadful dark miracle of incinerated tissue had descended upon the island in the night like snow.

Magnus set out to find what had happened, to try to discover, perhaps, where they were, what help might be at hand, to seek a meaning in the ash. He found a little cave, cool and narrow, and a slender stretch of white sand. You could bring a small boat ashore. If you had a small boat. Where are we, God in Heaven, where are we, and what are we going to do? The empty shells of nautilus were scattered on the sand, plump shining spirals gleaming in the light, dusted now with dark, sticky ash.

For two days Magnus, Minerva and Niña sheltered in the cave, a long hollow in the rock, with an overhang that protected them a little from the wind. In some places the red and black and white carbuncles of the pudding stone jutted out from the walls like jewels.

'Come here, Minerva. Come and see this.'

Minerva carried the baby into the narrow depths of the cave, in a twisted area to the left, past a rock that had been smoothed by the tight passage of many people long ago, where the air was cold and where there was a sweet sad smell of the earth. In the darkness at the back of the cave Magnus had found a rotting sofa lovingly made from rosewood, and covered with deep crimson velvet brocade. The curlicues and sweeps of the design were covered with a light film of dust. Stamped in dark-blue ink lettering on the back were the words: William Smee & Sons, No. 6, Finsbury Pavement, London. It came from the sea, but had long ago dried out, and had been dragged into the cave on its back. Beside and beneath the sofa were collected in piles the bones of small animals and birds, of limpet and abalone shells, and also the more recently scattered bones and feathers of a very large bird, an albatross, the head picked clean and perfectly dry, the bill smooth and shining, curved and huge. A memento — of what? Minerva's mind flew to the almost identical skull she had seen in Edward's hands. In the cave there seemed to be no human bones. The ceiling and upper walls were black with the soot of ancient fires. High and dry. Scattered on the floor were the dried and chewed remains of what smelt like turnips.

Minerva could sense all round her the enclosed air of tombs waiting for fresh bodies. She stood, Niña in her arms, and she turned from the albatross, with tears stinging her eyes, to look at the sofa. Astonishment. The sofa was a small replica of a golden couch from the house of her childhood in Lima. It was like an hallucination, a sudden gift that had drifted in dream from a drawing-room in London or Paris, and Minerva imagined she could see, lying upon it, the figure of a beautiful woman in a long silk gown. The woman was dead and cold, lying forever in the depths of the cave, in the sepulchre of Puddingstone Island.

'It's safe to lie on,' Magnus said. 'You could sleep here, you and the baby, sleep while I keep watch.'

But Minerva shuddered and shook her head. She longed to lie down, but she feared being separated from Magnus.

'We must stay together.'

She said this very quietly.

Later on she did lie on the faded crimson brocade, cradling Niña, while Magnus sat on the floor of the cave with his back to the side of the sofa. Niña had to be fed honey and rock water almost constantly. It was night and they were exhausted; no ghosts or fears could overcome the need for rest on the dry and dusty leftover of some other shipwreck, some other long-forgotten story. Niña imagined that the woman in the silken gown was herself, as she drifted into a deep, strangely untroubled and dreamless sleep, a blank, sweet sleep.

Some fresh water lay collected in hollows in the rocks of Puddingstone, but it was covered with a scum of ashy leaves. They pushed the ash aside and drank the water which tasted of salt and fire. They planned to save up the contents of the box for as long as they could, rationing them out. Minerva fed the honey to all three of them on her finger. It had the most astonishing and powerful flavour, smooth, floral, like lightning and sweet dew. The cave began to be a curious little home, filled with some of the contents of the bag, the trunk and the box. How long must they live there, the three of them together? Magnus searched for wild animals but found none. Birds? Fish? He imagined there could be savages, but saw none. Memories of the cannibal stories he had read in the *Glasgow Herald* sometimes crossed his mind, and then he would think of Glasgow, and his mother and sisters, and the warm dry house with the piano, and he felt that they had become part of a long-lost dream. He thought of Jenny, gone beyond, and experienced long bleak times of depression and despair. Perhaps he would join Jenny sooner than he had thought. But the island and the sea and Minerva and Niña brought him and his thoughts and hopes swiftly back to the desire for life.

Magnus scanned the horizon constantly for a sail but, in the pearly blue-grey mist of Bass Strait, no sail appeared. He found the battered figurehead from a wreck, sheltering in a wide crevice, tangled in seaweed, and he longed again for a light that he might set the wood on fire. It was the figure of a woman, straining forward, her hair blown behind her in the wind, flowers carved in her cloak, one hand on her heart. She was ancient, noseless and weathered, pitted by the salt air of the island, splashed with the droppings of the birds that wheeled above.

Once, as he was standing by the red umbrella, a large black dog leapt out in front of him, raced by, and was gone. Instinctively he started to run after it, but it had disappeared, as if it had never been. Perhaps he was seeing things.

'I saw a dog. It ran right in front of me,' he told Minerva. 'I know it was a dream. We will see visions and dreams now. We must be careful. They could lead us to terrible harm. I have heard of this kind of strange trickery. The dog was so very like a real animal. And a black dog is a bad omen.'

'These dreams are the image of things real, shapes and shadows,' Minerva said, and Magnus remained silent, not quite understanding what she could mean. Sometimes it was language that separated them; sometimes it was habits of thought. Never in their lives would they truly come to understand each other. It didn't seem to matter, on the island, or later during their long life together. An unbreakable link was forged between them the night the sea swallowed them and then threw them up on improbable Puddingstone Island.

Minerva tore strips from the baby's dress, soaked them in water and gave them to her to suck, squeezing them on her face, letting the water trickle into the half-open mouth. Over and over again she took scoops of water with her hand, held the water in her own mouth, and spat it slowly onto Niña's tongue. They put a tin dish and the china cups outside the cave, to catch the rain when it fell.

During the morning of the third day a little rain fell, sweetening the gauzy air, and the dish and cups were moist with a film of clear sweet water. Then close to her heart Minerva held the baby who tossed now with a fever, while Magnus ventured out to look again for help, or water, or food, or something. Again and again he went out, further along the shore, searching for whatever he could find, his eyes red with fatigue and cold and salty wind. Again the dog leapt out and ran in front of him, then away into some space between the rocks. Magnus's thick red curls whipped across his cheeks, into his mouth. It was a real animal that he saw. He called out to the dog, but it was gone. Sometimes Niña cried steadily; sometimes she fell into a profound and deathly sleep. Minerva was afraid to give her too much of the diluted laudanum, afraid that it could harm her, or even kill her.

Magnus and Minerva looked into each other's eyes, unable to utter the idea that Niña might die anyway. Then there was the deep and primitive thought that Niña could be their source of nourishment, a terrible reversal of the rule of nurture whereby Minerva's body should feed Niña. It was a sad and distorted reflection of the vivid stories about the cannibals from the *Glasgow Herald*.

Rock, rock, baby, in the evil wind that blows through the Strait. Will Niña in fact feed Minerva and Magnus with her own body? Could it come to that? They do not speak of it. In the remote nowhere of Puddingstone Island in Bass Strait, in February 1851, it could come to that.

Beneath the hot and swollen eyelids of the child were large bright eyes of forget-me-not blue. Minerva, weak and frightened, looked into them with her own inky gaze. Magnus killed a crippled silver gull with a stone hurled from a slingshot fashioned from a strip torn from his jacket. In the shelter of the cave the blood of the bird smelled clean and good. How were they to eat it? They were not yet ready to tear the sparse raw flesh apart with their fingers. The bird lay stiffly on a flat stone, waiting until they were ravenous, bringing ants and flies, smelling stronger and stronger of its own decay. Minerva mixed a little of the blood from the creature's wound, in the hollow of her hand, with drops of water. This she mixed in her mouth with her own saliva and then dribbled into the mouth of the baby, and then she licked her own fingers clean. She liked the taste. Magnus, learning astonishing new skills, caught a gannet in his hands and he wrung its neck. It too remained uneaten, a store in the larder. A rock in the sea, not far off from Puddingstone Island, was white with gannets.

Tough watery cactus grew in the cracks between the rocks. Minerva and Magnus chewed the silvery leaves, hoping the plant would not poison them. There were huge thistles also, offering no gesture of friendship, nor hope of nourishment. The thistles were like giant brown emblems of Scotland, horrible monster symbols of Magnus's homeland, spiny reminders of all that he had left behind, would never see again in this world. Magnus found the carcase of a rotting shearwater, a moonbird, on a narrow patch of sand. And with Rosa Hoffmann's knife he picked a handful of limpets from the rocks.

The waves of the incoming tide sent up a straw mattress, dumping it on the shore, on the one patch of coarse flat sand in the cove on the eastern side. A sudden gesture from the depths. Perhaps the mattress, regurgitated from the belly of the ocean, came from the *Iris*, perhaps not. It could be of no use to Magnus and Minerva, a bloated, sopping bridal bed beached between lonely rocks on the silent sand. In years to come the seeds from inside the mattress would sow themselves on Puddingstone Island. English grasses and periwinkles and poppies would blow and bloom in the crevices between the ancient speckled rocks, glowing in the sun, battered by the storm, fluttering beneath the spiky goblet heads of the thistles. When she first saw the mattress Minerva had a horrible vision of the sea sending up the body of Edward, flinging it at her feet. She saw his face had been eaten by fish; she saw small creatures swimming in the sockets where his beautiful eyes had been. She banished these images and ideas from her mind. She concentrated on Niña, willing the little girl, the little creature to cling to life.

'And how were they saved?' ask the children of Skye, cheeks pink, eyes wide, a picture of health ready to be pecked clean by gulls, sucked dry by underwater monsters that go shifting, gliding, slimy, more mysterious, more silent, more deadly than the deepest most sucking nightmare vision in the mud of the void. These children love to hear the story of their origins over and over again.

After days and nights a boat came, a fishing boat on its way back, almost empty-handed, from the islands. It was pointed at both ends, having once been a whale boat. The era of whaling and sealing in the Strait was over, and the boats had not yet been abandoned. It was returning also in bewilderment and fear, running home from the cloud of ash and crisp black leaves and insects that had filled the air in the Strait on February fifth.

Magnus stood high upon the highest rock of the island, beside the scarlet umbrella, scanning the sea, almost blind with the wind and the cold sunshine and the sight of that empty world. Then as if out of nowhere there came a black boat. Three men in a tough black boat, two oarsmen and one at the steer-oar, their backs to the island. Would they see him? He called, but his voice was whipped away by the wind, tossed into nowhere, spun off by the clouds. His bright wet hair was snatched from his brow, whipped about his head. He waved his arms and leapt in the air. The boat rocked up and down on the water, way below him, far off. They must turn round; they must see him. He willed them to look back, look up. Look here! Look here! He cried. Lord God make them look! The three men felt a sudden rush of blood-warm air at their shoulders and the boat turned, and the sailors looked up at the figure high on the rocky island. A mad and tattered scarecrow, seething with fever and crumpled dreams, beside a big red umbrella, he was calling to them. Coo-ee! Hold on! they called. Hold on! The sight of a man marooned on one of these islands was not new to them, they saw such things, such sights, from time to time. And they chipped and chopped through the steely waves, heading for the Puddingstone shore.

Almost half an hour, half an eternal hour, it took for the boat to reach the island. And the sun was high up in the sky. Magnus stood like a laird, half-naked, where the water met the rocks, and he prayed aloud to the Lord with thanks for this deliverance, and the hand that threw the bottle of water to him was solid, the eyes that looked into his, even at a distance, seemed as blue as noonday.

He caught the bottle in midair, like an expert catching a ball. Shipwreck, sailor? Shipwreck, he said. Me, me and a woman and a child. Alive? All alive. No more? All gone. A long draught of fresh water and it tasted like life, it tasted like love.

The blue eyes looked into his, a dark query, and two other pairs of silent eyes looked on and listened. Two rugged tanned faces, wrinkled and scarred, and a black. From the rock Magnus was unable to reach the boat in the waters below. We'll go round there to the cove. And come ashore. Water, he says, please give me water for the woman and the child.

A green glass bottle of pure fresh water was then thrown with a terrible confidence through the dangerous empty air, and now it was in Magnus's fist. As the sailors made their way by sea, pulling steadily on the oars, to the sandy inlet, Magnus followed on land, leaping the rocks with new vigour, with the energy of hope. He ran past the cave where Miverva and Niña were sheltering, Minerva in terror that the child was failing, quivering with cold and bewilderment and anticipation and a deadly fear of all that might be to come. The lights of hallucination danced and zipped before her eyes. Magnus rushed in at the opening and called to her. Magnus's face was glowing like the face of a madman as he came towards Minerva, the bottle of water gripped by the neck in his right hand. Water. A boat. We are saved. Take this, drink. Give some to the baby. Then follow me to the beach. The boat, the boat has come, the boat is here, we are saved.

Was this another vision, mirage, hallucination? But there in her hand was the bottle of water. Could there really be a boat so soon? Were they truly about to be delivered? Could they trust strangers in a boat? There were two codes on the seas; by one you could be saved, and by the other you could be robbed, raped and eaten by pirates.

Minerva drank the fresh water, she drank slowly and gently and gracefully, and Niña's eyes fluttered and her lips opened and she allowed drops of water warmed in Minerva's mouth, to trickle down her throat. Then Minerva, with a presence of mind for which she would become renowned, collected the pistols and ammunition from Rosa Hoffmann's possessions, along with the laudanum, and followed Magnus down to the water, with Niña bundled like a chrysalis in the blue shawl. Suntanned and grizzled men in heavy black jackets and caps were waiting, dark angels, by the boat. Their shoulders were dusted with ash, the surfaces of the boat decorated with the black imprints of ferns and leaves and insects, now smeared where they had been touched. Fire, they said, there was a big fire in Port Phillip. The whole country is on fire, the whole country is going up in smoke, turning to ash, turning to dust. It is the fire of hell. It is the Inferno. We had it from a whaler coming in from Cape Otway. It is the Last Judgement, the punishment, the fire of hell releasing poisonous smoke and ash over the rim of the horizon.

'And I saw an angel come down from heaven,
having the key of the bottomless pit and a great
chain in his hand.'

Because the catch was small, there was room for the two adults and the baby. There was a thick smell of rancid oil and the tang of salt. Minerva was quiet, shivering, sheltering Niña from the cold wet air; Magnus was ecstatic with the delirium of prayers answered in time of despair, his hair and eyes wild with a strange and burning light.

'And God shall wipe away all tears from their eyes.'

The sailors offered them more water, then from a tin box pieces of cheese, and strips of Irish salty pork to eat, slices of damper and cubes of rich muttonbird fruit cake with warm dark nips of rum. They took only the water and the rum. Magnus ate a little of the meat but Minerva felt she was about to vomit, to faint, to die from exhaustion and thirst. The fishermen stared in astonished reverence at the hot face of the baby, knowing a miraculous sea-rescue when they saw one.

And so, children of Skye, the red umbrella remained on the rock on Puddingstone Island for a long long time, and it was bright and it was brave, and it was tattered and fluttered by the winds, faded by the sun, cracked and split — until one day it just blew into the sea in a storm, and was returned to its dead owner at the very deep down bottom of Bass Strait. Barnaby Coppin, the man who owned the tin trunk, and his lovely leather umbrella with its chubby red rose at its apex, were together at last. God sees Barnaby, and thanks him for the timely use of his red umbrella.

One of the sailors, the one at the steer-oar, the black one, reached out with a long slender hand, cradling the baby's head. He bent over and placed his cheek on the child's face, and, without a word having been uttered, Minerva gave Niña to the sailor who moved forward, passing the steer-oar to Magnus. This moment, Magnus said to Minerva later, was the true miracle, for the sailor was a woman, and she put Niña to her milky breast, and Niña, limp and mewing faintly, began to feed. Dolly Thunderstone, in the watery wilderness of the Strait, became Niña's wet nurse. She was also the mother of two children, one a baby. One of the men in the boat, Thomas Riggs, was Dolly's father, the other, Inglis Finney, her husband. She sensed at once that Minerva was not the mother of this baby, and knew the baby needed to be nursed. Once, Niña choked and brought up a thin stream of pale brownish liquid, half mixed with Dolly's milk. Then she slept, and then she sucked again quite strongly for a long time, and then she fell asleep. It was a sweet and blessed sleep.

Thomas and Inglis spied the mahogany case exposed now on Minerva's lap, and they realised it must contain pistols. Minerva sat very still, wrapped in the blue shawl, with her long linen pantaloons showing. Her black hair had dried and now formed a shadowy nimbus around her face, her skin fine and golden, her dark eyes weary, troubled, alert. Round her neck she had her Claudina pendant as well as the amethyst from the leather bag. Magnus had the hunting knife in his belt. Before very long, out of the mist loomed the great rock that lies just off the coast at Circular Head. The sailors called it the Nut. Then they laughed and called it the Rock of Gibralta, and then somebody said 'Rock-a-bye baby', and they laughed again.

CHAPTER THIRTEEN

Earth

'The Monarch butterfly is common throughout the world, and migrates in flocks of millions, fleeing from the cold, returning always to the same places. From November to March they blanket the trees of a Mexican pine forest, spreading a soft murmur that is the collective music of their beating wings, bending the branches with their weight.'

CARRILLO MEAN, *The Butterfly Effect*

As the boat drew near to the wooden dock at Circular Head, Inglis Finney ran up a tattered red and white flag which was a signal of distress to the master of the little harbour. News of the disappearance of the *Iris* had already reached the community, and there was speculation about the possibility of survivors. A small crowd including Doctor Owen Tully was waiting, and Inglis handed his passengers over with but a brief explanation. Time and Tide wait for no man, he said to Owen Tully. We have done our part. Back to our labours. Certainly it is an ill wind, Doctor, that blows nobody any good. An ill wind.

In the flurry of astonished looking and talking and excitement that greeted the shipwrecked couple with the baby, nobody really took account of the fact that Dolly never came ashore. With some regret she handed Niña back to Minerva and waited in the boat. Before handing Niña over, Dolly tucked around the baby's wrist a bracelet woven from the sinews pulled from a wallaby tail, dyed with ochre, on which hung the pale pink frosty arm of a little china doll. Dolly had found the arm one morning early in the mud outside an abandoned shepherd's hut at Cape Grimm. The white shepherd and his white woman and their child had fled, leaving the hut half-burnt, one black man rotting under a bush, a bullet through his heart. The doll's arm lay gleaming on the surface of the mud, a little hole at one end where a string had attached it to the shoulder. This treasure had been hanging round Dolly's own neck for many months, and in a rush of love that was almost too painful to bear, she passed it over to Niña, linked herself in the only way she could to this lost baby from the waters of Puddingstone Island. The mixture of emotions criss-crossed Dolly's shiny black face, her eyes were glittering, and she wiped them with the flat of her hand. Dolly missed her own baby when he was not with her, and now her heart went out to Niña, small white survivor from the sea. The pale china limb of the doll resembled Niña's own human arms — Dolly wished to kiss and caress Niña's arms, hands, fingers, but dared not. She was briefly the black wet-nurse, and it was not her place to love the child. Dolly loved white babies and children, loved to watch them at play, loved to touch them gently, loved to look into their round eyes the colour of the sky or the sea, loved to hear them babble in real white language. The fishermen needed to make haste back out to the islands, for if Dolly had been spotted she would almost certainly have been impounded and taken to live — in fact to die — at Oyster Cove down south in Van Diemen's Land with the other tragic remnants of the native people. It was already twenty years since George Augustus Robinson had established his disruptive and quixotic programs called 'friendly missions', removing the natives from their land, making the colony a safer better place for white folk to live and prosper, and dedicating places where the native people too could live in peace. It is not surprising that the natives died from displacement, disease, depression, loss of hope, and the jagged fading of their broken, broken hearts.

The bracelet that Dolly slipped onto the baby's wrist remained in the Mean family, an object of mystery and reverence, coming down to the present day, worn by babies of many generations, a sacred lucky charm. The wallaby-tail sinew has been replaced several times, part of the original being always retained. Followers of modern child-care practice throw up their own arms in horror, saying the child will choke on the little china charm which is just a breeding ground for germs. No child has ever choked on it. Golden Mean was wearing the bracelet when she and her parents were captured at Cape Grimm on the night of the fire.

'What you never tell won't do no harm,' Inglis said to Magnus. There was salt and iron in his tone of voice, in his gaze. 'This Dolly's just a fisher-man, see. This us is three fishermen here. You understand me? Understand? Silence is worth your life you know. But for you there is a bargain. For your silence, we will promise to row back out to Puddingstone one of these days. One of these days. And we will bring you back the mess of things you left behind. One of these days. But you talk and you'll be sorry. One of these days. She's a wise little lady you have there now. She will know to be silent. Wise. She knowed to carry off the arms. Many a woman would ha' chose a bonnet instead. A wise one.'

Some of the things left behind in the cave were mysteriously returned, wrapped in an old length of sail, left at the Plough Inn at Circular Head one bleak morning in October, labelled for Magnus Mean. The fisherman had kept his word, had supposedly decided that Magnus had kept his silence and so could have his booty. 'One of these days' had arrived. Certain things that Minerva recalled as being in the box and bag were missing — the hand mirror, the olive oil, the gloves, the scissors and the wine. Perhaps she had half-imagined them after all. In any case, perhaps reasonable payment had been made in goods.

Having delivered the castaways to Circular Head the fishermen were gone, the wind behind them, oars pulling them fast out of sight. Owen Tully led the survivors to the Plough Inn where there was a fire, hot water, fresh clothing, food, drink, and remedies. The quilts on the beds were made with the down of the moonbird, so soft, so warm, so filled with travellers' dreams of the Pacific Ocean and the winds of eternal flight. There were a few rooms in the upstairs portion of the inn for travellers. A tall grandfather clock with sun and moon and stars on its face loudly ticked its welcome in the entrance hall. Ticktockticktock. Tidesturntidesturn. To Magnus this clock was one of the greatest comforts, the strong soft tick tick of the sweet old clock that resembled the clock in the hallway of the schoolmaster's house in Glasgow, a clock whose face was painted with an image of a sailing ship at sea, a clock bearing the motto, in gold and gothic letters: Time and Tide Wait for No Man. Yes, the clock in the hall of the inn was a comfort to Magnus, and yet the memories it stirred of his former life could cast him into deep reverie, sadness, and sometimes a grey despair. Tick-tick-tick. We are strangers to each other, brought together by the storm. Strangers? Strangers? Whose child is this? This sleeping baby girl. We do not know. Who does know? Nobody knows. Nobody knows. Oh woe!

Women in long cotton dresses, their shoulders covered with woollen shawls, and wearing thick boots, gather round Minerva and the baby in a chatter and a chitter and a sweet lavender worry that chants and flurries and whispers. Molly Smedley has a fat baby on her hip. She takes Niña to her breast and again Niña snuggles and mews as she feeds on warm strange milk. She is washed, she is examined by Dr Tully. She is a healthy white female child of six months, recovering from distress, some dehydration, exposure, hunger. Some bruising on the shoulders and the back. Blue-eyed and blonde. Presumed orphan. Now she is dressed in a long gown smelling of sunshine, a holy child, wrapped, and she falls into a deep, deep slumber, so still, waiting upon her dreams. Thrown from the ship, thrown up by the sea. Flotsam child. Alive. The china arm on the sinew bracelet is taken from her wrist and pinned to her gown, taken to be a token of good luck from the child's homeland, perhaps warding off the evil eye, phallic, porcelain, resembling a pale and frosty worm dropped by a fleeting gull.

The women, young and old, gaze at the child and run the backs of their fingers across her downy cheek, the tips of their fingers along her silky brow, the hollow of a hand cups the peachy silver ringlets lying damp as chrysanthemum petals on her baby skull. Firelight flickers on the group of women, on the baby, and now the child is sleeping in a rough wooden cradle. Someone has brought in a Chinese screen, making a tiny room where Niña can sleep. Strange tall white waterbirds are painted among the spikes and flags of iris of the screen. The candlelight is yellow.

In Niña's dreams, the sigh of the waves, the wing of the air, sweat of the sailors, smell of the rain on the sea. The air rushes past her ears, through her skin, salt on her tongue, in her eyes. A tumultuous violence riots through her blood. Dream, dream little Niña. Dream of the sudden jolting arc described by your flying body, propelled from the splintering deck of the *Iris*, buoyed by the wings of the hovering angels, lifted and landed and saved on the softest sliver of Puddingstone Island. Dream of storms and squalls and calm evenings, and the singsong harmonies of the women at the Plough Inn. Dream of your father's hands as they open to release you into life. Dream too of your soft mother's feathery silken neck, her forgiving breast, her dulcet, singing whisper-voice, long lost, at the bottom of the sea.

Minerva is offered steaming tea and a dish of hot water with soap and towels, clean petticoats and underwear, snowy white, trimmed with lace and ribbons, and a dress of dark-blue Manchester cotton, stockings and boots. She is given a brown shawl to wrap around her shoulders. She is wearing the uniform of the other women around her, but she will never resemble them. Something of the Indians and Spaniards of Peru marks her out as being quite, quite different, and something in the way she thinks, the way she feels, the things she knows, the way she moves.

Minerva is a very unusual and pretty name, Mrs Hinshelwood. And now Minerva weeps, for she hears in her heart Edward's English voice as the Welsh Dr Tully says — Minerva, that *is* a pretty name. Sometimes when her heart yearns for Edward, Minerva torments herself with memories of a story her English nurse used to tell her, the story of Alcyone and Ceyx. How Ceyx was shipwrecked and drowned, how he came to his beloved Alcyone in a dream, and how she went down to the seashore and leapt onto a great wave, transforming in that moment into a sorrowing bird of the sea. How Ceyx, his own wings new-formed, came to find her, and how the two of them flew away together, sharing fate, sharing an enduring love.

Now Minerva weeps great stricken tears, and she is inconsolable. They bring her brandy and sugar and warm water and opium, the common remedy for pain. She lies on a bed in an upstairs room at the Plough Inn as Dr Tully, in his black doctor's coat with the velvet collar and a white cambric shirt, takes her pulse and feels her forehead. He is like a priest in the clean quiet warmth of the room where the ceiling is low, the perfume of the air unfamiliar, the breath of safety sighing in the creak of the floorboards.

So, you were coming to Port Phillip with your new husband, Mrs Hinshelwood. Do you have family there? No? Ah, yes, well, Father Burke is coming by to see you. You would like to see him? Mr Mean has explained to me that you are a member of the Roman faith.

Magnus appears in the doorway, shining, washed and shaved and trimmed, dressed in boots and moleskins and a red cloth shirt. He is gleaming with soap and water. With him is Father Burke, black hat and face like some kind of funny monkey with round brown eyes and a smiling, wrinkled wisdom. He blesses Minerva with the sign of the cross and prays for her in Latin. His voice is a velvety voice, undulating, warm, golden — full of sunshine and lovely mists in this strange dark place at the upside-down end of the world. The tears flow more slowly; Minerva stops weeping, bows her head, then raises it and attempts to smile, summoning a feeling of hope now, from the depth of her sadness, bewilderment and lonely despair. The comfort of the murmured prayer, the music of the familiar words. The slightly elusive mingled smell of whisky and tobacco and perhaps incense is more familiar to her than the clean clear natural prehistoric air of this land. The holy busy fluttering bird-hands of the priest are making sacred signs in the foreign air, and Minerva's lips respond. She smiles with her eyes and she feels, again, hot tears of salty sorrow mingled with hot tears of swift relief.

CHAPTER FOURTEEN

The Path of the Insect

'And it came to pass that Magnus took Minerva for his wife at the village of Skye, within the boundaries of the pastures of the Van Diemen's Land Company, close by the rocky promontory known as Cape Grimm. And in the fullness of time the union was blessed with children.'

CARRILLO MEAN, *Camilo Carrillo and El Niño*

The Mean family Bible is a repository for loose leaves of manuscript, so many pages that the soft black leather binding of the great book has cracked at the spine, shattered at the edges, and must be handled with extreme care. It was left behind in the Temple of the Winds when Caleb set out to incinerate everyone in the Meeting Hall, and became an important source of information, a source through which folk would pore in attempts to discover the paths along which Caleb Mean had come, the paths that brought him into being, the paths that led him to annihilate his people. *Observe the path of the insect as it approaches the light.* Someone has inscribed these words in a flowing script above the vast and spreading family tree. What was the community of Skye, and who were the people that lived for generations in what was supposed to be utopian harmony, only to give themselves willingly into the hands of a crazed mass-murderer?

Here in the loose leaves scattered through the Bible a reader will find a newspaper account of the rescue of Minerva and Magnus, from the *Circular Head Gazette*. The piece of paper has been fingered and read by generations of the couple's descendants, has cracked in the folds, feathered at the edges, yellowed, the words read aloud by dozens of voices down the years.

> On the eighth day of February Mr Thomas Riggs, fisherman, of King Island brought ashore at Circular Head three survivors from the wreck of the *Iris* which foundered in the fierce storm on the night of the fifth day of February. The three, a man, woman, and child were rescued by Mr Riggs and his crew of two in a whaleboat off Puddingstone. According to the survivors the *Iris* has completely foundered, with loss of all other passengers and crew. A preliminary inquiry into the wreck will commence within the week at Launceston. The *Iris* was under the command of Captain Charles Delany. The survivors are said to be in good health after a remarkable ordeal and a miraculous rescue. Mr Riggs was commended for his action by the Warden of the Circular Head district.

A reader will learn that Caleb's ancestor Minerva grew up in Lima, and was the niece of Camilo Carrillo, the sea captain who, in 1892, first published work on the climatic effect 'El Niño'. Someone has written out on a piece of card, in careful copperplate, a translation of the words from Camilo Carrillo's treatise on the effects of currents on fishing.

> Peruvian sailors from the port of Paita in northern Peru, who frequently navigate along the coast in small crafts, whether to the north or to the south of Paita, named this ocean current 'El Niño' or 'Holy Child', without doubt because it has been most noticeable and is felt most significantly after the feast of Christ's Holy Nativity.

The Holy Child is El Niño, and his image in paint and sculpture is familiar to the children of Peru. He is a child resembling a small man, with a sweet kind face, a hat, a staff and a cluster of cockle shells. Minerva painted a small picture of the Holy Child and this is collected in the Bible, along with several copies made down the years by children in the family. For today's children seeking information on the climatic namesake, there are such sites as www.spacelink.nasa.gov

El Niño occurs in the Pacific Ocean. The normally cold surface waters along the coast of Peru and Ecuador, waters that supply the food for the fish, are temporarily replaced by warm water, starving the fish and causing dramatic effects on the climate. El Niño disrupts weather patterns throughout the world, giving rise to higher temperatures in the seas, causing strange storms and floods and droughts in places near and far. Long ago these warm currents seemed to occur at seven-year intervals, bringing violent and drenching rains, but in the twentieth century they became more observably erratic. When Pizarro began his conquest of Peru in 1531 it was a year of El Niño, and the rains meant that there was food and water for the Spanish troops, supplies that would not otherwise have been available. And in 1535, when the waters of the Pacific along the coast of South America were cool and full of fish, Lima, city of church bells and flower bells, was founded.

It is probable the storm that drove the *Iris* to the bottom of Bass Strait was part of El Niño of 1850–51.

Although she was not a particularly devout woman, Minerva had a fondness for Saint Rose of Lima, patron saint of all the Americas, and could trace her ancestry back to the saint's brother. She named her first daughter, the daughter of Edward, Rosa, in honour of the saint, and in memory of Rosa Hoffmann, the owner of the blessed wooden box washed up on Puddingstone Island. The rose bushes that Minerva brought from England in pots, watered and nurtured throughout the journey went to the bottom of the sea with poor Edward Hinshelwood and his cases of fossils and insects. His treasured books — *The Aurelian* by his hero Moses Harris; Maria Sibylla von Merian's glorious *Metamorphosis Insectorum Surinamensium* — his drowned books and his drowned heart, locked in the deepest, lightless ocean where the creatures are monstrous-alien, where the plants form feathery shawls of smothering fungi-shape as they sculpt the realms and temples of deepest ringing death.

From the moment Minerva saw a bowl of roses, cream, red and yellow, on a table in the parlour of the Plough Inn, her heart, her spirit, she ever-after believed, began to recover. Some resurrection took hold of her at the sight of those dear flowers, flowers as if risen themselves, risen from the depths of the terrible oceans. In this wild, cold, haunted place far, far from the patios and orange blossoms and jasmine flowers of Lima, the roses appeared to her bathed in a sharp supernatural light, surrounded by a faintly quivering halo of radiant haze. Their perfume breathed memories into the sparse parlour of the inn. These were blooms cut from the garden at Highgrove, the large house belonging to the governor of the Van Diemen's Land Company, and they were arranged in a simple thick white china bowl, the mixture of their colours creating a specific and mysterious gold, the cheeks of the soft blooms like the dewy skin of youth, of innocence. And as Minerva breathed in the sweetness of the roses, and as her spirit rose, she knew that deep within her another life was stirring.

Rosa Claudina Mean was — and there has never been any secret about this — the daughter of Minerva and Edward Hinshelwood. Magnus accepted Rosa — and Niña — as if they were his own daughters. Before Rosa was born, Minerva and Magnus sought to formalise the bond that had been established between them when they landed on Puddingstone Island, and which had since then grown into an unusual affection and trust.

There is some evidence to suggest that the strange and powerful religious habits that were practised over time by the Means of Skye and their descendants had their origins partly in the fact that Father Burke refused to perform the marriage ceremony for Minerva and Magnus, saying he needed to see the proof of the death of Edward Hinshelwood. And furthermore Magnus was not only not a Roman Catholic, but was hardly a man of any Christian faith at all. Why, Father Burke argued, could not Magnus, for the sake of Minerva and his own immortal soul, simply convert, first of all, as a preliminary measure, so to speak, in expectation that proof of the death of poor Mr Hinshelwood might come to light. But no, he would not. So there were many impediments to the union, in the wise old Irish eyes of Father Burke.

'By God's grace yourself was delivered to Puddingstone Island. Who knows but by a miracle Edward may be a-waiting on another island? It is possible, probable, my child,' said Father Burke. 'We in our un-wisdom are not given to judge until the day we see before our eyes the corpse of Edward Hinshelwood. A widow may, if she so chooses, in the course of time, take a husband; a married woman may not. I must accept your word that yourself and the good Edward were united in the Church of Saint Martin in London, and I may, if I choose, verify your word by correspondence with the clergy of that church. Such knowledge would only serve to strengthen my case. But whichever way we look at the facts, it is clear, my dear Minerva, that you are not free to marry. I am sorry, but it is the law and will of God. It is the way of things.'

Would Father Burke have seen the matter differently if Magnus had been Catholic, some people wondered. Having no real interest in matters religious, in spite of his love of the poetry of the Psalms and the Book of Revelation, Magnus could not bring himself to be converted to the Roman faith, here on this far wild coast, where simply to survive was what mattered most, and where the magic and mystery of the Roman Church mattered less than the way the wind was blowing, less than the time of the high tide or the low tide.

James Garrett, the minister to the Church of Scotland in the area, finally performed the ceremony of marriage in the parlour of the Plough Inn on May fifth 1852. It was not until 1855 that the Church of Scotland at Circular Head had its own handsome dedicated church building, a structure of iron and wood imported from London. This building cost the congregation four hundred pounds by the time it was finished, and Magnus Mean was listed as one of the subscribers. Anyhow, at the time when Minerva and Magnus tied the knot in the parlour of the Plough Inn, the little Mean family was well established on rented land at Skye, a few miles from Cape Grimm. Much later, as their fortunes rose, they were able to buy the land. Rosa was cutting her first teeth, Niña was running around, and Minerva was soon to be pregnant with their son, Magnus's firstborn, who was to be called Carrillo, a name that would echo down the generations. Nobody was ever able to verify the origins of Niña. The ship's records listed a Caroline Mary Sweeney, and a Victoria Caroline MacIntosh, and a Lucy Jane Orbell among the married women passengers who were accompanied by children, but the children were not named. Niña could have been the daughter of any of these women. Or perhaps she was the unlisted child of someone else. Most of the passengers were, in fact, young bachelors. Forever the family continued to speculate about who Niña could possibly have been, although she was taken into the family, and joyfully embraced as one of its own. She was a beautiful gift from heaven, a miracle, and that was how she was frequently described in the family narrative, as a miracle.

CHAPTER FIFTEEN

Secret Chronicle of Virginia Mean IV

'Whilst I stood gazing on this bloody cliff, me-thought I heard the shrieks of the mothers, the cries of the children and the agony of the husband who saw his wife, his children, torn forever from his fond embrace.'

GEORGE AUGUSTUS ROBINSON, *Journals*

I open my journal and I have the delicious luxury of saying: So let me see, what shall I write about today? What thoughts, what memories, what hopes, what fears? This is strange, this freedom to think whichever thoughts I choose, to write whatever tale or song or random waltzing thought comes into my head. There was a time, and it was not really so very long ago, when my days were parcelled out in hours of prayer and in spaces of devoted service offered to Caleb, and in working in the signery making the fancy painted heritage wooden signs to sell to people outside the community. I revelled in all the parts of my life and work, and there were days when Caleb and I would walk out to the Temple of the Winds and spend happy hours there alone. Sometimes on ordinary days, in the late afternoons, I would have some long moments where I could reflect and when I could make my personal notes and jottings in my journal. Now, however, it seems that I have all the time in the world. All the time in the world. That is an astonishing phrase. Father Fox has suggested that I should pour my heart out into this journal, writing whatever strange or banal thought comes flying into my mind. If I wished to write something down, he said, then I should write it.

I never know where to begin, but once I have made a beginning, there is little chance of stopping me. It is for you, Father Fox said, only for yourself, nobody else is ever going to read this journal.

Although I am hidden from the eyes of the world for my own safety, Father Fox has a plan to train me for the day when I may go out into society. I fancy I am somewhat like a girl in the nineteenth century in this, a girl who is being re-fashioned in order to be acceptable to others. A girl somewhat like Eliza Dolittle perhaps. Perhaps not. I do not know. I have read the magazines to learn about the world, to learn what I might wear, how to use make-up, and many thousands of other details that go to make up a young woman of my age today. Once upon a time my life was mapped out for me in Skye; now I must map it out myself. It is so strange no longer having a home, having to begin to imagine finding a home, making a home somewhere, at some time in the future. I watch TV which I find completely hypnotising, and there I learn probably almost everything there is to know about the world. I delight in watching movies, of which I have in fact seen many before, for Caleb had his own theatre room and he used to bring in videos which I was sometimes permitted to watch. Caleb — I will not think of him with regret. I try not to think of him but sometimes he breaks through my resolve.

I miss my family so very much. I long for them and I mourn for them. I miss my friends and all the children at Skye. My thoughts move round the community I used to know and I visit people one by one in my imagination, saying hello, saying goodbye. I never imagined it would be like this, so lonely and desolate and cut adrift from love. I am a sad lost remnant of a lost people, forever searching in my broken and bleeding heart for my sisters, forever longing for my home. Forever and forever.

Father Fox and Gilia and Michael say that the wounds I have suffered will heal, that I must heal for the sake of Stella and for my own sake. They never speak of Caleb. He has disappeared from the spoken air.

After the visit to the nuns Vincent drove us out here to the forest in the middle of the night. We did not stop once and it was a long and thought-filled drive. The relief I felt being in the car with Father Fox and with Stella in my arms is something I am unable to describe. I thought back to the terror of the night when I was first brought to Hobart, and the dreadful hours and days I had spent thereafter, and then I felt the warmth and the trust of Father Fox and I wept and I slept, in a kind of relief. When I met Gilia, her hair silvery in the lamplight, her eyes and hands so kind and sweet, I felt myself melt into her body with a sense of love all around me. I trust these people.

I see Gilia looking at me sometimes, and I think that she suspects I have weird thoughts, thoughts of being in heaven with my family. Then I hold Stella in my arms and I know that for some reason we have been given a second chance on this earth. We have a new life in a new and different world. 'Move on,' says Father Fox, and he looks at me quizzically, catching glimpses of my soul. The wisdom of our former lives I will hold deep in my mind and heart, and I will move on.

The day of the fire was a sparkling summer's day. Caleb and his men were occupied setting up the Meeting Hall for the big gathering in the early evening. He had had visions and messages telling him that the time had come, that there was a nuclear holocaust imminent, that the end of the whole world was upon us, and that the people of the light must leave this earth on the fifth day of February. The fire was to be a haven from the nuclear death. But the nuclear holocaust has not yet happened. It has not happened. Everyone with the exception of Caleb and the men, including me and Stella, spent the morning completing the Great Cleansing which had begun two weeks before. Every object from the smallest spoon in the kitchen drawer to the very surface of the roof had to shine like a silver pool in the moonlight. Processions went through the houses, the lanes, the orchards, the pastures collecting every piece of useless thing or scrap of rubbish, taking it to the ground behind the Meeting Hall and piling it up for the burning. Cleansings used to take place every month, but this was the very largest that we had ever undertaken, with brooms sweeping every cranny, dusters polishing every surface so that the whole village shone in expectation of the coming event. A place for everything and everything in its place, everything lined up, straightened up, waiting, ready. We went down to the beach and collected driftwood and dried seaweed and hauled everything up to the bonfires.

In the soft twilight of the final day, Stella and I rode out to Cape Grimm to wait for Caleb. Although it is government land we were always welcome there, considered to be more or less part of the wildlife. There was a great solemnity in the air, an anticipation. I knew what to expect and yet, in a strange way, I did not. I was in a self-induced trance and Stella and I were singing and playing little games. We tied the horse to a post and sat on the cliff and waited, listening to the lovely sounds of the waves down below us, watching the seabirds making their way home. I saw the shy albatrosses in the distance, wheeling like knives in the twilight air, their wings stiff as starch, and I thought sadly again of my father. Whenever I sit on that headland I remember the people who have died there over the years. It is impossible not to think of them, Aborigines and white folk, caught in the tragedy of time gone by, still haunting that place high up above the water on this crinkled lonely edge of God's earth where the air is pure and the winds hurtle in, bringing dragons from the open sea.

On the afternoon of the last day there was a feeling of elation among all the people. At midday the last procession set off, singing, wending its way out to the Temple of the Winds. We wound slowly down the main street of Skye. The doors of all the houses were open, the shops were open. All those places that were so soon to be destroyed in the fire when it leapt from the Meeting Hall and went racing up the street. We were inviting the spirit of the universe to enter everywhere, to visit each place as the winds blew through. There was in fact no wind until later that day. Out past the beehives and the poppy fields and onto the heath, up the gentle hillside, with a few sheep standing and watching us. This was part of the last great Feast of the Imagination, we sang of the beauty of the imaginary world and of the world to come.

I walked with Bethany and her little ones, '*guindilla, guindilla*,' she would call to them, Stella dancing in and out among them. One of the simplest and yet richest of our ceremonies and beliefs is the Feast of the Imagination. I believe we share this teaching with the Shakers of New England, yet we each arrived at the idea for ourselves. Theirs is called the Feast of Love, but it bears a strong resemblance to the Feast of the Imagination. We would process out to the Temple dressed in imaginary robes of gold, beneath them our usual earthly garments. Beside the Temple is an imaginary fountain from which we collect imaginary water in imaginary buckets. Then we remove all our clothing, both imaginary and real, and bathe in imaginary tubs, drinking imaginary juices, eating fruits from imaginary gardens, and cakes from imaginary kitchens while a group of singers intones from the temple, playing on musical instruments made over the years by the fine craftsmen of Skye.

Just as twilight was falling we dressed and robed and returned to Skye, to the Meeting Hall. Everybody except Stella and me filed into the hall in a mood approaching ecstasy. I knew exactly what was about to happen. Everybody knew. So they would have danced wildly round the floor, and then received their wine with the allotted drops of opium, and they would lie down to dream. The children were given strong drafts of a commercial sleeping drug. I did not see any of this, as Stella and I had already left for the clifftop at Cape Grimm. Caleb kissed each person in turn and blessed them. Then he secured the building, lit the fire, and rode off to meet us in preparation for our flight into the sea. The atmosphere of everything before I left was utterly serene and beautiful.

When I told this story on my writing pad, as well as I could, to the inquest I was still in a trance, or in shock. I wrote very slowly and thoughtfully, measuring every word I wrote, attempting to guess how my words would be interpreted. A woman in black read out my story, a few sentences at a time, and there was a strange and potent silence in the room. My words sailed out of me and onto the paper, and then they ballooned out of the woman in black and drifted about the heads of the people, and hovered in the air. Caleb was not present. I expected him to appear suddenly, of his own power, shining and glorious, but he did not come. All I ever heard about him was that he had been judged unfit to stand trial for murder and had been incarcerated in the Crystal Palace, never to be released. Never to be seen, never to be heard, never to be Caleb ever again.

As time went on, the world did not end. I wish . . . I wish I could be a child again, walking out to the Temple of the Winds with Caleb on a summer afternoon, breathing the sweet, sweet air of Cape Grimm, running and dancing on the hillside, in and out of the slender columns of the Temple, feeling the bones of the whales with the soles of my bare feet, feeling the bones of the whales along the bones of my spine as I lie on the floor of the Temple with Caleb — making love.

CHAPTER SIXTEEN

The Roses of Highfield

'The house contains drawing and dining and breakfast rooms, with five bedrooms, one dressing room, kitchen, pantry, store room, cellars and servants' apartments, with usual offices. It stands in a lawn of three acres. Surrounded by shrubberies and connected with a garden and orchard, comprising an area upwards of two acres.'

THE LAUNCESTON EXAMINER, 17 June 1856

On the hill to the west of Circular Head stood the house called Highfield, pretty, charming, airy, nestling in the landscape, imitating in its miniature way the great houses of the homeland. It was the domain of the Manager of the Van Diemen's Land Company, and so did service as the manor house for the people living in the countryside all around. It was approached through imposing stone gateposts, the stone imported from England for the purpose. There were rose bushes in the gardens at Highfield, and one day in summer every year the Manager, James Gibson, invited everyone from almost all levels of the isolated society to gather for a picnic and to admire the flowers. When she was a child Rosa Mean believed the roses had been planted in her honour.

The first time the Means went to the picnic, Minerva, dressed in her best blue gown, such as it was, and wearing, as ever, her silver pendant, was invited to join some of the other ladies for a stroll through parts of the house and the immediate grounds. The dimensions were smaller than those of the large houses she remembered, but the number of rooms, and the fabrics and ornaments made her both joyful and sad. She longed to live in such a place, and might have done so had she and Edward completed their journey together. Such thoughts could creep into her mind at night, as she was falling asleep, but she knew how to dismiss them and to go forward into everyday life, for she was alive, and she knew what a precious gift her life was. She was safe on dry land with a miraculous new husband and a strange wooden house, and Niña and another child, Rosa, on the way. But even knowing this, the roses in china bowls on the fine cedar tables, the silken drapes and the handsome piano, all brought a sigh to her throat. There was an embroidered Spanish shawl draped across a piano stool, a shawl that resembled in its glossy bright-blue flowers and its trailing fringe the shawls Minerva had lost at the bottom of the sea. Sunlight streamed through the window panes onto the pink Turkish carpet in the drawing-room. The long mahogany table with sixteen balloon-back chairs glowed in the dining-room. Minerva heard there were five bedrooms and an attic. There were quarters for the servants, and a vast kitchen where gleaming copper pans hung from the walls. The company walked out through the kitchen garden, across a paved courtyard, and were led by lavender hedges and a rose walk and flowerbeds filled with pansies and calendulas, out onto the lawns which were planted with young oak trees. There was an orchard where the Manager grew apples and pears, and a wide, neat vegetable garden smelling of fresh earth and onions, blue-green with cabbages, strawberries decorating the edges like embroidered motifs on a cloth. They went along the bowery walk to the honeysuckle bower where they saw the funeral urn commemorating the death of two-year-old Juliana Theresa Curr who had been thrown from her dogcart in 1834. Minerva wept as she heard the sad story, and held on tight to Niña who lay in her arms.

The Means were manufactured by the sea off Puddingstone Island, new creatures, three, actually four of them, Minerva, Magnus, Niña, unborn Rosa, tossed and thrown and blown from the bottom of the ocean to the shores of the wind-chewed edges of the rocky land on the edge of the heart-shaped world. They were fish gasping in the air, cold, sopping, scaly, crawling, finding their way blindly into the dry shelter of the cave. They were sea monsters with cracked skin and with satin staring eyes, washed with a primeval simplicity. Back, back into the darkness of the crumbly Puddingstone cave they moved in their darkest night thoughts, slowly, fearing the presence of fabled creatures, dragons, pirates, wild beasts, ghosts, vampires, cannibals, but seeking the warmth, the dry rocky floor, the embrace of the low roof, the womb of that musty space. They slowly surfaced from the deep hallucination of the slate-grey hell-black ice-green waters of the storm, feeling the gradual welcome of the land that had saved them, claimed them, made them new and strange and knotted together by fate and fortune and water and wind. On that first visit to Highfield, Rosa was the secret fourth member of the square, a tiny speck of mathematics dividing and multiplying in the salty warm waters slopping deep inside her mother, sparked by the seed of Edward Hinshelwood, poor drowned Edward Hinshelwood.

Minerva regretted many things, looked back in sorrow and loss, and one of these was the fact that she had lost the pepper seeds, seeds carried long before from the pepper tree in the garden in Lima, and seeds from red peppers as well. She had carried them to England, to the *Iris,* hoping to plant them, to grow great pepper trees and hot little pimentos on a green and sunny farm in the fabled pastures in the south of the world. But now the pepper seeds would rot at the bottom of the sea. Or they would take root in the eye sockets of drowned pirates and princes and would sprout new kinds of pepper trees, waving and drifting among silent corals and the jagged splinters of rotting decks. Remembering the phantom pepper trees and pimentos, Minerva would often call hot-tempered Rosa her little *guindilla*, and the nickname was affectionately passed down through generations of children in the family.

And those generations grew in all directions, fanned out, reined in blood from other families on the northwest, the northeast, until the growing community at Skye began to take on its own busy, industrious form, which was also a philosophical and religious form, with its Temple of the Winds and its remote pure ways of looking at the world, at life, at death, at work, and at the joys of sharing all in a frontier community.

CHAPTER SEVENTEEN

Mission

'It seemed to her that everything had already begun moving, crying, riding, flying round her, across her, towards her in a pattern.'

VIRGINIA WOOLF, 'In the Orchard'

Over time, when there is a closed community such as the one at Skye, two kinds of folklore grow up about it, one inside the community and one outside. All my life I had been familiar with the stories told from the outside, but from Virginia's chronicles and letters I am able to glean insights I could never otherwise have had. As children we used to think that inside the village of Skye was some kind of old-fashioned cannibal and incest hell, fascinating and repellent. Everything bad and mad and evil was contained in what we imagined were the walls of Skye. There were no walls. It was just a remote collection of houses and very small farms with a few workshops and a comprehensive general store. And a Meeting Hall, never discount the Meeting Hall. And the incredible and fabulous Temple of the Winds. It was a strange place, Skye, cut off yet probably harmless enough, until its time had come and it imploded. Until Caleb came along and took things so very seriously, it was at worst eccentric, at best harmless. To the people of Skye the world outside was full of the dangers of the devil's invention, and they saved themselves from all this when they left the planet. It is particularly difficult for Virginia who has been catapulted across the border and now has to adjust to the way things are done here if she is to survive. She can't stay forever in Ben Fox's hideout. And it's important to remember that she is very young, has been stamped by generations of Skye dogma, and believes she is still in love with Caleb. I suppose she is, but if so it will probably kill her. I wonder if she realises that a few other women have fallen in love with wicked celebrity Caleb too, and they write letters to him, letters he never receives. And so the folklore of inside/outside continues to fabricate and multipy, with a little help from the media, and the boundless imagination of the human heart.

It is certainly just as well we got Virginia (I find it hard to call her Claudina, I don't know why) out of the hospital in Hobart, as I think being there was driving her deeper into a kind of helpless and obsessive narcissism. She was hallucinating and could only be controlled by medication, whereas now she is in a kind of family set-up with Gilia and Michael, and she's got fresh air and ordinary activity such as gardening and cooking and caring for Stella. For a time she wrote down every minute detail of the house, was tracking the movement of the sunlight as it fell on the table, the floor, the bed. Then she would describe the moonlight, likewise. I asked her about why she did this and she said she had been trained always to 'follow the light as it moves across the surface of the world' and document it. Why? I said, and she said it was because the hour would surely come when the light would stand still, would die, and it was her responsibility to be there. I gave up on that line of questioning. The arrogance of these people is breathtaking and alarming. Never mind that if the sun stood still (the earth stood still?) the last thing you would need would be Virginia taking notes.

But some of her documentation of Skye is historically quite valuable.

Caleb was sixteen when Virginia was born. (So was I, for that matter.) She grew up knowing him as the handsome, powerful, charismatic preacher. To her he was not the Preacher Boy, El Niño, but someone altogether more magical, a young man to whom the whole community deferred. It is a testament, I suppose, to her nature (not to mention her youth and beauty) that he selected her to be with him after the fire, to be his proposed partner in the amazing leap into eternity from the clifftop at Cape Grimm.

The mission that people of Skye took to the world was really a small one, concentrating on rural Tasmania, never moving from a tiny corner of the island. There was a hope that they might establish a second centre on the east coast, but it foundered in quarrels over money and something to do with crayfish pots that I could never quite understand. Throughout his adolescence Caleb was driven all over the state by his father, preaching in church halls and school halls and to gatherings that came to see him principally, I understand, out of a rather idle curiosity. They wanted to see a freak show, and in a way that is what they saw. It is tragic that he was sincere in what he said, and so far from the point. He was interviewed twice for a TV news program, but never chose to do the obvious thing and sell his message that way. Caleb was well built and magnetic, yes, but there was something utterly alarming about his eyes, his teeth and his hair, his white or silver suit and he could resemble a crazed hedgehog. Sometimes the newspapers on the northwest coast would be short of local news and would write up some story or other about Skye, particularly about Caleb the Preacher Boy, but in a way it was all just part of the fabric of existence, nothing so special. I used to read these things avidly when I was young, impressed by the fame of this boy of my own age.

The way I see it there was something quite dark and creepy about the way Caleb and his father always quickly retreated to Skye, never straying far from base for long. On reflection I think they wanted the world to know that *they* had the answer, but did not particularly want the world to join them at Cape Grimm. It's quite a twisted way of doing things, but then twisted is what it all turned out to be. Caleb is a highly learned man, but with what we would have called in my childhood 'something missing up top' or 'a screw loose'. More than one screw loose actually. This is no way for a man of my profession to talk, but I find it quite descriptive and liberating. Several people did in fact choose to follow Caleb into the community. Virginia knew of two teenage girls from Scottsdale. Their families made desperate and futile attempts to recover them from Skye, but the more they tried, the less hope they had. The girls stayed at Skye, cut off all contact with their own people, and they died in the fire. I can only begin to imagine what it must be like to be the parents of those girls. And there were others. Enraged, bewildered and bereft, families occasionally went to the media, engaged cult-busters and so forth, but nothing ever came of it except in the case of a woman called, improbably, Marina Galaxy. (The Galaxys are in fact an old Chinese–Aboriginal family from Mount Olympus, near Lake St Clair.)

Marina Galaxy was about fifty, the mother of six children, grandmother of who knows how many, and she attended a meeting in a remote timber church underneath an old gum tree just outside Ringarooma one wild afternoon in spring. (We used to call it Ringaringaroses.) There was a small congregation, Caleb was in full voice, full flight, howling above the wind and rain, when the tree came crashing down on the roof, smashing everything in sight, narrowly missing the people in the pews. Marina, cut on the face by a splinter of flying glass, was within an inch of her life, yet rather than see Caleb as being maybe responsible, she decided to see him as her saviour. It was as simple as that. She washed her bleeding face under the tap at the gate, joined Caleb and his father on the drive back to Skye, and settled in, supposedly for life. But this was not taking into account her large, active, vocal and furious extended family who roared into Skye in a couple of Land Rovers and kidnapped her, holding the astonished members of the community back at gunpoint. I wonder about all this, actually, as I think perhaps Marina might have found her spiritual home. Who knows? There was certainly a fair element of Aboriginal story in the narratives and the thinking of the Skye community, and a decent quantity of Aboriginal and Chinese blood as well. The incident with Marina Galaxy put Skye in the news Australia-wide for a couple of days, but then things settled back into cloudy sleep, and other stories washed over the papers and the airwaves, and all was quiet at Cape Grimm. I sometimes wonder what became of Marina after that, after she went back to Mount Olympus. Where do stories end?

CHAPTER EIGHTEEN

Secret Chronicle of Virginia Mean V

'All is born of water. All is sustained by water.'

GOETHE

Father Fox has brought me a picture that I requested, a replica of one of the South American images my family treasured, part of our memory of Minerva. It is a painting of Jesus as a small child, dressed in the cloak and the hat of a traveller or pilgrim. He has cockle shells on his hat and a staff in his hand. It is El Niño of Atocha. When Gilia saw it she said I might also like to have a particular statue which was given to her by a gipsy woman outside an old cathedral in Spain one evening at twilight when the swallows were flitting round the stone towers, slicing the soft darkness, promising spring and hope. It is a statue of Mary standing on the waves above a little boat where two white sailors and one black one are battling the waves. Mary is in a bright-blue cloak with gold stars, and she has the baby Jesus, in a pink dress, in her arms. She has a huge crooked gold halo hovering above her head. I would very much like to travel to such places, see such things. Once I was uninterested in travel, being as I was so accustomed to visiting strange places in my imagination, but I have begun to have a real interest in foreign lands. How thrilling it would be to go to South America, to China, to Paris and New York. Father Fox laughs at me and says this is what comes from reading *Vogue* and watching television. When Gilia speaks of other places, even of Hobart, but particularly of faraway places she has been, I feel my mind stretching, out, out, around the world, flying along, and out I also go into space, visiting the stars and the planets. And I wonder what is my purpose in the world, what I am to do, beyond caring for Stella and washing and cleaning and cooking, drawing, writing, walking in the bush.

In my imagination I pull myself back into this house of safety, like a snail, encased in the whorls of its shell. I have made several sketches of seashells and nautilus shells, which are, I now realise, among my favourite objects of contemplation, and which are so very satisfying to draw. When I draw the nautilus I remember my father, the way he would say we were all trapped inside one. It was a strange and potent thing to say, and I never quite understood what he really meant. I need a specimen for my sketches, and so Father Fox has said he will bring me some shells, including a nautilus from Hobart next time he comes to see us here. He will buy them in a shell shop. How very strange that is to me, buying shells from shops, when I so often collected my shells on the yellow and white sandy shores of the northwest where the land, like shortbread, crumbles into the sea.

The walls in the central part of this house were originally made, long long ago, from logs, lined with clay and grasses, and then papered on the inside with sheets and sheets of newspaper which was glued and glued and then painted over. These days the colour of the paint is a dusky apricot, all soft and uneven, and like warm warm stone lying in the sun. And on the apricot kitchen wall, on a piece of board, there is a little oil painting that shows a sailing ship rocking on a wild sea. There are two human figures on the deck, and six at different positions up the masts. Three men, wearing black hats, are in a lifeboat, rowing towards the ship. There's a floating box, and one person swimming towards the ship. But the fantastic thing about this picture of rescue is the opening in the greenish-grey clouds of the heavens. Standing in the opening, the edges of which are peeled back like curling paper, is the Virgin Mary dressed as a queen, holding the child Jesus. They are standing above and behind a big brown bull, and Mary's face is quite grim and ugly. You might expect to see those heavenly figures appearing in the sky, but seeing the bull there is a great surprise to me.

Near the picture in the kitchen there is always a large green china bowl that is filled with flowers — lovely sprigs of pine heath, melaleuca, kangaroo apples and orchids. Gilia grows flowers and vegetables and fruit here, and whenever Michael goes to Hobart he brings back, along with all the groceries and other things, always some flowers. He says that the day when people do not love flowers will be the beginning of the end of the world. Father Fox always brings flowers too. He comes trundling up the wide bush track in his dusty old Land Rover, pulls up at the back door of the house, and jumps out with his arms full of flowers. He brings such things as great big white lilies and banana-yellow tulips and gladioli and roses, roses of all colours, so big and soft and dreamy — some from a garden in Sandy Bay and some from the shops in the city. I have never walked in the city streets. I imagine being able to go into a flower shop and buy bunches and bunches of every kind of flower. The most important plants are the native plants, but in a part of the garden where there is a statue of Saint Francis, very old and weathered, Gilia grows many kinds of old-world herbs, as well as calendulas, primroses and pansies, lobelia and daisies, hyacinths and daffodils — but they all have to be carefully contained and strictly cared for because we are living in the heart of an ancient and delicate forest, and the principal aim of Michael and Gilia is to care for and protect the forest that matters most in the world to them. Saint Francis is often visited by little native birds.

Michael works at his forest business most of the time, and he is always on the telephone, or away somewhere on important forest matters. He has a computer in his study and he prints out pages and pages of information that is sent through the computer by electronic mail. People from all over the world, but mostly in parts of Tasmania I think, gather information about the dangers to the forests, and they send them to the computer here. It seems exciting and mysterious to me, and I really love the idea of someone in somewhere like Greenland typing a letter to Michael, and sending it zap-zap-zap and zing-zing-zing through time and space quick as a flash, until it ends up in Transylvania and he can read it on his screen and print it out and file it in one of the big wooden filing cabinets in the hallway. All these documents and many of the conversations in this house are about the old-growth forests and the problems of woodchipping and logging. 'Green' is the most important word in our vocabulary. Green is good and logging is evil. How quickly I seem to have adapted to new ways of thinking and being. I have learnt to watch the clock on the kitchen wall and to measure time as Gilia and Michael and Father Fox measure time.

When I lie in bed at night, in this dark corner of the earth, in the solemn, starry silence of the forest, far far away from the troubles of the outside world, I can always hear, somewhere in the distance, the roar and grind of gears as trucks go up and down the mountain roads, great snaking, thundering, fire-breathing monsters loaded up with stacks and stacks of fat raw logs from the forest. There is a droning and a roaring, a relentless *gorrrrrrh*. The noise is the sound of the lazy hungry rage of a huge wild beast that roams the darkest night, seeking smaller animals with sweet flesh and delicate soft bones — travellers, children, babies, honeyeaters, fish, dragonflies — and the monster will open its jaws and swallow them whole or will chomp them with the saws of its sharp and gory teeth. It is difficult to imagine that there is a driver, a human being in the cabin of the truck, since the trucks have a life of their own, and they resemble enormous scaly medieval dragons, lumbering about eating up whole mountainsides of trees, snorting, snarling, slicing, biting. They hide out in caves larger than it is possible to imagine, leaving great steaming droppings that wipe out whole towns, cathedral spires poking up through the middle of the stinking mess with the shiny cross on top, like the decoration on a cake. Gipsies selling holy statues outside the cathedral are drowned in the dragon droppings, and little wooden images of El Niño float quietly to the surface and peer out at the sky.

Maidens in flimsy yellow-kid slippers and white dresses of swishing silk with thick blue-satin sashes and wreaths of fleshy rosebuds are sent up to the cave to keep the dragon's appetite down, and this slaughter will not stop until there is a special knight who dares to come and kill the beast. History sometimes follows a very repetitive and well-worn narrative. Today the wild old forests of Tasmania are at terrible risk, and Michael and Gilia and Father Fox are part of a group that is fighting to save them.

Old stories — stories about the shipwreck. I can sometimes dream of that night of the wreck — and how Niña was thrown from the drowning ship and landed on Puddingstone, and also stories about the wars between the shepherds and the sealers on one side and the Aborigines on the other. These things are traced through my sleeping hours, inhabiting my self as I dream. Niña is one of my ancestors, and so on one side of the family we do not really know who we are, since her identity was lost. Gilia has told me that with the latest scientific ways of reading the blood it would be theoretically possible to find out who Niña was. But where would you begin? And I ask myself the question — do I really want to know who Niña was?

In waking dreams I am sometimes aware of the presence of Niña as a child on the beach. She runs down the sand as far as the water's edge, and then she stops, and stands there in a long white dress, staring out to sea, with the little bracelet of animal sinew and the arm of a china doll. In this vision she never speaks. Then she fades. I do not know exactly what to call these things — are they hallucinations — should I just call them ghosts? It seems to me there is no word for the images I see. They are presences that visit me from the past and they frighten me, but not because they are frightening, but because I am helpless, impotent, unable to assist them, or even to cross the barrier between real and unreal that separates us. What is real? Apart from Niña, my only other waking dreams have been of the ghost of one young black woman who was shot by a sealer and drowned while trying to escape. Her name is Mannaginna — she told me her story on one still, still evening as we sat together in the shelter of a shallow cave halfway down the cliff. It was a desolate yet familiar and comforting place. It was the first time I had met her, a soft rain was drifting, clothing the world, and there was a feeling of menace in the air, a sense that something was about to happen. Such feelings come to me, and the messages they bring are seldom false.

I am sitting in the cave that is a place to which I go, a special secret place. The black girl swims towards me, beseeching me for help, and whispers a word that sounds like 'Mercy' over and over again. Even though she is far below me in the water I can hear her whispered moans and sounds and words as they climb through the air towards me, up the cliff. Ladders of whispered words ascend the split and crumbling battered flecky stoneface of the crenellated cliff. And as a strange reddish light descends on the hills behind me, and as a low whistling rustle shifts through the gorse, and as a sharp little wind flurries up, Mannaginna rises from the waters below and materialises quite suddenly in the cave where I am sheltered. I feel no fear and I feel also that she is comforted by my presence. I hope I comfort her. We sit in the cave, side by side, facing out to sea, thinking together, silent as ghosts. Ghostly tears roll down her face, my own cheeks are wet with tears and the air seems to tremble, to quiver around us in a haze of terrible sadness. We trickle sand and shells through our fingers, we gather energy and then we collect pebbles from the dry floor, and we hurl those pebbles out, out into the ocean. A hundred rolling pebbles flying out across the spectral air, slicing the sky, then plunging to the ocean, penetrating to the heart of the deepest silky sea. Mannaginna is no ordinary spectre. Did I dream this, Mannaginna? Black girl, did I dream you? You show me the tracks of ants, you lead me to the nests of strange and edible insects. You teach me the names of trees, of winds, of mysterious pathways. I touch your hand and it is real.

The pebbles we throw stir up a whole theatre of the imagination, of the memory, of the dream as they slice the sky and split the water. Often in the sea air I can smell the scent of violets — the sea has a dark-blue perfume, sombre and sweet, creeping into the recesses of my memory and imagination. We look out to the horizon and we see tall ghost ships sailing along with purpose and intent just behind a scrim of gull-grey drizzling gauze. We see small flashes of the red coats of the soldiers, we hear the sound of guns, the rough cries of the men in chains, the lofty ideas and the practical measures, and the jokes and the miasma of disease. We see a company of black men on the shore, throwing spears, we see black women who are stolen, and black women who are pleased enough to leave the tribe to travel with the sealers. We see black people making sad mistake after sad mistake, and white people making different violent sad and mad mistakes as the chaos grows and the rain falls and the animals flee and the forests fall. And swiftly death comes to haunt the tribal lands, death in the guise of war and of disease and sorrow. We watch it as it happens. It is as though the sea before us, the hills around us, are a floating, drifting, open stage, and the things that happened here can be played upon that stage to those with eyes to see and hearts to understand.

We see the things that happened here, and that still haunt the cliffs and hills. I have heard people say that it is not what happens to you that matters so much as how you respond to what happens. But how would anyone respond? In truth how would people react to those mysterious powerful phantom gliding great swan ships freighted with surprise and misery and death, death by the strangulation of starvation and poison and the raging fever of dismay? If strangers suddenly have the power to inhabit the land and take the wives and kill the children, how do the people respond? How would a man respond if his wife had tiptoed out one night to join a murderous crew of raucous sailors clubbing seals? The moans of sorrow and despair curdle the craggy darkness beneath a grey-striped marbled sky.

Like George Augustus Robinson, I hear the shrieks of the mothers, the cries of the children, the agony of the men. And I see the people, and I see the massacres, and they move across and through the phantom landscape of my sight.

The images fade, the moans, the cries, the whispers die away. I am a dreamer, but Mannaginna herself is not a dream. I sense in myself a great, great longing to merge with this dark bright spirit who sits beside me in the cave. But the sky turns to ivory and lilac, the gorse on the hill darkens, the gulls wheel and call their empty mournful call, mist begins to cloud the horizon, and Mannaginna slips without effort into nowhere, merging with the thickening air, dropping like an invisible feather onto the surface of the ocean. She is gone. The beautiful pain of this absent vision, this hallucination, this quiet visit stays with me for hours and hours, for days, paralysing and infecting everything I try to do. Only a few times has this happened, but Mannaginna is part of my life, part of my soul.

I try to think of all the words I know for ghost — is she a phantom? Is she an apparition? I suppose she is all those things, and none of them. She is fifteen years old, and tiny, and beautiful. Her eyes, even though they are the eyes of an apparition, glint and glitter, they are black, gleaming, gliding in their gaze, shifting brightly, sadly, across her world. I think she resembles Trucanini, from pictures I have seen, and from descriptions I have read. They are from different groups, different peoples, but the girl who sat beside me in the cave up above the ocean could almost have been Trucanini, the ghost of Trucanini when she was young.

The last time I saw Mannaginna was a long time ago now, I must have been only thirteen myself. Without her I have never had the power to see the ships and soldiers and tribes of men and women and their struggle. Perhaps I will never see them again, will never again see Mannaginna. But I will never forget. I have told no-one about all this, as it seemed to be correct, to guard the knowledge of something that is really beyond words, beyond understanding, which seems to me to be sacred in ways that I do not understand, that I can not explain, that slip away from me even as I try to recall them. It is pointless to try to tell anyone such stories, for who would believe? Who could believe? I know I have been honoured in a strange way, honoured, yes, that's what it is, honoured. And gifted. I can only treasure that fact.

I don't believe that Mannaginna will ever find peace, will forever and forever haunt the ocean and the cliffside. She will never find peace; I will never find peace. My life is a tattered epilogue to the theatre of the holocaust that is itself a flaring epilogue to the story of the disintegration that began — oh, but who can say where such things begin? — even before the *Iris* disappeared in Bass Strait, before the whalers and the sealers and the soldiers and the farmers came to Van Diemen's Land. Where in the world do stories begin? They begin, I believe, in the air, and in the waters of the ocean, in the rocks. Thoughts of Mannaginna bring up in me thoughts of my own deep, deep sorrow, a sorrow that I can not even name.

These are strange thoughts of how and when things start to go wrong, start to crack, start to unravel — there must be hundreds of ways to say this, and none of them means what I want it to mean — when things collide and start to disintegrate there is nothing you can do but watch it happen. You learn to watch as I learnt to do in the cave beside Mannaginna, to watch as we watched the theatre of dreams. For when the ships with their cargo of soldiers and sailors and prisoners entered the horizon, the moment of fracture before the violence and before the disintegration had arrived. But the ships had been coming for a long long time. The idea of the fatal visit had been some years building in the minds of the great swan ships and the people who sent them here, and the ships themselves had been out upon the water for many months. But Mannaginna and her people were not expecting the visit. They were not prepared for the world to change.

The land where I grew up was always haunted. And now in recent times it must be inhabited by the ghosts of all the people who died in the fire at Skye. And my own heart goes round and round in dervish circles, flying round the world like a moonbird seeking a home. For this house in the forest with Gilia and Michael is not to be my home forever. I must discover how to seek a home.

CHAPTER NINETEEN

The Ghosts of Suicide Bay

'The only object of the early colonists was to stamp the natives out. The settlers would surround their camps by night and destroy every man, woman and child.'

MRS CHARLES SMITH, from *The Westlake Papers* of 1908–1910 (edited by N.J.B. Plomley)

After reading Virginia's story of the ghost of Mannaginna I began thinking more about the sorrowful history of the northwest of the island. Flocks of sheep and their shepherds gather by the remote stone huts where the shepherds live. Fur seals and elephant seals move in the seas and on the islands around the coastline of Van Diemen's Land. Swirling shifting shawls of shiny iodine-brown seaweed, slap in drifting straps and beaded chaplets through grey waters, against silvery-blue rocks. The empty sky, the stretch and curve of empty ocean dream of long ago. And long ago men in small tough boats came to harvest the seals. Pale eyes looked out from the bearded weathered faces of these white men of enterprise, bright dark eyes glittered from the black faces of the black men. One group carried guns, the other spears. The white men were expecting to find the black, with their strange habits and ways, but the black men had not expected to see the white, with theirs. It took almost twenty-five years for the blacks to realise they were going to starve, and for the whites to realise that the blacks of Van Diemen's Land could be more than a tedious nuisance, could be a serious threat. The sealers and the shepherds were trussed up in dark wool jackets, thick hide boots. Except for some animal skins, the black people were naked, their bodies strong and lithe, the hair of the men in ringlets dyed red with precious ochre, resembling the dreadlocks of the 1990s. The breasts of the women were gloriously visible and inviting, decorated with sinew necklaces hung with little shells and seeds that were polished from gentle contact with the skin.

Little details gleam out of a mist of lost stories and lives, and I see the shepherds, the sealers, the tribesmen and women as bleary smudges in a faraway landscape that sits, looms, hunches, weeps in a forgotten corner of the past, not quite real, not quite invented, less defined than a well-known fairytale or the story of Adam and Eve.

The forlorn and ragged end-of-the-earth cliffs at the northwest corner of Van Diemen's Land are soaked in the mingled nineteenth-century blood of white and black. Long before the incredible tragedy at Skye, Europeans came here at the very beginning of the century to kill the seals that bred on the islands. I have read no documents written by sealers, who were not a reflective or literary lot, but I have seen in the library in Hobart diaries and other accounts giving testimony of violent, desperate, half-crazed creatures of the wild waters who would club the animals like so many giant flies, shoot the black men, steal and rape the black women, and keep those women chained up in caves on the islands. There are accounts of strips of black women's flesh being eaten round the sealers' fires. This earth, these waters are stained bloody crimson, a deep sad opal crimson that churns endlessly through the waves of the sea and forever nourishes the ghosts that walk the land, those ghosts that Virginia has the ability to see. The air today is constantly monitored and measured for its content, for the detection of impurities, but no gauge can ever quantify the broken human souls that haunt this wild and windswept edge. I say 'haunt' and I don't say that lightly. You can often enough hear people saying that this island is haunted by its past, and I go along with that, but I am here talking about more specific haunting, about revenants, ghosts who may be encountered in the twilight, or on the midnight hour. I have never met a ghost at Cape Grimm, but while I realise second-hand reports of the supernatural are easily dismissed, I have to say I believe not only Virginia, but the accounts of others that have been reported to me.

A stench of mournful abject violence hangs in the air, howls in the waves, moans in the wind, rustles in the heath and stirs among the adamantine rocks. Call them ghosts. Call them the sorrow that inhabits the atmosphere, but they are not shapeless, they have the form of tormented human beings, restlessly returning to the place where their lives were lost or taken from them. Even on a sun-filled summer afternoon the land, the sea and the air in this place are haunted. Some ghosts are white, most are black. The figures and voices of sorrowful men who died in the attempt to protect their own lives, and the lives of their women and children. The mournful cries of the violated, mutilated women who saw their babies dashed against the rocks, saw their family groups scattered and dispossessed. There is nowhere a report of a black man raping a white woman — if such an event had taken place it would surely have been recorded? There could be several reasons for the blank space where rape might be expected — for one thing I suppose the few white women around at the time on the far northwest coast were well shielded from such harm. These ghosts of which I speak are the ghosts that haunt the cliffs and rocks and waters of Suicide Bay and Victory Hill.

Clear and unbiased documentation on massacres in this region is difficult to come by. George Augustus Robinson visited here in 1830 and made an attempt to find out what had happened back in 1827 and 1828, but already the truth was clouded by time and emotion, and the account in his journal makes it fairly clear that the facts can never really be known. Virginia's story of Mannaginna is another part of this record, and I believe it should be heeded. It is probably crazy of me to suggest there is anything to be gained by listening to ghosts, but I throw the story into the mix, for what it's worth. It is part of a tale of a time of dark violence, and it involves the sealers and the shepherds, and three Aboriginal tribal groups: the Parperloihener, the Peerapper and the Pennemukeer. I am fascinated by the sounds of those names. When we studied History at school, we didn't learn any of this.

There were at least two main sequences of this violence, one with sealers and one with shepherds. The first one went something like this: In 1827 a group of sealers, armed with muskets, ambushed a group of Parperloihener people with the purpose of stealing the women. When a black man hurled a spear at one of the sealers he was shot dead. Seven women were then taken to Kangaroo Island which is off the coast of South Australia, never to be seen again, nevermore to enjoy their tribal lives in the northwest of Van Diemen's Land. The sounds of their terrified voices, their desperate attempts to escape and swim to safety stopped by the threat of the muskets pointed at them from the boats. A few weeks later another bunch of sealers hid out in a cave on one of the islands where naked Aboriginal women were collecting shellfish and moonbirds. When the women set off with their baskets of supplies to swim home the men with muskets herded them into a hollow, in Suicide Bay, tied them up, and, with the exception of one woman who drowned in the frenzied capture, sailed them off also to Kangaroo Island. The desperate black men retaliated by capturing three sealers and clubbing them insensible and leaving them to die.

The second sequence went more or less like this: In late 1827 a band of Peerapper people collecting moonbirds were confronted by the strange sight of a flock of sheep. These people had never seen such strange bulky creatures before, and had probably not seen white people up close. Imagine seeing a sheep for the first time! Shepherds appeared from their huts and invited the Peerapper women to enter. The black men attempted to stop this from happening, the shepherds insisted, until violence broke out and a Peerapper was shot, a shepherd wounded. Determined and enraged Peerapper men, howling and screaming and wielding waddies and spears then herded a lot of sheep to the edge of the cliff and saw them topple in hysterical panic into the sea.

I imagine these sheep in two ways — see them first as the ragged, bewildered, frightened creatures they must have been, crying out in terror and losing their grip on the earth as they fell swiftly onto the rocks or into the water, ending up as smashed corpses of bloody wool, or as floating rugs. Then I see them in flight, white, fluffy, angelic, a pure and blameless flock streaming off the cliff, into the pure air that buoys them up, lifts them out, out in a magnificent arc. And they fly, sail on into the wide blue yonder, heading for the horizon, silently entering the pathway of the moonbird, and setting out on the long long journey of the figure eight, all the way to Alaska and back again. I never see them coming back, just leaving, setting out in serene and godly hope. The moonbird (muttonbird) is called the flying sheep of the Pacific, so I have conflated two species to make a kind of angel sheep.

When the first lot of sheep had gone over the cliff, demented Peerapper then clubbed at least a hundred more to death. I don't understand why the hundred stayed around to be sacrificed, but it seems they must have done so. Then a few weeks later at Victory Hill shepherds shot about thirty men from the Pennemukeer people and tossed them into the sea.

Such written records as exist of all this were kept by white people. Yet among their accounts there are too few names for my liking, too many vague groups like 'shepherds' and 'sealers'. Many are the dark smudges of facts blurred and stories twisted. Most of the records concentrate on attacks of blacks on whites — and this is I think unlikely, since under the circumstances the white men had the advantage, the guns and the motive, which was the desire for land and pasture. The blood and the horror were real in the lives of all people, black and white. Virginia's journal throws up a name for one of the black women, a name that has been spoken to her, Virginia says, by the woman's ghost. The name is Mannaginna. Virginia's record is one of strange and personal hallucination, or visitation, or vision. Who would believe her, she says. Who indeed?

Historians and others continue to do battle over the lost truths of the conflicts between black and white in the remote little corner of Van Diemen's Land at Cape Grimm. I entertain a fanciful notion that the cataclysmic grisly violence of the nineteenth century infects the air and the land and the sea around Cape Grimm, and that this disease erupted again in the conflagration of 1992. But the fire did not cleanse, nor did it exorcise. The company of tormented souls that haunt the hills and cliffs has multiplied, and a greater sorrow moans its plaintive way along the winds, intones its deep lament across the groaning waters of the bays. Virginia Mean holds a key to the ancient truths at Suicide Bay, but who would listen to the stories of a mute girl in witness protection, the lover of a mass murderer? When people can listen with the heart to dreams and poetry, then they will know the truth.

For some time I had been reading extracts of Virginia's journals, and before that exchanging brief letters with her through the Catholic Welfare Office. She had, after a while, agreed that I could see the journals as part of my work with Caleb. This was a big breakthrough in trust for her. When I thought about her visions of the massacres I experienced in a flash a simple yet incredible truth — Virginia is not only a witness to the holocaust at Cape Grimm, but a witness to the massacres there in the 1820s. She crosses time. George Augustus Robinson spoke to people some years after the events at Cape Grimm; Virginia spoke directly to the ghost of one of the victims and saw visions of the tragedies. I know this evidence will be laughed out of court if anyone tries to enter it in the debates of the historians. But my belief in what Virginia wrote in her journal prompted me to find her and talk to her. At first I thought this would be impossible, but then I became obsessed with seeing her, talking to her, believing she held the key to something deeply important, anxious that she would die or disappear before I could make contact with her. There was no reason to believe this, but I was overtaken by the imperatives of a dark desire to know — to know what — I am not really sure. I feared that the insubstantial pageant of her life could dissolve like the waves on the seashore, crumble, as she puts it, like shortbread. And so I wrote to Ben Fox, explaining some of my ideas and reasons. I happen to know he has a family history of seances and ghostly happenings, and perhaps this predisposed him to consider my argument favourably. In any case I didn't want to quiz Virginia about Caleb at all, and I explained that to him. My interest was in her psychic powers, in the quality of her visions. I began to feel the excitement of a new discovery, the thrill of being on the threshold of a fantastic link with the truths of history. There's a woman somewhere in America who channels the music of great composers; could it be that Virginia is 'channelling' the bloody history of Van Diemen's Land? They will say I am mad.

I had met Ben Fox several times on Welfare business, and my credibility with him was high, although he was still very protective of Virginia. He wanted to be perfectly sure I was not intending to go to the media. He had permitted me to correspond to an extent with Virginia, to read the diaries, to give her the simple truth about Caleb, telling her he was still alive, something she is sometimes inclined to doubt. And now he has said in fact that he feels I might provide a clearer understanding for her, might be the one to explain to her that although he is alive she will never be able to see Caleb again. As she herself is fond of saying 'forever and forever'. Ben Fox is a real character in Hobart, one of those down-to-earth saints working for the poor and the downtrodden and the criminal and the mad, while hobnobbing with the landed gentry and the law and high society and the media and the arts. He is distantly related to the Fox sisters who started the fashion for mediums and spritualism in New York in the middle of the nineteenth century. It is no secret that Ben gets around with a well-known forger, a brilliant man they call Vincent van Gogh. Ben arranged for Virginia to be brought to a convent in North Hobart where I could interview her. She could only communicate by writing notes.

I flew to Hobart one glorious summer morning, planning to pick up a car in Hobart and stay with my sister and her family at Tinderbox.

So it was early summer, the day I met Virginia for the first time. I walked across a courtyard with Ben and Sister Margaret, a no-nonsense middle-aged Dominican in grey skirt and cardigan, with stereotypical twinkling nunnish eyes and peaches-and-cream skin. Virginia was sitting on a bench in the cloister, the air minty-green around her, wearing the simplest clothing — a white tee-shirt and blue jeans. Behind her there was an old cherry tree covered in dark-red fruit, and a statue of Saint Rose of Lima, patron saint of gardeners, stood beneath the tree. Everything was quiet, and there was a stillness in the air. She stood up and we shook hands, then Ben and the nun left us alone. The light in Virginia's eyes was soft and deep and strange, and her silence only added to the silence in the cloister. She smiled sadly. She was the most lovely young woman I had ever seen in my life. The intersection of our lives at this point, in this way, was odd, to say the least, and all I could do for a moment was stare at her like a fool.

We sat together on the bench and I asked her about her journal and her visions, if they were visions, of Mannaginna and her people, and the massacres that had passed before her eyes, that had floated above the cliff, that had faded out to sea, lamenting and wailing. She wrote on her notepad (which was decorated with a pale image of Mrs Tiggywinkle): 'Mannaginna is solid, but her people appear to me as figures of thin substance, like real people, but they are constructed of gauze or smoke. As they move across the landscape, the landscape moves through them. Mannaginna is the only one who speaks to me; the others — shepherds, blacks, soldiers — they perform their vision-lives as they lived their earthly lives, and I see the soldiers and the shepherds as they kill the black women and men and children and drive them over the cliff at Cape Grimm. It is like a film.' That was all she could say or write.

I nodded, and I think she could see in my face that I believed her.

'But how can you prove this to other people?' I asked her gently. And she wrote that she could not, that she was speaking the truth of what she had seen and that she could not be concerned with what other people believed.

'Ben believes me.'

'I believe you. But is there nothing you can suggest that will prove the truth of your story to others?'

'No,' she wrote, 'and what does it matter anyway? There are still people who do not believe in the visions of Saint Joan, or the visions of Saint Bernadette. It makes no difference. My people move across the stage of the world in a terrible procession. If nobody believes this, it makes no difference. It is true.'

'It would make a hell of a difference to — well, to the way Tasmanian history is told.' I felt completely idiotic saying that, and Virginia smiled and wrote: 'Quite so.' And then she closed her notebook as if the interview was over. She was going to keep her ghosts close to her heart, safe in their own phantom world of truth, untroubled by the marketplace of history-making and media limelight. I was conscious that in her eyes I had not really fulfilled my part, had not brought up the question of Caleb's future. I know she expected me to say something. Virginia looked at me quizzically, as if she knew I had more to say. Then she opened her notebook once more, smoothed a fresh page with her hand and wrote: 'You have not spoken to me of Caleb.'

'I am sorry,' I said. 'I am not sure where to begin.'

'I had a dream. He was not in the dream. But an angel came to me and said that I would never see Caleb again.'

This was my cue to tell her the truth, that the angel in the dream was right. I hesitated for too long, and she wrote: 'That is true, I know. I will never see him again on this earth. Tell me it is true.'

'I believe it is true.'

'Thank you. I knew I could trust you to tell me. And now, tell me this, is he alive or is he dead?'

'He is alive.'

'Thank you. I needed to hear that.'

She showed no emotion, closed the notebook and stood up. She gave me her hand in a goodbye gesture. I felt very sad and somehow bereft. I thanked her for talking to me, and I felt stupid again.

Ben quickly gathered her up and she was back in the car and on her way to wherever they had come from almost before I could think what was happening. I wanted her to stay, I wanted to sit in the garden and look at her and talk to her and watch her as she quietly and thoughtfully bent her head over her notebook and wrote her notes in her perfect flowing old-fashioned handwriting that reminded me of the handwriting of my grandmother. I wanted to look at her for endless moments.

I was under her spell. I wanted her to stay forever. But she was gone with Ben and Vincent, disappeared.

The sky darkened and it began to pour with rain. I was in a trance in the front parlour of the convent, having a cup of pale tea in a fine bone primrose-yellow cup with forget-me-nots on the rim, when Sister Margaret came sailing in carrying a black briefcase.

'Goodness gracious, I forgot to give this to Father Fox,' she said, 'and I am somewhat at a loss. I know he needs to give it to Michael urgently. Now, what do you suggest I do?'

The rain was drumming on the windowsill. I heard the clock strike five. She was smiling up at me.

'Perhaps he will realise and come back?'

'Ah yes, perhaps. I shall telephone Michael for advice.'

She was gone for some time, and I watched the rain beating against the window as the twilight thickened and a shroud of slate grey descended on the world.

'Michael says that he would like you to take the Land Rover and drive the briefcase out to him at the house, if that is at all possible.' Sister Margaret's voice contained the imperative of a mother superior. She was telling me what to do. I wonder if she knew that she was also fulfilling my most urgent wish, to follow Virginia Mean into the wilderness? It was really rather remarkable that I was to be entrusted with knowledge of the secret location. I must have passed some reliability test or other — or they were very desperate indeed for the contents of the briefcase to be delivered — possibly both things applied.

Driving the convent's ancient Land Rover, wearing a Driza-Bone also from the convent, I followed a printed set of instructions and a map that Sister Margaret had given me, driving through rough terrain, thick forest, and black, black storm. When I got into the tangled heart of the wilderness there were reflecting arrows stuck into the side of the track at fairly long intervals. Out of mobile range, I boyishly felt I was on a desperate mission. I was elated, moving on a level of adrenalin-driven hallucinatory excitement — in other words I was a little mad. I was actually chasing off into the unknown southwest wilderness after a woman I had no business chasing. It was just one of those moments. I did what I had to do — the briefcase containing whatever it was that Michael had to have, on the seat beside me. I knew it would be papers relating to their anti-government work on forests and conservation of the environment, conducted in a kind of jesuitical cloak and dagger manner that seemed to appeal to them. I listened to my favourite Mozart CD, the flute and harp concerto, over and over, with the growl of the engine and the lashing of the rain as a wonderful, a glorious, an unreal background, the forest a dense world of shadow on either side of me. To tell the truth I scarcely noticed anything as I drove, the headlights slicing through walls of water, the wipers cutting their half-moon shapes, not quite fast enough most of the time. I was utterly intent on seeing Virginia again, revelling in my good fortune at being entrusted as a courier. Once I stopped to pee, and I stood for a while in the sombre, sullen blackness, where the phantom jungle shapes of eerie myrtle and celery-top bruised the world of soaking silence a darker shade of purple-black. I did not feel alone. There was a cloak of comfort, even of warmth wreathed around me, breathing deeply in the gnarled and matted wall that was the forest on either side of the track. The rain had stopped briefly, and the leaves seemed in my demented mind to quiver in response to the moment.

I must have killed about three twilight wallabies early in the drive — but there was less wildlife about than I might have expected in finer weather. Four hours after leaving the convent I was guiding the Land Rover up the rough drive that leads to the house where Michael and Gilia live, where I would find Virginia. The house was lit like a cottage in a European fairytale, nestling deep in the embrace of the forest. With the strategic briefcase under my arm, I pushed through the rain to the lighted porch. The door opened, and I was greeted like the prodigal son, the long lost cousin, the angel bearing good tidings. Michael, a man I had never even met before, hardly acknowledged me, but fell upon the briefcase and disappeared into a room down the hallway. Gilia took the Driza-Bone and hung it on a peg behind the door.

I dined with Gilia and Michael and Ben and Vincent and Claudina (for such she had truly become in the forest house) that evening, and I recall that we talked mainly about the problems of how to preserve the precious wilderness — the air, the plants, the trees, the rivers, the animals, how to save the island from rapacious mining, felling, damming. The child, Stella, laughed and played and was very busy and bustling helping Gilia with the cooking. Claudina was a silent presence at the end of the table, and I was conscious only of the strange depths of this silence. Vincent was sketching her portrait. Anything I said about the trees or the rivers was uttered in a kind of routine way, as I was concentrating on trying not to stare at Claudina — but nobody really seemed to notice what I was doing. They were passionate in their efforts to subvert the state government and the timber industry from encroaching on the wilderness of Transylvania. At least ten times the phone rang, and ten times I could hear Michael or Ben in muttered conversation with their callers. Gilia served the food and the three men raved on and Claudina sat while the artist did her picture — I watched and half-listened. Claudina was wearing a blue jacket over her white shirt, and I know it sounds obvious, and stupid, but as she sat there, still as marble, she resembled medieval pictures of the Virgin, her soft hair cut short like an angel. It serves no real purpose to describe her in that way, except that is exactly what she looked like, a figure in a painting, perhaps a Vermeer.

I was actually a bit disgusted and horrified by myself, by my reaction to this woman whom I had gone to the convent to interview for illumination on the spirits and ghosts of Cape Grimm. I had even expected to gain some insights into history, and into Caleb. Perhaps I had indeed gained those insights. At that moment I had almost forgotten the spirits of the Aborigines, and I no longer cared anything much for Caleb Mean. I knew in my heart of hearts that I had fallen in love with this woman through her journals months before, and that my visit to her in Hobart had been a pretext, and I could tell that Ben, for one, knew or sensed this as well. Had he deliberately left the briefcase behind? Surely not. It was much too precious. Or was it? I will probably never know the answer to that question.

Gilia began to sing a soft lullaby, and Stella fell asleep in Gilia's arms, and, as if bidden by a force outside herself, Claudina stood up, stretched, and began to dance on the dark geometric rug in the middle of the room. She moved as if in a trance, swaying to the music, and slowly from her throat there came a sound, a song, a silvery melody. It mingled, it braided with the song that Gilia sang. It was an old Welsh lullaby and it haunted the room. Candles flickered on the table and Claudina moved in and out of light and shadow, and she sang. Nobody spoke. Claudina, in her song, in her dance, moved from the candlelight into the shadow, and out through the passageway, and was gone. She did not return to the living-room that night.

The company was silent. The first to speak, after a long, long time, was Ben.

'So it has happened,' he said. 'It was only a matter of time before her voice began to come back. Any day now she will speak. I have seen it coming.'

'But why now?' asked Gilia.

Ben did not reply, and then the phone rang again, and they were all off on their desperate and hopeful campaign to save the forests, the contents of the briefcase possibly having furnished them with some vital piece of documentation.

CHAPTER TWENTY

Secret Chronicle of Virginia Mean VI

'The eyes are the third great gateway of the psyche.
Here the soul goes in and out of the body,
as a bird flying forth and coming home.'
D.H. LAWRENCE, *Fantasia of the Unconscious*

He stood in the lighted doorway, the flooding rain pouring down on him, drowning. Yet through the oceanic drumming tempest sheets of water his eyes could glitter, his smile could gleam, and about him glowed a fine nimbus of ethereal radiance. And from somewhere, I know not where, in my throat, from my heart, I hear myself frame a whisper: 'Paul?' He did not hear my voice over the sound of the falling rain, but to me the faint whisper, the flutter of wings, was like the breath of God. I knew that I had spoken a word for the first time since the night of the fire, and I knew with that word I had betrayed my past, had betrayed Caleb, had betrayed love, had changed everything forever. Paul. Who was he? Why did he appear before me as a spectre in the teeming night, wrenching from within me the sound of his name? Standing in the light, framed by the darkest gloom, his spirit reaching out to mine, like calling to like. I was powerless to resist the truth of what had happened in that moment, in that twinkling of an eye, a blink, a wink, a long slow weeping dancing tear. 'Paul?' I whispered. And the angels heard the sound. Paul. The day after, Paul was gone. He had not heard me, but I knew that he and I were linked and I knew also that he was aware of this.

In the night-time I began almost to sing, to make a low chanting sound in my throat which was sadly unaccustomed to the exercise. But I knew that I had begun my journey to speech. Nobody commented upon it, and it was some days before I began to sing old songs to Stella. I slept a great deal, and I wept a great deal, and eventually I began to speak to Gilia, to Michael, to Ben, and I left my notebook behind in my bedside drawer. It was almost as if I had never been silent, except I could read the relief in the eyes of those around me, those kind people who have cared for me and sheltered me all this time.

CHAPTER TWENTY-ONE

Taos

'Unless the Lord had been my help, my soul
had almost dwelt in silence.'

PSALM 94:17

I held in my heart all my sudden feelings of amazement and joy, and I returned to Black River, where there was soon a letter from Virginia simply telling me that she had begun to speak again. I replied warmly but almost impersonally, so fearful was I of upsetting something I felt was coming into being between us. We communicated very little over the following months, indeed over the following years during which time I did not see her, but I felt profoundly secure in the knowledge and the hope of a happy resolution in a future not too far distant. I threw myself into my work, as people may do when faced with the impossible in their emotional and romantic lives. In the late nineties we began to use email and, I am sorry to sound so banal, it was email that finally brought us together, email through which we were able to explore the possibilities of our lives, for she was in the wilderness house, Stella was in school in Hobart, and I was at Black River. It would be still some time before Virginia was able to break free of the past and emerge in person from the forest.

My meeting with Virginia in the wilderness on that night long ago had awakened in me sharp memories of the first time I met my wife, Paloma García, the circumstances so different, the feeling of swift enchantment that goes far deeper than physical attraction, almost the same. I fell in love with Paloma; I fell in love with Virginia. But these events were many years apart in time, and many worlds away. As I longed to take Virginia in my arms, I trawled in my mind and heart back over my history with Paloma, seeking self-knowledge, seeking an illumination that I knew I needed before I could proceed.

When Caleb was sent first to the Black River facility I was far away in New Mexico. My coming back to Tasmania is full of mingled feelings and reasons, some to do with the pull towards Black River, some to do with the break-up of my marriage to Paloma. I think, if I am honest, that the break-up was the dominant factor in my return. Although I generally feel like blaming Paloma and Jesus the Jesuit for the break-up, I must admit that some fault existed on my side. No, I wasn't interested in another woman at the time, but I was impossible to live with — I realise that now about myself. I was writing a lot of bad poetry and falling into a close identification with D.H. Lawrence, a writer Paloma, a feminist, certainly could not stand. I have always admired Lawrence's poetry and essays and I just went into a kind of fugue of crazy closeness. I am fascinated by the fact that Lawrence owed some of his inspiration for *Kangaroo* to Willem Siebenhaar, the brother of my ancestor Claesgen, whom Lawrence met several times in Perth. Paloma and I originally went to Taos to ski, mingling with hundreds of people, most of whom were suffering from a mid-life crisis. To Paloma Taos also meant *Easy Rider*, but when I realised Lawrence and Frieda had lived there for two years, I went a little mad. Before that I had never even heard of the nine Lawrence paintings that came to be known as the

'Forbidden Paintings'. When I saw them, in the manager's office at the Commercial Hotel, I was hooked. They're not great works of art, but thinking they were painted by the hand of D.H. Lawrence made me go hot and cold. Paloma grudgingly admitted that she also liked them, so that was something. People these days generally go out to the shrine at the Kioma Ranch to pay homage to the writer, but the thought of Lawrence's ashes out there in the cement of the altar is a heavy-hearted thought to me. He should never have been mixed up in cement. In my opinion. To me the trees and the sky arching over Taos speak of the poet, but the shrine is dumb and numbing. The memorial seems to me to be so ordinary, so predictable, like a shrine to anybody. The scent of the damp earth, the gushing water at the fountain, the sudden rustle of leaves at twilight, the brutal blonde intensity of the sun, that is Lawrence. This kind of talk drove the rational, pragmatic Paloma wild.

I suppose you could say I was unfaithful to Paloma with Lawrence. Some friends have even suggested that I could in fact blame the poet for my loss of my wife. I don't know. She fell in love with another man while my attention was temporarily diverted by the magic and the poetry of a place. Why could she not share my fascination? I loved to breathe the air Lawrence had breathed, see the sunsets, the trees, the country he saw, talk to the people, imbibe him. The place has changed a lot since he was there, there are fewer adobe houses, and more folkloric restaurants and museums and general tourist traps which he would have hated. But I still thought I could commune with him, and I was at the time lacking in any irony regarding all this. I was like some mad undergraduate would-be poet, and now I can scarcely recognise myself. I really meant it, and Paloma got fed up. She called me, in her cute little accent, a wanker, and she was right, horrible as it is to admit. Also a loser. It is painful to write this, because there was a time when we would laugh together in the very joy of our existence. But I suppose that's the way of love, it comes and goes. Now laughter, now tears. Because of the fragility of that love, I am very wary of my feelings for Virginia, who has suffered so much.

Paloma and I had rented a tawny adobe cabin, with simple wooden furniture covered with local native rugs, bright against the softness of the walls. I say 'we' rented it, but the truth is that I was the one who rented it. It was less than ordinary to Paloma, who saw it as a fake Spanish-American-Indian hovel tarted up for tourists. There was a small painting of Nuestra Senora de la Salud, which was a bit ironic. She was all blue cape and stars and roses. Paloma was right, the place was only a childish tourist facsimile of an original cabin, but I didn't want to acknowledge this at the time. High up in one wall there was a window in the shape of a hemisphere, like a jellyfish. When we were first there, and we were still in love, we both enjoyed looking at the moon through the jellyfish, making love by the light of the moon through the funny wobbly glass. I wrote a song about it, and about us, and about love — the madness and all the rest of it — but as time went on and things went downhill between us, she began to call me her jelly-jellyfish and to look up at the window with a sneer. I hated seeing that in her, but there were awful things about me too. I know that and I admit it. We traded some very ugly insults in our new misery.

I was, in my demented state, convinced I had developed tuberculosis, a reference, mirror-image of Lawrence's disease, and I refused to see a doctor. I would cough all night and half the day, meanwhile lying on a long seat, half under a Ponderosa pine, half in the sun, reading books and writing poems, my Lawrentian beard just visible beneath my big straw hat. I started writing a play but it came to nothing. There seemed to be an urgency about getting the poems written, driven by the disease. It was in fact

Jesus who finally insisted I go along to the medical centre, and there I was told by an old-fashioned American doctor in a soft blue shirt and braces, with a white moustache and sad doggy eyes like Einstein, that I had nothing to fear, a viral cough, it would clear up. He prescribed a cough syrup that was principally codeine and so not unpleasant. But nothing to fear? I had Paloma to contend with. She was merciless in her scorn at my hypochondria and my obsession with Lawrence, a man, she said, who writes poems addressed to flowers and treats women like dirt. What kind of a man is that? It is a fact that as the love-object (by which I mean Paloma) degenerates and fades, everything about her becomes — well — a matter for disgust. Paloma, once so perfect and seductive in my eyes, so warm, sexy, adorable, beautiful, graceful, intelligent, became so tarnished, flat, and above all irritating. I didn't hate her exactly. But I hated her voice, for some reason. It got to grate on me, whereas once it had only delighted me. I did hate tall handsome dark Jesus though, and I thought that he was a disgrace to his church, but I felt only bewildered and sad about Paloma, once so desirable, now so trashy. Love is blind. Well, so is hate I suppose. I was hurt, deep down hurt by the whole thing, I don't deny that. Insulted. Love destroys judgment and, afterwards, a man can feel he has been tricked by it, not by the woman, but by love itself.

I suffered from terrible, brilliant dreams, dreams of insects with the detail and glitter of precious jewellery. I could make no sense of them, except as an escape from, a defence against, my present life predicament. I confess that these dreams were not unrelated to the times I spent with Dr Einstein — he was lonely too, and his real name was Henry Millar, which is funny enough in itself, when you consider I was still doing my impersonation of Lawrence at the time. We started driving out to his cabin and sampling his stash of magic mushrooms, and he was fascinated by the fact that my family grows opium commercially. Really, he said in amazement, fields of opium at your own back door? I said I would send him some pictures after I got home, and I think maybe it was then I started to put my numb mind and my dull heart to the idea of coming home. Home. The magic mushrooms really spelled the end of Paloma and me. I began to think seriously about leaving them to their thing and going home. The last few weeks in New Mexico are quite strange to me now, but I finally broke free of the scene, free of Henry, free of Paloma, and headed home to Christmas Hills. True to my word I did send Henry pictures of the farm, my nephew on the new tractor, a bleeding scarlet ocean of tulips in the spring, undulating waves of dreaming green-grey-pink poppies, my mother and father grinning on the verandah of the old house. I never heard from him, never heard what he thought. I realised the pictures that would have really interested him were the ones of the poppies — he seemed so amazed that way off in Tasmania — which was practically mythical to him, as it is to many people in other countries — there were opium fields, something he associated with a place like Afghanistan. Is it wild like Afghanistan? he asked me. He spoke of paying us a visit here, and maybe some day he will.

The bright morning Jesus came with the rose and his basket of fruit and stole Paloma away, I was chopping up apples in the narrow kitchen, in preparation for an attempt at making my mother's cinnamon apple slice. Paloma had never heard of such a thing, never tasted or imagined tasting such a thing. I was trying to make my way back to her, to get past the poetry and the mysticism and back to the way we had been or the way I thought we had been. Henry had said the night before, make her one of your mother's apple pies, son. And he gave me a special bottle of Californian wine. So that's what I was doing, chopping the apples for the cinnamon slice. And Paloma was fresh from the bath, all amber and glowing and dressed in white linen, with red sandals and silver bracelets, and through the russet-red wooden door, through its wibbly-wobbly panes of old glass, I could see the image, the sun behind it, of a tall man in black with a basket of oranges and a rose.

After everything I came back home, the first member of the family to leave Australia, the first to return. I came back without Paloma, whom my family had never even met, and after a time of working on the farm I began to recover from whatever it was that had been bugging me, exorcised the ghost of D.H. Lawrence, and looked around for a job. My family asked me so little about Paloma, it was as if she had never existed, and my mother and aunts engaged in strategies to get me to meet the local women, but nothing came of any of that.

As I worked at Christmas Hills among the fruit trees and the poppies and the tulips and the chrysanthemums — which we used to call chrysanthe-mothers when we were kids — as I went fishing with my brother, as I sat in the pub listening to the local band and drinking Australian beer, as I played at mild flirtations with the few unmarried women hereabouts, I recovered from the condition of unrest and depression that I had been suffering, and began to look ahead again. Looking back it now seems that destiny guided me, that I was meant to be on hand when the job at the facility came up.

I had heard with horror and fascination all about Caleb's murderous rampage, and I had also heard about the facility, which is an object of interest in some international circles, and suddenly there it all was before me, falling into place. I would come here to Black River and make a close study of one of the world's most notorious criminals, a man who grew up in my own district, a figure from my own past. Caleb Mean. As well as Caleb, I have to say, there are other inmates who are well worth studying.

Caleb was the first leader of the Skye sect to turn the community's beliefs back onto the people and in doing this he murdered one hundred and forty-seven members of his church, of his own flesh and blood. An unusual aspect of this is that he did not also destroy himself, as such leaders usually do. I compare his case with the suicides of the Heaven's Gate people near San Diego in 1997 — Marshall Applewhite, known as King Do, died with his followers. Among his papers at the Rancho Santa Fe they found notes and newspaper articles about Caleb and the community at Skye. He had written that Caleb's one mistake was to allow himself to be taken prisoner. King Do believed Caleb should have taken the leap off Cape Grimm with Virginia and Golden, and he also wrote approvingly of the fact that Jim Jones died with his people in Guyana in 1978. There is some evidence that Caleb meant to race off the cliff on his horse, but something held him back. What this was nobody will ever know, although you can speculate that somewhere in his thinking, or in his heart, there was a powerful impulse for self-preservation. Having had some time to study him, I would certainly argue that. This deep desire to continue to live on earth over-ruled his own image of himself and his little holy family sailing off the clifftop into the air before dropping into the sea.

Caleb was treated as holy from the beginning, a kind of non-Catholic incarnation of El Niño, a concept leftover in the family from the time of Minerva and Magnus Mean. He spent very little time with other children, concentrating on his studies and his preaching. I don't know how often he made appearances like the one he made to us at Duck River, but when I look back I see him that day as being so poignantly tragic. He was a child like us, but his only contact with us was as a freak shouting scripture from the top of a rock.

I heard of one time when he appeared at the Eisteddfod at Devonport, competing in a bagpipe-playing contest. He was thirteen. His performance was outstanding, the best playing of 'Amazing Grace' the judge said he had ever heard. And he requested the boy to return to the stage to play again for the audience. Caleb took up his position, raised the pipes, the tartan bag beneath his skinny arm, and then, slowly and deliberately he bent down and placed the bagpipes on the floor. He straightened up, flicked back his hair with his left hand, and fixed the audience with his outer-space stare. Then he started. It was a more childish version of the sermon on the cliff at Cape Grimm, delivered in the just-breaking voice of an adolescent. On and on he went, his voice soaring and falling and railing, his message full of angels and devils and the light of understanding to be delivered to the faithful and the chosen. Those who heard him say that he was totally magical, persuasive, convincing, mesmerising. They wished he would never stop. But he did stop. Quite suddenly, as if he had not said a word, he picked up his bagpipes and again he played 'Amazing Grace'. The audience applause was like a giant waterfall crashing around the Devonport Town Hall on a sullen Tuesday afternoon.

A turn of fortune's wheel brought me to Van Diemen's Land where I would find, at the very heart of the dark and evil narrative of that same Caleb, the woman I would love. I returned from my visit to the convent in Hobart and to the house in Transylvania with the certain knowledge that one day I would make Virginia my own. I did not know how this would be accomplished, but I had a perfect sense that it was going to happen, and a kind of serenity came upon me. I had never experienced anything like this before, such calm certainty. But still I had to tread most carefully. Virginia was not in the legal sense married to Caleb, but how to proceed with her in hiding, with her new identity — the whole thing was beyond action. I am capable of great patience. I decided to wait, to wait and see, to trust destiny, fate, whatever power it is that might be thought to control the lives we lead. I did not conceal my feelings from her. She did not conceal hers from me. It was a love affair conducted by infrequent letters, postcards, email, and the occasional phone call. I suppose it was old-fashioned. It was as if we were on different continents, months apart by sea, in the nineteenth century. It was painful and difficult, but it *was* romantic. And it was real. And yes, I forgot for the time being all about her mystic powers and her visions of the history of early Van Diemen's Land.

CHAPTER TWENTY-TWO

Letters to the Dead

'The worst of madmen is a saint run mad.'

ALEXANDER POPE

And so, while I conducted my love affair with Virginia at a remove, life at BRPDF went on. Dr Sophie Goddard was the first Director here, and with her hand-picked team the facility was gaining considerable recognition overseas for its work with the rehabilitation of the inmates. Among the thirty-odd patients housed here when I arrived was a man called Declan Dequidt, known as Dee Dee, a professor of art who had strangled his wife and three other women as well and fed smallish frozen segments of their bodies into the sewer system over a period of years, keeping the parts in large freezers at the back of the convenience store that he ran with his brother. He admitted that he also kept in the freezers surplus boxes of ice-creams and frozen vegetables that he would later sell in the store. He also admitted that there were times when he had taken portions of the frozen women to local neighbourhood barbecues where they were enjoyed as cuts of choice pork. It is possible that he sold some of the portions to customers, but he would never clarify this one way or the other.

His brother was apparently innocent of all these goings-on. Pieces of Dee Dee's women's remains would surface from time to time in a swamp or a billabong or somebody's vegetable patch, having travelled through the sewers of Hobart. The damage Dee Dee caused to at least four families beggars belief, and this is an area, the aftermath of severe trauma of this kind, that interests me greatly. I have made a considerable study of the psychology of criminal homicide which includes the effects that reach far far into the future of the friends and families of victims. Imagine if you were Dee Dee's wife's sister, or her father, if you were the husband or child of one of the other women. You would never know when another part of the dead woman was going to come up to the surface somewhere, bring with it all the suffering, all the pain, all over again. In the case of Caleb, everyone in the closed community was killed, leaving only Virginia and her child to carry the burden of long-lasting trauma.

Dee Dee was the only member of the Black River cohort to rival Caleb in the shocking details of his case. He spent most of his time studying art, anatomy and music. He was by temperament a rather sweet quiet man who never could be brought to see the problem that other people found with what he had done to his wife and the other women. These four had disappointed him, had fallen short of his standards of devotion to him, but more particularly they had fallen short of his standards of beauty which were fixated on Botticelli's Venus. I would have thought that this fact put at risk ninety-nine point nine per cent of the female population, but he had chosen to concentrate on the four selected victims as part of some larger project that was never clear to me.

Obsessed with the Botticelli Venus, Dee Dee has the remarkable gift of being able to reproduce small linocut prints or oil reproductions of this image of the goddess of love which bear a startling likeness to the original. Uncanny, people say. There is a certain proportion of the oil paint that is mixed with his own blood and semen and urine and excrement and, naturally, his room reeks of linseed and blood and shit and piss and turps. Another of Dee Dee's gifts is the ability to cause his own nose to bleed to order. When he wishes to get some blood for mixing he will simply lean over a fresh or half-finished canvas and command his nose to gush shiny scarlet lacquer onto the surface. It is a kind of party trick he will perform to the delight of fellow inmates. 'Turn on the tap Dee Dee,' they say, and if he is in the mood, he will. He gave me a picture which hangs on my office wall, and it really is quite, quite beautiful. Otherwise he sells them outside the facility through a dealer, the money coming back to us, and he always has at least one on his own wall. While he paints he listens over and over to the music of the harp, a CD titled *The Birth of Venus* by an Australian harpist called Marshall McGuire. People deliberately go past his door so they can listen to the music of Bach, Handel or Purcell, which is like crystal and dreams floating along the curved and gleaming walls of the spooky Norwegian corridor. The sounds also travel through the plumbing into Caleb's room. Caleb and Dee Dee exchange, as prisoners often do, anecdotes and information of various kinds via their toilet bowls. Dee Dee naturally has a special interest in sewer systems.

Caleb and this man are the only members of our community whose files are stamped 'never to be released', however it is in fact unlikely that many of the other people enclosed here will ever leave. Caleb's walls are densely papered with images cut from magazines, all of them pictures of Marilyn Monroe. There is a strange purity to this repetitive and obsessive form of decoration, but it is, when you first see it, a shock. Caleb Mean, the Christ Child, surrounded by this exquisite banality? The reproduction of the image of the same beautiful woman over and over again seems somehow to rob her of her magic, I have found. There were just so many pictures of Diana I could look at before she lost her charms for me, and the same goes for Marilyn. Andy Warhol was definitely onto something, I think. With Caleb I might have expected to see pictures of the Christ Child, or of Caleb himself — but then who knows what to expect — perhaps Marilyn is entirely predictable. Caleb is after all, when all's said and done, a man like any other — which is a horrible thing in itself to contemplate. If he is like me, am I like him?

In any case, his cell is certainly most striking, being a box lined entirely — walls, ceiling, door — with images of the goddess Marilyn. The only comment I know Caleb has made about all this is found above the door in his inscription: Where there is Beauty there is God. He does not seem to have given much thought to the woman and the child he took with him to the clifftop. I suppose one of the advantages of having individual religious beliefs is that nobody can really argue with you. You believe what you believe, and that's that. I often wonder just what those other one hundred and forty-seven people believed. Virginia has quickly modified her thinking to come into line more or less with something like the humanism of the people around her. I wondered for a time if she would ever follow Gilia and Michael and Father Fox and convert to Catholicism. I doubted it, but then, one never can tell. Father Fox himself has a certain amount of charisma.

Caleb spends much of his time, when he is not working out, particularly on the rowing machine, writing letters. There are four people to whom he writes. One is Marilyn herself, and the others are his ancestors Minerva and Magnus Mean and the Belgian philosopher and playwright Maurice Maeterlinck. All these people are dead and so can not reply to his letters, but that doesn't seem to matter to Caleb. I have no idea what to make of the coincidence of the double M in all the initials. Caleb refuses to discuss any of this. I realise that one of the keys to the beliefs of the people of Skye was the power of the imagination, the reality, if you like, of the imagination. Caleb cartainly has a wild imagination that he follows as he pleases. He appears to believe that these people are receiving his letters which are charming, friendly, intimate, and that follow sequences suggesting a kind of conversation. Although he now has a computer in his room, Caleb chooses to write the letters by hand on blue airmail paper. He has asked for email but has been refused. I thought it would be interesting to see what messages would come back from Marilyn and the others out of cyberspace, but it is too risky. The letters are all officially filed and one can get access to them only by special application. Caleb seals them in airmail envelopes and then hands them over to be posted. I do not know how much he believes in the truth of this charade. He is mad, after all.

The facility is largely Sophie's brainchild. It was designed by her lover and so this makes Sophie very much a central figure here, it is almost as if the building itself were part of her, rather than she part of it. Sophie Goddard is a force to be reckoned with at Black River, whichever way you look at it. The lover, Thor Gulbransen, is no longer in the picture, having returned to his wife in Norway where he died in a hotel fire. The irony of that is never mentioned, but it occurs to me that there is a sort of nasty symmetry with Skye and a hellfire coincidence. I am too imaginative. For quite a few years, some short time ago, Sophie and Thor were a big item in Sydney, and it was one of those arts-political scandals that he got the commission to design the facility at Black River. That kind of thing happens all the time, and is the way the world goes round. There is very little that is new under the sun.

Like calls to like, and people find the people they will need for good or ill. Sophie had been dreaming of building and directing this particular type of modern facility for years. Then she had it designed by Thor, saw it approved, built, and then she found herself appointed Director. And *then* who should arrive within its walls but Sophie's perfect patient, Caleb Mean. Caleb became effectively Sophie's prisoner, and also her pet project. Sophie and Caleb were made for each other, and the facility was made to be their — their private palace, their playground where each can play out the fantasies of the other. Rapunzel's tower in the story was interesting not because it was safe, but because it was *not,* in the end, inviolate. You can't really keep human beings in if their desire for freedom is strong enough. For that matter you can't keep them out either, if they really want to get in. If there is one thing I have learnt about human beings in my years of study and work in this field, it is that they are devious, and they are incredibly clever. That's how we got where we got. Devious is the one word that really covers Caleb and Sophie, a wonderful, horrible word. Devious. Is this strange language to choose when I speak of a mad inmate and his doctor? If readers can detect a certain bitterness running in my tone here, then they are right. My work with Caleb who had for so long been a figure in my dreams, my heart, my imagination, was now held at a remove, the way being partly barred, the object of my interest obscured by the interference of Sophie Goddard.

I believe that all the Caleb material belongs by rights to me, that there is no real argument to be had about that. Caleb has been *my* object of fascination, my obsession since that day long ago when he shouted the Psalm at us at the picnic at Duck River. 'He telleth the number of the stars; he calleth them all by their names.' For so long now I have hesitated to compose all this into a narrative, to write it down for other people to read. I held back for many reasons — mainly for fear of transgressing professional and ethical boundaries. All — or at least much of the information concerning the facility and the patients is public knowledge — what's different here is the way I have interpreted it, and the way I have put it together, the way I have reported things, strange things, putting them into their context, which is, some of the time, my own context. I have tried to set aside my professional language, and to speak openly, using words such as 'mad' and 'crazy' whenever they seem to me to be the honest words. So much language in all professions is specialised and hedged about by a razor wire of prohibitions. There are terms and categories into which Caleb is classified by his doctors, but I can't see any point in using them here. He is mad, crazy, evil. I am not exactly his doctor either, I am his — I search for the word — nemesis. I was shocked when I found that word on my lips, but on reflection I think that it is accurate. And I rebuke myself for all the years that I paid him so little attention, when I could have been making close observation of a remarkable phenomenon right under my nose, when I was aware he was running a bizarre and potentially dangerous commune out at Skye, but like everyone else I used to laugh about it, although in my heart of hearts I knew, *I knew*! I'm not simply saying that in hindsight I believe I was aware, even before he made his visit to our picnic, that there was something of strange and terrible significance about the little boy they called El Niño.

The people who could tell me things now, or even give me other access to information about Caleb before the fire, are the tragic people who were lost in the fire. There are relatives at Woodpecker Point, but they have generally no desire to discuss anything that will bring up memories of the tragedy. It is in fact the most sensitive material ever to be buried in the minds and hearts of the people of the far northwest coast of the island. The folks at Woodpecker Point have long since cut themselves off from the people at Skye. Talking to Caleb himself is always interesting and to a certain extent revealing, but you can never be sure he is telling the truth, since he gives in often to the flights of his phoenix imagination — which are interesting enough in themselves, but not especially useful if you are looking for the truth. He is an artist. The main hope of anyone researching Caleb's life was to talk to Virginia, but for a long time she was legally out of reach. Sophie has shown no interest in Virginia at all, and I find this quite significant. She places all her emphasis on Caleb himself, ignoring the young woman and the child who are surely a vital clue to the madness that fuels his purpose.

There is a terrible irony in the fact that Virginia and I are in love.

CHAPTER TWENTY-THREE

Butter Dream

'The soul of Matthew Flinders lives in every boy
who points the prow of his little skiff to sea.'
ERNESTINE HILL, *My Love Must Wait*

'Row, row, row your boat gently down the stream
Merrily, merrily, merrily, merrily
Life is butter dream.'

It was late at night as I sat typing. I was in a house in the remote southwest wilderness of Van Diemen's Land and the television was on in the corner of the room. The fourth item in the news bulletin, read of course by the charming smiling clone-woman in the pink suit, told of the escape of 'life-term patient Caleb Mean from the maximum security detention facility for the criminally insane at Black River in the state's far northwest. Mean,' she says, smiling and steady, 'is the man responsible for the deaths by fire of one hundred and forty-seven people in the village of Skye in 1992.' I have such a weakness for pretty women in pink dresses.

Years ago this story would have been the material for an exciting newsflash, but it is now nearly ten years since the fire, and Caleb is lucky to make it to item number four. I wondered for a while what Sophie had been doing, how it was that she would let this happen, and I entertained wild thoughts that she had conspired with Caleb in his escape. I rang through to the facility only to be reminded that Sophie was at a conference on the mainland.

The story is that Caleb escaped through a skylight and lowered himself to the ground on a thick woollen rope he had manufactured himself in the spinning and weaving workshop at the facility. Guards reported no sign of the patient in the grounds, nor was he sighted at the main gates. The walls of the facility are fully protected electronically with security back-up. Personally, I doubt that thing about sliding down the rope James Bond-Musketeer-style. I doubt that very much. I imagine he might have hung the rope from the skylight as a decoy. No, I think he simply stole Sophie's passkey, and let himself out through the complicated staff exits dressed as — what — maybe a driver. I must never lose sight of the fact that this is a consummate con-artist, capable of talking and acting his way past anyone who might have challenged him. And he was also possessed of a kind of super-human strength that had its origins in his belief that he was divinely inspired, and always right. He had also been working out for years in the gym at the facility.

He left a note behind addressed to me, actually. It was on his blue airmail paper, sealed up in a thin blue envelope. He offered me his cell with all his pictures of MM, saying he knew how much I loved her. He was going, he said, to join Dr Goddard at the Hyatt on Collins, and they were in due course going away together to start a new life. He knew I would be pleased and asked me to look after Dee Dee, and to forward any mail he might receive to him care of the Hyatt.

I sat in my office in the gathering cobwebs of twilight, Caleb's letter in my hand, and wondered about Sophie. How much had she realised, known about Caleb's state of mind? Was she unaware of his coldly demented plans? She saw him, I believe, as the *case* that would take her career to greater heights. She was also crazy about him, was under his spell — of that I am certain.

In the cool mist of a July morning Caleb made his way through the sombre forest, heading for the sea. It was the first time he had been at liberty in nine years. The air was sweet, perfumed with the honey of freedom, the sounds of the forest musical and heavenly. Wearing blue jeans, a white tee-shirt and black trainers, he was a man like any other walking in the woods. He carried a bottle of water, a Cherry Ripe and a parcel of dried fruit, and he wore a watch. His shining eyes, full of electric excitement at his project, swiftly moved to left and right, round, up and down, alert for any sign of danger. But he knew he was invincible, perhaps even invisible. He was fit and he could move between the trees and rocks like a wild animal. He rejoiced in the glorious beating of his own strong red joyful heart.

In a strange way he is high, he is walking on air, intoxicated by success and by the anticipation of the bright and gleaming world opening up before him. He knows when he is getting closer to the sea, to the mystical wide opening of Bass Strait that beckons him. He can smell the water.

No sound of alarm comes from the prison. No hint that he is missed or pursued. He begins to forget that he is an escaped prisoner, and sees himself as the swift and glorious voyager he truly is. God's anointed, God's obedient son, God's holy messenger. God's favourite. He is the son of his earthly father, but he is also the son of the son of God.

He has listened very carefully when Sophie has spoken of her house, its location and the small blue dinghy tied up on the shore. Through the tea-tree on the edge of the forest, between the tall trees and the sandy scrub, he can glimpse the silvery-grey cedar shingles and the glint of the wall of glass bricks. Thor has designed another perfect landmark, almost like a lighthouse, and now Caleb has it in his sights. Skirting the house he follows the sandy track down to the foreshore, and there, sure enough, knotted to a tree-stump, upside down on the gravelly sand, there in the slow, shimmering morning sunlight is the blue-green dinghy of his dreams, oars crossed on the sand. The little Seagull motor Sophie had spoken of must be up at the house — Caleb looks round and he considers going to look for it, but a fear of being seen decides him. He will row the boat to mainland Australia in the primitive old-fashioned way. On the prow Sophie has painted the name *Tom Thumb* after two of the boats used by Bass and Flinders. Caleb smiles to himself when he sees that. Flinders is one of his heroes, the man who named Cape Grimm.

For a few minutes Caleb pauses and stares out into the Strait, his arms uplifted as he takes deep joyful breaths of the sweet, sweet air. God will be his guide across this stretch of water, which today is flat and almost still. Looking-glass, millpond, ornamental lake. Blue, green, silver, gold. He knows it is one of the most treacherous straits in the world, he knows that deep down there somewhere lie the remains of the *Iris.* He knows the Roaring Forties can come roaring in without warning. He hangs his shoes around his neck and wriggles his toes in the cold wet sand. Then he turns the boat over, drags it to the water, collects the oars, pushes out, hops in, sets the oars, and he's away! Sailor boy.

I have to remember, as if I could forget, that Caleb is — not to mince words — mad. I find, strangely enough, that the mad are on the one hand interesting, but on the other kind of one-dimensional and boring, like a cheap cartoon animation such as the Road Runner. I suppose what I am saying is that they are sort of children with a screw loose — but dangerous and not to be underestimated.

Caleb is an escapee from an institution for the criminally insane, to which institution he has been consigned for the rest of his life. He has no compass, although he is sharp enough to be able to navigate roughly by the sun. Rowing? Yes, rowing across Bass Strait from the northwest coast of Van Diemen's Land to the mainland of Australia. In many, some would say most, ways, he is a child on an adventure, a child having the *best* time. He is likely to burn up in the daytime, freeze at night, starve, die of thirst, drown. Where does he think he is going? In so far as he is thinking at all, he is fixated on the idea that he will go to Melbourne and find Sophie and together they will take on the world. Something like that occupies his imagination. He can smell crushed raspberries, taste crushed raspberries, warm and bleeding in the sun. And high in his dreamless mind he sees himself as he was when he took out his old bagpipes and played his beloved tunes. In his mind, on the water, he starts to hum.

Speed bonny boat like a bird on the wing
Onward! The sailors cry.
Carry the man who's born to be king
Over the sea to Skye.

Caleb *is* El Niño, stuck in his holy babyhood. That fact is what has shaped him, disfigured him, warped him — however you want to say it. He is the Baby Jesus who never grew up, bobbing along in the choppy wavey watery adventure of Bass Strait.

He feels the lovely strength in his arms as the oars dip and rise, dip and rise in the water. He is Peter the Fisherman, he is Matthew Flinders, he is Rat, he is Mole. Messing about in boats. He is the Owl and the Pussycat. He is on his way to the land where that bong tree grows. He is the Steadfast Tin Soldier making his faithful way to his beloved ballerina. Fast. The oars are the oars of a man who has worked out on the rowing machine for the past three years, waiting and planning his journey to freedom. For three hours he travels out, sighting nothing but a very small rocky island where a few storm-petrels are lined up staring into the wind. Every hour he takes a sip of water. He plans to keep the fruit and chocolate for later. His bare feet push against the friendly wooden slats in the floor of the boat. And lying beneath his feet is an old rainbow string bag Sophie has left there.

Snatches of texts he has read float whole onto his lips: 'Your goats have gone wild, your orchards fallen into decay, your birds flown, and the only sound is the cry of the sparrow-hawk as it circles the valley of rocks. And as for myself, I am as a friendless friend, a father who has lost his children, a traveller who roams the earth where I alone remain.'

A brisk wind picks up on the water, blows him along, out, out towards the horizon. Then before he knows it a steel dark cloud begins to roll in from the west, and the water that has welcomed *Tom Thumb* like a child's yacht on an ornamental pond begins to rock and then to churn and the boat is tossed and spinning. And the cloud rolls on and it drops great sheets of rain like drenching black night, and Caleb in his boat of salvation is helpless.

He can not hear in the distance behind him the sudden piercing wail of the facility siren. *Weeaaroooh-weeaarooh*! As Caleb spins and tips and puts his faith in God.

O Holy Spirit who didst brood
Upon the waters dark and rude
And bid their angry tumult cease
And give for wild confusion, peace.
O hear us when we cry to Thee
For those in peril on the sea.

The storm takes hold of the waters and rolls and roars in over the land, so that the police helicopter can't take off, and although all stations are on alert, the land search can not begin until the weather clears. It has not yet occurred to them that Caleb might have set off by sea. In fact it never really occurs to them at all. Three days later, when the whole north of the island is in a state of jitters because there is a maniac on the loose in the woods somewhere, Caleb's black trainers stamped on the inside in red 'BRPDF' and knotted together, are washed up on the rocks at Penguin. It is likely that Caleb Mean has drowned while attempting to escape. Nobody has yet discovered that *Tom Thumb* is missing.

'The boat at last spun round four times and became filled to the brim with water. It began to fall apart, and as he thought of his love a line from a poem came to him: Death comes so swift and cold. The boat fell apart and he would have drowned had not a greedy fish swallowed him. The fish was caught by a fisherman and taken to the market and sold. The kitchen maid found the Steadfast Tin Soldier inside the fish when she opened it up to clean it. So she picked him up and took him in to show him to the family. And there in the dining-room he saw his dancer, his love.'

It was three weeks before the whole world read the headline: GIANT SQUID TAKES HOLOCAUST PREACHER. As you can imagine, TV went berserk.

On the beach at Boat Harbour, as they were setting off for their morning swim, Josh and Jenny Astor found to their amazement the sprawling, stranded body of a sea monster. Sixteen metres long, pink with eight tentacles each as thick as a man's leg, liberally studded with powerful suckers that bloom all along from where they join the body of the beast to the tips. Jet propelled, the giant squid, feeding close to the surface in these times of warming seas, discovered the *Tom Thumb* with its fit and healthy sailor boy, and with all the elegance of a ballerina of the sea, wrapped the package in a firm embrace and powered off into the stygian deep to enjoy the feast. Let's call it the Kraken. Forgive me if I sound callous as I tell this story. It is after all about the horrible nightmare death of one of my patients, but there is something so other-worldly about all this that I have quite a bit of difficulty getting the right tone.

When scientists opened up the Kraken, they discovered nothing that could be identified as human residue, for these creatures chew their food thoroughly, and it must pass through their brain before it reaches their digestive system proper. But, lodged in one of the tentacles were a few shards and splinters of wood, faintly painted blue-green, and on one of these could be deciphered the letters 'UM'. In the eight-day interval between the finding of the shoes and the finding of the Kraken, it was decided that Caleb had possibly drowned. Then they tested the stuff in the belly of the beast, but they could not say that any of it was human. The poet in me — or you could say the cynic — wanted to hear they had found skin on which was drawn the image of a bluebird of happiness, but that was impossible. They didn't find that. They didn't find anything. Because of the discovery of the fragment of the boat, it was assumed and officially accepted that Caleb had been taken by the squid. Forgive me now, but I must give in to an urge to quote from Tennyson.

> 'There hath he lain for ages, and will lie,
> Battening upon huge sea-worms in his sleep,
> Until the latter fire shall heat the deep:
> Then once by man and angels to be seen,
> In roaring he shall rise, and on the surface die.'

There's also a part that talks about the Kraken's 'ancient, dreamless, uninvaded sleep'. I thought that was nice, given Caleb's own notorious inability to dream. I couldn't get the tone, could I, but at least I have passed on the essence of the narrative. Caleb's Kraken weighed two-hundred and sixty kilos, which is not so big when you think of whales, but it is big.

There was a sad funeral at the facility, unremarked in the press except for one small paragraph in a national paper, although someone got some pictures to put up on the website. It was attended by no members of Caleb Mean's family and conducted by Father Fox. The poor remains — the shoes and the bit of boat — were cremated and later scattered into Bass Strait one eerie grey afternoon off the Bluff at Devonport — again by Father Fox who has become the de facto guardian cleric to the remnants of the Means. So finally Caleb was drowned, eaten, burned and scattered. One day Virginia and Golden and I drove out to the Bluff and said a brief farewell to Caleb. Virginia had brought with her a bunch of Highfield roses and as we stood on the cliff, our faces to the open sea, the grey wind in our eyes, we hurled the heads of the roses into the waves below. They floated for an instant, blushing dots of colour on the riding foam, then sank quite suddenly from view, consumed.

CHAPTER TWENTY-FOUR

Heb Dhu Heb Dhim

'The hitherto lifeless earth springs into green. Gross flowering plants appear, bright, lush, as high as a horse's head.'

CARRILLO MEAN, *Making Love to the Air*

For myself and Virginia and Golden there is a happy ending. Years after I met her beneath the cherry tree in the convent, years after she spoke her first word, my name, years after I left her behind in the wilderness, we found our happy ending. I accepted a two-year appointment to a job in Tallahassee at Florida State University and the State Prison in Starke, and before we left Van Diemen's Land Virginia and I were married in a simple outdoor ceremony at Christmas Hills, among a stand of she-oaks above a sea of scarlet tulips and dream-coloured poppies. Virginia was wearing pearly pink. Father Fox gave the bride away, and Golden, who had re-claimed her name, and two of my nieces were the flower girls. Virginia resembled an angel in a Botticelli picture, and I can not begin to describe how beautiful she was. I was in a trance of joy, experiencing feelings I have never known before, feelings I have read about in poetry without truly understanding. This was bliss, indescribable bliss for me. I saw that Virginia was so calm, so serene, so pure and lovely, and it was almost as if I had been bewitched. I feel a fool, going on like this, but that is how it was. Something transcendent occurred when Virginia appeared beside Father Fox in the little glade at Christmas Hills.

The party afterwards was one of my mother's biggest efforts ever, with all the women from miles around roped in to cook and lend their tablecloths and their best plates and silverware and crystal. The tables underneath the trees were heaped with flowers and fruits and wine and more food than you can imagine. One of my cousins had come up from Hobart to play the harp, and she was like another angel under the trees. Virginia decided to take my name, to become Mrs Van Loon, and Golden also, my adopted daughter, has taken my name, becoming Golden Van Loon, removing from herself the strange script written by her father into the words 'Golden Mean'. Perhaps we have been able, to some extent, to exorcise the spirit of Caleb Mean, but only time will tell. There was no shadow of his presence that I could feel at the wedding that day. The only darkness, a deep and abiding sorrow, lay in the fact that all of Virginia's family was missing. Also, I knew that my father was shocked that I was marrying her, one of the Means, when he had had higher aspirations for me. The phantom of Caleb and the fire, the horrors of the union of Bedrock and Carrillo, the whole mad tribe of unsavoury Mean characters hovered in a cloud around my father that day. He looked very old.

There is a great pleasure in explaining all the normal, ordinary details of the wedding, as they come in the wake of such bizarre and extraordinary events, events that have coloured and fragmented our lives over the past ten years. I plan to write a Christmas email this year, and there I will be able to elaborate on the many small triumphs that have marked our lives over the past twelve months. But for now Cape Grimm and the tulip farm and Black River and Transylvania are all far, far away from me, as if in another world and time. The winds of destiny have brought us here to Florida, to the place where the fate of the world was decided in 2000 by the flutter of the chad in the US presidential elections. The pregnant chad, the dimple chad, the butterfly ballot and the caterpillar ballot — how organic and charming and innocent it all sounds. How sadly it now all resonates with the present stories of the world at large.

So the winds of destiny have brought us to the Gulf of Mexico, just a stretch of water — a large enough stretch of water — from where I met Paloma during that incredible earthquake years ago. It is so long now since I have thought of her, but the close and real presence of the place where we met sometimes reminds me of past happiness and sorrow. In moments of reflection I recall the bike ride from the hospital, through the ruined city, to the small neat house, untouched by the earth tremors, where her uncle was sitting quietly in the kitchen as if waiting for us, his old hands on the knob of his walking-stick, his bright brown eyes twinkling with pleasure at the sight of us. I recall also the unknown man who died at our feet as we embraced in the hellish darkness of the emergency room. I remember these things like episodes in a distant tale, connected and yet disconnected to myself.

So, the winds have brought Virginia and me to the Gulf of Mexico.

After the wedding at Christmas Hills we travelled out to the ruins of the village of Skye, our principal aim being to visit the Temple of the Winds. Virginia once believed that she would never have the courage to go back, but together we found the strength, together we made our way to the Temple of the Winds. We had to pass through the ruined and abandoned village that was a forlorn whistling skeleton through which morning glory and blackberries and grasses had moved, giving the effect of softening, decorative, even artificial greenery. It was a fairyland of woody, leafy arches and hollows and windows and arcades. Through the leaves of a riotous honeysuckle I read a fading but undamaged sign in blue and white that said: 'Flying Sheep Café'. Trees sprouted from the rusting skeletons of burnt-out cars. As if spirit people had suddenly fled before a powerful, creeping, verdant force. The most potent thing was the wind itself, the way it twined and softly wailed, raising flurries of pale sand from the ground, a sand that had all but obliterated the patterns on shattered pavement tiles. The breath of desolation was carried on the wind.

The place where the Meeting Hall had been was cleared and flattened, covered with grass knee-high. In the graveyard next to it were rows of uniform white crosses, like on an old battlefield in some far-off country. We walked slowly up and down the rows, and silently read the names — Virginia's whole family was buried there. We were both weeping softly. Since then we have never spoken of this time in the graveyard, and perhaps we never will. It was beyond words, beyond emotion, beyond understanding. The miracle was that Virginia and Golden had escaped, had lived to take up their lives in joy and hope. As I looked at Virginia while we stood by the graveside of her mother and father and brothers and sisters I was overcome with a great amazement that she should be beside me, that she should be so vital, so filled with a shining energy and beauty, that she should be mine.

Together we knelt and kissed the earth and then we slowly made our way out of the ruined village, and took the winding path that leads out to the Temple of the Winds. It was a clear day, blue and lilac, with a sweet and gentle breeze ruffling the grasses. As we strolled along it was difficult to believe in the reality of the violent history of this place. Petrels and gulls wheeled, lazy in the air above us. We passed the disused, ruined beehives that had supplied the people of Skye with their wonderful honey, honey that they had exported all over the world. We have our own honey at Christmas Hills, but the Skye honey was always better, much better. Their bees were believed to be direct descendants of the first European honeybees to come to Van Diemen's Land in 1821. Where are they now, those honeybees?

The Temple of the Winds has the look of something that has always been there, of something that will last forever, as if the ancient Greeks had sailed here to this remote and lonely hilltop and had brought with them a perfect little temple kit that they assembled here against the sky before leaving for other lands, other seas. To be inside it is to be inside a great seashell, at the still point of the world. The pavement is a mandala made from the vertebrae of whales, and from a selection of the sworls and spirals and speckles of all the seashells of the world.

We came back towards Cape Grimm but were unable to enter the government enclosure where the weather station stands. Somewhere over there in the distance was the cliff where Caleb and Virginia had waited on their horses the night of the fire. This same young woman I now hold in my arms. Somewhere over there was Suicide Bay where Mannaginna died. I believe in the ghosts of the Aboriginal people who lived on these lands, and who died here so violently at the hands of sealers and shepherds and others in the nineteenth century. You can sense their presence here — it is in the rocks, the waves, the air, and it will never be erased. And I believe wholeheartedly in Virginia's visions of them, but the world will never really know.

Our street in Tallahassee is lined with wise old magnolias and live oaks, and these are decorated with the silvery drifting fairytale beards of Spanish moss. Across the street, Miss Henrietta Missildine sits in her rocker in the shade of her porch. She is nearly ninety, and every morning early, when I pass her as I am about to jog round the park, she waves to me and calls out. 'Have a nice day!' she cries, and then she laughs and adds, 'Oh, have a nice dream, it lasts longer.'

In a pecan tree in our garden we have a resident pileated woodpecker tap-tap-tapping like something in a cartoon, flashing red, black and white stripes as it flies. I asked a colleague about the extinct ivory-beaked woodpecker, mainly because old Philosopher Mean fancied he saw one on the northwest coast of Van Diemen's Land long ago, and hence the name Woodpecker Point. There are no Australian woodpeckers at all. Impossible for him to see an ivory bill, said my colleague, but he also explained to me that although the bird is believed to be extinct, there are occasional excited sightings. Like the Tasmanian tiger I suppose. The last one of those died in sordid captivity in the Hobart zoo in 1936, yet people dedicate their lives to believing it still lives in the bush. And in fact they see it, and some scientists are also hoping to clone it from some old preserved tissue. How we long for the lost animals to return to grace us. These days the tiger exists in a TV commercial for beer. He hides in bright and unconvincing fabulous forest ferns and is finally revealed as a tame, firm, and rather wooden character, beside a large bottle of beer. He is, as a handsome graphic, the symbol for tourism in the state, and his image also adorns the council rubbish bins in some towns. Poor dead lost animal, he must now carry the weight of all the fantasies and romances of Van Diemen's Land. Once he was hunted out of existence, a bounty on his head; now he is the key to paradise, an obsession, and a tragic joke.

Virginia is enrolled as an undergraduate at Florida State, studying the Poetics of Evolution and Ecology. I have given her a Swiss watch that belonged to my grandmother, to help her to get to lectures on time. She loves this watch, linking her as it does to my ancestors and my past. She is very punctual — in fact she is strangely meticulous in all things, but is specially particular about time. She never speaks of Caleb, although when we had a celebration for my birthday, she stopped for a strange moment, a breath, a hiatus before picking up her fork to eat a piece of birthday cake, and she said, 'Yes, you were born in 1959 too. That was a very memorable year.' That was all she said.

Then she opened her mouth and popped in a mouthful of angel cake, and life continued its flow that had for that brief space been arrested. The theme of birth is very much in the air as we are expecting, at Christmas time, not one child but two, and Virginia sat serenely at my birthday table with her hands folded on her belly, a medieval madonna with a little Swiss watch glinting on her wrist. The twins are a boy and a girl. Fraternal twins are something of a tradition in Virginia's family. And already we have named them Jane (in honour of Lady Franklin who first took the stories of the Brothers Grimm to Van Diemen's Land) and Jakob (after one of the Brothers). Thus we remember our place of origin.

Golden is now a student at Godby Junior High School, looking much like any other high school student from around here, except that she still sounds different, but that will change. Her first name is not at all eccentric among her peers at Godby where there are kids called Silver and Nomad and Shadow and Hannibal and Helvetica as well as twins named Vanity and Sanity. The strange journey she has followed thus far must make it in some ways difficult to adjust to her new life, but maybe coming here, right away from everything that used to be home, is going to turn out well for her. Human beings are so fragile, and yet also so resilient. She'll be OK, but I confess I am sometimes thrown by the ice-bright blue of her eyes, and by her dazzling, captivating smile. Where have I seen those before? A chill goes through me as I recall the dark cold chamber that was the heart of Caleb Mean. At least Golden has not been brought up to believe she is God's anointed. In so many ways she seems to be my own daughter, and yet I know in my heart, as she too will always know, that the late Caleb Mean was in truth her father, and who can tell what shards and splinters of that frightening man's strange composition lie within her soul? When we stood on the top of the Bluff, the three of us, Golden faced the open sea, and she said, very loud and firm: My father is my father and my father is dead.

Virginia recently wrote a creative paper for her Poetics of Ecology tutorial, giving it the title: 'What the Hedgehog Knows'. I found it deeply interesting, but at school it received only a C+ grade. The comment on it was highly critical of her spelling and punctuation which are, to say the least, whimsical. I have a feeling that the tutor didn't actually read the story. I later corrected it myself out of interest, and I think it was pretty good.

It goes thus: 'I am the Scribe. Long long ago, once upon a time, in a far far country, on the edge of the world, at the tip of the land where the sky meets the sea and the sea meets the land and where the light of heaven meets the shadow of the inferno, there lived a man and his wife. Now this couple had been thrown up by the sea itself, born as Venus was born, floating towards each other on the wings of a great and purple storm of rhinoceros proportions, she on the platter of a cockle shell, he in the pearly chamber of a nautilus. They stood together in their nakedness on the shining tip of a rocky island, and on the foam of the swelling wave which flowed across the ocean, they saw, as they searched the horizon for the boat they hoped would rescue them, a huge and silky poppy, pink as sunset in the tropics, soft as the skin of an unborn goat. And upon the poppy lay a child, a small and perfect female child who wafted in, in, in towards them on the wave, and they forgot their hunger, and they forgot their thirst, and they waited for the child with open arms, and they gathered her up and they loved her. "For she is the child of our dismay, and we are called to love her and to nurture her and to put her before our own good. We must name her Niña." That is what they said. The man, whose name was Magnus, was a fierce and warlike Scot; the woman, who was named Minerva, was a strangely beautiful creature from Peru. Their languages, in consequence, were not compatible, and neither were their given faiths, for he was a Scots Protestant, and she was a South American Catholic with a deep strain of Inca superstition still bubbling joyously in her blood.

Why had these two with their divergent tongues and gods come together in this haunted icy place? Well, before long a ship hove into view, and the captain of the ship was amazed to see the man and the woman and the child as they stood waiting for him, naked, beneath the gleaming scarlet canopy of an oriental parasol. He fell to imagining, as the ship drew closer to the mirage upon the rocky shore, that he could discern a jewelled elephant, a banyan tree, and a dark-green glittering serpent beneath a joyful double rainbow, beneath a burning azure sky. He blinked and shaded his eyes the way such sea-captains must do, and the glow of mysterious haze fell from the scene, and the ship sailed closer, and before the afternoon sun began to glide over the rim of the mulberry horizon, the man and the woman and the child were safe in the bosom of the good ship which was called, by a coincidence, *Marvel of Peru.* And the ship delivered the little trinity from the small island to the larger island of Van Diemen's Land, where they would dwell forever more. But the people of that land were troubled in their hearts by the naked truth of the little family, by the supernatural mood of the cockle shell and the nautilus shell and the silky, milky poppy, and they glanced at the trio out of the corners of their eyes, and they whispered little stories out of the whip whip whip of the corners of their mouths, and the couple and their daughter were not so gently waved and wafted out out out to a distant corner (where, as I said, the sky meets the sea and the sea meets the land and heaven runs into hell) and there they stayed. And they built a house of bark and logs, and they called the house 'Skye' after the island where Magnus was born in the far away Hebrides. They shared a strange and deep understanding and a profound and pearly faith in a new and sea-born providence, and they discovered, as time went on, that they had been gifted with a secret new religion, had been sent from the sea to the end of the world to seed the new way to the Great Good. And by their quiet and shining example of courage, diligence and charity, they gradually gathered about themselves a community of like-minded folk who followed Magnus and Minerva as if they had been the Prophet. And the little community of Skye grew and prospered, and their faith was in the earth and in the stars and in the power of that pink and silky poppy wherein Niña had floated to her destiny. They established a large and healthy family of their own, and when the time came, Magnus handed to his eldest son, the Chosen Son, the torch of the faith of Skye, and in the fullness of time that son too died and handed on the torch. And so it went. The community developed a devotion to the winds and to the air itself, and to the simplicity of following their Chosen Sons. The star of their faith was the limitless human and divine Imagination, fed by music and by the poppy itself, until there came a time, in the fullness of all Time when all of God's species were beginning to wane, and the Chosen Son knew that the Time had come, and he, who was known as the Hedgehog, saw that the faithful should fall into a final slumber, and should return by fire to the stars. When this was done he handed on the Knowledge to the Scribe, that the story might be told. I am the Scribe.'

So there it is. I thought it was quite revealing, in its naive way.

In the evenings I am reading the old *Mabinogion* with Golden, as if I were after all perhaps her father, or her uncle, or her friend. I am in fact none of these; I am her mother's husband, the father of her unborn half-brother and half-sister, and I can sense in the air between us, something knowing and resigned, some fine reserve that will perhaps exist forever between this child and myself. She reads some of the book aloud, I read some.

'A most strange creature will come from the sea marsh, as a punishment for iniquity, and his hair and his teeth and his eyes shall be as gold. . . '

We are fascinated by the idea of his gold teeth and are swept along gleefully by the narratives. We have completed *The White*

Book and are about a third of the way through *The Red Book*. Golden says she plans to write her own *Black Book* as part of her English Study Assessment. That will be an interesting thing to see, but so far she has been very secretive about it. She says she is going to set it in Florida State Prison, and is making some connection between 'Mabinogion' and 'Mabo', the word 'mab' signifying both 'son' and 'story' in Old Welsh. I taught her to make Aunt Edda's gingerbread men, and she took them to school where they were highly acclaimed. She says, in this post-millennium, late post-modern age, that she is going to incorporate the gingerbread men into her assignment. Run, run as fast as you can.

I became interested in Florida State Prison myself in the late eighties, when Ted Bundy was on death row. The issue of capital punishment has always been one of my most passionate interests, its meaning and purpose. In Australia we don't have the death penalty any more, which probably accounts for Caleb and Dee Dee and others being at places like Black River for life. The last execution in Australia took place on the day when a woman named Victoria Field was murdered in the grounds of Sophie Goddard's father's Mandala Clinic — more than an irony, I think, more like a message signifying the pointlessness of the punishments human beings can devise. I followed Ted Bundy's progress towards his execution in 1989, and I kept in touch with James Dobson who was the last person to interview him. I am only being fanciful when I say that I can sense the spirit of Ted Bundy in the place where I now work. But as I have already made clear, I do believe in ghosts. I can't explain them and I have not made a study of them, but yes, I do believe in them. I confess to a frisson of excitement when August, the man next-door, told me that Bundy is believed to have spent a week hiding out in his house. Sometimes as I sit on August's porch I fancy I can feel Ted behind me in the empty study, or above me in the attic, looking down in his cool, handsome way.

To reach the prison I drive through pines and live oaks, past the old farms and cattle pastures of North Florida until I come to the iron sign that arches above me like a wingless insect: 'Florida State Prison'. I get my first glimpse of the pale-green buildings that stretch, an excrescence across the landscape. The guards in brown, the prisoners in blue. If I mentally compare this place with the tiny frosted castle of Black River, where there is such a small population, and where prisoners like Caleb and Dee Dee are stamped 'never to be released', where there is no chance of state-assisted death, I see them simply as two extreme faces of the same problem. The problem of where to put the people who offend against society's sense of the good, and what to do with them when you have put them there. Obviously, in the case of Caleb the solution to the question was very faulty. But the Bundy solution served no real purpose either, as far as I can see. The Black River experiment is not the answer — I suppose there is no answer. The question defeats me, anyhow. Thor Gulbransen applied his vivid imagination to the question of how to house the criminally insane, but maybe the pale-green multiplying boxes of Florida State are just as good, just as bad, as Black River anyway. Just as good, just as bad. Maybe there is something terribly wrong with the luxury — for staff as well as prisoners — at Black River. In hindsight, for one thing, imagine giving Caleb access to the rowing machine.

Another mistake — and we make these mistakes over and over again in our work — was to deny Dee Dee his ration of tobacco and at the same time to give him access to the linocutting tools in the craft hall. It was part of a Health Department directive to save money on nicotine patches. Dee Dee was a heavy smoker suffering from withdrawal when he went berserk with two knives and before he could be stopped he had stabbed not only the man across the table, but also Dr Sophie Goddard. The other prisoner lost an eye but he recovered; Sophie Goddard died.

In my opinion Dee Dee had developed a violent hatred for Sophie, blaming her for the loss of his companion, Caleb. The withdrawal of the tobacco ration was the last straw, I imagine.

There will be an inquiry, the same intense deliberations that occurred after Caleb's escape, Dee Dee will get his tobacco, his linocuts will be worth a fortune and will probably be collected and published in a handsome coffee-table volume for Christmas. The value of the Venus on my office wall has risen considerably.

I have, in fact, made a decision to move out of prison work and to set up somewhere, who knows where, in private practice. And I need to write poetry again. The muse is upon me, she speaks to me from the inky waters of the Florida swamps, from the sweet sharp perfumes of the citrus groves, from the mysterious ecstasy of the rocket launch, from the eerie slow finality of the death penalty, from the starving reality of drought and flood, from the loom of war, the bursting star shapes of disease. There are people who suggest that Caleb and all the other modern prophets such as Jim Jones and the guy at Heaven's Gate might have had an inkling of the right idea, that the end of the world perhaps is nigh. I don't know — we are just enjoying life in Florida, and heaven seems very far away. We took Golden down to Orlando one weekend — you couldn't bring a child to Florida and not go to Disney World. It was incredibly clean, smelling of a disinfectant that reminded me of the facility at Black River. That place seems now to be light years away — far off in time and space. And I think with horror about what happened to Sophie; I wonder about mad Scandinavian Thor Gulbransen who died quite pointlessly in the hotel fire and who never got to hear about what Caleb did, what Dee Dee did. I suppose just about everybody in the world read some version or other of 'GIANT SQUID TAKES HOLOCAUST PREACHER', and perhaps many people also read about what came to be called the 'OCCUPATIONAL THERAPY MURDER'.

I sit here on the porch, the sky above me lit with a faint glow of indigo, and make notes and nod to my neighbours, calling out a greeting now and then. And it seems I can't escape Scandinavians, for August, the man in the house next-door, is from Sweden and he is so homesick he is trying to plant a whole Scandinavian rock garden, but this is not working, and the place is reverting to a Florida jungle complete with tiny deadly coral snakes. August comes over sometimes and we discuss the gardening problems over a drink. We are both strangers in a strange land, and so we have mint juleps in an attempt to follow the local customs. He smokes Ritmeester cigars, and I am getting quite a taste for these. It could be that my old homeland is calling to me, August says in his rather ponderous way. He imagines he might find prehistoric remains in the garden, and he tells me about the huge skeleton some French palaeontologists are putting together in a remote place in Pakistan. It went extinct, August says, over twenty million years ago. I said if he digs in the right place perhaps he will find a little memento left behind by Ted Bundy, but August didn't laugh when I said that.

Most of the gardening around our house is done by Golden, and she is very keen to grow the native plants that flourish here, as well as the traditional flowers that are dear to her heart. She says she hopes to grow the tallest sunflower in the world — the tallest one so far being, apparently, seven metres high. One day when she was digging in the earth at the back of the house, planting her arsenic green envy zinnias, and her tulips and pussycat pansies and sunflowers and marigolds and dahlias, she uncovered shards of old pottery and a little wooden statue. It was Spanish, El Niño in his hat with the cockle shells, probably a relic from the missionaries of the sixteenth century. His paint had almost disappeared, his face was pitted, and his little childish arm, which should have been raised in blessing, was broken off at the shoulder. Father Fox once told me that it was in Tallahassee in 1539 that the priests said the first Navidad mass ever to be celebrated in North America.

I held the sad and ancient object in my hands, and I sensed a power and a force within it, and I found myself very moved by it. I felt I was going to weep.

'What's the matter?' Golden said.

'I don't know,' I said. 'It just seems really strange and sad — it's so old, so full of messages and meanings.'

'What is it though — is it El Niño?'

'Yes,' I said, 'it's a very old statue of El Niño.'

'Oh, isn't it weird,' Golden said in a voice that was gathering a Florida lilt, 'how things like that can just lie there underneath the earth for so long, and then suddenly come to the surface.'

'Yes,' I said, 'that is weird, but the past can throw out very long shadows.'

'I suppose one day everything under the earth and everything under the sea will probably come up to the surface.'

'Not everything,' I said.

'Yes. Everything.'

And she went on digging, searching for the arm, which she did not find.

'That will be the end of the world,' she said, smiling at me.

'Yes,' I said, 'the end of the world.'

Epilogue

'People have found that as the climate shifts over time the distribution of butterfly populations changes as well. They are, in a sense, the litmus test of the environment.'

DUNCAN MACKAY, Flinders University

All is but fortune.

As for everything else, why, only time will tell.

India has won the toss and has sent Australia in to bat.

The Claudina has been declared extinct.

Time and Tide

The material in 'Time and Tide' is presented in linear chronological and alphabetical sequences for the convenience of readers. The meanings embedded in 'Time and Tide' are in fact non-linear, and they intersect and interact in many diverse patterns and manners with the material of the narrative of *Cape Grimm.* 'Time and Tide' is a tuning fork that hums and riffles back into the narrative. Readers are invited to strike it and listen to the sounds.

Paul Van Loon
Florida

Time

'The sands of time are just around the corner.
The winds of change are swiftly running out.'
CARRILLO MEAN, *The Mining of Meaning*

TIME

BC 1500	Introduction of the iris from Syria to Egypt.
BC 710–676	Lifetime of the Greek poet Archilochus, who invented iambic verse and to whom is attributed the saying: 'The fox knows many things but the hedgehog knows one great thing.'
AD 784	Death of the Irish Saint Virgil (Ferghil), an astronomer monk who taught the existence of the Antipodes, which was also the Fairy World of Irish folklore.
1170	Birth of Fibonacci (Leonardo of Pisa).
1182	Birth of Saint Francis of Assisi.
1202	Publication of Fibonacci's *Liber abaci* which brought the Hindu-Arabic system of numerals to Western culture.

1404, 1421 AND 1424	The Saint Elisabeth floods which inundated and devastated vast areas of the Southern Netherlands.
1440	Invention of moveable type by Johannes Gutenberg.
1485	Painting of *The Birth of Venus* by Sandro Botticelli (1445–1510).
1525	Death of Thomas Münzer in the massacre of the faithful in Frankenhausen.
1531	Onset of El Niño in Peru.
1531	Franciso Pizarro began his conquest of Peru.
1539	First Christmas Mass in North America (at Tallahassee).
1642	Discovery of Van Diemen's Land by Abel Janszoon Tasman.
1705	Publication of *Metamorphosis insectorum Surinamensium* by Maria Sybilla Merian.
1719	Publication of *Robinson Crusoe* by Daniel Defoe.
1726	Publication of *Gulliver's Travels* by Jonathan Swift.
1766	Publication of *The Aurelian* by Moses Harris.
1776	Birth of E.T.A. Hoffmann.
1785	Birth of Jakob Grimm.
1786	Birth of Wilhelm Grimm.
1796	Zinnia seeds introduced from Mexico.
1798	Discovery of Bass Strait by Matthew Flinders and George Bass.
1801	First visit of John Franklin to Australia, travelling with his uncle by marriage, Matthew Flinders.
1803	Arrival of first convicts and soldiers at Risdon Cove in Van Diemen's Land.
1805	Francis Beaufort devised the Beaufort Wind Force Scale.
1812	First publication of folk tales by Jakob and Wilhelm Grimm.

1821	Introduction of European honeybee to Van Diemen's Land.
1823	Publication of the first English translation of the Grimm Brothers' *German Popular Stories*, translator Edgar Taylor.
1824	Sir George Arthur became Governor of Van Diemen's Land (until 1836).
1828	English dogs (greyhounds, pointers, setters) and birds (thrushes, goldfinches, blackbirds, yellowhammers and bullfinches) imported to Van Diemen's Land by Captain Langdon on the *Wanstead.*
1836	Sir John Franklin became Lieutenant-Governor of Van Diemen's Land.
1837	Death of Mannaginna.
1841	Jane Franklin established a 'Ladies' Society for the Reformation of Female Prisoners' in Hobart Town.
1844	Charles Sturt's expedition, carrying a boat to the centre of Australia in search of inland water, discovered only a dry ocean of deep red sand whose ridges undulate like waves.
1845	Meeting of Jakob and Wilhelm Grimm with Hans Christian Andersen in Berlin.
1846	Publication of *The Mabinogion*, translated by Charlotte Guest.
1847	Death of Sir John Franklin in the Arctic.
1847	Establishment of Launceston Horticultural Society with an exhibition.
1847	Establishment of Aboriginal settlement at Oyster Cove.
1848	The young Fox sisters, Mary and Kate, first hear the ghostly rappings in their house in Hydesville, New York.

1850	The first thylacine exported from Van Diemen's Land to Regent's Park Zoo, London.
1850	Letter from Jakob Grimm to Jane Franklin.
1850	Invention of the perambulator.
1851	Final visit of George Augustus Robinson to Oyster Cove where only thirty Aborigines had survived.
1851	Wreck of the *Iris* off Puddingstone Island in Bass Strait.
1851	Discovery on Beechy Island by Captain Erasmus Ommaney of three graves and scattered relics of the Arctic expedition of Sir John Franklin.
1851	6 February: Black Thursday — fire in Port Phillip.
1851	Publication of *London Labour and the London Poor* by Henry Mayhew.
1851	First discovery of gold in Victoria.
1851	Opening of the Great Exhibition at the Crystal Palace in London's Hyde Park. From 8 August to 11 October copies of a weather map were produced and distributed (for a penny a copy) by Electric Telegraph Company. The map was based on weather observations telegraphed to the Exhibition's printing press. This was the first time a weather map was available on the same day as the weather described. Samples of knitted woollen gloves, stockings, socks and shawls made by the children at the Queen's Orphanage in Hobart Town were sent to the Great Exhibition.
1851	Death of Mary Shelley, author of *Frankenstein*.
1851	El Niño event.
1852	Marriage of Minerva and Magnus Mean.

1852	Death of Ada Byron King (born 1815), daughter of Lord Byron. She was a mathematician. During her last illness Charles Dickens visited her and read to her extracts from *Dombey and Son*, which was the first of his novels adapted for public reading.
1852	First discovery of gold in Van Diemen's Land, at Fingal.
1853	End of convict transportation to Van Diemen's Land.
1853	Invention of the hypodermic syringe.
1854	Cyrus Field began to lay the transatlantic telegraph cable linking America and Europe. In 1858 he invited Queen Victoria to send the first message to President Buchanan, but three months after that the cable broke. The project was completed successfully in 1866.
1856	Name of Van Diemen's Land changed to 'Tasmania'.
1856	Exhibition of *A Primrose from England* painted by Edward Hopley (1816–1869).
1856	Seeking a cure for malaria, William Perkin discovered synthetic dyes made from coal tar. He patented the dye for the colour mauve.
1857	The little yacht *Fox* was bought by Jane Franklin and sent, under the command of Francis McClintock, to seek her husband John in the Arctic. Captain McClintock discovered at Point Victoria the written record of the fate of John Franklin and his men, as well as such relics as five watches, books, a Bible, spoons, forks and the Franklin crest.
1859	Publication of *Origin of Species* by Charles Darwin.

1860	Prince of Wales introduces the American grey squirrel to England.
1867	Alaska sold by Russia to the United States of America.
1868	The first time an Australian cricket team travelled to England to play. This was an Aboriginal team from the Western District of Victoria.
1870	Death of Charles Dickens.
1871	Walter Douglas, an itinerant preacher, imprisoned at Circular Head for causing a disturbance by singing hymns in the street.
1871	Discovery of tin at Mount Bischoff by Philosopher Smith.
C.1872	Birth of George Ivanovitch Gurdjieff (d. 1949).
1874	Floods at Oyster Cove.
1876	Death of Trucanini.
1886	Colonial and Indian Exhibition in London to celebrate Golden Jubilee of Queen Victoria. Niña Mean sent a collection of Tasmanian butterflies as a contribution to the display.
1892	Publication in *Boletines del Sociedad Geografico Lima* of the 'Disertation sobre las Corrientes Oceanicas y Estudios de la Corriente Peruana de Humboldt' by Peruvian navy captain Camilo Carrillo. In this dissertation, which was first delivered at a Geographical Society meeting in Lima, Camilo Carrillo said: 'Peruvian sailors from the port of Paita in northern Peru, who frequently navigate along the coast in small craft, either to the north or to the south of Paita, named this current "El Niño" without doubt because it is most noticeable and felt after the feast of the Holy Child.'

1898	First marketing of heroin (by Bayer) as a cough remedy.
1900	Birth of Minnie Mean (grandmother of Caleb).
1913	Publication of *The Fall of the Dutch Republic* by Hendrik Van Loon.
1937	Death of last Tasmanian Tiger.
1949	Death of Maurice Maeterlinck.
1959	Birth of Caleb Mean.
1959	Birth of Paul Van Loon.
1967	Hanging of Ronald Ryan, the last man to be executed by the state in Australia.
1967	Murder of Victoria Field at Mandala Clinic, Melbourne.
1975	Birth of Virginia Mean.
1977	Scattering of ashes of Trucanini at Oyster Cove.
1978	Deaths at Jonestown, Guyana, of the People's Temple Cult.
1985	Marriage of Paul Van Loon and Paloma García.
1989	Execution of serial killer Ted Bundy.
1990	Birth of Golden Mean.
1992	Mabo decision on Native Title in High Court of Australia.
1992	Centenary of the publication in Lima of Camilo Carrillo's first official naming of El Niño.
1992	Deaths of one hundred and forty-seven people in the fire at the Meeting Hall in Skye.
1997	Deaths of members of Heaven's Gate sect near San Diego.
2001	Election of George W. Bush to presidency of USA.
2001	Death of Caleb Mean.

Tide

A

ALCYONE AND CEYX

Alcyone was the daughter of the King of the Winds. She was the wife of Ceyx, whose father was Lucifer after whom was named the star that heralds the day, the light-bringer, the morning star. Lucifer, the fallen angel. And Ceyx was the king of Thessaly, in Ancient Greece. Alcyone, fair of skin and with eyes as soft as moonstones, and Ceyx, high-browed and powerful, were devoted to each other. Yet there came a time when it was necessary for Ceyx to journey far across the seas to consult a mysterious distant oracle. Because Alcyone had grown up in the palace of the King of the Winds she knew the dangers that might be encountered by men who sail in ships at sea: the pirates, the storms, the shipwrecks, the sirens and the mermaids, the wars and the forgetfulness. The dreams. And she was very troubled at the thought of Ceyx, her husband, lover and friend, adrift atop the dark blue waves, at the mercy of wind and wave and all the fearful monsters of the deep. On the night when Ceyx put to sea a great black and jasper storm did in fact break, and the shining ship was thrown upon the mounting waters, flying through the wild air, and then sinking down into the lightless depths. All the men on board were drowned.

And as the cruel dark waters closed for the final time over Ceyx, the last word upon his noble lips was the sweetest word he knew: 'Alcyone'.

Time passed, and Alcyone waited patiently for word of the expedition and for the return of her dear husband. She prayed to Hera to safeguard Ceyx. Now the goddess knew that Ceyx was already drowned, that already he lay at the bottom of the ocean, that his flesh had fed monsters large and small, and that his bones were but the architecture for a fleet of colourless fish whose fins and tails fanned lazily across the brow and through the jaw and in and out the ribs of the man so beloved by fair Alcyone. Hera was touched by Alcyone's prayers for a man already dead, and so she sent the widow a dream that she might know the truth.

In this dream Morpheus, son of the god of sleep, assumed the shape of Alcyone's beloved Ceyx, and he spoke to Alcyone saying, 'Dearest Alcyone, look, your husband is here. I am here.' And Alcyone's soft eyes glistened with tears of joy. But then she heard the dream-vision say: 'I am dead. I am your dead husband Ceyx. Is my face changed in death? I beg you to give me your tears, that I may not go down into the shadowy underworld unwept.' Alcyone stretched out to touch her husband and cried aloud, begging him to wait for her that she might go with him, and her own voice awakened her from sleep, and she knew that Ceyx was dead.

In the morning, when the sun rose and the sky was streaked with salmon and pearl, Alcyone ran to the seashore. As she stared out over the still and gleaming water she saw in the shining distance an object floating towards her. As it got closer she saw it was a body, and she knew in her heart that it was Ceyx, and before long she knew for certain that it was the body of her husband. She ran through the surf, splashing in the waves, and suddenly, as the gods looked on, she was flying, flying on winged feet over the water to her husband. The gods took pity on Alcyone and Ceyx, and they rewarded their love and constancy and changed them into two sorrowing birds of the sea. He was a kingfisher and she was a gannet.

Every winter there are seven whole days when the sea is perfectly calm, and these are the days when Alcyone, the gannet, broods over her nest floating on the sea, and when Ceyx, the kingfisher, accompanies her. These days of perfect peace are named after her, Alcyone. They are the halcyon days.

ALEUTIAN ISLANDS

The home of the Aleuts since 2000 BC, and the northern destination of the Bass Strait moonbirds. The Aleutian Islands are part of Alaska, which was bought by the United States from Russia in 1867. They are a chaplet of small islands separating the Bering Sea from the Pacific Ocean, and they form an arc-like segment of the chain of volcanoes called the Ring of Fire. Some of the volcanoes are active. There are fourteen larger islands and fifty-five smaller ones, as well as many fragments and islets. The principal groups are the Near Islands, the Rat Islands, the Fox Islands, the Islands of Four Mountains and the Andreanof Islands. The shores are wild and rocky and dangerous to ships, with the land rising abruptly from the shore to grim, steep, forbidding mountains. There is a persistent fog in the Aleutians, and there are few trees, but the islands are brilliant with green grasses, moody with sedge and, in the summer, ablaze with wildflowers such as pink and blue lupins, yellow saxifrage, delicate miniature orchids and chocolate lilies. The fauna includes the arctic blue fox, sea lions, whales, reindeer, fur seals, an abundance of fish and hundreds of species of birds; for the music of their names, there's the red-faced cormorant, the red-legged kittiwake, the crested auklet, not forgetting the restless, roaming moonbird, the aerial wanderer that linked the indigenous peoples of Van Diemen's Land with the people of the Aleutian Islands, who wove fine grass baskets not unlike those of the Tasmanians. It was the Northwest Passage between the Fish River and the Bering Strait that John Franklin was seeking when his ships became trapped in ice, the whole expedition dying from starvation, exposure and lead poisoning.

ANGEL CAKE

THE SONG

When you're gazing out the window
And you're feeling kinda blue
And you're standing in the kitchen
And you don't know what to do
You get no joy from cups of tea
The missing thing's a recipe
So you can have your angel cake
And eat it too.

Everybody's got to have
Those dry ingredients
The secret is to sift eleven times
You've got to sift through little bits
Of nitty-gritty grit
Sifting through the grit of life
Will help you quite a bit.

You can be a drifter
Or choose to be a sifter
For happiness will come swifter
If you sift.

You've got to pinch the salt
And beat the egg whites till they're stiff
The key is to be gentle but be firm
You've got to get a balance

Between discipline and lovin'
From the mixing of the batter
To the heating of the oven.

If you put it in and bake it
You'll be sure to make it
Every body needs an angel
Everybody needs an angel
Everybody needs an angel cake.

RECIPE

INGREDIENTS

4 oz plain flour
1 teaspoon cream of tartar
10 oz castor sugar
11 egg whites
1 teaspoon pure vanilla essence
good pinch of salt

METHOD

(The dry ingredients will be sifted eleven times.)
Sift the flour four times.
Add cream of tartar and sift.
Sift sugar four times.
Combine dry ingredients and sift twice.
Beat egg whites until stiff.
Using the sifter, gently add the dry ingredients to the whites while the whites are still beating.
Add vanilla and salt to the mixture.
Flour but do not grease the cake tin.
Bake in a moderate oven for 40 minutes.
Leave cake in the tin until it is cold, then turn it out and ice it completely with rough white vanilla frosting.

The cake should not be cut with a knife, but gently pulled apart with two forks placed back to back, as the wings of an angel.

ARCHILOCHUS (710–676 BC)

Greek poet best known for his statement: 'The fox knows many things but the hedgehog knows one great thing.'

B

BEAUFORT WIND FORCE SCALE

This is a system for estimating the strength of the wind without the use of instruments. In 1805 Admiral Sir Francis Beaufort of the British navy detailed the Scale to describe the effects of different wind strengths on a fully-rigged man-of-war. The Scale was later broadened to include descriptions of the effects of the winds on land features as well, to obtain a more unified evaluation of the weather.

The Scale is divided into values from 0 to 12, 0 being the strength of calm and 12 being the strength of a hurricane. Each force is accompanied by wind speeds in miles per hour and in knots, and by descriptions of the effects of the wind on the sea and on things such as smoke and trees. Where the wind speed is between 25 and 31 miles per hour, or between 22 and 27 knots, the waves will be large, between 8 and 13 feet high, and there will be many whitecaps and much spray. The large branches of trees will be seen to be in motion, and there will be heard whistling along the telegraph wires. This is a 'strong breeze', and the number on the Scale is 6.

BEE

Hobart Town Gazette, 7 April, 1821: A hive of bees in the best possible state of health and condition has been brought by the ship *Mary* from Liverpool and has been presented by Mr Kermode, owner of that vessel, to the Lieutenant-Governor. The bee has not before been imported into Van Diemen's Land.

BERNARDIN DE SAINT-PIERRE, JACQUES-HENRI (1737–1814)

A French naturalist and author, and a friend of Rousseau, by whom he was strongly influenced. His chief work was his *Etudes de la Nature*, in which he sought to prove the existence of God through the study of the wonders of nature. A section of this work was the sentimental prose idyll, 'Paul et Virginie', which was very popular in its time and had a strong influence on the French Romantic poets.

BLUE BIRD

The play, *The Blue Bird*, was written by Maurice Maeterlinck in 1908.

'It is not in the actions but in the words that are found the beauty and greatness of tragedies that are truly beautiful and great; and this not solely in the words that accompany and explain the action, for there must perforce be another dialogue besides the one which is superficially necessary. And indeed the only words that count in the play are those that at first seemed useless, for it is therein that the essence lies. Side by side with the necessary dialogue will you almost always find another dialogue that seems superfluous; but examine it carefully, and it will be borne home to you that this is the only one that the soul can listen to profoundly, for here alone is it the soul that is being addressed.' (From 'The Tragical in Daily Life' by Maurice Maeterlinck in *The Treasure of the Humble*, 1916.)

BUNDY, TED

Born 1946 to Eleanor Louise Cowell in the Elizabeth Lund Home for Unwed Mothers in Burlington, Vermont. He confessed to the murders of twenty-eight women in twelve states of the USA, although it is believed he killed many more than that. After escaping from custody he lived for three months on the run in Tallahassee, Florida, and was executed in the Florida State Prison on 24 January 1989.

C

CALEB

The name means 'dog' in Hebrew. In the Old Testament this was the name of one of the twelve spies sent by Moses into Israel. Of the Israelites who left Egypt with Moses, Caleb and Joshua were the only ones who lived to see the promised land.

CALENDULA FISH SOUP

RECIPE

INGREDIENTS

4 heads of snapper
2 onions
teaspoon olive oil
milk
plain flour
2 tablespoons sweet sherry
salt
thyme, bay leaf, garlic, black pepper, marjoram, nutmeg
petals of calendula (fresh or dry)

METHOD

Cook the chopped garlic and onion in oil until transparent. Add heads of snapper, salt, herbs and cover with water.
Poach slowly until fish flesh falls from bones.
Put flesh aside.
Strain liquid and add sherry to make fish stock.
Make a white sauce from the milk and flour.
Gradually add the fish stock to this while the sauce is hot.
Stir in fish meat.
Season to taste with salt and pepper.
Add a handful of calendula petals and a sprinkle of nutmeg to each serving bowl.

CARRILLO, CAMILO (1839–1901)

Uncle of Minerva Mean. He was a Peruvian sea captain who, using information he obtained from fishermen about the apparent relationship between warm currents and the dramatic fluctuations in the seasonal size of the catch, publicised the name 'El Niño counter-current'. Warm waters appear off the coast of Peru around Christmas time, temporarily replacing the cold waters which provide the nutrients for the fish upon which the fishing industry depends. At roughly seven-year intervals the warm current lingers on well into the new year, and the result is disastrous for the fishermen. Carrillo wrote his paper on the subject in 1892, and the name 'El Niño' is now widely applied to the dramatic and disastrous cyclical climate changes and associated events that include tornadoes, droughts, famines, floods.

CHRISTMAS ISLAND

This remote limestone atoll is part of the Commonwealth of Australia. It lies 300 kilometres southwest of Java in the Indian Ocean, and was one of the last of the large tropical islands to be settled by humans, an event which occurred in 1886 when phosphate mines were established there. With the humans came the black rat, and with the rat a disease that attacked the local Bulldog and MaClear's rats, both of which are recorded as being extinct by 1903. It is probable that the native rats kept in check the red crabs, which since the beginning of the twentieth century have multiplied to such an extent that they are now one of the most precious species on the island because they attract tourists. The red crabs are in turn being threatened by the crazy ant. Christmas Island is the location of the Australian Federal Government's detention centre for people seeking political asylum in Australia, and was the destination of the boat known as the SIEV-X, which sank in the waters off the island.

CLAUDINA

The Claudina butterfly (*Agrias Claudina*) depends for food on the wild relations of the coca plant. It is close to becoming an endangered species and the Sunshine Project aims to ensure that it does not become extinct (www. sunshine-project.org). The US project of war on narcotics plans to test and apply a microbal fungus to attack all plants (wild and cultivated) that produce coca, opium and marijuana. Consequently the Claudina is likely to become extinct.

D

DREAMING

Sophie Goddard's doctoral thesis, *A Glimpse Within the Labyrinth — a neurobiological and psychobiological study of the dreaming and the dreamless brain*, published in California in 1990, is a ground-breaking work in the ongoing research into the nature and importance of dreams. It follows on from the 1950s' work in Rome of Dr Santo de Santis, whose research suggested that the more hardened a criminal was, the less likely he or she was to dream. De Santis proposed that this lack of dream life was caused by a general anaesthesia of sensibility in the conscious life. Goddard's thesis naturally takes account of the advances in technology and research over the intervening period, but does not make reference to the 1968 monograph of Carrillo Mean, *Platypus-Hedgehog Dreaming*, in which Mean, in his examination of the unconscious of the monotreme, foreshadows some of Goddard's material. The ant-eating echidna has been one of Goddard's key areas of interest. In the late 1980s she worked on a performance piece with the Tasmanian company, Tasdance, called *When Echidnas Dream*.

E

ECHIDNAS

Related to the platypus, Tasmanian echidnas or spiny anteaters are small egg-laying mammals whose backs are covered in honey-coloured or red-black spines, resembling a hedgehog. They are part of a wider Mammal group which is found throughout Australia and New Guinea. They are nocturnal, although they are sometimes seen foraging in daylight. They are shy and slow-moving, sheltering in hollow logs or burrows. When they are disturbed or frightened they dig rapidly with powerful claws and disappear into the earth. They are good swimmers, will amble across the beach to swim and groom in the sea, and are infested with the world's largest flea. They feed on insects caught by the long and rapidly-moving tongue which is covered with sticky mucus. They are prey for the Tasmanian devil. (See entry on Monotremes.)

EL NIÑO

El Niño is a global climatic perturbation first recognised in Peru, publicly named by Camilo Carrillo in 1898, and now known to affect weather and to alter climate throughout the world.

El Niño is the Spanish name for the holy child Jesus. One of the most popular invocations of El Niño in the Spanish-speaking world takes the image of the child as pilgrim. It is known as the Prayer to El Niño of Atocha, and is addressed to the Blessed Virgin, asking for her intercession with her son. A faded and framed copy of this prayer, with a nineteenth-century English translation, was one of the Mean family's treasured possessions, along with the memorabilia regarding Camilo Carrillo.

'Purísima Madre del Santo Niño de Atocha, amorosísima Esposa del Espíritu Santo, abogada de los pecadores y bondadosa Madre mía, espero de tu amor y generosidad que intercederás poi mi con tu

Hijo para que me conceda lo que tanto deseo. Ruégale que venga en mi amparo y que me asista con su santísimo poder, porque Él es quien todo lo puede y de Él depende toda mi felicidad. Amén.'

'O most pure Mother of the Holy Infant of Atocha, most loving Spouse of the Holy Spirit, bountiful Mother, advocate for sinners, in your love and abundance I trust, that you may intercede for me with your Son, that He grant my heart's desire. Beseech him that he come to my aid with His most holy power, and that he watch over me, for it is He in whom all things are possible, and on Him rests all my happiness. Amen.' (Translated by Alonzo Crucero, SJ, in *Dedicaciones*, Lima, 1852.)

ELISABETH

Saint Elisabeth of Hungary (1207–31) was the wife of Louis IV of Hungary and was known for her humility, compassion and good works. In 1227 Louis died of plague while away on a Crusade and his brother drove Elisabeth from the court. She became a Franciscan tertiary and built a hospital for the poor near her house in Marburg, Hesse. She lived by an austere regime, serving the poor by spinning, weaving, fishing. A story is told of her being stopped by her brother-in-law as she was carrying bread to the poor. When asked to reveal what she was carrying under her cloak, she opened the cloak to reveal a basket of roses. Her feast day is 17 (formerly 19) November. The floods in Holland in the early fifteenth century are named for her as they occurred three times on her name day.

F

FIBONACCI (1170–1250)

The pen name of Leonardo of Pisa, the author of *Liber Abaci*, which introduced Arabic numbers into Western culture. He was the first person to record the numbers that generate the golden proportion (section or mean), which centuries earlier Plato described as being the key to the physics of the cosmos. Fibonacci was a contemporary of Francis of Assisi.

www.mcs.surrey.ac.uk/Personal/R.Knott/
www.vashti.net/mceine/golden.htm/

FIELD, CYRUS (1815–1896)

A wealthy New York businessman, with interests mainly in the paper industry. In 1854 he developed a plan to lay a telegraph cable from America to Newfoundland. Then he established another cable between America and Europe. In 1858 he invited Queen Victoria to send the first cable, a message to the American President, James Buchanan. Cyrus Field was the great-great-uncle of Victoria Field, who died in Melbourne, Australia in 1967. Victoria Field was murdered in the grounds of the Mandala Clinic for the Mentally Ill by one of the inmates. Dr Ambrose Goddard, father of Dr Sophie Goddard, was the director of Mandala (see entry below).

FINGAL

Site of the first discovery of gold in Van Diemen's Land, in February 1852.

FOX

Mary and Kate Fox, having moved to a new home in Hydesville, New York, in 1848, heard rapping noises in the house. They discovered that if they clapped their hands in a rapping code they devised, they could ask questions and elicit responses from the spirits. In this way they discovered that the rapper was a peddler who had been murdered and then buried under the house. A skeleton and a peddler's tin were later uncovered beneath the cellar. Mary and Kate, accompanied by another sister, went on to conduct seances that set the fashion for mediums throughout the

United States and Europe for many years. Their uncle Silas Fox emigrated to Van Diemen's Land, taking up land at Lower Snug, where he became active in the humane treatment of local indigenous people, and where he set up a series of inconclusive seances in an attempt to clarify events that had occurred at Risdon Cove in 1804. One of his descendants, Father Benedict Fox, became a Jesuit.

FRANKLIN, JANE, NÉE GRIFFIN (1791–1875)

The energetic daughter of a silk-weaver, she accompanied her father on journeys to Russia, Scandinavia and Spain, writing descriptions of her travels in her journals. She married John Franklin in 1828 and, with his niece Sophia Cracroft as companion, she continued to travel, joining her husband on board the *Rainbow* in the Mediterranean whenever possible. She was very active in the cultural, social, educational and political life of Van Diemen's Land, where Sir John was Governor from 1837–43. She organised a campaign to rid the island of its many deadly snakes, and was generally a patron of the arts and sciences, as well as a determined social reformer, setting up the 'Ladies' Society for the Reformation of Female Prisoners' in 1841. In the bush outside Hobart Town she built a small museum, Ancanthe, in the style of a Greek temple. She adopted and then abandoned an indigenous child, Mathinna, who later died most tragically at the age of twenty-one. During Sir John's arctic expedition of 1854 Jane travelled with Sophia in America and the West Indies. Between 1850 and 1857 she organised five search expeditions to look for Sir John, seeking the assistance of Napoleon, the President of the United States and Lord Palmerston. Sir John had died on the ice in 1847, and this was established by the 1857 expedition led by Francis McClintock in the yacht *Fox*. McClintock clarified the fact that John Franklin had discovered the Northwest Passage. In recognition of her contribution to Arctic research Jane was the first woman ever to be honoured with the Royal Geographic Society's Gold Medal, in 1860. Jane Franklin died in 1875.

FRANKLIN, JOHN (1786–1847)

Born in Lincolnshire, England. He was in charge of signals at the Battle of Trafalgar, commanded the ship *Rainbow* in the Mediterranean, and in 1801 assisted in the mapping of the coastline of the Great South Land with his uncle, Matthew Flinders. He was a Fellow of the Royal Society, and was knighted in 1829. From 1836–43 John Franklin was the Lieutenant-Governor of Van Diemen's Land. He had always dreamed of proving the existence of the Northwest Passage, a water route from the Atlantic Ocean to the Pacific Ocean through Canada. After two previous attempts to find the Northwest Passage, in 1845 he sailed from England with an expedition of one hundred and twenty-eight men to Canada once again. His ships, the *Terror* and the *Erebus*, became trapped in ice, and the men, desperate, freezing and suffering from the poisonous effects of the lead in their food containers, resorted to eating the dead bodies of their companions. In 1848 the first expedition to look for them set out, but it was not until 1857 that any trace of them was found, when Franklin's wife, Jane, sent the little yacht *Fox* to look for evidence. It was then established that John Franklin had died in 1847.

G

GINGERBREAD

RECIPE

INGREDIENTS

3 cups plain flour

3/4 cup sugar

4 teaspoons ground ginger

1 teaspoon allspice

1 teaspoon ground cinnamon
pinch of salt
1 cup milk
125 grams butter
3 teaspoons bicarbonate of soda
1 cup treacle
2 eggs

METHOD

Mix flour, sugar, spices and salt.
Heat milk and dissolve butter and soda in it.
Add treacle and well-beaten eggs.
Stir this mixture into the dry ingredients.
Mix well.
Bake in a lined and greased tin for 45 minutes in a moderate oven.

GODDARD, AMBROSE (1934–1974)

Psychiatrist, founder of the Mandala Clinic for the Mentally Ill in Melbourne, Australia, and advocate of the controversial Deep Sleep Therapy. Died by his own hand in 1974.

GODDARD, SOPHIE (1960–2002)

Psychiatrist, daughter of Ambrose (see above), who was murdered by one of the inmates of the Black River Psychiatric Detention Facility while in the performance of her duties.

GOLDEN APPLE SNAIL

The golden apple snail was introduced into China from Florida and Mexico in the 1980s by snail farmers who planned to export the snails to European markets. The venture was unsuccessful, and the snails escaped and spread through the waterways until they found an ideal habitat in the rice fields where they are now a serious threat, being capable of destroying whole crops in a very short time.

GOLDEN GATE

Name of the gold mine at Mathinna, near Fingal in Van Diemen's Land.

GOLDEN MEAN

This pattern appears clearly and regularly in the realm of things that grow and unfold in steps, the phenomenon being very obvious in such structures as the shell of the paper nautilus and the seed head of the sunflower which grows in clockwise spirals overlaid on counterclockwise spirals, according to Fibonacci numbers. It may also be observed in the configuration of the inner ear.

H

HANS-MY-HEDGEHOG

Story number 108 from the *Nursery and Household Tales* of the Brothers Grimm.

Once upon a time there was a man who possessed lands and monies sufficient to his needs, yet there was something lacking in his happiness, for he and his wife had no children. One day when he was at the market some of the merchants questioned him on the subject of his childlessness, and he and his wife were mocked. Humiliated and sad, the man grew angry, and when he returned home he found himself saying to his wife that he *would* have a child, 'even,' he said, 'if that child should be a hedgehog.' His wife laughed at his remark, and when she became pregnant there was great rejoicing in the house. The couple were naturally forgetful of the husband's careless words uttered in sadness and rage.

Then the wife had a baby, and the top half was a hedgehog with long sharp quills and the bottom half was a boy. When the woman saw the baby, she was horrified and she remembered at once her husband's words and she said, 'Now see what you have wished upon us!'

'It can not be helped. The boy must be baptised,' said her husband.

In her great sorrow the woman said that the only name they could give him was Hans-My-Hedgehog.

The astonished priest who baptised him said, 'Because of his quills he can not be given an ordinary bed.'

So they put a little heap of fresh straw behind the stove and laid him in it. In truth his father wished him dead, such was his misery at having fathered such a creature, but his mother saw to it that her child had sufficient nourishment, and so Hans-My-Hedgehog grew and thrived. He lived behind the stove for eight years.

One day the man was going to a fair in the neighbouring town, and he asked his wife what gift he might bring home for her.

'A little meat, some bread, and a little red jug for the table.'

Then he asked the servant girl, and she requested a pair of silken slippers and some fancy stockings.

Finally, to be fair, the man went behind the stove and said, 'Hans-My-Hedgehog, what would you like?'

'Father,' Hans said, 'bring me some bagpipes.'

When the peasant returned home he gave his wife the meat, the bread and the little red jug. Then he gave the servant girl the silken slippers and fancy stockings. And finally he went behind the stove and gave Hans-My-Hedgehog as handsome a set of bagpipes as you could ever imagine.

When Hans-My-Hedgehog saw the bagpipes he was very happy and he said, 'Father, would you go to the blacksmith's and have our fine cock-rooster shod like a stallion, that I may ride away and never more come back?'

So the father had the rooster shod, and when it was done Hans-My-Hedgehog rode away, taking with him some pigs and some donkeys, for he planned to live in a certain style in the forest. The cock-rooster flew up into a tall tree, carrying Hans-My-Hedgehog with him. There Hans sat for four long years and watched over the donkeys and the pigs until they had grown into a fine herd. And all the while as he sat in the treetop, he played his bagpipes and the music he made was beautiful.

One day in the spring a king came riding by on his elegant white horse. He had heard the music of the pipes from the edge of the forest, and he was beguiled and followed the sound deep into the woods until he became quite lost. When the king arrived at the tree where Hans was sitting, he looked up and was surprised to see a little hedgehog astride a little cock-rooster sitting in the tree making the music. The king called up into the tree, thanking the player for the music, and then saying he had lost his way and asking for directions back to the kingdom. Hans-My-Hedgehog had much knowledge, and he had been thinking about things for many years. He now climbed down from the tree and explained to the king that he would show him the way if the king would promise to give him the first thing that greeted him at the royal court upon his arrival home. When the king said nothing Hans-My-Hedgehog handed him a quill and a leaf of paper and requested the promise be recorded in the king's own hand. So the king took the quill and the paper and he wrote something down. Then Hans-My-Hedgehog, who had never learnt to read, showed him the way, and the king rode safely all the way to his palace.

His daughter saw him coming from afar, and was so overjoyed that she ran to meet him and kissed him. The king thought about Hans-My-Hedgehog and told her what had happened. He said he had lost his way in the woods and had met a strange animal riding a cock-rooster and playing sweet and mysterious music on the pipes. The animal had given him directions to the palace and had expected him to keep a promise in return. But the king had written nonsense on the paper, and he felt the life of his daughter was safe. His daughter laughed when she heard the story, and there was great rejoicing in the kingdom for the king had returned.

Hans-My-Hedgehog wondered what had become of the king and his promise, but he was of good cheer and tended the donkeys and pigs, and sat in the tree playing his strange melodies on his pipes.

Now it happened that a second king heard the sound and that he too was beguiled and he too became lost. When he saw Hans-My-Hedgehog he asked for directions and Hans again replied as he had done before, asking for a written promise.

'Promise me you will give me the first living thing that greets you when you reach the gates of your palace.'

The king said yes and signed a promise to Hans-My-Hedgehog. But this time Hans told the king that he would lead him to the palace, and so, riding on his cock-rooster, Hans led the procession of the king's horses and men until they came to the gates of the palace where Hans left the king and rode away.

Now the second king also had a daughter and she was fair and beautiful. She ran out to greet her father, threw her arms around his neck and kissed him. She asked him where he had been during his long absence, and he told her how he had heard some strange music, and had followed it, and had lost his way in a great forest. He told her he had come upon the musician, who was half hedgehog, half human, astride a rooster sitting in a tall tree playing his bagpipes. Then he looked into her eyes and told her that he had made a promise which he must honour. He had promised the hedgehog that he would give it the first living thing that greeted him when he arrived at his kingdom. The princess was shocked and afraid, but she said that she would gladly honour her father's promise and go with the creature when he came for her.

Hans-My-Hedgehog rode then into the kingdom where the first king ruled. The king had issued an order against any person who was carrying bagpipes and riding on a rooster. This person should be killed at once, should be shot at, struck down and stabbed to prevent him from entering the castle. Thus, when Hans-My-Hedgehog rode up, they attacked him with bayonets, but Hans was swift, and he spurred his rooster on, and they flew high up, up, up, over the gate and up to the dishonest king's window. Landing there, Hans shouted to the king. 'Give me your daughter as you agreed, or you and your daughter will die.'

The king grew afraid of the strange magic that attended this creature, Hans-My-Hedgehog, and so he told the princess to go out to him, in order to save his life and her own as well. So the princess put on a white dress, and her father gave her a carriage with six horses, many servants, a bag of gold and seven fine houses. She rode out on a white horse and Hans-My-Hedgehog took his place beside her with his cock-rooster and his bagpipes.

The king was very sad and thought that he would never see his daughter again, and he lamented that he had attempted to trick Hans-My-Hedgehog. However, it did not go as he thought it would, for when the princess and Hans had travelled a short distance from the city, Hans-My-Hedgehog stopped the horses. He alighted and he asked the princess also to alight. She was more afraid than she had ever been. Then he pulled off her white dress that shimmered with bright jewels and she stood naked before him. Then he attacked her in rage and he stuck her with his quills until she was covered in blood from head to toe.

'This is the reward for your father's deceit. Go away. I do not want to see you ever again.'

And, weeping with pain and sorrow, the princess wrapped herself in a blanket and mounted her white horse, which was soon spattered and smeared with bright red blood. She rode away home, and when her father saw her he cried out and died from grief, and she was cursed as long as she lived.

Then Hans-My-Hedgehog rode on to the second kingdom. Here the king had ordered that if anyone resembling Hans-My-Hedgehog should arrive, he should be saluted and brought to the royal castle with honours and should be escorted by a guard of soldiers in full regalia. So Hans arrived, and he was met with great ceremony at the gates of the kingdom and made a royal progress to the king's reception hall. There the princess saw him for the first time and she was faint with horror and amazement and fear. Yet she was honourable as her father was honourable, and she sat with Hans at the royal table and they ate and drank together. Later that evening, in the courtyard of the palace, the princess and Hans-My-Hedgehog were married amid great celebrations, among mountains of fresh flowers, to the sounds of royal music and accompanied by a display of Chinese fireworks.

As dawn was breaking it came the time for Hans and the princess to retire to the royal bedchamber. She was most afraid of his quills, but he told her to have no fear, for he would not hurt her. Then he requested that four men should come to the recess outside the bedchamber, and that a large fire should be burning in the grate beside the door. When this was done he shed his hedgehog skin and gave it to the men, who burned it utterly in the fire where it flamed and crackled and spat until it was reduced to ashes.

When his hedgehog skin was gone, Hans lay upon the bed in the shape of a beautiful young man. But his skin was charred, as if blackened by the fire. The princess requested the attention of the king's physician, who washed Hans with good salves and balms until he was cleansed and soothed and pure, and there was rejoicing for another week in the kingdom.

Some months later Hans travelled with his wife to visit his father and mother, who still lived in the house where Hans had spent so many long sad hours behind the stove. When he said he was their son they said they had no son. Then the woman said there used to be a son, but he was dead, and he had been born under a spell, with quills on his back like the quills of a hedgehog. Hans then took out his old bagpipes and started to play, and the cock-rooster came running up crowing, and the father and mother, with tears in their eyes, knew that this young prince was indeed their son, and they rejoiced and embraced Hans-My-Hedgehog and his bride the princess.

My tale is done, and away it is run, to little August's house.

I

IRIS

Iris, counterpart of Hermes, is the female messenger of the gods of Olympus, having the power of the word. She is in the service of Hera, has golden wings and feathered slippers, and bears the kerykeion, or snaky wand, in one hand and the box of the word in the other. She is the only one who can enter the cave of Hypnos, the god of sleep, to deliver a message without being overpowered by drowsiness. Iris is also a psychopomp who accompanies the souls of women to the other world. The rainbow is the bridge between Iris and the earth, and is also the 'eye of heaven', lending the goddess's name to the coloured disk of the human eye.

The luminescent colours of the iris flower led to its being named for the rainbow. The iris is one of the most ancient cutivated plants. It was taken from Syria to Egypt fifteen hundred years before the birth of Christ. Because of the association with the goddess who carries the word, the flower is a symbol of eloquence.

Indians of the Californian desert wrapped their babies in the leaves of the iris to protect them from dehydration, and they also used the leaves as fibre for cord, snares and fishing nets.

The legend of Clovis from sixth-century France explains the inspiration of the iris as the model for the fleur-de-lys. Clovis's army was trapped by the Goths, when Clovis saw yellow irises growing in the Rhine. He realised the water was therefore shallow enough for him and his men to cross. He escaped to safety and adopted the iris as his device and it became the emblem of the French royal house. When Louis VII adopted it as his emblem during the Crusades in the twelfth century it came to be known as fleur-de-Louis and then the fleur-de-lys.

In the twelfth century, when the magnet was first used for the navigation of ships at sea, the fleur-de-lys was chosen as the symbol to indicate North and it has appeared in that capacity on all compasses and maps ever since.

The name of the ship that sank off Puddingstone Island in 1851.

J

JOACHIM THE PROPHET

He was born at Celico in Calabria in about 1130 and died in 1202. Joachim was a visionary and prophet who, early in life, adopted an ascetic life. After a pilgrimage to Palestine, he entered the Cistercian Abbey at Sambucina. In 1176, he became abbot of Corazzo, and about 1190 founded his own monastery at Fiore, forming a new Cistercian congregation. He predicted a Golden Age when infidels would unite with Christians, and when the hierarchy of the Church would become unnecessary. Dante names Joachim as one of the people in Paradise.

THE JUNIPER TREE

Story number 47 from the *Nursery and Household Tales* of the Brothers Grimm.

Once there was a rich man who had a beautiful wife but no children, and the wife prayed for a child by day and by night. In front of the house there was a courtyard where there stood a juniper tree. One day in winter the woman was sitting beneath the tree, peeling apples with a knife, and as she was doing so she cut her finger and three drops of blood fell upon the snow. Then she longed for a child who was as red as blood and as white as snow, and in that moment she felt sure that this would come to pass.

A month went by, and the snow melted. And two months, and everything was green. And three months, and all the flowers came forth from the earth. And four months, and all the trees in the woods grew thicker, and the green branches were all entwined in one another, and the birds sang. Then the fifth month passed, and the woman stood beneath the juniper tree and her heart leapt for joy. She fell to her knees. When the sixth month had passed, the fruit was heavy on the trees and then the woman rested. After the seventh month she picked the juniper berries and she ate them greedily, but then she grew sorrowful. When the eighth month passed the woman called her husband to her and she said, 'Husband, if I should die, bury me beneath the juniper tree.'

Then she was comforted and happy until the next month was over, and then her son was born, and he was as red as blood and as white as snow, and when the woman heard him cry she smiled, and as she smiled, she lapsed and died, and grieving, her husband buried her beneath the juniper tree.

The months passed and the husband took a new wife, and this wife had a little daughter whose name was Anne-Marie and whom she loved very much. When she looked at the little boy, this woman felt a bitterness in her heart, for she knew that the boy would always stand in her daughter's way for her husband's property. But the little girl loved her brother and they played together happily all year long. However, her mother frequently grew angry with the boy and he could find no peace in the house. The woman was secretly planning to rid herself of this impediment to her daughter's fortune.

So one day in the autumn, when the boy came in from school, the woman said to him, 'You must be hungry. Would you like to have an apple from the chest?'

The boy was surprised, but he was not suspicious, and when the woman opened the chest he leant over and picked a bright red apple from inside, and as he did so the woman let the great heavy lid of the chest fall down *thud* on his neck so that his head flew off and rolled among the apples in the chest. Then the woman was overcome with horror and fear at what she had done, and she fetched a large white handkerchief, and set the boy on a high stool, placed his head upon his shoulders and tied the handkerchief around the wound. Then she placed the apple in his hand.

When Anne-Marie came into the kitchen she said to her mother, 'My brother is sitting at the door, and he looks so very strange and white and has an apple in his hand. I asked him to give me the apple, but he did not answer me and I was very frightened.'

'Then go back to him,' said her mother, 'and if he will not answer you, then you should box his ears.'

So Anne-Marie went to him and said, 'Brother, please will you give me the apple?'

But he was silent, and so she boxed his ears, and immediately his head fell off. Anne-Marie screamed in horror and she ran to her mother and told her what had happened and she could not be comforted.

'Anne-Marie,' said the mother, 'what have you done? Be quiet and do not tell anyone about it. It can not be helped now. We will cook him into stew.' Then the mother took the little boy and chopped him into little pieces, put him in the pot and cooked him into rich and savoury stew. Anne-Marie stood by weeping bitterly, and all her tears fell into the pot.

Then the father came home, and sat down at the table and said, 'Where is my son?' And the mother said that he had gone to visit his uncle in the next village, and then she served up a large, large dish of stew, and Anne-Marie cried and could not stop.

'What is he doing there?' said the father. 'He did not even say goodbye to me.'

'Oh, he wanted to go, and asked me if he could stay six weeks. He will be well taken care of. Do not fret.'

Then the man said, 'Wife, this food is delicious. Give me some more.' And the more he ate the more he wanted, and he said, 'Give me some more. You two shall have none of it. It seems to me as if it were all mine.' And he ate and ate, throwing all the bones under the table, until he had finished.

Anne-Marie gathered all the bones from beneath the table and tied them up in her silk scarf, then she carried them outside the door, crying tears of blood. She laid them down beneath the juniper tree, and after she had put them there she suddenly felt better and did not weep any more.

And when the girl had stopped weeping the juniper tree began to sway. The branches shifted quietly apart, then moved together again, just as if someone were rejoicing and clapping their hands. At the same time a pearly mist rose from the tree, and in the centre of this mist was a burning fire, and from the heart of the flame flew out a beautiful bird that sang a sweet song. The bird flew high into the air, and when it was gone the juniper tree was just as it had been before, but the cloth with the bones had disappeared. And Anne-Marie was as happy and contented as if her brother were still alive, and she went into the house and ate her bread.

Then the bird flew away and lit on a goldsmith's house, and it began to sing:

'My mother she killed me
My father he ate me
My little sister Anne-Marie
She gathered up the bones of me
Tied them in a silken cloth
To lay beneath the juniper tree
What a beautiful bird am I.'

The goldsmith was sitting in his workshop making a golden chain, when he heard the bird sitting on his roof and singing. The song seemed very beautiful to him and he stood up, but as he crossed the threshold he lost one of his slippers. However, he went right up the middle of the street wearing only one slipper. He had his leather apron on, and in one hand he had a golden chain and in the other his tongs. He walked onward, then stood still and said to the bird, 'Bird, bird, how beautifully you can sing. Please sing that piece again for me.'

'No,' said the bird, 'I do not sing twice for nothing. Give me the golden chain and then I will sing again for you.'

The goldsmith said, 'Here is the golden chain for you. Now sing that song again for me.'

Then the bird came and took the golden chain in his right claw, and sat in front of the goldsmith and sang. Then the bird flew away to a shoemaker, and lit on his roof and there it sang again. And the shoemaker came out of doors in his shirt-sleeves and begged the bird to sing again, but the bird said he must give him the pair of little red shoes from the window of his shop before it would sing again. So the shoemaker's wife fetched the shoes, and the bird, all red and green and gold like fire, sang the song again, and all who heard it marvelled at the beauty of the music and wondered at the strange meaning of the words. The eyes of the bird shone like stars. And the bird took the little red shoes in its left claw and flew away.

In the right claw was the chain and in the left claw were the shoes. The bird flew far away to a mill, and the millwheel went clickety-clack, clickety-clack, clickety-clack. In the mill sat twenty apprentices cutting a stone and chiselling chip-chop, chip-chop, chip-chop to make a fine new millstone. And the bird, all red and green and gold, sat on the linden tree and sang its song.

'My mother, she killed me . . . '
Then one of them stopped working.
'My father, he ate me . . . '
Then two more stopped working.
'My little sister Anne-Marie . . . '
Then four more stopped working.
'Gathered up the bones of me
And tied them in a silken scarf . . . '
Now only eight were chiselling.
'And laid them underneath . . . '
Now only five.
'The juniper tree . . . '
Now only one.
'What a beautiful bird am I.'

Then the last one stopped also and heard the last words.

'Bird,' he said, 'how beautifully you sing. Please sing again for us.'

But the bird said no, and then explained that if they gave it the millstone it would sing again for them. So they gave the bird the millstone, and again it sang the song, and then, with the chain in one claw and the shoes in the other and the stone around its neck, the bird flew off into the sky. It flew until it reached the house where little Anne-Marie was sitting at the kitchen table with her mother and father.

'I feel very uneasy,' the mother said, 'as if a storm were brewing.'

Then the bird flew up, and as it seated itself on the roof, the father said, 'Oh, I feel so truly happy, and the sun is shining so beautifully outside. I feel as if I were about to see a dear old friend again.'

But the woman's teeth were chattering, and she felt she was suffering from a fever, and there was a fire in her veins, and she tore at her bodice until it was torn to shreds. Then the bird alighted on the juniper tree and sang:

'My mother, she killed me,' and the mother stopped her ears and shut her eyes, not wanting to see or hear, but there was a roaring in her ears like the fiercest storm, and before her eyes the world burned and flashed like lightning.

The father said, 'The bird is singing so sweetly, and the sun is shining so warmly, and the whole world smells like rich dark cinnamon.'

And the man went outside and looked up at the bird, and the bird dropped the golden chain so that it fell about the father's neck. And the woman was amazed and terrified and she fell down on the floor, her cap rolling off her head. But Anne-Marie ran out into the garden to look at the bird, and the bird threw down the little red shoes which she put on her feet and they fitted her perfectly. Then the woman jumped to her feet and she went out the door, her hair standing on end like flames of fire. And as she came to the juniper tree the bird dropped the millstone on top of her and she was crushed to death in an instant.

Smoke, flames and fire rose from the juniper tree, and when the smoke had cleared, the little brother was standing there, handsome and smiling. He took his father and Anne-Marie by the hand, and all three were very happy, and they went into the house, sat down at the table and ate their supper.

K

KRAKEN

This is a legendary giant underwater monster with many tentacles, capable of sinking large ships. Its counterpart in the real world is the giant squid, which is known to be capable of wrestling a sperm whale. In recent years the bodies of giant squid have been discovered on beaches in increasing numbers.

M

MONOTREMES

The duck-billed platypus and two species of echidna (see entry for Echidna) are the only living monotremes, being mammals possessing a single opening for urinary, genital and excretory functions. Their habitat is Australia and New Guinea. They are primitive mammals because, like reptiles and birds, they lay eggs instead of giving live birth. Modern adult monotremes have no teeth. Like other mammals, however, they produce milk, have hair, a single lower jaw bone, three bones in the inner ear, and high metabolic rates. A good source of information on monotremes is the website of the University of Tasmania: www.healthsci.utas.edu.au/medicine/research/mono/References.html.

MOONBIRD

This is one of the names for the muttonbird or shearwater, a petrel that constantly wanders the earth, as if seeking a home, laying eggs in remote parts of Australia, such as the islands of Bass Strait, and flying north to the Arctic Circle. Its nest is a burrow for one solitary chick, and the noise and musty smell of the breeding ground is distinctive. The moonbird is sometimes called the flying sheep of the Pacific, but its more romantic title of 'moonbird' relates to the legend of the origin of the Pacific Ocean. The story is that the moon was formed when a great round chunk of the earth flew out, leaving the void of the Pacific. The moonbird follows the path, in a figure eight, of the whole Pacific Ocean, from north to south and back again. The birds feed on fish and shellfish during daylight, and sleep in groups on the surface of the sea.

MÜNZER, THOMAS (C. 1489–1525)

A German Protestant pastor who taught that the inner transformation of the spirit, coupled with the external transformation of society into a theocratic state, would result in obedience to the divine will. He established such a community in Mühlhausen, and was beheaded during a massacre of the faithful at Frankenhausen in 1525.

P

PAXTON, JOSEPH (1803–1865)

He was a gardener's boy who became the head gardener to the Duke of Devonshire at Chatsworth, where he cultivated the Victoria Regia or Giant Water Lily. A photograph was taken of his daughter standing on one of the giant leaves, and it was the principal of the lily-leaf's construction that inspired Paxton's design for a glasshouse. This design he later used in his blueprint for the Crystal Palace. He sketched the building on a piece of blotting paper and completed the design in ten days. His later career included the designs for many public parks and the grounds of country houses.

PEOPLE'S TEMPLE

The name of Jim Jones's cult, whose members committed mass suicide with cyanide in 1978 at the settlement of Jonestown in the jungle of Guyana.

R

RAMPION

Rapunzel, *Campanula rapunculus*, a congener of the common harebell. It has a long white spindle-shaped root, which is eaten raw like a radish and has a pleasant sweet flavour. Its roots, leaves and young shoots are also used in salads.

RAPUNZEL

Story number 12 from the *Nursery and Household Tales* of the Brothers Grimm.

There was once a man and a woman who had long wished for a child. You may imagine that these were the same people who had the son they called Hans-My-Hedgehog, but although the beginnings of the stories are similar, this is a different couple. However, in these and other tales, when the desire for a child is thwarted, the lengths to which the parents will go, the risks they will take and the strange effects their actions sometimes have, are quite remarkable. Children — lost, found, stolen, borrowed — are powerful and desirable commodities in these narratives. Consider the scene in *The Blue Bird*, where the character of Light reveals the thirty thousand halls where all the unborn children live. 'When fathers and mothers want children, the great doors are opened and the little ones go down. There are enough children to last to the end of the world.'

But to continue with 'Rapunzel': At length the woman had reason to hope that God was about to grant her desire. Now the couple had a little window at the back of their house, and from this window they were able to see into the neighbour's garden, a garden filled with the most beautiful flowers and herbs. It was, however, surrounded by a high wall, and no-one dared to go into it, because it belonged to an enchantress who had great power and was dreaded by all the people for many miles around. One day the woman was standing by this window and looking down into the garden, when she saw a bed which was planted with the most beautiful rampion. It looked so fresh and green that she longed for it, and had the greatest desire to eat some. This desire increased every day, and as she knew that she could not get any of it, she began to pine away.

'If I can not get some of this rampion, I know I shall surely die,' she told her husband.

So that evening, at twilight, the husband climbed up and over the wall and into the garden of the enchantress. He snatched up a handful of rampion, climbed back over the wall, and took the green herb to his wife on a clean white platter. But the wife ate it with such relish that the next day she longed for twice as much rampion, and so the husband at twilight scaled the wall, picked the herb and returned to his wife. But the wife ate it with such gusto that she then required three times as much, and so on the third night the husband climbed the wall again.

But this time the enchantress was waiting for him, and she was very angry and he was very afraid.

'Thief,' she said, 'why do you steal my rampion?'

'Ah, forgive me,' said the man, 'but my wife saw your rampion from our window, and she had such a longing for it in her heart that she knew she would die for lack of it. Please, good madam, let mercy take the place of justice, for my wife is to bring our child into the world before many months have passed.'

At this the enchantress was delighted and she smiled a sly smile and she said, 'Then you may take as much rampion as you wish,' and the man bent down and, as he thanked her with some surprise, he took a great handful of the herb. But the enchantress continued, 'I make one condition. When the child is born you must deliver it to me. I will care for it like a mother.'

The man in his terror consented without thinking, and returned home. For three more months the woman was happy because she could eat as much of the witch's rampion as she wished. Then the day came when the child was born. As the wife was holding her newborn daughter in her arms, the enchantress appeared at once, took the child, and swept out of the room and was gone. The mother cried out in shock and despair, and the father shook with shame and sorrow, and they were bereft.

It is worth noticing that the parents drop right out of the narrative at this point, never to return.

Rapunzel grew into the most beautiful child beneath the sun. Her skin was like snow and her hair was long and flowing red-gold like a river in the sunlight. When she was twelve years old, the enchantress shut her into a tower, which stood in a forest, and the tower had neither stairs nor door, but high up at the top was a little window looking out onto the sky. When the enchantress wanted to enter the tower and visit Rapunzel, she stood on the earth beneath this window and cried, 'Rapunzel, Rapunzel, let down your hair.'

So Rapunzel would wind her braided tresses around one of the bars of her window, and would then let them flow down the tower wall until they reached the ground.

After a year or two, it came to pass that the king's son rode through the forest and passed by the tower. Then he heard a song that was so sweet and seductive that he stood still and listened. It was Rapunzel. In her solitude she would play her lute and sing sad songs of her own invention. The prince listened as the music drifted down from the tower and across the forest. As he was listening, he heard another sound: 'Rapunzel, Rapunzel, let down your hair.' Then he saw to his astonishment the long tresses of red-gold hair that swiftly fell from the tower window, and then he saw the witch as she climbed up with a small basket of fresh fruit and vegetables. Intrigued by the sight and seduced by the song, and marvelling at the beauty of the silken rope of hair that he had seen, he waited until dark and then the prince stood at the foot of the tower and called out: 'Rapunzel, Rapunzel, let down your hair.'

Almost at once, hair fell down in the moonlight, and the king's son, pleased and a little anxious at what he might discover, climbed up.

At first Rapunzel was bewildered and afraid, for she had never seen a man before. But the prince reassured her, explaining how much he admired her song, and she looked at him and saw that he was very young and handsome. Then Rapunzel lost her fear, and at once he asked her if she would take him for her husband, and she looked into his eyes and she said yes, and laid her hand in his. But how were they to escape from the tower?

Together they devised a plan. Every time the prince came to visit Rapunzel he would bring with him a skein of yellow silk. With this Rapunzel would weave a ladder, and when the ladder was finished she would climb down and meet him, and they would ride away together. So the prince came to visit Rapunzel every night for forty nights, and the witch came to visit her by day. Now Rapunzel was a girl of certain guile, but even the most diligent liars and tricksters will one day be unable to keep concealed the truths that occupy their hearts. And so it was that one day Rapunzel said to the witch, 'How is it that you are so much slower and heavier than the prince?'

Then the witch guessed what had happened, and in her rage she fetched her enormous scissors from her belt and she chopped off Rapunzel's long red-gold tresses then and there, and made of them a ladder down which she and Rapunzel, who was weeping with despair, climbed. It was the first time Rapunzel had ever walked upon the earth, and she stumbled as she was dragged along to the witch's house close by.

Here the witch secured her to the bedhead with a rope made from the sinews of a fallow deer, then set off back to the tower where she lay in wait for the prince on his nightly visit. And when he called out for Rapunzel, the witch let down the yellow braids in the moonlight, and the prince swiftly and lightly leapt up the wall in joy, only to be greeted by the witch in all her hideous rage.

'Your beautiful bird sits no longer singing in her nest, for the cat has taken her, and the cat will scratch out your eyes and you will never see Rapunzel again.'

In his distress the prince rushed to the window and cast himself from the tower, to land in a thicket of wild roses where his eyes were pierced by thorns and bled bright blood across the white petals of the rose. The witch returned in triumph to her house, where she looked upon Rapunzel with great disgust and hatred. And after a time she took Rapunzel far, far out to the edge of the forest, to where the desert begins, and there she left her.

The prince wandered blindly in the forest for several years, eating roots and berries and weeping for his loss, until he came one day to a place where he could hear a woman singing. She was singing to her children, a little boy and girl, and the song that she sang was the song he had heard on the night when he first met Rapunzel. He approached the voice, and when she saw him Rapunzel knew him, and she fell upon his neck and she wept. Her tears fell across his face, and rivulets of her tears flowed into the prince's eyes, and his eyes opened, and grew clear again, and he could see his beautiful Rapunzel and the children who were his own twin son and daughter. He led them back to his kingdom where they all lived long and happy lives.

On the day when the prince found Rapunzel again, a strange thing happened deep in the forest. A hare that was carrying a lighted candle in its teeth bounded into the witch's little house and the enchantress was burned to death.

ROBINSON, GEORGE AUGUSTUS (1791–1866)

When George Robinson sailed for Australia in 1823 he left behind his wife and five children, but they later joined him in Van Diemen's Land. He set about civilising and Christianising the indigenous peoples of the island, being appointed the first Chief Protector of Aborigines in Australia. He travelled great distances on horseback and on foot throughout both Van Diemen's Land and the Australian mainland in pursuit of his duties. He made some of the earliest records of local culture and language. One of his most notorious projects was the failed attempt to round up the native peoples of

Van Diemen's Land by capturing them in a human net which moved across the island. He tried to investigate and report on the stories of black and white deaths at Cape Grim, but his account is only one version of the events that took place. Robinson remains one of the most problematic and interfering figures in the tragic early history of Van Diemen's Land.

ROSE

Saint Rose of Lima (1586–1617) was canonised in 1671, and her feast day is 30 August. She was born Isabel de Flores y del Oliva in Lima, was always known as Rose, and was the first person in the Americas to be canonised. Rose's family was very poor and Rose supplemented the family income by growing and selling flowers, embroidering and selling collars. She refused to marry, and when she was twenty she became a Dominican tertiary and lived in a summerhouse in the garden of her parents' property. She was particularly devoted to the Virgin of the Rosary and to the Black Virgin of Atocha. She lived a life of strict prayer, rigid penance and mystical experience, and she became the subject of a church inquiry but was found to be beyond reproach. She ministered to slaves, to Indians, to the sick and the poor, and was considered to be a saint in her own lifetime, establishing the first free health clinic in the Americas. One of the most dramatic and popular stories of Saint Rose tells of the day in 1615, when Lima was threatened by Dutch pirates led by Jorge Spitberg. When the pirates advanced through the port and stormed the church in search of rich loot they were confronted by the sight of Rose, in her black and white habit, in a state of ecstasy, arms outstretched and barring their way to the holy tabernacle of the altar. The sight of her was blinding and frightening, and they fled. The next day the black sails of their fleet had vanished from the port.

S

SHOO-FLY PIE

RECIPE

INGREDIENTS

Medium-size unbaked pie shell

TOPPING

1.5 cups flour

1.5 cups sugar

1 teaspoon baking powder

1/2 teaspoon salt

1/4 cup butter

BOTTOM

1/2 cup molasses

1/2 cup boiling water

1/2 teaspoon baking soda

METHOD

Preheat oven to 400°F (200°C).

Mix all topping ingredients together, squeezing and crumbling to make crumbs the size of small peas. Set aside.

In another bowl, dissolve baking soda in boiling water. Add molasses. Stir well.

Pour into unbaked pie shell and add crumb topping, BUT be careful not to blend the topping with the molasses mixture.

Bake at 400°F for 15 minutes, then at 350°F for 35 minutes.

Cool and serve.

SKYE

This island to the west of Scotland, between the mainland and the islands of the Outer Hebrides, was first populated by Norse sea-roving peoples.

The tiny community of Skye in northwest Tasmania was burnt out in 1992 and is now a ghost town.

STEADFAST TIN SOLDIER

Written by Hans Christian Anderson and first published in 1838.

There were once five and twenty tin soldiers, all brothers, for they were the offspring of the same old tin spoon. Each man shouldered his gun, kept his eyes well to the front, and wore the smartest red and blue uniform imaginable. The first thing they heard in their new world, when the lid was taken off the box, was a little boy clapping his hands and crying, 'Soldiers, soldiers!' It was his birthday, and they had just been given to him.

All the soldiers were exactly alike, with one exception, and he differed from the rest in having only one leg. For he was made last, and there was not quite enough tin left to finish him. However, he stood just as well on his one leg as the others on two. In fact he was the very one who was to become famous.

On the table where the soldiers were being set up were many other toys, but the chief thing that caught the eye was a paper castle. You could see through the windows, right into the rooms. Outside there were some little trees surrounding a small mirror, representing a lake, whose surface reflected the waxen swans that were swimming about on it. And the prettiest thing of all was a little maiden standing at the open door of the castle. She, too, was cut out of paper, but she wore a dress of the lightest gauze, with a blue ribbon over her shoulders by way of a scarf, set off by a brilliant spangle as big as her whole face. She was stretching out both arms, for she was a dancer, and in the dance one of her legs was raised so high into the air that the tin soldier could see absolutely nothing of it, and he supposed that she, like himself, had but one leg.

He thought she was so beautiful and that she would make him the perfect wife. But then he realised she was much too grand for him, as she was a princess in a palace. However, he decided he would try to make friends with her and so he lay down full length behind a snuffbox which stood on the table. From that point he could have a good look at the dancer, who continued to stand on one leg without losing her balance.

Late in the evening the other soldiers were put into their box, and the people of the house went to bed. There was a goblin in the snuffbox, and he saw the tin soldier staring at the dancer, and he said, 'Have the goodness to keep your eyes to yourself.'

But the tin soldier pretended not to hear.

'Then you just wait till tomorrow,' the goblin said.

In the morning, when the little boy got up, he put the tin soldier on the window frame, and whether it was just a puff of wind, or whether the goblin gave the soldier a little push, no-one can tell, but the window flew open and the tin soldier tumbled from the third storey and landed with his bayonet wedged between two paving stones and with his leg in the air. The maidservant and the little boy ran to look for him, but they could not see him, and they almost trod on him. Presently it began to rain, and the drops fell faster and faster, till there was a regular torrent. When the storm was over, two boys came along.

'Look,' said one boy, 'there's a tin soldier. He shall go for a sail in the gutter.'

So they made a boat out of a newspaper, and put the soldier into the middle of it, and he sailed away down the gutter. Both boys ran alongside, clapping their hands. What waves there were in the gutter, and what a current. The paper boat danced up and down, and now and then whirled round and round. A shudder ran through the tin soldier, but he remained undaunted, and did not move a muscle, only looked straight before him with his gun shouldered. All at once the boat drifted under a long wooden tunnel, and it became as dark as night. At this moment a big water rat, who lived in the tunnel, came up.

'Have you a pass?' asked the rat. 'Hand me your pass!'

The tin soldier did not speak, but clung still tighter to his gun. The boat rushed on, the rat close behind. He gnashed his teeth and shouted to the bits of stick and straw, 'Stop him, stop him, he hasn't paid his toll! He hasn't shown his pass!'

The current grew stronger and stronger, and the tin soldier could already see daylight before him at the end of the tunnel. But he also heard a roaring sound, fit to strike terror into the bravest heart. Where the tunnel ended the stream rushed straight into the big canal. He was so near the end now that it was impossible to stop. The boat dashed out, out into the waters of the canal. The boat swirled round three or four times, and filled with water to the edge. It must sink. The tin soldier stood up to his neck in water, and the boat sank deeper and deeper. The paper became limper and limper, and at last the water went over his head. Then he thought of the pretty little dancer, whom he was never to see again, and the thought of her made him brave.

At last the paper gave way entirely and the soldier fell through, but at the same moment he was swallowed by an enormous fish.

Oh! how dark it was inside that fish. But the tin soldier was as dauntless as ever, and lay full length, shouldering his gun. The fish rushed about and made the most frantic movements. At last it became quite quiet, and after a time a flash like lightning pierced the terrible darkness. The soldier was once more in the broad daylight, and someone called out, 'Look, a tin soldier!' The fish had been caught, taken to market, sold, and brought into the kitchen, where the cook cut it open with a large knife. She took the soldier up by the waist with two fingers and carried him into the parlour, where everyone wanted to see the wonderful man who had travelled about in the stomach of a fish. But the tin soldier was not at all proud. They set him up on the table, and, wonder of wonders, he found himself in the very same room that he had been in before. He saw the very same children, and the toys were still standing on the table, as well as the beautiful castle with the pretty little dancer.

The dancer still stood on one leg and held the other up in the air. The soldier was so much moved that he was ready to shed tears of tin, but that would not have been fitting. He looked at her, and she looked at him, but they said never a word. At this moment one of the little boys took up the tin soldier and, without rhyme or reason, threw him headlong into the fire. Perhaps the little goblin in the snuffbox was to blame for that. The tin soldier stood there, lighted up by the flame and in the most horrible heat. He looked at the little dancer, and she looked at him, and he felt that he was melting away, but he still managed to keep himself upright, shouldering his gun.

A door was suddenly opened, the draught caught the little dancer and she fluttered like a sylph straight into the fire. She fell upon the soldier, blazed up and was gone. By this time the soldier was reduced to a mere lump, and when the maid took away the ashes next morning she found him, in the shape of a small tin heart. All that was left of the dancer was the spangle from her scarf, and that was burnt as black as a coal. The tin heart and the spangle were welded together forever.

STRUWWELPETER

The character from a nineteenth-century children's rhyme by Heinrich Hoffmann.

'Just look at him! There he stands
With his nasty hair and hands
See! His nails are never cut
They are grimed and black as soot
And the sloven, I declare
Never once has combed his hair
Anything to me is sweeter
Than to see Shock-headed Peter.'

T

TASMAN, ABEL JANSZOON (1603–1659)

Born in Lutjegast, Holland; when he died he left twenty-five guilders to the poor of his village. His property was divided between his wife, Jannetje, and Claesgen, his daughter by his first marriage. Tasman is attributed with the discovery of Van Diemen's Land, of New Zealand, and the Tonga and Fiji Islands. He was the first known navigator to sail all around Australia.

In 1633 he was employed by the Dutch East India Company and soon commanded several of their ships and made a number of voyages to the East Indies. In 1639 he was dispatched by Antonio van Diemen, Governor-General of the Dutch East Indies, on a voyage to the northwestern Pacific in search of 'islands of gold and silver' believed to lie east of Japan. On this voyage Tasman visited the Philippines and discovered and mapped various islands to the north. In 1642 he set out with the *Heemskerck* and the *Zeehaen* on his first great expedition to map the Great South Land, calling at Mauritius for repairs to the ships. He sighted Van Diemen's Land on 24 November 1642. Tasman named the place after the man who had sent him. The first two mountains he sighted on the west coast were later named Mount Zeehan and Mount Heemskirk. He named an island 'Maria' after van Diemen's wife. When he found and landed in New Zealand some of his men were killed by local warriors. And again he named the northern-most point of New Zealand after van Diemen's wife. Islands of Tonga were later named Amsterdam and Rotterdam. After his return home he again sailed to Australia, where he mapped the north coast, naming the Gulf of Carpentaria. He resigned from the service in 1650, after having failed in an attempt to defeat ships of the Spanish fleet.

TRUCANINI (1812–1876)

Trucanini was a small and very beautiful member of the southeast tribe. By 1830 the Governor of Van Diemen's Land was offering a bounty of five pounds for every adult native caught alive, and two pounds for every child. Trucanini was one of a small group who, in spite of receiving brutal treatment by many white people, tried to co-operate with the government and to improve the lives of Aborigines, as well as the relations between black and white people. For many years she was considered to be the last of the race of Tasmanian Aborigines, but the term is a dramatic inaccuracy since there are in the twenty-first century living descendants of the race. Her name is, however, emblematic of the tragedy visited upon the Tasmanian Aborigines by their white invaders.

V

VAN LOON, HARRY

A senior research associate in the Climate and Global Dynamics Division at the National Center for Atmospheric Research, Boulder, Colorado, and working in the area of El Niño.

VAN LOON, HENDRIK WILLEM (1882–1944)

Born in Rotterdam, Holland, on 14 January 1882 and later moved to the United States where he graduated from Cornell, working for the Associated Press in New York City; Washington, D.C.; Moscow and Warsaw. He lectured at Cornell on European History from 1915–16. In 1921 he received the Newberry Medal for *The Story of Mankind*. He made his first radio broadcast on Christmas Day, 1929, and in 1939–40 his radio broadcasts were directed to Holland from WRVL in Boston. He died in Old Greenwich, Connecticut, on 11 March 1944. He is probably most remembered for his many books, which include *The Story of Mankind*, *The Home of Mankind* and *Van Loon's Lives,* some of which are illustrated with sketches and watercolours by the author.

VIRGIL

Saint Virgil was an Irish monk and astronomer of the eighth century, his Irish name being Ferghil, who became the Bishop of Salzburg. Pope Zachary had some reservations about Virgil's teachings on the real existence of another world beneath this world, a world of Irish fairies, which he labelled Antipodes. Virgil's date of birth is not known, but he died in 784 and his feast day is 27 November.

W

WARDIAN CASE

Edward Hinshelwood, who drowned when the *Iris* was wrecked in Bass Strait in 1851, had with him at that time several plant specimens preserved in wardian cases, miniature glasshouses which had proved effective for the transportation of plants from England to the colonies and back. As early as 500 BC, plants had been kept under bell jars for the purpose of exhibition, but it was not until 1829 that a London doctor, Nathaniel Ward, observed that a healthy fern had grown in the soil at the bottom of a covered jar in which he was keeping the cocoon of a moth. Unlike the ferns in his garden, which had suffered from the effects of factory fumes, this fern was flourishing. So Nathaniel Ward developed his fern cases, miniature terrariums, which have come to be known as wardian cases. He published an article in 1834 in *The Gardener's Magazine* called, 'On Growing Ferns and Other Plants in Glass Cases, in the Midst of the Smoke of London'; and 'On Transporting Plants from one Country to Another by Similar Means'. His book, published in 1852, was called *On the Growth of Plants in Closely Glazed Cases.*

WARNING

Notice on the white picket fence at the entrance to the seaside cemetery at Stanley: 'Circular Head Council — Warning — Soil Unstable — Take care as you walk due to rabbits burrowing.'

X

SIEV–X

Suspected Illegal Entry Vessel, the boat that sailed from Indonesia and sank off Christmas Island on 19 October 2001, drowning three hundred and fifty-three people who were seeking the safety of political asylum in Australia. I realise that this entry belongs under 'S', but I have placed it under 'X' because the X seems to me to be a particularly significant and sinister element of the acronym, and because the X stands poignantly here as a reminder of the 'Christ' in 'Christmas Island'. *If I die in the sea, don't leave me here alone.*

Z

ZINN, JOHANN GOTTFRIED (1727–1759)

A German anatomist and botanist who published a monograph on the human eye. He is remembered in the name of Zinn's ligament, which is the fibrous ligament surrounding the optic nerve, and Zinn's zonule, the ring-shaped suspensory ligament of the crystalline lens of the eye. His name is more commonly invoked by the name of a vivid flower, the zinnia.

ZINNIA

A complex daisy-like flower with a lollipop, pom-pom storybook appearance. The surface of the petals of these flowers is seemingly dusted with a fine powdery bloom, rendering zinnias brilliant yet faintly dreamy, faded and other-worldly. They may be rose, pink, purple, lilac, scarlet, orange, cadmium yellow or white. And there is one that is a vivid chartreuse green that is called Green Envy. They belong to the *Compositae* family, which includes calendulas, dahlias, sunflowers and chrysanthemums, and are native to South America and Mexico. The first examples of zinnias reached Europe in 1750, although seeds were not available there until 1796 when they were taken to Spain. They grew in profusion in the gardens of Montezuma, where it was said that the Aztec gardeners would prick their ears and scatter the blood on the leaves of young plants to encourage growth. A common name for the zinnia is 'Youth and Age', and in the Language of Flowers it stands for Simplicity, and also for Thoughts of Absent Friends.

Acknowledgments

Author's thanks for kindness, support, inspiration, information, translation, conversation and music to:

Dr Susan Ballyn, Camilla Bird, Dr Sally Burgess, Fran Bryson, Elvira Cabballero, Matthew Condon, Dr Alan Crosier, Jane Edwards, Dr Sarah Ferber, Dr Timothy Flanagan, Linda Funnell, Dr Michael H. Glantz, Peter Goding, Ian Hamilton, Joan Hammonds, Philip Harvey, Rosaleen Love, Michael McGirr, Marshall McGuire, Hilary McPhee, Dinny O'Hearn, John O'Meara, Jan Owen, Sharon Peoples, Dr Gregory Power, Dr Cassandra Pybus, Vanessa Radnidge, Lisa Roberts, Dr Gerardo Rodriguez Salas, Dr Des Roman, Meredith Rose, Professor Daniel H. Sandweiss, Peter and Jane Walford, Dr Brenda Walker, Dr Shirley Walker, Dr John Wormuth.

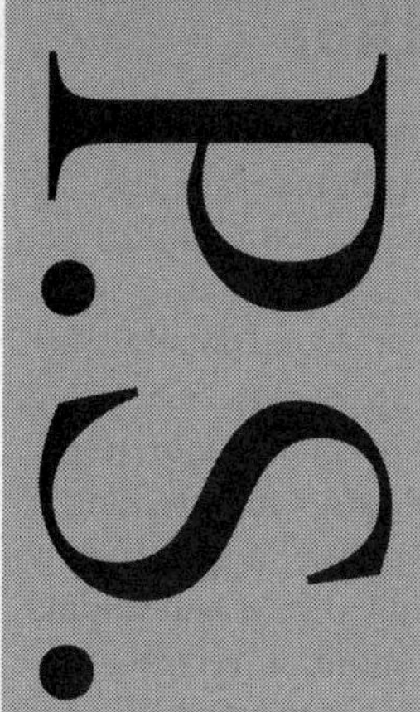

Ideas, interviews & features included in a new section…

About the author

About the book

Read on

Meet the author

CARMEL BIRD was born in Launceston in 1940. 'My heritage is Tasmanian,' she says, 'and when I lived there, as a young child, I thought a lot about the island's past; it fascinated me.' She is the second daughter of an optometrist, and grew up close to her three girl cousins, who lived next door. Her only brother was born eight years later, and she adores him, she says now. She grew up with a dream of escaping to Paris and studied French and Literature at the University of Tasmania before leaving for marriage to a Melbourne lawyer in 1963.

She travelled to the United States with her first husband, and spent a year in Los Angeles before driving in a leisurely fashion across the States. She spent a year in Paris, and travelled in England, Germany, Italy, and Spain where she became fascinated by the language. On returning to Australia she studied Spanish at Monash, and has since made several journeys back to Spain, the latest in 2001 when she was researching her upcoming novel. In the seventies she re-married, and in 1975 her daughter Camilla was born. Her first published short story appeared in the *Women's Weekly* in 1963, and she won many prizes in short story competitions before the publication of her first book in her forties.

Carmel says she has always loved reading and writing, constructing narratives in a kind of attempt to make sense *and nonsense* out of the world of her experience. She is fascinated by words and language, and the possibility of a kind of playing, of making something (a story) out of just words and nothing else, of drawing images with words alone. As a child she wrote plays for herself to direct and other children to perform, and for 'various kind, long-suffering' adults to witness as members of the audience.

Now, Carmel Bird is considered one of the most exciting and original writers in Australia today. She was also one of the pioneers of Australia's creative writing programs, when in the early '80s she introduced the first short-story writing course at the Council for Adult Education in Melbourne. As well as mentoring developing writers and teaching creative writing, she's written two popular books about the writing process — *Dear Writer* (one of the first such guides to appear on the market and a benchmark for the genre) and *Not Now Jack, I'm Writing a Novel*, and is working on a third, *What Possessed You?*

Her other writing ranges from non-fiction to multimedia, and includes novels for adults and works for children. Her novels include *Red Shoes, The White Garden* and *The Bluebird Café*, all of which were shortlisted for the Miles Franklin Award, and she has published several volumes of short stories as well as editing anthologies including *The Penguin Century of Australian Stories* and *The Stolen Children — Their Stories.* The story 'A Telephone Call For Genevieve Snow' from *Automatic Teller* was made into a film directed by Peter Long, which won the Silver Lion award in Venice in 2001. Carmel lives in Melbourne, Victoria. ■

> ‘Carmel has always loved reading and writing, constructing narratives in a kind of attempt to make sense *and nonsense* out of the world of her experience.’

Life at a glance

BORN

Launceston, in 1940

EDUCATED

University of Tasmania

CAREER

Has worked as a teacher of French and English, currently Writer in Residence at Latrobe University.

PREVIOUS WORKS:

NOVELS
Cherry Ripe (1985)
The Bluebird Café (1990)
The White Garden (1995)
Crisis (1996)
Red Shoes (1998)
Unholy Writ (2000)
Open for Inspection (2002)
Cape Grimm (2004)

SHORT STORY COLLECTIONS
Births, Deaths and Marriages (1983)
The Woodpecker Toy Fact (1987)
The Common Rat (1993)
Automatic Teller (1996)

CHILDRENS
The Mouth (1996)
The Cassowary's Quiz (1998)

NON-FICTION
Dear Writer (1988, revised and expanded 1996)
Not Now Jack — I'm Writing a Novel (1994)

AS EDITOR

The Writing on the Wall: Collection of Poetry and Prose by Women (1985)
Relations: Australian short stories (1991)
Red Hot Notes (1996)
Daughters and Fathers (1997)
The Stolen Children: Their Stories (1998)
The Penguin Century of Australian Stories (2000) ■

About the book

The critical eye

'GIVEN HER due' begins professor of Australian literature Peter Pierce's *Sydney Morning Herald* review, 'Carmel Bird would be recognised as one of Australia's finest storytellers and connoisseurs of story. In her latest novel, *Cape Grimm*, the stories that families and region inherit, and others they make for themselves, are the principal subject. With the addition of a single letter, Cape Grim, on the north-west coast of Tasmania and site of the purest air in the world, is transformed into Cape Grimm, a site where horrid and marvellous tales are generated and harboured.' He concludes: 'It is a bravura performance, a fantasia of and on storytelling, that makes all the stranger the tale Bird has added to the many told of Tasmania.'

Writing in the *Bulletin*, journalist and reviewer Anne Susskind feels that 'Carmel Bird makes no concessions in *Cape Grimm*, a portentous, threatening whirlpool of a novel about a cult suicide which dives deep into the recesses of madness ... it is nightmarish, about the dark side of life and, more particularly, the effects on the Australian psyche of the treatment of Aborigines.' Bird shows here that she is 'a powerful and lyrical writer, and *Cape Grimm* makes compelling reading'.

Nicola Walker, reviewing for the *Age*, comments on the author's own writing about, well, writing: 'Carmel Bird once noted that "the writer is a kind of confidence trickster whose job it is to get the reader in". All fiction is an artifice, and a good writer is by definition convincing, but the idea that the reader needs to be gulled is rather curious. Perhaps it is because Bird likes to play with the fantastic that she feels like an illywhacker. Or perhaps it is that after 20 books in as many years, she is as much concerned with the reasons writers make up stories as with what's in them … There are plenty of clues to the sparks of her own zesty imagination in the prologue and end pieces of her new novel, *Cape Grimm*.'

'It is clear from the start that *Cape Grimm* … is to be a mythic tale … By setting the novel in north-western Tasmania, Bird brilliantly combines a landscape and seascape that seem made for myth with a story of mass murder,' writes Dorothy Johnston in *The Canberra Times*. 'The massacre and death by disease of the indigenous inhabitants are woven in, as are aspects of Tasmanian history that other writers have developed into a strong fictional tradition. But not until *Cape Grimm* have the various elements been brought so powerfully together … Bird's prose style delights in coincidences and conundrums, in the playful and dangerous blend of fact and fiction. She is not afraid of spinning out the many glittering facets of a theme. One last plus — the cover is a beauty.' ■

‘a powerful and lyrical writer’
Anne Susskind
The Bulletin

Behind the scenes

Carmel Bird on Writing

ON IDEAS

'People often ask writers where their ideas for their fiction originate; I have truly never known the answer to that question, and I think that now I know even less.' From 'Chinese Carpets'

ON JOURNALS

'My journals are really notebooks, large black books with scarlet spines and corners, in which I write drafts, disjointed drafts and short notes … I collect here scraps of information about things that fascinate me … I love to write about fruits and flowers. I write family trees and other details for the characters in my fiction; I write the notes that go with the editing of my manuscripts and proofs; and I paste in cuttings from newspapers. Sometimes I paste in pages I have written on scrap paper or on the backs of envelopes. I keep notes from my reading of references. There are also photographs I have taken of things I think are significant to a manuscript, and there are images from newspapers, postcards and other scraps. I collect pictures of houses I dream of buying in Tasmania … The journals are the chaos; the fiction is the order manufactured from this disarray.' — from 'Reflections On Keeping A Writer's Journal'

ON BURNING DESIRE

'The longing to examine and expose my ideas in words is something emotional and physical. Ask me where I get my ideas from and I can tell you I don't really know; but ask me how I feel when I have an idea for a story, and I can tell you that I have a fabulous burning sensation behind the eyes ... For me it's as if something hot is melting in and around my eyeballs, and my hands can't wait to get to the keyboard, to set in motion the statement, the dramatisation of the thoughts that have ignited somehow in my imagination ... I write fiction, and the simple reason I give for doing that is that I believe writing fiction is the thing I do best.' — From 'Burning Desire: a reflection on writing, inspiration and imagination'

ON FACT AND FICTION

'Life is a crude inventor; fiction will only be convincing if it is more artful than life. To make fiction take the reader in, you have to leave out lots and lots of remarkable things that happened in life, you have to re-assemble, you have to *make* ... I enjoy reading facts, but when I write, I mostly write fiction... Elements of reality and memory inspire me. I am interested in the play between fact and fiction, interested in the moment when the metamorphosis takes place, when the grub of fact becomes the butterfly of fiction ... Sometimes the only way to tell the truth, to get to the meaning of what you are trying to say, is to tell it in fiction.' — From 'Fact or Fiction: Who Knows, Who Cares' ■

Author's top ten favourite books

Lolita
by Vladimir Nabokov

Speak, Memory
by Vladimir Nabokov

Austerlitz
by W.G. Sebald

Metamorphoses
by Ovid

A Heart So White
by Javier Marias

Le Grand Meaulnes
by Henri Alain-Fournier

Bleak House
by Charles Dickens

Moments of Being
by Virginia Woolf

Finnegans Wake
by James Joyce

Timequake
by Kurt Vonnegut

The inspiration

ALTHOUGH *CAPE GRIMM*'S apocalyptic cult and its charismatic leader Caleb Mean were only loosely inspired by historic events, 'those utopian communities always fascinated me', Bird says. 'They can be good and sweet and creative but I see something creepy and arrogant and dangerous and potentially deadly'. The novel's community of Skye is 'an amalgam,' she says, 'of David Koresh and *Heaven's Gate*, and deep within it is the inspiration of the actions of a number of mass murderers who surfaced at the end of the twentieth century.' This is the third of Bird's trilogy of novels inspired by the idea of 'charisma and evil' — the others are *The White Garden*, based on the controversial deep-sleep therapy of Chelmsford hospital, and *The Red Shoes*, which draws on the cult known as The Family.

But, as readers will have seen from *Cape Grimm*'s extensive epilogue, the inspirations and symbols go far deeper. Facts and fables are included as a series of notes, a kind of glossary to the novel, and reflect just some of the influences the author absorbed during the eight years (with a few breaks to write essays and a couple of 'racy' crime novels) it took to finish *Cape Grimm*. She is even able to describe the inspiration for some of the smallest details: the 'small blue dinghy' Caleb Mean escapes in comes from a passing reference in court transcripts to a boat owned by the family of Martin Bryant, for example.

Tasmania, too, is a constant source of inspiration. 'Although it is the end of the earth; although it is beautiful; although it is

> ‘… utopian communities always fascinated me. They can be good and sweet and creative but I see something creepy and arrogant and dangerous and potentially deadly.’

quiet and strange and funny, Tasmania is as vulnerable and dark as anywhere else. That [Martin Bryant] shot thirty-five people in a tourist park set in the ruins of a vile old prison on a place that resembles a little piece of paradise on a sunny Sunday in autumn is an evil, but not such a very surprising fact', Carmel wrote in 1996, soon after the event. She has also 'always been fascinated by the racial histories of this island.' Even as a child, she has written, she 'had what was considered at the time to be an unnecessary, unhealthy and dangerous interest in convicts, Aborigines and other old things best suppressed. I would spend hours in the Queen Victoria Museum and Art Gallery in Launceston, sort of breathing in, imbibing, the old things there … I experienced Tasmania as a strange and haunted place.' On the release of *Cape Grimm*, though, she worried that 'people [would] groan: "not another book about Tasmania". It became fashionable for a moment and now it's unfashionable. It doesn't matter — I write about what I want to write about … Although I haven't lived in Tasmania since I was 25, I visit frequently and still have family and very close friends there. That's how I would identify, as a Tasmanian writer.' ■

Have you read?

The Woodpecker Toy Fact
(1987, US edition titled *Woodpecker Point*, New Directions, 1988, ISBN 0811210731)
'Bird's stories are, by turns, beautiful, ambiguous and eccentric … seamlessly crafted … both finely wrought and emotionally affecting. In all, the author's foray into "another reality" is illuminating and unsettling.' *Publishers Weekly*

'I think Carmel Bird's stories are terrific, and the first thing any review should say is, simply, buy them … There is something of Vonnegut or Mark Twain in her deadpan, mock innocent ironies, and something of Barbara Hanrahan's wide-eyed breathlessness in her detailed description of weird events.' Peter Goldsworthy, *Sydney Morning Herald*

'These short stories are of the rare sort that you should avoid reading alone. They are full of good bits to read aloud and giggle at with someone, which yields double the pleasure. Carmel Bird's touch is deft, bright, and accurate.' Viki Wright, *The Australian*

Dear Writer
(1988, Random House, revised and expanded edition 1996, ISBN 0091833973 another edition in 2004)
A series of letters to a woman who is learning to write fiction, and now a classic fiction writing guide. Includes practical advice on everything the novice writer needs to know — from where ideas come from to submitting a finished manuscript.

'*Dear Writer* — God, I love it!' Mem Fox

'There are a number of good reasons to buy and read this book, not only if you're an aspiring writer but also if you're a student of literature, or anyone who loves to read about writing' — Kerryn Goldsworthy, *Australian Book Review*

The Bluebird Café
(First published by McPhee Gribble, 1990, US edition from New Directions, 1991, ISBN 081121155X)
A small girl of mixed race disappears overnight from her home in a remote Tasmanian copper-mining town. When big business later builds a facsimile of the town, and places it beneath an enormous glass dome, the search for the child is reawakened. Shortlisted for the Miles Franklin Award.

'... written with the precision of a Nabokov.' *Kirkus Reviews*

'A down-under Vonnegut.' *Californian Review*

The White Garden
(UQP, 1995, ISBN 0702228214)
A compelling portrait of a man whose lust for power is expressed in his treatment of psychiatric patients. Seven women die in deep sleep therapy; the doctor rapes his patients in the Sleeping Beauty Ward. The sister of one of the doctor's victims becomes his nemesis ... Shortlisted for The Miles Franklin Award.

'Carmel Bird's latest novel is a pleasure ... a clever, wise and humane triumph.' Michael Sharkey, *The Australian*

'a splendid, plangent, and memorable achievement, and a permanent contribution to Australian literature.' Nicholas Birns, *Antipodes*

' A down-under Vonnegut '
Californian Review

Crisis
(1996, republished by Arrow in 1999,
ISBN 0091840384)
A comic novel. His wife leaves him for a man who makes grass overcoats. He yearns for the girl in the lingerie shop. He finds diversion in babes and booze, and inspiration in the lives of cast-off husbands …

'a rollicking yarn of middle-class low life'
Frank Hardy

Red Shoes
(Random House, 1998, ISBN 0091834015)
An angel is assigned as guardian to an evil woman who leads a millennial cult of which the foundation is baby girls stolen from their mothers. The angel must continually examine his own moral position as he hovers beside the woman and observes child-stealing, violence, rape and murder committed in the name of religion. And the angel's voice is one of cool, seductive clarity.

'Original, imaginative and thoughtful.'
Stephanie Dale, *The Weekend Magazine*

'A horribly fascinating story… worthy of the Brothers Grimm at their grimmest.'
Ann Skea, *Australian Book Review*

The Stolen Children: Their Stories,
edited by Carmel Bird
(Random House Australia, 1998,
ISBN 0091836891)
Based on *Bringing Them Home*, the Report on the stolen children which was published by The Human Rights and Equal Employment Opportunities, these are the deeply moving and compelling actual stories told in the Report by the stolen generations of their experiences.

Unholy Writ
(HarperCollins, 2000, ISBN 0732267471)
Brooke Anderson never had a chance to finish her novel. The brutally murdered Brooke was just one of Quill's lovers — that's William Quinlan, Director of the College of Creative and Professional Writing. He's married to Juliana, former student at the College. Juliana knows what happened (or so she says) but who really killed Brooke? Courteney Frome, girl journalist, is out of her depth with this cast of slightly mad, if glamorous murder suspects. Will the beautiful Courtney join the list of mutilated corpses? Shortlisted for the 2000 Ned Kelly Awards.

The Penguin Century of Australian Stories,
edited by Carmel Bird
(Penguin, 2000, ISBN 0140284672)
This landmark collection brings together the best Australian short stories written in the twentieth century.

'It's a treat … Buying this book is a kind of investment in Australian culture. It's a book you'll dip into and come back to time and time again throughout your life.'
Sian Pryor, ABC Radio National

Open for Inspection
(HarperCollins, 2002, ISBN 0732269903)
Lizzie Candy lies in the luxurious spa of her luxurious home. She is 32, she is gorgeous, she is dead. Set in the world of expansive bay views and renovator's delights that is the real estate market, this is the second crime novel featuring journalist Courtney Frome.

'It is serious, and it is satire; it is black and it is very funny … [Bird] offers the edginess and unexpectedness of a novel of our times, set in the present moment.' Marion Halligan, *Canberra Times* ■

Find out more

ON THE WEB

www.carmelbird.com

The author's website, with extracts from her previous work, reviews and biographical information, and copies of her regular column on writing.

http://home.vicnet.net.au/~ozlit/

A database and resource for anyone interested in Australian writing and writers

www.nationalgeographic.com/grimm

One of the many sites dedicated to the Brothers Grimm, this one includes audio files of the 1914 translations of their stories.

www.csj.org

The website of the American Family Foundation, a major independent US group on cult awareness and counselling, which contains resources about psychological manipulation, cult groups, sects, and new religious movements.

READ

Nursery and Household Tales by the Brothers Grimm

VISIT

Tasmania
see www.discovertasmania.com.au
Queen Victoria Museum and Art Gallery
www.qvmag.tas.gov.au. ■